AUGUSTA

AUGUSTA

Patricia Read

The Book Guild Ltd

Sussex, England

The Book Guild Ltd
25 High Street
Lewes, Sussex
First published 1991
© Patricia Read 1991
Set in Baskerville
Photosetting by Kudos Graphics
Slinfold, West Sussex
Printed in Great Britain by
Antony Rowe Ltd
Chippenham, Wiltshire

British Library Cataloguing in Publication Data
Read, Patricia
  Augusta
  I. Title
  823.914 [F]

ISBN 0 86332 575 0

In dedication to
Joan French
to whom I owe so much.

1

The south-bound stage-coach rolled and rattled over the endless terrain, trailing a cloud of terracotta dust in its wake. The heat from the midday sun was totally unbearable. Nerves were fraying as the four occupants inside the coach eased themselves into more comfortable positions.

The young man sitting in the right-hand corner thumped heavily on the roof of the coach and called out to the driver, 'Jesus, how much longer before we meet up with civilization?'

The coachman did not reply. This unexpected movement by the young man caused the corpulent gentleman slumped beside him to mutter angrily to himself before drifting back to sleep.

The two women sitting facing them turned and smiled at each other. The elder of the two, a drab and somewhat careworn person in her early fifties, was pondering hard on what this attractive, young woman was doing travelling on her own and in such a wretched place. But as stilted conversation over the past week's journeying failed to render anything of a substantial nature, she decided not to pursue the matter. She too, opted for catching up with lost sleep.

Left in peace with her thoughts, Augusta Harrington was asking herself the same searching question. How many times during these seemingly endless weeks of travel had she thought of stopping off at one of the many past trading posts to wait for a returning coach? But what was there to go back to? The die was now cast. Her fate lay in the hands of another.

Augusta Charlotte Harrington settled back in her seat and reflected on her past life. Here she was, in her twenty-fourth year, in excellent health, extremely attractive and very newly-wed. To the outside world this seemed an enviable position to be in, but to Augusta the future was far from that. She remembered the last time she had felt this insecure, when her parents told her that they would have to part from everything they held dear in England to start all over again in a strange new land.

Her father, Edmund Percival Alfred Harrington, once held a promininent position at Court during the reign of George IV. Her mother, Frances Elizabeth, was regarded by many to be a beauty.

In the earlier years of his married life, her father had been an admirable man, full of enthusiasm for his profession and family. But over the years, due to constant upheavals in England and the shameful follies indulged in by the King and his followers, with whose company he was closely associated, he gradually began to suffer and this had brought about his own downfall. So, like the rest of his contemporaries, he succumbed to gambling and drinking, just to keep in with them. Once in the company of notorious rakes such as Sheridan, Garrick and Charles James Fox, ardent supporters of the past Regency, it was impossible to settle for anything less than a wild, flamboyant way of life.

Things went from bad to worse and the last straw came when he was forced to relinquish his lovely house. This his wife found impossible to come to terms with and her health deteriorated. Respite came, with the chance to make a fresh start, when her husband was offered an overseas posting with the Diplomatic Corps in the 'New Country' - Australia.

☆ ☆ ☆

They arrived in Australia on Augusta's nineteenth birthday. She was now a slim, auburn-haired girl with a delightful nature, her parents' only offspring and often over-indulged but her character had not weakened in any way.

On moving into Government House, they were received warmly by the Governor-General himself and were delighted to be given an elegant suite of rooms overlooking Sydney Cove.

After the settling-in period was over, Augusta found herself reasonably contented with her way of life. There was always plenty to do around the new State. Her parents tried hard to adjust to life in the colonies, but the coarse and callous behaviour of many around them did little to help. Her mother's spirits sank lower and lower until she ceased to care for herself. With her mind and body rapidly declining, she managed to carry on for eighteen months and finally passed away.

Her father tried hard to make a go of his new position, but after the death of his wife, he became increasingly morose and dissatisified with life and as the months went by, Augusta also found it hard to cope. She missed her mother and all she had grown used to at the Court of St James.

Gazing momentarily at the barren vastness of the Australian terrain, her mind began to dwell upon Sydney and Government House. It was in that rambling, red-bricked building that her father had died suddenly of pneumonia. Hot, stinging tears welled in her eyes as she remembered the place and the miserable time she had there mourning her parents' deaths.

The months dragged on and still she felt thoroughly wretched and exceedingly bored, sending out invitation cards and escorting visiting diplomats around the colony. Awakening one morning and looking round her poky room, she decided it was time to make a new life for herself. Where to start? There was precious little in this country a single woman could do.

Opportunity arose the same day when she visited the local store. Browsing amongst an assortment of gaily-coloured ribbons, she accidentally bumped into the storekeeper, causing the articles he was carrying to spill over the floor. Apologising profusely, Augusta bent down and helped him retrieve them. Her curious gaze fell upon a sharp, black-edged card.

The storekeeper looked up at her and said casually, 'I was just about to pin that on the door frame. It's been lying here for some time.'

It said simply: 'REQUIRED, PERSON OF GOOD QUALITY TO MANAGE LARGE HOUSE, WITH STAFF. EXPERIENCED, GOOD REFERENCES. AND FREE'.

The word 'free' amused her greatly. On mentioning this to the storekeeper, he suggested it probably meant, 'not being married and definitely not a convict.'

'Well,' she thought, 'I am neither married, nor a convict and I could manage a large house, given enough staff. Who knows, this could be the opportunity I have been looking for?'

Handing the card back to the storekeeper, she said 'Please inform me where I reply to. I may consider this for myself.'

The storekeeper soon produced the grubby piece of paper bearing the sender's name and address and promptly handed it to her. After thanking him most warmly, Augusta left the store, fully determined to apply for the position immediately.

On best quality note paper, she carefully listed her qualifications, starting with her upbringing in England, hoping that this would enhance her chances, especially as her father once held a high position in the English Parliament. Also she pointed out that she was neither affianced nor attached to anyone. Prudently she admitted that her past friendship with a young aide was not officially terminated, but since he had secretly returned to England, without asking her to accompany him, she decided there was little hope in pursuing this association. Concluding the letter with accounts of her activities at Government House and a list of important names that the recipient could approach in terms of her worthiness, she popped the letter into an envelope, sealed it with her father's seal and addressed it.

She had not the faintest idea where the address was, or the dangers she could be exposed to, but this concerned her not the least. Now her mind was made up to something, precious little would detract her from it.

On the following morning she left the letter with the driver of a departing mail-coach and slowly walked back towards the compound of Government House. Although this event had greatly excited her, she decided then and there to push all unforeseen thoughts from her mind and return to the dreary reality of the present day.

It was months before she received a reply, but an ebony-edged card had been left at the local store for her to find. On retrieving it she quickly read; 'ARRIVING IN SYDNEY

SHORTLY. WILL CONTACT YOU BEFORE I RETURN. YOURS TRULY R H A FITZROY ESQ.'

Daily, with mounting tension, she waited for him to arrive and wondered what her reaction would be towards him. Finally the day came and the local messenger boy scurried over to Government House, enquiring if Miss Augusta Harrington would be available to meet a 'certain gentleman'. Panicking, she thought, 'Good gracious, it has actually happened. At last he had arrived.' What should she wear? What should she say to him? Informing the boy that she would be at the store within fifteen minutes, she hastily tore off her drab morning-dress and donned a green, taffeta skirt with a frilled blouse tucked neatly inside and with trembling fingers she rearranged her hair into a more flattering style.

Now she was ready to meet him. With a quickening of heartbeats she made her way over the stony ground, towards the spot chosen for their first meeting. To her dismay, on reaching the store it was only to find several of the local inhabitants lounging around. Hesitating for a moment, she wondered whether she ought to return. Perhaps this was not such a good idea after all. But, just as she was about to turn tail a tall figure of a man stepped out of the store and confronted her openly. In a heavy drawl he asked, 'Would you be *Miss* Augusta Harrington?'

This made her stop dead in her tracks and arch her back to look at him and, in so doing, an icy chill ran down her spine. Moving forward, for he had not attempted to walk towards her, she held out her hand. Pausing slightly, he in turn, gripped it tightly beneath his own, causing her to wince with pain. Pulling her hand free and rubbing it down the side of her skirt, Augusta meekly nodded and replied; 'I am pleased to make your acquaintance, Mr Fitzroy.'

At that remark the man threw back his head and laughing loudly said, 'Damn me alive. Do you take me for Fitzroy? No Miss, I am the Head Overseer. Adam Smith's the name.'

Augusta heaved a sigh of relief and hoped he had not noticed how much she had been taken aback. Alas, he had. For he was not the kind of man to miss something like that. Firmly taking her by the elbow he asked, 'Is there somewhere we could go to discuss this matter without being interrupted?'

She hesitated, wondering where to take him. Not to her

room, thereby running the risk of being talked about. That was definite. She had to find somewhere less conspicuous. Then, remembering a favoured spot nearby, she offered, 'We could walk to the pond. It is not too far and it would be cooler.'

Adam Smith nodded in agreement and proceeded to follow her. On reaching the pond, Augusta made her way over to a rustic seat and, after wiping it clean of fallen leaves, she sat down and motioned for him to do likewise. It was a luxuriant place abounding with tall, willowy, blossoms. It appeared so tranquil, which was more than could be said for the way she was feeling as she constantly fidgeted with the frills around her wrists.

Adam Smith did not sit beside her but leant against the trunk of a eucalyptus tree, smiling to himself as he raked his eyes over her trim figure. Running his fingers through his tousled hair, he figured now was the time to impress her by telling her why he and not his boss was meeting her.

Plausibly he explained how, due to a nasty fall, Mr Fitzroy was prevented from any form of travel. It was suggested that he, Adam Smith, should take his master's place. Glossing over the fact that vast sums of money were being spent on the estate and that a housekeeper of sorts was employed who was getting on in years he said, Mr Fitzroy was extremely ambitious and he needed someone reliable amd efficient to manage the house:

'So Miss,' he continued, 'seeing as it's left for me to judge, I reckon you will do very nicely indeed.'

Colour rose swiftly on Augusta's face and, without waiting for her to reply, he added cunningly, 'By the way, he was mighty pleased with those references you sent him. Trouble is, you may be too perfect for the position. Still, I'll report back and say everything seems fine and dandy to me and guess you'll have to take it from there.'

Knowing it would be useless to ask how long she might have to wait, she replied, 'Thank you, Mr Smith. No doubt we will meet again.'

'I would like to think so, Miss Harrington, but, on my return, I intend leaving the employ of Mr Fitzroy.'

Augusta looked surprised. 'Really? May I be permitted to enquire why, or is it personal?'

Studying her for a moment, he replied, 'Let's just say that he and I don't always see eye to eye over things. Still, that mustn't put you off. It's a nice place and you might get to like it.'

When the interview had come to an end, Augusta stood up and after thanking him for his trouble, turned smartly on her heels and just left him standing there.

Chuckling to himself as he watched her walk calmly away, he wondered how she would have reacted, if she knew the real reason why Richard Fitzroy was unable to meet her in person.

☆　　☆　　☆

Richard Fitzroy had been drinking heavily and, being unable to sleep, he had staggered downstairs to the dining-room to pour himself a drink. On entering the room, he found Kathryn, a young convict girl, bent over the table, clearing away the supper remains. The sight of her shapely buttocks protruding through her thin, miserable dress, instantly aroused him. Rubbing his bleary eyes, he stumbled towards her and playfully smacked those buttocks. The girl was stunned and as she spun round to face him, fear etched her face at the thought of being alone with him. Lewdly he eyed her nubile and supple body. He sensed her fear and made a grab for her, flinging her to the floor. Within seconds he had torn away the top part of her dress. 'Here was fair game,' he thought as he rummaged beneath her skimpy underclothing.

Suddenly the door swung open and in stepped Mrs Potts, the housekeeper. Hearing her come in, Kathryn jerked her head to one side and let out a strangled scream.

Mrs Potts rushed over from where the scream had emerged and with a choking gasp took in the scene before her. Richard Fitzroy was so engrossed in his mission of lust that it came as something of a shock when Mrs Potts attempted to haul him off. In a choking, but controlled voice, she cried, 'Sir, sir, have you lost your wits? This is most unseemly, if I may say so.'

Coming to his senses slowly, he stared down at the girl, who by now was in a deep faint. Mrs Potts was at her wits' end, not knowing what to do next. Looking around, her eyes were drawn to a large vase of flowers on the table and, without hesitating, she emptied its entire contents over Fitzroy's head, muttering apologies as she did so.

Cursing her vehemently, Fitzroy dragged himself away from his victim and flopped, spent on to a chair, while Mrs Potts proceeded to slap the girl's face. He stared at them mesmerised. What had he been doing? Thank God it was only the housekeeper who had found him and not one of his friends.

The girl came round and in a broad Irish accent screamed, 'You bastard, you dirty old bastard. It's not my fault that I'm a convict, more the fault of another. My father, another dirty bastard, got us sent here. Just thank God that my ma's not alive, or she would have slit your guts for what you've done to me.'

Suddenly, Fitzroy leaped up and swiped her full around the face.

'Shut your foul mouth, you little bitch,' he roared, 'Who do you think you are talking to?'

Before he knew what was happening, Kathryn picked up a heavy candlestick and hurled it at him. It caught Fitzroy on the left side of his temple, causing blood to spurt forth like water from a fountain. Clapping his hand to his forehead, he could feel the sticky warm life-blood ooze slowly through his fingers. Screaming at the top of her voice, Mrs Potts tried to push her way past him. But as she did so, he swung out and violently pushed her onto the couch, shouting hoarsely, 'Stay where you are, Potts, I'm not having you caterwauling all over the place and waking the rest of the household.'

At that moment Kathryn saw her chance to escape. Darting past him, like a boxer avoiding a punch, she sped through the open doorway, just as Fitzroy looked up to see her disappearing from sight.

Much to Mrs Potts' relief, he flung her to one side and, muttering an evil oath, hoisted his bulky frame through the door to chase after the girl, tearing along the hallway, down the steps that led to the servants' quarters and over the flagstone passage to the back of the gardens.

To her dismay, Kathryn turned around to see the gap closing between them. Fitzroy was panting heavily and only the will to catch her gave his bulk the strength to continue his pursuit of the young convict.

Making her way deftly through the twisted paths of the kitchen-gardens, she hoped this would hamper his progress. Being young and agile, she knew she could flit easily between the rows of vegetables without falling.

She came to a low wall at the end of the patch, jumped it neatly and rounded the corner. The light from the full moon allowed her to see clearly where she was going. On the other hand, Fitzroy, blinded by sweat from his unusual exertion, did not see the wall and plunged right over it, coming down hard on the stony ground below.

He tried to move but pain seared through his spine. Screaming and cursing, he tried with all his might to hoist himself up, but to no avail. He was left with no alternative but to cry, 'Help me someone! For God's sake; help me.'

Eventually, lights appeared at the windows and people began to run in all directions. Fitzroy could just make out little shapes moving about on the lawns.

'Over here, you fools,' he fumed.

It was Adam Smith, the overseer, who finally found him and, with the help of Mrs Pott's son Jack, they managed to propel him back to the house and up to his bed.

Fitzroy's body was badly bruised all over and he could not move his right leg. It seemed to be broken.

'Must get a doctor over in the morning, sir,' said Adam Smith. 'I'm afraid he will not come any sooner.'

'Damn the doctor. That old fool is utterly useless and the sooner he pops off the better. Now fetch that silly bitch Potts here, so that she can clean me up a bit and leave me in peace.'

Mrs Potts arrived in the room looking ashen and trembling. It had all been too much for her. Gingerly creeping towards him, she trilled, 'Oh, my lawks. What have you been and gone and done sir?' as she observed the state he was in.

'Don't ask such bloody stupid questions, Potts,' he snapped back at her. 'Just do what you can till the quack arrives.' Then in a more determined tone he added, 'Tomorrow, when that Irish whore is found, she is to be given one hundred lashes and, if she survives, I want her taken to the lake and thrown in to drown.'

True to his word, two days after the incident, Kathryn was put to the whipping-post. But it did not take one hundred lashes to finish her off, just seventy-three. Later that day, her body was cut down and thrown into the lake.

A week later Mrs Potts asked if she could be relieved of her post, suggesting that the position would now suit someone younger and abler than herself. She even hinted that he should take a wife. It was this last plea which had sown the seed of the scheme in Fitzroy's mind and had led to the advertisement in Augusta's local store.

Under no circumstances could Adam Smith inform Augusta Harrington of his Master's plan.

2

It was about two months after her interview with Adam Smith that a bulky envelope arrived. This time it was addressed personally to her at Government House. Tearing it open, Augusta read with amazement the words that were written in a neat hand. It was from none other than Richard Fitzroy and now he was not just offering her the position of housekeeper, but proposed marriage as well. It seemed that the overseer's report on her must have held some sway over his employer for, in great detail, he stated 'how he badly needed a wife and even though they had never met, she appeared to be the ideal choice'.

On turning the page, it went on to say 'that although they knew absolutely nothing about each other, he did consider himself to be a very good catch for someone of her mature years, always on the understanding that her heart was not involved with another.' Then, there was a set of instructions stating that 'as it was still difficult for him to travel he was, however, sending his overseer, whom she had met previously and someone of 'some standing', as he put it, to take his place in a 'marriage by proxy'. He finished the letter adding, 'I trust you will give this sincere proposal your full consideration and accept without too much delay.'

Holding the letter limply in her hand, Augusta stood motionless for a few minutes for this last piece of news had completely dulled her senses. Then she found herself reading it again, to convince herself of its contents. Suddenly, she threw back her head and laughed until the tears coursed down her face.

'The man must be insane,' she cried aloud, 'for I have never heard of anything so preposterous in all my life.'

When she had stopped laughing, she began to take stock of

17

the situation. No, she decided. The very idea of marrying a man she had yet to meet was too ridiculous for words. Yet what was worse, was the sheer effrontery of this man. How could he contemplate that she would consider his proposal, yet alone accept it?

Back in the sanctity of her own little room, she threw herself across the bed and tossed the letter onto the bedside cabinet. On reflection, the best way to deal with the situation would be to forget all about it and hope that Richard Fitzroy in turn would do likewise.

Trying to find herself a worthwhile occupation was harder than she realised. There had merely been one response to her enquiries and that had turned out to be for a housemaid on a large sheep farm several thousand miles away. If something a little more challenging did not turn up soon, she vowed, she would turn her back on the New Country and return to England.

However, she need not have harboured such drastic thoughts. For the next day something happened which was to change her way of life completely.

Returning from an afternoon stroll around the square, she was just nearing the newly-built Catholic Church of St Saviour's, when she heard someone calling her name. Spinning round, she came face to face with Adam Smith.

'Mr Smith,' she cried in surprise, 'I had not thought to meet up with you again.'

'Well now, Miss Harrington, how do you like that? I was hoping to cross your path.'

'I trust you are no longer in the employ of Mr Fitzroy,' she replied, gaining her composure hastily.

'Just for a short time now, Miss,' he said, shaking his head slowly, 'as there are one or two loose ends to tie up and one of them concerns you.'

'Pardon me, Mr Smith, but I am at a loss as to what you mean. Perhaps you could enlighten me.'

Adam Smith coughed loudly and loosened his neckerchief. Choosing his explanation very carefully, he began,

'Miss Harrington, this is going to come as something of a shock to you but I would like you to come to the new lodging-house with me, as I have someone there for you to meet.'

Augusta looked horrified. It was just not the done thing to

ask a respectable lady to go unchaperoned to a lodging-house.

In a dignified tone she uttered, 'No, Mr Smith, I will not. That is not unless you explain the reason for this mysterious visit of yours.'

'Very well then, Miss Harrington, I will do so. But only because there is someone waiting for me there.'

Augusta agreed and together they made their way slowly across the square towards the lodging-house. This was a large, sandy-brick building, considered by many to be the main attraction of the square and, naturally enough, officers from the nearby garrisons often frequented the place and had cheekily decked it out with their own scarlet banners, in the hope of attracting visiting officials.

By the time they reached the reception area, Augusta's head was in a complete whirl. She had been trying desperately hard to take in the news that Adam Smith had just conveyed to her. For, according to him, the letter she had sent to Mr Fitzroy had gone astray and he was still under the impression that she was going to marry him.

A strong whiff of stale tobacco smoke caught her breath and she almost choked the words, 'There must be some mistake.'

To which, Adam Smith shook his head and went on to explain that, although Mr Fitzroy's leg had mended, it was still impossible for him to make the journey, as he was engaged upon other serious matters. However, a marvellous idea had occurred to him. On hearing that there was now a Catholic Church in Sydney, and especially as he had found someone extremely suitable to stand in for him, he would now like Augusta to marry him by proxy.

He also stressed that Adam Smith was to be one witness and all she had to do was to find another. Apparently there was no need for her to worry about new clothes for the journey. He promised faithfully to provide her with a complete trousseau as soon as the marriage ceremony had been performed properly.

A wide grin started to spread over Adam Smith's face as he kicked open the saloon door. For he could not help gloating over the fact that Augusta was probably feeling a trifle uncomfortable at being seen in such a rowdy place.

Shouting above the noisy babble, he bent towards her and said, 'So, Miss Harrington, I would like you to meet your suitor by proxy.'

Augusta stopped dead in her tracks and stared at him coldly.

'Mr Smith,' she exclaimed, 'I think it is only fair to tell you this, but I have no intention whatsoever of marrying Mr Fitzroy.'

Adam Smith was extremely annoyed by her apparent prevarication, He had travelled many weary miles to do Richard Fitzroy's bidding and all he wanted was to get the wretched performance over and done with. After that, they could all go to Hell as far as he was concerned. Gripping her arm tightly, he steered her through the crowded room, muttering between clenched teeth, 'We will see about that.'

The saloon was lined with red-flock wallpaper, the ceiling high and well-moulded. Three large hide settees and several armchairs were placed cosily around the room. Pots of sprightly aspidistras and amber-coloured oil lamps added a touch of homeliness to the place.

Augusta looked warily about her, as some of the guests turned their heads and began speculating on the reason for her arrival. She was quite beginning to wish she had never ventured here in the first place. Suddenly, from the far corner of the room, a tall slim-built man in his early thirties strode towards them. Adam Smith immediately clasped his hand and introduced him to Augusta by saying, 'This is Doctor Charles Hadleigh, the gentleman in question.'

Augusta's heart missed a beat at the sight of this well-bred Englishman, with his piercing, blue eyes and dark, curly locks. The only heir of the Worcestershire Magistrate, he had fallen out with his father by refusing to follow the same profession. Charles Hadleigh had little liking for English law, especially as it was such a complicated affair. Therefore, he chose to become a doctor instead. It was while he was on a 'Grand Tour' of the Continent that he developed a passion for travelling.

Unable to settle in England, he decided to venture much further afield to try his luck in Australia. Moving around from one colony to another, he finally reached New South Wales. Good fortune had come when the old doctor at Fairlawns recently passed away and Richard Fitzroy requested him to take his place. However, as was so often the case with Richard Fitzroy, there was a condition to the commencement of his new position. It had been implied that only by going along with Adam Smith, to act as stand-in at Fitzroy's legal binding proxy ceremony to Miss Augusta Charlotte Harrington could the position be his.

He greeted her almost casually, his lips brushing across the back of her hand. A slight tremor, barely suppressed, was running through her entire being. For it seemed to both Augusta and Charles that some sort of magnetic force was surging through them within the first split second of their meeting.

Standing there, amidst the noise of the customers in the saloon around them, Adam Smith was attempting to go over the arrangements of the proposed marriage. He was convinced that Augusta and Charles were both taking in what he was trying to convey. For were they not going through the motions of nodding their heads in agreement to this, or showing signs of disapproval to that?

But as it happened, neither was listening to him at all. Silently congratulating himself on how smoothly everything seemed to be going, Adam Smith would have been surprised indeed if only he knew the turmoil that was brewing in the hearts of the two people standing next to him.

For some inexplicable reason, Augusta actually found herself agreeing to these absurd marriage proposals and, to his horror, Doctor Hadleigh suddenly realised that the one thing that had been expected of him and had plagued his conscience since leaving Fairlawns, he found he was now quite prepared to do.

Two weeks passed. It was a hot, sultry day in the year 1837. Augusta Charlotte Harrington and Doctor Charles Hadleigh were now standing side by side in the new Catholic Church, exchanging their vows. Only Charles' vows were being said on behalf of Richard Fitzroy, Augusta's yet unseen partner in marriage.

To her it all seemed slightly unreal and faintly theatrical. Even the church lacked that awesome, inspiring feeling that was so evident in the old churches back home in England. The fact that the entire congregation, including the Priest,

21

consisted of only five people, did not help to give the vows religious significance.

Even though it was a marriage by proxy, Augusta had taken immense care to appear bridal. She had been especially fortunate in acquiring a beautiful, cream-coloured, lace dress worn by the Ambassador's wife at last year's Colonial Ball and given to Augusta as a parting gift. Perched on top of her elegant up-swept hairstyle sat a very fetching, little hat, concocted entirely of small, fluffy ostrich feathers.

Doctor Charles Hadleigh also looked very dashing in a new morning-suit. And, adding a twist of irony to it all, Adam Smith, who had rarely taken his eyes off the couple during the seven minute ceremony, could not help thinking what a charming and well-matched pair they looked. He would even admit to a slight shock on hearing the Priest's low tones confirm, 'Augusta Charlotte, nee Harrington, I now pronounce you truly married by proxy to Richard Henry Fitzroy.'

It was over. It was done. The knot was well and truly tied. And now, sitting around the specially-prepared buffet table of the Lodging House, Augusta thought that the atmosphere was more in keeping with a wake than a wedding. The barman was totally convinced that it was a 'shotgun affair'. But as the champagne flowed and the room temperature soared, so then did everyone's spirits.

Just as they were beginning to enjoy the absurdity of it all, Adam Smith suddenly realised that it was time for him to take his leave. However, in making his farewells to Augusta, he did remember to pass on the fare and the necessary instructions needed for her long journey to Fairlawns.

Doctor Hadleigh appeared almost reluctant to go but maintained there was still plenty of unfinished business for him to attend to. After exchanging pleasantries with Augusta, he departed, but not before saying to her,

'Goodbye, Miss Harrington. I wish you a safe journey and don't forget to look out for me when I eventually return to Fairlawns.'

With her eyes misting over and a tiny lump now rising in her throat, she watched him as he leapt upon a waiting horse and cantered off through the endless, dusty plains.

3

Augusta saw the house through the hazy morning sunshine. It was a low, two-storeyed building, part brick, part wood and surrounded by a white, colonnaded verandah. Tall, graceful evergreens flanked its side and the acreage of fenced-in land appeared indefinable. Everywhere looked impressive and seemingly well-maintained.

As the stage-coach jolted her along the twisting, sandy carriage-way, Augusta, now the sole occupant of the stage-coach, forced herself to sit up so that she could fully absorb the first impressions of her new home.

Gradually the stage-coach came to halt. Wiping the grit away from her eyes, she stared towards the front porch. Nothing stirred, nor did there appear to be any one around. It was so still and quiet. The coachman, anxious to be on his way, alighted from the postern and hauled down her battered valise.

Striding towards her, with a puzzled frown on his perspiring face, he enquired, 'Are you sure you're expected Miss?'

Glancing nervously about her, she wondered whether this was, after all, the right place. She was about to question this when suddenly the front door swung open. A small, swarthy-skinned man strode out of the house, followed by a small retinue of people – presumably the servants. Ceremoniously, they trooped out, one by one, to form a semicircle in front of her. The swarthy-skinned man then introduced himself as Mr McTavish, the head-man at Fairlawns.

A miraculous feeling of relief swept over her as the man welcomingly stretched out his hand and said, 'Good day to you Ma'am, and I apologise for the delay in receiving you but, unfortunately, the Master has been called away unexpectedly and it has taken me sometime to re-organise things.'

Augusta managed a wan smile and released his hand quickly. The coachman, eager to be on his way, clambered back aboard, wished her a pleasant stay, then swung away down the carriage-way.

With the greetings dispensed with, Augusta turned towards Mr McTavish, the head-man, and whispered, 'May I go to my room first, for I am very dusty and tired after such a long journey?'

'Just as you wish Ma'am', he replied brusquely. Then, raising his forefinger, he beckoned to the housekeeper and commanded, 'Mrs Potts, will you oblige me and show the Mistress to her room?'

Mrs Potts, a tall, thin-lipped woman in her late fifties, nodded her head in assent. A prim expression graced her face as she escorted Augusta silently along the wood-panelled hallway and up the spiral staircase that led to the bedrooms. By the time they had reached the end of the long whitewashed corridor, the servants below had scuttled away to their own domains.

On reaching the end of the corridor, the housekeeper suddenly stopped and, after fumbling in her pockets, produced an enormous bunch of keys. After searching for the right one, she niftily inserted it into the lock and pushed the door ajar.

The room itself was fairly large. A few rag rugs lay strewn across a polished woodblock floor. Bare, khaki-coloured wallcoverings served to add to its overall drabness. In front of a bay window stood a pine dressing-table, with a tarnished mirror atop of it. Poked in one corner was the customary wash-stand, complete with basin and ewer. In the opposite corner a faded green chaise-longue reposed. Glancing swiftly towards a pair of heavy, dun-coloured curtains, Augusta came to the now obvious conclusion that this was a man's room, plain but functional. She could not help thinking that even her little room back at Government House had afforded her far more warmth than this one did.

Mrs Potts sensed Augusta's inevitable disappointment and bustled around her exclaiming, 'Well, Ma'am, perhaps this is not quite what you expected but with the Master away, like, we were not sure where to put you. For you see, the upper part of the house is still in some sort of disarray.'

Hands on hips, spread wide and pausing for breath, she secretively confided.

'I shouldn't be telling you this, but on the other hand, I have to speak my mind.'

Augusta listened in disbelief as the housekeeper shamelessly prattled on.

'It all happened a couple of weeks ago, when the Master had several of his old cronies stay here. A fine old time they had I must say. Everyone of them ended up blotto. Some of them not even knowing what day of the week it was. They left us a right old mess to clean up.'

Hitching up her sagging bosom, she went on, 'So, I thought it was only proper that you should have a room to yourself and the Master's belongings have been moved next door.'

Augusta's head was now beginning to ache. Her feet were sore and her limbs felt numb. Moving over towards the open window, she rested her hands upon the window-sill and drew in great gulps of clean air.

All she really craved for was to sleep, but the housekeeper continued by saying, 'I'll arrange for a chest or a cupboard to be fixed up so that you can have somewhere to place your clothes.'

Tired as she was, Augusta could not help feeling touched by this woman's honest way of speaking and replied, 'Thank you, Mrs Potts, that would be greatly appreciated and if I could just have some hot water I would be more than grateful.'

The housekeeper looked thoughtful. Hot water was not usually available until evening time. Still, the Mistress looked as though she could use some.

She added tersely. 'I'll see what I can do to hustle the servants along a bit.'

Augusta heaved a sigh of relief and, within seconds of the housekeeper leaving the room, she pulled off her black, laced-up boots, flopped down on top of the bed, too exhausted to move.

It has been left to Betsy, the young maid, to drag in the hip-bath and assist Augusta in removing her travel-stained garments. However, once the ablutions were over and the cans of dirty water removed, a silver tray was placed before her containing a bowl of turtle soup, several slices of cold meats, some crusty bread and a refreshingly cool beverage.

Betsy was a pretty girl with rosy cheeks and bubbly, yellow locks. She flitted to and fro as she sorted through Augusta's belonging. This did not take too long as Augusta had brought very little with her, seeing as she had been promised an entire trousseau on her arrival.

A little later, the housekeeper's son, Jack, struggled in with a large mahogany chest. He was a lanky, pimply-faced youth who puffed and panted loudly as he dragged the chest across the floor. On looking around the room his eyes lit up at the slight of Augusta reclining on the chaise-longue. Now attired in a pale-blue, muslin gown and with her rich, auburn hair tumbling around her creamy shoulders, she was, he thought a 'fetching sight indeed'.

Betsy caught the leering look he had cast in the direction of her Mistress. 'Hurry up, Jack, and get back to the kitchen at once,' she cried disparagingly.

Shifting uneasily in her seat, Augusta offered silent thanks to Betsy for reprimanding the boy and looked away coyly as he scuttled out of sight.

With everything packed neatly away into the chest, Betsy tiptoed out of the room, leaving Augusta to slip beneath the counterpane.

Later that evening, Augusta was awoken sharply by the housekeeper's agitated cries of; 'Wake up Ma'am, wake up, the Master returned to the house about an hour ago and says he wishes to greet you.'

Augusta stared at Mrs Potts crossly. No-one had ever demanded anything of her before in that tone. Rubbing the sleep out of her eyes, she struggled towards the wash-stand and began to douse her face with cold water. Barely waiting for Augusta to dry herself, Mrs Potts pulled a plain lavender-coloured gown out of the mahogany chest, thrust it over Augusta's head and commanded her to hurry. Then without warning, she seized a heavy-backed hairbrush and began working it backwards and forwards through Augusta's mane of gleaming locks.

With her hair pinned neatly in place and her feet shod in a pair of matching slippers, Augusta slipped through the open doorway before Mrs Potts had the chance to douse her in stale-smelling rosewater.

'Welcome to Fairlawns, my dear,' cried Richard Fitzroy approvingly as he rose from his study-desk to greet her. Crushing her tiny fingers beneath his own, he caused Augusta to wince, then flinch at the first sight of her new husband.

He was a large, bulky man, broad-shouldered and with heavy thighs. Dark, wavy hair, greying at the temples, framed a pair of startling blue eyes. His mouth was thin-lipped and the chin very determined. His clothes, although well-pressed, looked a trifle old-fashioned. She had the distinct impression that here was a man used to having his own way - in every way. He motioned her to sit opposite him. She did so, allowing him to scrutinise her appearance in every detail.

Passing the back of his hand over his clean-shaven chin, he thought how clever he had been in asking her to marry him, instead of her merely becoming his housekeeper. He had not thought to be so lucky, for the idea of marriage had never appealed to him before. He had preferred to travel alone along life's difficult paths.

'Well,' he admitted, 'I must say, my dear, you look splendid after your tiring journey. But then, all things considered, you have just spent the entire afternoon resting.'

Unsure of how to take this remark, she let it go unheeded. Poking a chewed, clay-pipe firmly between his teeth, Fitzroy softened his tone by apologising for not being at the house to greet her.

'But, I did have important duties to attend to, as you will shortly discover. For to tell the truth, I am never in one place for any given length of time.'

Looking towards the vast array of pewter and hunting trophies heaped upon the tall mantelshelf, Augusta wondered whether that idea would appeal to her. For, if she were to fall madly in love with him, the actual prospect of his not being around sounded far from ideal. However if, on the other hand, she found that she could not love him as was expected of her, it might not be such a bad thing after all.

Fitzroy caught sight of her far-away look. So he thought he would use the moment to explain, 'Augusta, now that you are here, it is only fair to tell you my reasons for asking you to marry me. And by proxy at that.'

Colouring deeply, she met his steady gaze. The thought of him divulging his personal feelings so soon caused her a pang of anxiety. And he noticed the effect of his last remark.

Swiftly, he pulled a gold, fob-watch from his waistcoat pocket, studied it, then said, 'However I suggest we discuss this over a hot meal.'

Augusta's attempts at a reply, were merely brushed aside.

'Come along now, one must learn to be prompt for dinner,' he added, 'for it keeps the servants on their toes, don't you know.'

Leading Augusta into the dining-room, Fitzroy walked straight towards the table and promptly pulled out a chair for her to sit upon. He hovered around her for a few seconds, making sure that she was comfortable. Tugging at the bell-rope, he then returned to his own chair and waited somewhat impatiently for the servants to serve the evening meal.

With the remains of the turtle soup cleared away, Richard Fitzroy clicked his teeth impatiently.

'My dear, I fully realize that you have had precious little time to inspect the place, but it could not have escaped your attention how large the house and surrounding grounds are. Quite a feat in this young and struggling country, don't you think?'

She thought how bumptious he sounded, so turned her attention to what was around her. The room was wood-panelled in light-oak, which gave it a more homely appearance. Heavily-scented, tallow candles permeated the sultry air. Above the reddish-stone fireplace hung a beautiful gilt-edged mirror, probably of French origin. Two rocking-chairs fitted snugly into the recesses either side of the fireplace. Placed in the centre of the dining-room table was an attractive flower arrangement of golden, wattle blooms.

Coughing loudly he attempted conversation once again.

'May I suggest that as soon as we have finished our meal, you allow me to show you around the house? And if you are not too tired, perhaps a stroll around the grounds to follow. Then, early tomorrow morning, you might care to see some of the outer surroundings.'

'I shall indeed look forward to that,' she confirmed.

As he poured himself yet another glass of wine, Richard Fitzroy sat observing Augusta. She was tucking into a plate of thickly sliced mutton, surrounded by a goodly quantity of root vegetables. Her first meal at Fairlawns was proving to be a wholesome delight, especially after the scant and tasteless food she had encountered on her journey.

Dabbing the corners of her mouth with her napkin she looked up and caught him unawares. Floundering for a moment, she tried to think of something interesting to say, for she had a premonition of what he was about to say next.

Nothing seemed to come to mind. However, as if reading her thoughts, he leant across the table, caught hold of her hand and boldly asked, 'Now shall we get on with discussing the other little matter I mentioned before?'

'The other matter?' Augusta enquired innocently.

'Now don't trifle with me. You know perfectly well what I mean.'

'Oh, yes, the marriage. Forgive me, please,' she recalled, twisting awkwardly in her chair. For she had not wished to cause offence.

Richard Fitzroy picked up a toothpick and began picking away at his teeth. He paused.

'Perhaps I had better remind you why I suggested marriage and not just a housekeeper, as was my original intention.'

'There really is no need to reiterate,' interrupted Augusta, 'for Adam Smith did go into some lengthy detail when we last met.'

'Adam Smith, Adam Smith,' he cried, banging his fist down hard upon the table, causing Augusta and everything around him to shake. 'This has nothing to do with the overseer. This is my affair and I intend telling you, in my own good way.'

Augusta could hardly believe her ears. She sat rigid in her chair. Her face was flushed. Suddenly she turned a pair of smouldering eyes towards Fitzroy's direction. They had only just met and here he was, already displaying a nasty temper. If his behaviour towards her was going to be like this right from the start, what would it be like in years to come?

Pushing her chair away from the table, she cried in a choking voice, 'Mr Fitzroy, I have made a terrible mistake in coming here. Please have my things packed and left in the hall. I shall return to Sydney as soon as arrangements can be made.'

☆ ☆ ☆

She had gone to her room, locking the door behind her. Downstairs, Richard Fitzroy was sweating heavily and coming to terms with the hard fact of the impressions he had just created. They were far from good. He had behaved like a perfect fool. Why, oh why, didn't he take things gently to start with? 'After all,' he reminded himself, 'he was only married to her by proxy. She could easily change her mind and back out of the proper ceremony altogether.' There was only one thing he could do.

Praying that the servants could not hear him, he rapped on the bedroom door.

'Augusta,' he cried in a conciliatory tone, 'I did not mean to startle you by speaking so brusquely.'

There was no immediate response. He tried again.

'You see, my dear, life out here is hard and for so long I have been on my own. I'm sorry I forgot my manners.'

Eventually she came out of the room and agreed to join him in the small sitting-room downstairs, but only because she did not wish to appear churlish. After all that had been said, it was still his house. Finding himself greatly overcome by her gracious behaviour, Fitzroy fervently promised 'that he would never again treat her so shamefully.'

Standing with his back to the open grate and with Augusta sitting upright on the chesterfield, Fitzroy tried to convince her into believing that she would make him the perfect wife.

'I need a real woman about the place. Someone young. Someone to keep me in order, make me more respectable. I want to entertain more. The men out here will not bring their wives over to visit if there is no Mistress of the House. There are very few single women here. Most of them marry at very early ages and, naturally enough, to men of their own age. So when Mr Smith came back and told me all about you, I became interested. I also realised, as he so rightly pointed out, that it would be awkward for you to remain here just as a housekeeper. That's when I decided to try my hand at marriage.'

Noisily downing the rest of the port, he admitted, rather embarrassed, 'There's something else I must impart. Although I'm a plain man and not known for flowery speeches, I do consider you to be very attractive and pleasing to my eyes.'

Augusta had listened amazed by all he had imparted. At the same time, however, she could not push aside the niggling little thoughts now creeping into her mind.

He moved towards her, pausing briefly to give her hand a reassuring squeeze, then completely surprised her by saying, 'By the way, I am nearing forty-seven. Does that worry you at all?'

Hesitating for a moment or two, she shook her head slightly and wondering, with some trepidation, as to what might be said next.

Fitzroy, refilling his glass, turned to Augusta and with a strange glint in his eyes said,

'Well that settles it. Now my mind is made up, I suggest that we go through with the proper marriage ceremony within the next few days.'

Augusta felt her heart pounding beneath her ribs. Turning a fearful pair of eyes towards him she stammered, 'So soon?'

'Why in heaven's name not? Shilly-shallying is not in my nature.'

But before she could make her own feelings known on the subject, he strode over to the fireplace, grabbed hold of the bell-cord and pulled it fiercely.

Then looking backwards he confirmed, 'That settles it then, I will arrange for the ceremony to take place the day after tomorrow.'

The following morning Augusta awoke late. For a split second she wondered where she was. Then it all came flooding back to her. Pushing back the counterpane, she scrambled out of bed, made her way towards the window and pulled aside the heavy curtains. Directly below were the gardens that she was to have strolled around the previous evening. But this, and the tour of the house, did not materialise. For, to her astonishment, no sooner did their evening's discussion come to an end, when Richard Fitzroy settled himself into his favourite chair and after several more glasses of port, nodded off into a deep sleep.

She could not help smiling to herself when, earlier on, he had accused her of being too tired to take a stroll. Still, on reflection, she remembered how her father was wont to take a nap after partaking heavily of the port. She must have waited a long time for him to wake up, for it was not until the housekeeper had crept in to extinguish the candles that she sensed how late it was. Mrs Potts realised what had happened and suggested to Augusta that it would be best if she were to retire. Admitting that it had been an exacting day, she allowed the housekeeper to take a lighted candelabrum and lead the way upstairs.

Hastily pushing last night's thoughts away, she sought to savour the new sights and scents around her. Presently she became aware of other sensations, for the pangs of hunger were creeping slowly over her. Still wondering why no one had bothered to wake her, she went over to the door and turned the handle. Nothing happened. She tugged at it again. Then bending down, she looked through the keyhole. To her horror, she realised that someone had locked her in her room.

No, there must be some mistake. She was about to bang on the door and cry for help, but decided that this might be construed as childish on her part. Running towards the bed, she ran her hands around the wall to see if a pullrope could be found.

Yes, there it was, almost concealed by the homespun sampler hanging against it. Pulling it three times in quick succession, she waited breathlessly. Soon footsteps could be heard hastening along the corridor. The lock turned. The door opened and in burst a slightly, flustered Mrs Potts. Augusta at once demanded to know why she had been locked in the room. Surely they did not think that she would be so childish as to run away.

Placing a pile of freshly laundered towels beside the washstand, Mrs Potts tried to make light of the situation.

'Well Ma'am, knowing that the Master was well away in his cups last night, he might easily have wandered into this room quite unintentionally. So, on reflection, I thought it would be far more prudent to lock the door.'

This explanation had more than a ring of truth about it and Augusta wondered why this thought had not crossed her own mind.

Mrs Potts hastily urged, 'If you care to have your breakfast on a tray, Ma'am, you may just catch the Master before he completes his rounds.'

Dressed in a sombre-coloured gown, with a wide-brimmed hat crammed upon her rich auburn locks, Augusta made her way towards the sitting-room. Although it was empty, she thought how different the room looked with the midday sun streaming through the tall windows. This was not an elegant-looking room but a comfortable one. Adjoining the room was a narrow archway that led into a beautifully panelled library. How marvellous, she thought to herself, to have such lovely books around her.

Turning to Betsy, who had just entered the room, she pointed to the glass cabinets and enquired, 'Do you happen to know where Mr Fitzroy acquires his books?'

'Not exactly, Ma'am, he just seems to collect them wherever he goes. Are you interested in books?'

'Why yes, Betsy, I am. Considering I was just a girl, and a very lucky one, books played a large part in my privileged education. My father set great store by learning. They were one of his delights. Mother, on the other hand, adored verse. She was always quoting certain passages. Apparently her great passion was Mollineaux.'

Suddenly they were disturbed by a loud commotion coming from the hallway.

'Good heavens, it sounds like the Master,' Betsy wailed. 'Quick put that book away Mam, it's best not to keep him waiting.'

Augusta did as she was bid and carefully patted the tiny volume of verse back where it belonged.

Sweeping into the hallway, she found Richard Fitzroy dressed in some kind of riding attire, stalking up and down, shouting abusively at one of the servants. On seeing Augusta emerge, he stopped.

Annoyed at being caught shouting again, he apologised and said, in a far quieter tone, 'It's good to see you at last, my dear. And about time too, if you are to join me for the last part of my rounds.'

Augusta confirmed that she was indeed ready.

Taking her arm and leading her through the main door, he uttered. 'I must say my dear, you seem to be spending an awful lot of time abed. Still, I daresay this bad habit of yours will shortly be remedied.'

Feeling a trifle vexed she replied, 'Why, yes sir,of course. I intend to do my best.'

'Good Lord, woman, what's all this 'Sir' business? The name is Richard. So from now on, will you kindly get used to calling me that.'

On reaching the bottom of the porch steps, she was surprised to find a two-horse buggy waiting there. Climbing in beside Richard, she wondered what this lovely day would have in store for her. Outside the air was scorching hot. Trying to protect her face from the sun's fierce rays, she pulled her straw bonnet down even further.

Fitzroy thought how funny she looked and laughingly said, 'Gracious me, girl, where did you get those awful clothes? That hat hides your face. We must do something about getting you some new ones.'

Augusta winced and said in a slightly peeved tone, 'I'm glad that you have mentioned that, as I did not like to venture the point myself. But it was agreed that I was to be provided with a trousseau.'

Flicking his whip across the backs of the horses, Fitzroy simply chose to ignore this last remark.

Augusta, however, was not going to let this one slip.

Insistently she prodded, 'I sincerely trust that it has not slipped your mind?'

'Not in the least,' he was forced to say. 'Tomorrow at twelve noon is the time that I have arranged with the Minister for us to be married. And, as soon as we return from this little jaunt, you will instruct Mrs Jameson to run you up something pretty to wear.'

It wasn't quite what she expected. But she thanked him all the same. She had a sneaking suspicion that where he was concerned, one had to be thankful for small mercies. He probably had no notion at all when he suggested that Mrs Jameson, the needlewoman, 'should run her up something for tomorrow', that the poor woman would doubtless be up all night working on it. The thought of the tomorrow's events suddenly sent a shiver down her spine.

Settling back in the buggy, Augusta decided not to dwell on such thoughts, but to concentrate on the scenery around. On either side of the carriage-way tall, willowy, acacia blossoms swayed in the breeze, their delicate beauty highlighted amidst the grey-green leaves of the eucalyptus trees behind them. Silver-tongued lizards slithered around rocky boulders, while vermilion-tipped butterflies hovered directly above their heads.

Presently the buggy swung out over a stony track, passing by a noisy forge and leaving several large barns in its wake. Now rushing ahead towards the wide-beyond, Augusta was forced to direct her rapt attention towards her new husband.

'My dear,' he boasted, 'you will now see my latest enterprise. For it is my intention to put Fairlawns well and truly on the map.'

'Really,' she replied, a little taken aback. 'And may I ask, what scheme you have in mind?'

He looked ruefully at her a moment or two. What a strange question for a woman to ask. Normally their heads were full of nonsense.

'Yes,' he replied after a long pause, 'I plan to grow hectare upon hectare of sugar-beet and golden, God-like corn.'

The buggy came to a standstill. Gingerly climbing down, Augusta stared towards the endless wilderness surrounding her. Scrubby patches covered the rocky dunes where they almost merged with the dense, wooded areas that soared away to the far-off hills. She was not going to admit that she failed to see how Fitzroy's flight of fancy could be so easily transformed into hard-headed reality. The ground they were now standing upon was parched and rock-hard. And this apparently was the area that Richard Fitzroy had chosen to grow his hectares upon hectares of golden, God-like corn! Feeling hot and sticky, she returned to the buggy. To her amazement she found she was covered from head to toe in reddish-brown dust.

As the buggy jolted along, kangaroos and wallabies could be seen frisking about. Augusta looked about her, entranced. On turning to look at her profile, Fitzroy was pleased to see that she appeared to be enjoying herself. Tomorrow could not come soon enough. It might be fun, he thought, having someone like her to impress.

Was it merely imagination, or was everything around her looking greener and much more luxuriant? Augusta strained her ears. Was that running water she could hear?

Steering the buggy into a wide clearing, Fitzroy stopped suddenly, for cascading down a huge craggy rock, surrounded by twining leaves and emerald-green foliage, was a crystal waterfall, plunging into a swirling, frothy stream below. Huge moss and lichen-covered boulders and bright, crimson flowers hung precariously over the edge of the stream. How far it flowed was impossible to tell. Swirling and frothing in the wider regions, it then narrowed and meandered on, at its own gentle pace. This shining stretch of rippling water, surrounded by the hues of exotic plants, nestling alongside its grassy banks, proved to be a miraculous sight indeed.

Perched on the edge of a mossy rock, Augusta pulled off her dust-stained cotton gloves and thrust her hands into the icy-cold stream below. The sensation was delicious. Dipping in her lace kerchief, she dabbed at her face and neck. Close behind her, Fitzroy bent down and cupped his hands together forming a bowl-shape, for Augusta to drink from.

Filling his tightly-clenched hands with water, he suddenly thrust them under her chin and said, 'You can drink from this stream too.'

Augusta recoiled, for this sudden intrusion to her face faintly disturbed her.

Deftly moving aside, so as not to hurt his feelings, she said coyly, 'I never drink water from strange streams. One never knows if they are contaminated or not.'

Undeterred, Richard drank the water.

'My dear, this is as pure and sweet as you are.'

Lowering her eyelids, Augusta chose to ignore the patronising remark.

He took her by the arm and pointing to the gurgling

stream announced, 'Now this is what I intend to irrigate my land with.'

'This, this lovely little stream,' she cried, horrified at its impending desecration. 'Forgive me, but it sounds totally absurd. For there is so much more of the land and so little of the stream.'

'That is where you are quite mistaken, my dear. You see, in certain areas, I plan to dam it. Therefore, the damming will force the water to change its course, and hopefully to flow freely onto my fields.'

Augusta stared in disbelief. First at the beautiful stream, then towards the stubbly knotted mess of the interior that they had previously traversed.

'There is no need to look so astounded, for I have no intention of doing it myself. No, my dear, my aim is to employ enough workers to construct it for me. Just you wait and see, my girl, when my mind is set to do something, nothing nor no-one ever interferes with my plans.'

And with that he pulled the horses round sharply and headed back to the house.

4

The following morning came round sooner than Augusta expected. The moment had come and here she was, entering the threshold of a new life.

Heads turned as she entered the room. She looked stunning in her creamy-lace gown. The off-shoulder neckline accentuated her swan-like neck. Tiny frills cascaded down the front of the tight, nipped-in bodice that fell into wide pleats below. The long, fine-laced veil was held in place by a dainty circlet of seed pearls and marcasites. A large droplet pearl suspended above the up-swept hairstyle complemented her high cheekbones and porcelain-like textured skin. Her sapphire-coloured eyes sparkled with apprehension. Clutched tightly in her hands was a bouquet of fragrant-smelling lilac blossoms.

Glancing around her, she noticed that the shabby and featureless parlour had been transformed into a most attractive scene by the determined efforts of the household staff. Festooned around the walls and the chandeliers hung gaily-coloured ribbons and flowers of every hue.

The room even smelt fresher. At the far end of the room stood two large sideboards, heaped high with silver dishes containing various canapes and other delectable delicacies. The house itself was very nearly filled to capacity. Fitzroy's friends and colleagues had been arriving since early morning. Augusta wondered how she had managed to sleep through such a commotion.

Fitzroy was now standing beside her. She noticed he had taken great care with his appearance today. His bulky figure was well-contained in a silver-grey morning-coat. A high-necked, crisp white shirt stood out sharply from between the folds of his dapper waistcoat. His grey-tinged, oftimes-unruly hair, had been well-sleeked back behind a pair of slightly, protruding ears.

The Minister was now going through the usual ritual. His words flashed hazily by as he placed the ring upon Augusta's outstretched finger. Where it came from, she had no idea. But strangely enough, it fitted exceedingly well. Looking down at the wide, gold-band on her left hand, Augusta realized the significance of it all.

Shaken suddenly out of her reverie she heard the Minister proclaim, 'You are now man and wife. Richard Fitzroy, you may kiss your bride.'

But he did not. He merely took both her tiny hands into his large ones, raised them to his thick lips and brushed his bushy, moustache across the back of them.

Soon the champagne corks were popping. Glasses were raised to the happy couple and everyone was talking nineteen to the dozen. Then before she knew what was happening, Fitzroy was whisking her aound the room and introducing her to his friends. Where they had all emerged from she had no idea. For this seemed to be the only large estate around for miles. She soon discovered that a number of them came from the new colonies, further south of Fairlawns. Apparently Fitzroy had made their acquaintance coming over on the clipper. Some had been travelling for several days. To her dismay, Augusta found that she was not overly impressed by them.

However, the guests appeared to be enjoying themselves. For occasions like this were a treat indeed. Presently the fiddlers arrived and took up their positions in the hall. To everyone's astonishment, Fitzroy proudly swung Augusta into the middle of the floor. Needless to say, it was not too long before the rest of the guests began jigging and cavorting around.

As the day wore on, so the temperature became hotter and hotter. Dust and flies were everywhere. As the wine flowed freely, so did the tongues. How one danced and jostled around in this heat was beyond Augusta's belief. Mr McTavish noticed that her glass was empty and instantly rushed over to refill it.

A little later on and, after several more refills of ruby wine, Augusta discovered that her head was not just aching but positively thumping. Her new shoes rubbed her heels and were beginning to create blisters. She longed to sit down under the cool bough of a leafy tree.

Glancing around her, she saw that Fitzroy was busily chatting to his guests. Would he notice, she wondered, if she were to creep outside for a breath of fresh air? She doubted if any of the ensemble would even notice her absence, judging by their state of intoxication.

Stepping outside onto the verandah, Augusta made sure that she was not being observed. Crossing behind the garden-seat, she tossed her veil and head-dress over the back of it. God, how hot it was! Tugging at her gown, she tried desperately to lower the neckline an inch or two.

Turning away from the direction of the house, Augusta soon came across a clump of eucalyptus trees. Cool breezes fanned seductively over her. Darting amongst their spreading boughs, she soon discovered a leafy glade. The rays of the sun shafted through the tall evergreens, flooding the earth below in an ethereal light.

Augusta flopped down beneath the tree and tried to collect her jumbled thoughts. It was a relief to be able to escape from all that frenzied noise. Trusting that she was not being observed, Augusta furtively raised up the hem of her gown and swiftly removed her blue garters. Placing them beside her, she then wriggled her bare feet in the dusty ground and luxuriously leant back against the bark of tree. From afar came the distant sound of the fiddlers. Augusta closed her eyes and allowed her body to sway to the lilting strains of an old Irish tune.

The pain in her forehead was easing away. Soft, refreshing breezes played over her bare legs. They reminded her of breezy summers spent in England. Dear God, she thought, it all seemed so far away. She began to think about her parents. It was the first time she had thought of them for ages and suddenly she realised how much she was missing them.

Searching for her kerchief, she cried angrily to herself, 'If you were both alive now, I would not be sitting here today, feeling so lonely and unloved.'

For today was supposed to be the happiest day of her life.

'And where was the groom?' she asked herself. Probably too busy enjoying himself to notice that she was even missing.

Augusta wiped away her tears. Angrily she thought about all those people in the house. Some she had never even encountered before. All creating mayhem for a supposedly, happy couple. And here she was sitting under a tree all alone and nobody even seemed to care.

Slowly the tears trickled down her cheeks. Fiercely she dabbed them away. In doing so, Augusta had not noticed the deep shadow of a man standing several feet away from her. He was watching her with a bemused look on his face. Then, suddenly she was aware of him. Augusta looked up and stared in amazement at the tall figure of Doctor Hadleigh.

'May I offer you my congratulations, Mrs Fitzroy?'

'Charles, oh Charles,' she gasped. 'I had not thought to see you here.'

He remained perfectly still. Jumping to her feet, Augusta flushed crimson, as she realised how untidy her appearance must look.

Looking hastily away from Doctor Hadleigh's persistent gaze, she did not know what to do first. Straighten her crumpled dress? Rearrange the now deeply-plunging neckline? Hide her discarded hose and garters or slip her bare-feet back into her discarded slippers? Her arms and legs appeared to be going in all directions.

Doctor Hadleigh found it difficult to contain his mirth any longer. He laughed so loudly that Augusta, fearing that he might be overheard, protested in horror.

'Dear me, Augusta,' he cried, 'what a state I find you in.'

Still laughing, he watched her as she attempted to pin back the strands of loose-flowing hair.

Pausing for breath, he went on to say, 'Would it interest you to know, Augusta, just how far I have travelled to see you and Fitzroy properly wed?'

Augusta lowered her eyelids in deference.

Doctor Hadleigh pretended not to notice and said mockingly, 'Naturally enough I had expected to find the bride looking regal in her bridal attire, but alas, what do I eventually see? A bride sitting all forlorn and tearful, her hair all awry, legs barely covered.'

Then, catching sight of her heaving bosom, he threw up his hands in mock despair and added, 'gown in complete disarray . . .,' and here he broke off, realising that Augusta was finding his gentle taunts far from amusing. Turning away from his prying eyes, she tried to cover herself up, but, became even more confused when he said quietly,

'But looking far more beautiful than I ever imagined you to be.'

Augusta found this remark to be even more impertinent. She decided she was not prepared to face this man or the present situation any longer.

Gathering as much dignity as she could muster, she held out her hand and said falteringly, 'It's been good to make your acquaintance again, Doctor Hadleigh. But I really must go back to the house, as my guests will wonder what has happened to me.'

Without waiting for a reply, she flitted past him and ran across the spiky grass as fast as her skirts would allow.

Doctor Hadleigh remained where he was until Augusta vanished from sight. He thought her behaviour most strange, for at first, she appeared quite pleased to see him. She even called him 'Charles'.

'Why then,' he repeated to himself, 'did she suddenly revert to addressing him more formally as Doctor Hadleigh?'

Returning towards the house, he pondered on why he had found Augusta in the grounds alone and looking so distressed. Shrugging his shoulders, he decided that it was none of his business anyway. However, being a doctor, one soon came to hear of these things, if not from one source, then surely from another.

Augusta crept up to her room without delay. Taking several deep breaths, she tried to steady her shattered nerves. Catching sight of herself in the mirror, she gasped in horror. Was this reflection truly hers? Face all hot and flushed, eyes sparkling like sapphires? She sat down on the bed and began to remove the strands of coarse grass poking between her toes. Instantly this reminded of the encounter with Doctor Hadleigh. Running her fingers through her tangled hair she thought, 'Goodness, what must he have thought of me?'

More to the point, what was he doing here so soon? For she had not expected to see him again for some months.

Stepping out of her wedding-gown, she hurled it across the bed.

'Why oh why, did he turn up today?' she asked herself.

Today of all days. Especially when he knew that today was for real.

Reality soon overcame her. For why should his sudden return bother her at all? After all, she was nothing to him, or vice-versa. He had been but a substitute for the required occasion and had merely performed a duty for Richard Fitzroy. So why should she care? Strangely enough, she found she did care. The more she thought about it, the more bothered she became. Right now he was probably thinking what a childish person she was, running away from her new husband and behaving like some hoyden. Well, she would show him and the others gathered downstairs just how cool and collected she could be.

Augusta entered the room and all noise gradually ceased. However, aware that all eyes were focused upon her, she soon found her newly-found composure slowly ebbing away.

As luck would have it, one of the guests came swiftly to her rescue.

Openly admiring Augusta's rose-coloured gown and sophisticated, chignon hairstyle, she linked Augusta's arm through her own and loudly exclaimed, 'My dear, how positively divine you look. I wondered where you had disappeared to.'

Leading Augusta into the centre of the room she added, 'Mind you, if that stunning outfit of yours is anything to go by it's certainly proved to be worth waiting for.'

Innocuous tittering filled the room.

Then someone shouted in Augusta's ears, 'Where's that husband of yours? He's been most concerned about you.'

More titters ensued, but louder this time.

The same woman spoke again, 'Talk of the devil, here he comes now.'

All eyes shot towards the French windows and watched in amusement as Richard Fitzroy came staggering through them. Attempting to support him were two old cronies, who looked far worse than he did. On seeing Augusta making her way towards him, Fitzroy tried to stand unaided, but failed miserably. With his knees heavily bent, his bow-shaped legs looked even more pronounced.

Someone nearby was heard to say, 'Gor blimey, look at Fitzroy. He looks more like a violin than ever. If some sod lends me his cane, I'll see if I can wheedle a tune out of him.'

43

Fitzroy was not amused.

Ignoring the sniggering behind his back, he managed to say, 'Dear me, Augusta, where have you been hiding yourself all this time? And what has happened to your beautiful bridal gown? You haven't ruined it already have you?'

'No, Richard, of course not. I decided to change into something more appropriate for the late afternoon.' she lied easily.

Fitzroy was thinking how ravishing she looked. That colour really suited her. For the satin-like texture of Augusta's gown further enhanced her slimness and added extra radiance to her delicate colouring. Boldly he placed his arm around her waist. Feelings of desire started to pulse through his veins. Pulling her closer to him, he began whispering intimate words in her ear. Suddenly, he felt her body stiffen beneath his touch. Thinking he had offended her, he moved quickly away. In doing so, he became aware of Augusta's agitated look. But the look was not intended for him. For coming through the French windows was none other than Doctor Hadleigh.

'Why, Charles,' Fitzroy exclaimed, 'good to see you again. This is a surprise. Didn't expect to see you at Fairlawns for some time yet.'

Pushing Augusta towards him, he lisped, 'Meet my new wife once again.'

☆　　☆　　☆

The tallow lights along the carriage-way had long been extinguished. The last of the guests had finally departed. Downstairs the great clearing-up was already in progress. In the kitchen a great deal of commotion and silent drinking was still going on. Upstairs all was reasonably quiet.

The last vase of heady blooms had been removed from Augusta's bedroom. Betsy the maid, was silently preparing her Mistress for bed.

Mrs Potts was just about to leave, but not before she called out to Betsy, 'Don't forget to tidy those away,' pointing towards an untidy pile of clothes strewn across the bedroom floor.

Augusta was about to bid Betsy goodnight, when suddenly

44

it occurred to her that she had forgotten to give Richard a wedding gift. She did not know what to give him. Then, instinctively, she remembered her father's parting gift to her. Augusta knew it was nothing special, although she herself valued it greatly for it was the solid gold fob-watch presented to her father by King George IV. Fervently she hoped that Richard would also appreciate the significance of this. Wrapping the watch carefully into a piece of tissue paper, she then sealed it with a blob of candle wax and instructed Betsy to leave the gift with Mr McTavish.

Promising to make sure that the Master would receive his gift the following morning, Betsy firmly added, 'Sleep well Ma'am. And let's hope that tonight you remain undisturbed.' Betsy was more than just concerned about leaving her Mistress alone, even though the Master was supposedly sleeping in his dressing-room. She knew it was silly to think this way, for in the eyes of God they were man and wife. But she also knew the circumstances surrounding this marriage. She prayed that the Master would give her Mistress time to settle in. Still, knowing men, and especially the Master, she very much doubted it.

Augusta lay still in the big bed. The strange happenings of the day were still churning around in her head. It hardly seemed like a Wedding Day. She thought the proxy marriage-service to Doctor Hadleigh seemed more real than this one did. She wondered if it was because she was now married to a man she hardly knew.

Mercifully for her, Richard had not insisted on sharing the same bed with her. So hugging this thought to herself, Augusta doused the candles and finally succumbed to sleep.

Sleep, however, was the last thing on Fitzroy's mind. He had just woken up from a fitful doze and began to feel dry about the mouth. Hoisting himself into an upright position, he reached towards the water jug on the bedside table. He drank the water thirstily, then tried to go back to sleep, but found it impossible to do so. Tossing and turning, he could not make out why the bed seemed to be so uncomfortable. Then suddenly it dawned on him. He was sleeping on the day-bed in the dressing-room and not in the four-poster bed in his own room.

Stumbling towards the tiny window, he managed to gather his thoughts together. Quick as a flash it came to him. Yesterday he had wed a beautiful woman who was now sleeping in the next room, while he had been obliged to sleep in this poky dressing-room. Well, now was the time to put things into perspective. By God's Ordinance he was entitled to his conjugal rights. They were his for the taking. Time he did something about it.

'Yes, by gad,' he cried to himself. 'Mustn't let the side down. What! what! as the Old King was wont to say.'

Stark naked, he shambled towards the inter-connecting door. Turning the handle, he found it was locked. In frustration he began to twist and rattle it violently, so much so, that the large, metal key on the other side of the door landed on the bare boards with a metallic crash.

Augusta woke with a jump. Searching for the tinder-box, she managed to light the candle without burning herself. Springing out of bed, she tip-toed towards the dressing-room door and listened intently. The rattling noise began again, only more forcefully this time.

Augusta shook with fright as the door suddenly swung open and Fitzroy came bursting through. Mesmerised, he stared at the slight figure trembling before him. The subtle glow from the bedside candle accentuated every part of her body. The fine lawn nightdress became almost transparent. Crazy with desire, Fitzroy lunged towards her. She tried to scream but fear paralysed her vocal cords. Shaking with intense fright, Augusta attempted to back away from him. She tried desperately to ward him off, but he kept moving closer towards her. Then suddenly her heel caught the foot of the bed. She froze instantly. Now there was no escape.

'At last,' he slurred as he caught her tightly in his arms.

Swinging Augusta onto the bed, he swiftly forced himself on top of her. She lay there, scarcely breathing. She found she could not move, for he had pinioned her arms around the back of her head. Her legs he had thrown God knows where.

The smell of his stale breath nauseated her as he slobbered over her. Fat, hairy-hands pounded over her body. She felt as if she were made of clay. Each time she tried to struggle away from him, his ardour became more demanding.

A knife seemed to be shooting through her. She tried to scream out, but Fitzroy clapped his hand forcefully over her mouth. The pain was excruciating. She wanted to die. On and on it went. Now it was becoming faster and faster. Harder and harder. Perspiration was oozing from every pore of Fitzroy's body. Presently, he let out a shuddering sigh and finally rolled away from her.

She ached all over. Vainly she cried for help. Knowing full well that she would have to attend to herself, Augusta crawled out of bed. Creeping towards the dressing-room door, she stepped inside. The room was bathed in moonlight.

Searching about the unfamiliar room, she had no notion as to what brought her here in the first place. Her thoughts were all mixed up. But somehow she had to get rid of this awful stickiness about her.

Gradually her eyes became accustomed to the room. She could focus more clearly now. There was just enough light filtering through the bare windows for her to inspect herself more clearly. The front of her nightdress had been ripped completely open. It hung about her like a torn sail from the mast of a ship. Kicking it aside, she soon discovered that the lower half of her was heavily stained. The same staining covered her thighs and legs. Slowly, it dawned on her. It was blood, her own blood.

Blood that was not expected for at least another two weeks.

'Oh, God,' she cried aloud, 'what has that monster done to me?'

Aware of her narrow upbringing, Augusta knew that she was ignorant of the more intimate aspects of married life. She had, after all, seen couples kiss and fondle each other quite openly, but this brutal assault to her body was something she could not comprehend or forgive.

Hot, salty tears began coursing down her cheeks. Then the sobbing started, slowly at first, then quickening, till her body was racked with pain.

Some time later, she managed to pick up the remains of her

nightdress, tore it into strips and began the irksome task of trying to cleanse herself. Pulling a blanket from off the single bed, she wrapped it around herself securely and then tried to settle down to sleep.

5

Augusta was sitting on the verandah, her head bent over a piece of embroidery.

The mid-morning solitude was shattered suddenly as Richard remarked abruptly, 'I have decided to leave Fairlawns straightaway. I need to find a new overseer. It is becoming impossible to manage without one.'

This forthright announcement of Richard's did not greatly surprise her, for his belligerent and preoccupied manner over the past three months was steadily becoming worse.

Looking up from her embroidery she asked, 'How long do you propose to be away?'

Richard shrugged his shoulders.

'Don't know exactly. But I do need to find someone trustworthy. Don't want any old bod, you understand.'

Augusta nodded her head in agreement. Tapping her on the shoulders lightly, he went on.

'By the way, I have given full instructions to that damn-fool bunch of idiots in there,' and here he pointed towards the lower part of the house, 'that as my wife, you are to be treated respectfully. And, if you wish to make certain changes about the place, you just give the orders and then make sure that they are obeyed.'

Augusta replied that she would.

Planting a kiss on top of her head he asked, 'You will be all right here? Won't be too damn lonely without me?'

'No, Richard, of course not. It is only right that you must go. You must find someone, as you say, to manage things.'

Stumbling and stuttering around her words, she managed to say, 'I trust the journey will not be too arduous. Or that your leg does not give you too much pain. Remember to take the ointment with you.'

Turning on her Richard angrily exclaimed, 'Not that goddam stuff. Do you expect me to walk about smelling like some old tom cat?'

Afraid that this line of conversation could lead up to an untimely quarrel, Augusta tried to placate him by answering, 'Richard, I was only trying to help.'

Waving her explanation aside he added tersely, 'Can't stand here gossiping all morning. I've important business to attend to. Now, take care of yourself till I return.'

Augusta watched him depart and a feeling of relief swept through her. She knew she was being disloyal, but how wonderful to be free of him, she thought, if only for a short time.

Sitting there, Augusta could not help but reflect over the ghastly mistake she had made in marrying this man, What a complete and utter fool she had been. Now that the knot was well and truly tied, how could she possibly untie it? Often as not she had thought of running away, but where to? This new country was so vast and inhospitable. Outside of Fairlawns was such a wild and lonely place. She wished that she had made more friends when she had been at Government House. Perhaps she should have stayed there. For at least there, people knew of her existence.

Days later, she tried to analyse what it was about Richard that made her despise him so much. Could it be that it was because he differed so much from her own father? Although known to be irresponsible and even reckless at times, he had nevertheless been the perfect gentleman, especially where the fairer sex were concerned.

No, she decided, it was Richard's rough and offhand manner that she found so offensive. He had little regard for other people's feelings or opinions. Here was a man of strong desires and intense dislikes. Why did she always feel so ill at ease in his presence?

She knew his moods to be unfathomable. The least thing said to him could set off his temper. One morning she tried to approach Mrs Potts about his constant criticisms only to be told, 'It must be something to do with his Virgoan trait.'

With Richard away the ensuing days became tranquil and uneventful. As a rule he was known to be away from the house until early evening. Then with his boots still on, his normal procedure, was to stomp through the hall, charge at the stairs and summon all and sundry to be at his constant bidding. While in the kitchens below, pandemonium reigned supreme as the staff busied themselves, heating the numerous cans of water need for his daily ablutions. Orders and commands were issued at an unrelenting pace to whomsoever happened to be in earshot.

Supper was never a very pleasant experience. It always had to be dead on seven o'clock and nobody was ever allowed in the dining-room until Fitzroy gave the orders, plus the fact that he was never particularly interested in what he ate. The intake of food, in his opinion, was something one did to keep body and soul together. But, drink, well that was something entirely different. Augusta ceased to be amazed over the vast quantities of wine and port that he managed to consume each evening. Conversation during the meal nearly always verged on how he came to acquire Fairlawns.

Even when she scanned the shelves in the library, Augusta felt she could recite backwards his version of 'How as a young man he had arrived in Australia almost penniless. Barely surviving a treacherous sea-crossing with only the clothes he stood up in and a package of rare books that his father had the fortitude to force upon him.'

Undoubtedly life in his early years had been unspeakably hard. Several times he had only just cheated death. Trying to settle in newly-found colonies became hard-going and restrictive to his ebullient disposition. He lived entirely off his wits and luckily had the ability to turn his hand to all kinds of labours. After many hard years of toil and struggle he finally managed, partly by selling some of his books and by scrimping and saving, to acquire a piece of land of his own. For several years he lived in a makeshift old shack, spending all his time cultivating and nurturing the place until he was able to make a reasonable living from it.

Of course, he was more than well rewarded for his hard-earned efforts. He had achieved something to be really proud of.

Augusta often tried to interest him with anecdotes and trivia that had happened during her day, little light-hearted episodes, like how young Jack, the errand boy, had actually locked himself in the new wardrobe that had been made for her, while trying to assemble it in the dressing-room. Or how Mrs Jameson, in her haste to put the new bolster case on the bolster, had inadvertently stitched it up all the way round, leaving no gap to slip the bolster into. Or the incredible story of how, after Betsy was dragging Richard's dirty bath water into the back yard to empty, the stable boy had accidentally been sprayed in urine from one of the horses and had sneaked up to the back yard and requested the Master's left-over bath water to cleanse himself with. Normally this would not be allowed, but Betsy could not endure the stink of him so she relented and poured the water into a wooden tub for him to use, but not before she had emptied a cask of carbolic fluid into it. All would have been well if the lazy boy had emptied the tub himself, but no, he slunk off without even bothering. Some hours later, the gardener came through the yard carrying some exotic blooms he had been trying to nurture, when on seeing the water in the bath and what with the now dry spell, he thought he would give the plants a good dousing. So he popped them in the tub and dragged them off out of sight. Imagine his dismay the next morning when he discovered that all his beautiful blooms had withered and faded away from carbolic poisoning. But none of these amusing stories held any interest whatsoever for Fitzroy. He only became more and more annoyed about the philander-ings and misdemeanours of others.

The late evenings were usually spent with Augusta and Richard returning to the Parlour: she to play the old-fashioned spinnet or read prose and he to take his favourite companion, the decanter of Port.

All this Augusta endured pretty well, because by nature she was normally a self-contained type of person. Life in general, did not get her down, only the behaviour of certain people. She found she responded far better to people who were witty, clever and amusing, partly because this was the climate in which she had been brought up. Her parents had always surrounded themselves with the most intellectual and flamboyant members of society. This new country lacked the polish and sophistication of the English upper classes. Now and then her mind would drift back to those wonderful lavish parties and the exciting masquerades that even as a very young girl her mother had allowed her to indulge in. Still, on second thoughts, it was probably not a good idea to dwell on the past too much, as on greater reflection it had been the notoriety and the prolific way of life that had eventually destroyed both her parents. No, she must venture forward and try to meet each new challenge boldly. But it was very trying to maintain this ideal, especially with someone like her husband, who seemed to her to become bolder and bolder once they were in bed. Since that dreadful first night, Richard had insisted on moving back into the bedroom with her. The dressing-room door had been fully restored and several new pieces of home-hewn furniture had been added to the room. But it was still a dreary room and lacked pretence of any real warmth. The single bed had been removed from the dressing-room, as Richard obviously had no intention whatsoever of returning there.

It was to the nightime that Augusta's thoughts constantly returned. Anxiety would suddenly sweep over her, as she prepared for bed. Would he make those odious demands on her tonight? Or would he be too far gone in his cups to bother her? Well, there was precious little that she could do about it. Apparently, after having a somewhat embarrassing conversation with Mrs Potts about it. Mrs Potts had replied, 'That it was the lot of all women and best to grit your teeth and get it over and done with as quickly as possible.' But try as she could, Augusta still found the whole act something in the region of animalism.

The crunching of wheels retreating down the carriage-way jolted her thoughts. Flinging her embroidery aside, she leapt out of the chair and ran as fast as she could down towards the large spreading tree. Finally, on reaching the tree, she clasped her arms about it and broke down and sobbed with relief. Sheer relief at being able to be on her own for a while. If only for a short while.

The following weeks at Fairlawns were probably the happiest that Augusta had spent there since her arrival. She tried to fill her days with useful things to do. During the mornings she would instruct the staff to try and rearrange the furniture, to clean and polish all the woodwork, give the meagre display of silver an extra shine. She had ordered that the chandeliers be removed and cleansed thoroughly of the reddish sandy dust that penetrated into everything in sight.

The guest rooms that had been perpetually closed had now been opened, cleaned, polished and thoroughly aired. The late afternoons were spent trying to teach Betsy how to arrange flowers decoratively, instead of just thrusting them in vases looking for all the world like a bunch of soldiers on parade. Mrs Jameson was being taught how to accomplish very fine tapestry work so that Augusta would be able to fill some of those bare walls with her efforts. She also constantly toured the grounds to make sure that they were not neglected. Then in the early evenings, she would have one of the stable boys saddle her a fine mare and canter off around the paddocks. This Augusta loved most of all. She was a good horsewoman, having been taught at an early age how to ride and handle a horse. Back home in the Old Country, she and her father had spent many an enjoyable Sunday morning cantering around the pretty Surrey lanes. Eventide was the most boring time of all, as there was no-one with whom to communicate. She disliked sitting in that large dining-room all on her own, with only the occasional appearance of Sally to bring in the next course. She never lingered over her supper and as soon as she had finished, she readily retired to the small sitting-room to work on her embroidery. Mrs Potts and Betsy, however, were becoming anxious about the amount of time that Augusta was spending on her own. It was a great pity that there was no-one in the immediate vicinity that Augusta could make the acquaintance of. There were no decent neighbours to speak of. Richard Fitzroy had built Fairlawns virtually in the middle of nowhere.

Then as if in answer to a prayer, a few days later, quite unexpectedly a visitor did arrive. Augusta had just returned to the house, fairly late one afternoon from her daily ride, to be met in the hall by a smiling, but somewhat dusty looking Doctor Hadleigh.

'Good evening, Augusta. How are you?' he exclaimed. 'I am pleased to see that you are looking so well.'

Noticing that she was wearing her riding attire, he purposefully added, 'I trust that I have not called at an inconvenient hour.'

Augusta quickly brushed aside a loose strand of hair and hastily replied.

'Why, no, Doctor Hadleigh. You are welcome here at any

time. But I am afraid that Richard is away at the moment.'

She shifted uncomfortably from one foot to another, as Charles started to explain why he had turned up without any forewarning.

'Well, not to worry, I shall not stay then, just thought I would inform Richard that I am now ready to take up my position here at Fairlawns. Apparently he wants me to move into one of the shacks on the estate until I find somewhere permanent of my own.'

Augusta looked up into his deep blue eyes and said, 'Oh, I see, well, thank you for informing me.'

Then as an afterthought, 'Is there anything that you need before you move in?'

Charles eyed her levelly and said with a smile, 'No, not really. I have someone who is seeing to everything. Thank you. But before I go, perhaps I may be permitted to borrow one or two of your husband's books. I hear he has quite a collection.'

'Yes, of course. I am sure that Richard would not object to such a request. If you would care to follow me to the library, you may choose what you will.'

With that Charles did as Augusta requested.

Once in the closeness of the tiny library, Augusta quickly became very aware of how unladylike she must look. In fact, she thought, she looked quite comical. She did not possess a riding habit of her own as one in general did not seem to go in for them here. Mrs Jameson had very kindly improvised on an old pair of riding breeches that had become too tight for the Master. She had taken them in and altered them to the best of her ability. Though why the Mistress had insisted on wearing breeches, instead of a skirt like everyone else she could not fathom. But Augusta loved to ride around the paddocks sitting astride the horse and not riding side-saddle as was expected of her sex. Fortunately the plain lawn shirt that she had tucked bulkily inside the breeches did not look too out of place. Her hair, like the last time she had encountered him, was a tangled mess around her face. He turned towards her, with a book of verse in his hands and in so doing, he caught her critically examining herself. Augusta looked up at him and read his thoughts.

Colouring slightly, she uttered, 'Forgive me, Doctor Hadleigh, please. What a sight I must look. But I believe I looked far worse the last time we met and I behaved very badly in running off and leaving one of our guests to his own devices.'

'There is nothing to forgive you for, Augusta. It was I who was in the wrong to have disturbed you in the first place,' he gently replied.

Then, tapping her arm lightly with the book, he went on to say, 'By the way, I think that it is high time you called me Charles instead of Doctor Hadleigh.'

Augusta laughed nervously and said flippantly, 'Well, if that is what the Doctor orders who am I to disobey his commands, and to make further amends, won't you stay to supper tonight? I am sure Richard would never forgive me if I turned away one of his friends without offering them so much as a bite to eat.'

She stared at him quite coyly waiting for his reply.

'If you are quite sure you want me to, Augusta, I would be only too delighted,' he answered her quietly.

'Why yes, most definitely. It is so boring here in the evenings. I could do with someone to talk to. Now if you will excuse me, Charles, I must go and ask cook to organise something nice for supper. Please feel free to wander around and if there is anything that you should need, just ring for Mrs Potts.'

Augusta turned on her heel and was about to leave the room but not before she added with mock severity, 'Supper, I will have you know, is at seven o'clock.'

And with that she disappeared from the library leaving a bemused Charles still holding on to the book. Turning the book in his hand he discovered that it was William Blake's *Songs of Innocence*. A strange book for someone like Fitzroy to possess, he thought.

Supper that evening proved to be a most delightful one. Charles's light-hearted manner and easy repartee were not lost on Augusta's intuitive mind. Because his background and breeding were similar to her own, they were both able to discuss in the most infinite detail virtually every subject that they broached. There was no awkwardness or restraint between them. The conversation just seemed to flow natural-ly. Even the food and wine seemed impeccable tonight. Needless to say, Augusta had taken great care with her appearance too. She was determined to let Charles see that on certain occasions she could look elegant and ladylike. She had chosen well and the creamy silk gown adorned with Fitzroy's wedding gift to her, a beautiful aquamarine necklet with matching earpieces, conveyed a very regal Augusta. Charles thought she looked quite devastating and at times found it immensely difficult to avert his eyes from her. It annoyed him greatly to think that all this beauty and talent should be wasted on Richard Fitzroy. Oh, well, the ways of the heart were never straight.

When supper was finished, Augusta did not take Charles to the small sitting-room as she did not think that this was the proper thing to do but ushered him instead into the more formal drawing-room. Charles was quick to notice that the spinet had been placed in the centre of the room. This was obviously Augusta's decision. Nor was it his imagination in thinking that the room looked a little more homelier and cleaner than when he was here last.

'Do you play, Augusta', he asked as he pointed tentatively towards the spinet.

'Yes, Charles, a little,' was her shy reply.

'Would you care to play for me then. It is some time since I heard the melodious tinkle of a spinet.'

Augusta nodded briefly and walked over and sat down on the stool. Lifting the lid of the spinet, she hesitated for a few seconds then gradually began to play. It was a nocturnal little piece, something she had been taught by her Governess. She was not even sure who had composed it, or what it was called, but she adored it, especially as it sounded so hauntingly lovely played on the spinet. Charles closed his eyes and allowed the sweet refrain to wash over him. He felt a wonderful feeling of peace and contentment, something he had not experienced for a very long time. In his profession one witnesses such awful events most of the time, that occasions like these were something of a rarity.

But it all came to an end far too quickly. For just as Augusta had finished playing the piece, Mrs Potts knocked on the door, rushed in and in a panic stated that the 'stable boy was in great agony as he had just received a very nasty kick in the stomach from one of the horses and could the Doctor attend him straight away?'

6

Augusta did not receive any more visitors after Charles had left. Nor did she see him again until the day Fitzroy returned home. It was some four weeks later, when one sultry evening as she was dining alone, that she and the entire household experienced a tremendous amount of noise and commotion going on outside of the house. Jumping up from the table and running towards the open windows, Augusta looked out to see who or what it could be. Suddenly sweeping into view came Fitzroy's buggy followed by a procession of what looked like ox carts being drawn by the mangiest looking beasts she had ever seen. There were about eight or ten of them, all following each other in a slow but organised fashion. Then she gasped and flung her hands across her mouth, for seated in these carts were scores of men and women. Who were they? What were they doing here at Fairlawns? Seconds later, Fitzroy's buggy and only his halted at the top of the carriage-way. Augusta watched him as he slowly stepped to the ground. She was about to rush down to where he stood and demand an explanation as to what these people were doing down there, when out of the buggy stepped a tall, powerfully built man, dressed in nankeen breeches and a tasselled shirt. He strode purposefully to where all the carts were standing motionless. In his right hand was a lethal looking bull whip. To Augusta's eye, there seemed to be something sinister about this scene, something that seemed out of place. Anxiously she watched as Fitzroy followed this man towards the carts. On reaching them, they both seemed to be engrossed in some kind of discussion. There appeared to be a lot of arm waving and finger pointing going on. Still they stood there, Fitzroy obviously issuing orders and giving instructions and the other person acknowledging them knowingly. And all the time the occupants of the carts dumbly sat still. Soon the discussion was over and with a resounding crack of the whip, the man turned towards the little groups huddled together and began shouting at them. One by one they filed slowly out of the contraptions that they had been sitting in for so long. Slowly they formed some kind of semicircle in front of Fitzroy. As they moved they were accompanied by a dreadful clanking sound. From where she stood, Augusta could not properly make out what it could be that was causing this noise as the buggy was obscuring the view.

Picking up her skirts, she swiftly ran out of the house and out into the grounds towards her husband, By this time the rest of the staff were gradually appearing, all clearly anxious to know what was happening. As Augusta reached the end of the carriage-way and crept around past the buggy, she stared in amazement at the small procession of men and women shuffling along in a straight line down the gravelled path towards the enclosed area. Watching them depart, a sudden lump welled into her throat as she saw that this straggly, dejected, and filthy looking bunch were all shackled together. Of course, she should have realized at once what they were: convicts, all of them. She should have guessed that the clanking sounds she had heard at the beginning were of the chains being dragged along the ground. No!, oh no! What was her husband thinking of? How could he bring convicts here? She knew of course that this went on in the New Colonies. On infrequent occasions, it had been mentioned that a couple of them had been put to work in the kitchens at Fairlawns. But they had since been removed. The last thing she wanted was for her husband to be involved in this kind of thing.

Feelings of anger and resentment swept through her body at witnessing this spectacle of human degradation. She decided to act at once and tackle Fitzroy forthwith. Gathering her skirts and lifting them as high as modesty allowed, she bore down and skirted as widely as possible along the rough track and ran swiftly past the convicts, past the man who was herding them along and on to where Fitzroy was leading them. But her actions did not go unheeded. For as she swept past the man in the nankeen breeches he turned, and with a thunderous crack of the bull whip, lashed out, narrowly missing her ankle by inches. Augusta screamed and jumped to one side, but did not stop. She just kept on running forwards. The man who lashed out at her stared in anger, then in disbelief at the shapely figure speeding past him. At first he had thought it was one of the convicts trying to excape, but by taking in her clean and fashionable clothes he realised that she was not. Silently thanking God that he had not caught her with the bull whip, he hastily tucked the handle of it through his leather belt. Fitzroy, on hearing the sharp crack of the whip, stared aghast at the tiny, fast moving figure of his wife as she ran towards him.

'Richard, Richard', she practically shouted at him, not heeding as to who might be listening to her. Then with a quickening pace, he started to run towards her.

'Augusta, have you lost your reasoning? What are you doing here? Get back to the house at once.'

'Have I lost my reasoning, Richard? How dare you ask that of me,' she retorted angrily.

They now stood facing each other, each with eyes ablaze and nostrils quivering.

'Are you answering me back, woman?' he almost spat at her.

She stopped dead in her tracks and looking around, she realized that they were not alone. By now the convicts were standing just a few feet away from them, standing there in mute silence, all of them relishing the scene that was being performed right under their noses. Both Augusta and Fitzroy refrained from making any further comments to each other, but continued to eye each other warily. To add to the fray, the man in the nankeen breeches had also caught them up.

He cut through their predicament by enquiring in an extremely curt tone, 'Where should I shack up the convicts for the time being?'

Fitzroy, looking heavily disconcerted, took hold of Augusta's arm and led her towards the man and said a little more politely, 'Augusta, this is my new overseer, Ned Cookson.'

Then turning to the man in question he added, 'Cookson, meet my wife, Mrs Fitzroy.'

Cookson stared at her, doffed his hat and in a heavy nasal, back of the throat voice, uttered a rough, 'Evening, Ma'am.

How-do-you-do?'

Augusta returned his solicitations very formally and took
an instant dislike to the man, Apart from looking rough and
crude, he also behaved in the same manner. Then quite by
chance, a slight breeze sprang up and miraculously cooled
the heady atmosphere. But simultaneously, although the
breeze was creating a refreshingly cool sensation for those
standing about, especially for Augusta, who was particularly
sensitive in this area, another kind of sensation was slowly
wafting towards her, namely, the warm, highly pungent, fetid
and nauseating stench of unwashed bodies. Clearly and
looking towards where the poor, miserable dejected bunch of
convicts stood, shuffling and pulling at their cruel chains, she
soon realized from whence it came. Of course, she had failed
to notice straightaway, being so concerned at finding them
here. But now, as she stood still and took stock of the
situation, she felt even more outraged and confused.

Fitzroy and the new overseer had started to walk away
from her and made their way over to their frightened
captives. With several more cracks of the whip, the overseer
pushed them towards the carts and had them follow him
towards the direction of the stables. Augusta watched the
little procession move off once again at a painfully slow pace.
She felt that she wanted to cry out and help them in some
way, at least to offer them a bowl of water, but she knew it
would be useless even to try, for Fitzroy would not stand for
her interference again. So, she turned her back on it all and
started to walk slowly in the direction of the house. Barely
had she taken a few steps when Fitzroy began shouting at her
again.

'Just a minute, Augusta. I want a word with you before you
return.'

She stopped where she was and waited for him to catch her
up. Nor did she answer him but straightened her back, raised
her head high and looked at him cooly.

'Your behaviour back there', he flouted at her, 'was
inexcusable. Do you hear me, Madam, inexcusable? How
dare you show me up like that! Running and shouting about
like a spoilt child. To interfere in my business affairs. Damn
you, woman, it is of no concern of yours.'

Forced to reply she said heatedly, 'Yes, it is, Richard. It is now my home too. Or had you forgotten that? And I do not want it on my conscience for the rest of my life that I willingly had convicts working for me. Just look at them, Richard, the poor wretched souls. It is not fair.'

'Fair, fair, what has being fair got to do with it?' He snapped back at her. 'Just you listen to me, you pious wretch, I have not travelled half-way round the world, fighting to stay alive on a fearful ocean voyage, only just surviving an attack of beri-beri due to lousy tainted food, crawling across all kinds of ghastly terrain, meeting up with hazards that I would not care to tell you about, before I finally chose this place to call my own and now, just when I find a way of putting into action all the things I dreamed and imagined of doing with the place, now that I have bought enough hands to help me accomplish what I have craved for all these years, now you tell me that you do not wish to have it on your conscience. Your conscience, Madam! Who the hell cares about your conscience?'

Augusta felt like bursting into tears at this despicable outburst but somehow managed to avoid doing so. With his arms waving wildly in the air, he continued to vent his anger on her.

'This is all mine. My lands. My property. My home. My workers. My horses.'

Then, dramatically going down on all fours, he went on, 'My soil. Even the air here that I breathe is mine. Mine, mine. Bought with my money and my toil. You have contributed nothing to it, nothing. You Madam are ONLY my wife. And if the truth were known, I did not even want you to become that. I really only needed a housekeeper. But for decency's sake, I gave up my freedom and took you aboard as a wife just to spare your feelings around the place.'

Pausing for breath he went on, 'Talking of place, I suggest that you get back to yours and stay put until I need you further. Women should know better than to meddle in their Master's affairs and may I inform you also, Madam, that I am perfectly capable to be able to deal with the accommodation and welfare of those damn stinking convicts, without taking advice from you.' With that he strode off towards the stables where he intended to house his 'workers' for the time being.

For a moment Augusta felt totally numb and void. Her

body felt limp and drained. The shock of receiving such an ebullient outrage and having those demeaning insults hurled upon her eventually caused floods of hot prickly tears to swamp her eyes. Her throat felt dry and constricted. Now her head was spinning and her face felt as though it was on fire. She knew that she could not stay here any longer without fully breaking down. Somehow she had to return to the safe and familiar confines of the house.

☆　　☆　　☆

The following morning, to the cook's amazement, found all the servants seated around the scrubbed kitchen table. They had all emerged for breakfast, but no-one was partaking of any food. The events of the previous night were being discussed in tense, hushed sibilant whispers. Of course the servants were all used to their Master's viterperative outpourings. But to lash them on to their new Mistress was unforgiveable.

'And she such a lady,' ventured Mrs Jameson.

'I knew it would come to no good. I feel really sorry for her. She's far too good for him,' replied Mrs Potts.

'Yeah, and I can tell you a thing or two about his indecent behaviour,' chimed in young Jack.

'Oh, no you don't,' his mother primly reprimanded him. 'Enough is enough. Hurry up and get on with your food and then you can put your idle back into doing an honest day's work.'

He glared at her sullenly. Why, he was just beginning to enjoy himself.

'She looked as if she had been visited by the dead,' said Betsy quietly, who was genuinely concerned for her Mistress. 'I don't think she even remembers me putting her to bed last night. She never uttered a word, you know. Not a word. She must have been terribly shook-up by it all.'

'Thank God we have no-one staying here to witness what has been going on,' Mr McTavish said aside to Mr Jackson. 'I mean, the way he kept raising his voice. It wouldn't surprise me if half the entire colony did not hear him.'

'Talking of him, I had better go and attend to his needs, before he fires off at me', replied Mr Jackson, jumping up from the table and rushing over towards the door and inwardly praying that the Master would be in a better frame of mind on this bright sunny morning.

☆　　☆　　☆

Augusta had slept in late, unaware that Mrs Potts had slipped into her nightly beverage a soothing tisane to help her sleep.

Fitzroy had woken much earlier and, feeling a trifle uneasy about his rude behaviour of late, decided to slip away as quietly as he could and leave himself as much time as was necessary before having to apologise to her. Betsy had hovered around upstairs, waiting for the Master to disappear before going in to attend to Augusta. Normally she would have waited for her Mistress to ring for her, but she was slightly worried about the appearance of her Mistress lately and, although it was not her place to do so, she had decided to take the bull by the horns, so to speak, and entered the room without being summoned. Tip-toeing up to the side of the bed, she was surprised to find Augusta lying there, with her eyes wide open, staring into space. She lay there motionless. Betsy coughed nervously behind her hands. Augusta turned her head and looked at her.

She stared at her for a while, before saying in a flat tone, 'Good morning, Betsy. Is it very late? I had trouble waking this morning and my head feels terribly woolly.'

'No, Ma'am. Don't you fret. I took the liberty of coming in to see if there was anything you wanted. Pardon me for saying, but you didn't look your usual self last night,' Betsy answered her rather hesitantly.

'That was thoughtful of you, Betsy, but no, there is nothing I need, except some hot water and my clothes laid out as usual,' Augusta replied flatly.

'Very good Ma'am, I shall see to it right away.'

Augusta lay there quite still for some time after Betsy had gone. The brilliant rays of the sun filtered into the room and outside cheery birds could be heard chirping merrily away. A large vermilion butterfly hopped onto her window-sill, fluttered about briefly, then gracefully flew away. The tiny mosquitoes and endless flies could be heard whirring around the room. This is silly, thought Augusta, I have to get up and put on a brave face to life. Swinging out of bed and reaching for her robe, she suddenly experienced a most startling sensation. The room began to dance about in front of her eyes. The floor seemed to be moving beneath her. Then, before she could do anything to prevent it, she vomited all over the counterpane. Everything went black and she remembered nothing until a frightened Betsy came to her rescue by splashing cold water over her face. Seized by panic, Betsy tried to lift Augusta back on to the top of the bed. But could not manage it for Augusta's usuallly lithe and supple body suddenly became like a dead weight. The movement had naturally enough brought Augusta round and she managed to call out rather feebly.

'No, no, not on the bed, Betsy. I cannot make it and anyway I have despoiled it. Whatever possessed me to do such a thing?'

Betsy had not noticed the spoilt counterpane. The first thing she had seen when on re-entering the room was her Mistress crumpled up on the floor. Hastily gathering up the counterpane, she bundled it under the bed. Then swiftly placing a pillow under Augusta's head and tucking a clean sheet around her body, Betsy fled out of the room to fetch Mrs Potts.

Several hours later Augusta was sitting up in bed attired in a clean night-shift. Her hands and face had been well washed and her hair carefully brushed. Mrs Potts, leaning over one side of the bed busily fussing about, while Betsy was carefully smoothing out a clean counterpane on the other side, did not hear Doctor Hadleigh enter the room.

They both looked fairly startled as he burst forth with a 'Good morning, ladies. Mr McTavish told me to come straight up.'

Without waiting for them to reply, he walked straight over to Augusta's bedside. Lifting one of her limp hands into his he gently enquired how she was. Augusta attempted a weak smile and said she felt a little better now.

Doctor Hadleigh began to root around in his little black bag for a moment, then, looking straight at Mrs Potts and Betsy, he motioned them to leave the room. They did this rather reluctantly.

Snapping the bag together tightly, Doctor Hadleigh moved towards the bed again and enquired, 'Well, my dear, what have you been up to now?'

Augusta began to repeat to him what had happened in the bedroom and only in the bedroom, and taking care to omit what had happened the previous evening.

Doctor Hadleigh rubbed his chin thoughtfully and said, 'Yes, I think it is time I gave you a quick examination. Luckily, I have my bag with me. For I was in the middle of administering to a very nasty burn that the blacksmith had incurred, when young Jack spotted me and fairly dragged me away, stammering and stuttering that you had been taken queer and needed me right away.'

'Oh dear, Charles, how dreadful. It seems as if everyone knows about my predicament. News spreads like wildfire out here.'

'Out here is no different from anywhere else where gossip is concerned,' he smilingly said. 'Now, pull back the bedclothes and let me take a look at you.'

Doctor Hadleigh proceeded to examine Augusta, after which he asked her a few personal questions. Augusta found the whole episode very embarrassing and did not know where to hide her face. She thought that he would tell her straight away what was wrong with her, but no, he paced slowly up and down the bedroom floor for a few seconds wearing a thoughtful look on his bronzed handsome face.

Watching him a trifle impatiently, she called out, 'Charles, what is the matter? Is there something terribly wrong with me?'

He stopped pacing about and said, 'No, of course not, my dear. There is nothing wrong with you at all. In fact, you are in perfect health.'

Augusta did not believe this for one moment.

'Then why did I faint? Why was I so sick?' she questioned him eagerly.

Charles rushed over and sat on the bedside chair and in an incredulous tone asked, 'Augusta, do you really mean to tell me that you have no idea at all why you felt so ill?'

She shook her head in disbelief.

'You silly goose,' he laughed at her. 'You are with child. You are "enceinte", as they say in France.'

Augusta looked dumbfounded and said in a shocked voice, 'Are you sure? Are you absolutely sure?'

'I trust you are not questioning my professional integrity,' he replied with mocking severity.

He hoped that she would reply in a similar vein, but she just shook her head from side to side, wearing an expressionless look on her face.

Moving away from the bedside, Charles went towards the dressing-table so that he could put his stethoscope back into its case. He pretended to be preoccupied with sorting out the various instruments that he carried around with him. All this was done in the hope that in his silence Augusta would make some kind of comment or movement. But nothing ventured forth. After a while his patience snapped.

'Augusta,' he said, trying to speak in a level tone, 'is there something else you wish to tell me? Has anything unpleasant happened to you just recently? I have just informed you that you are with child. You should be overjoyed. Does Richard suspect, do you think?'

She shook her head again.

'Does he want sons? Has he even mentioned it? Are you worried about telling him? Would you like me to inform him? Although I think it is your proper duty to tell him.'

An answer was not forthcoming for heavy footsteps could be heard coming along the corridor and suddenly the bedroom door was flung wide open. Richard Fitzroy marched into the room and, on seeing Charles there, went straight over to him, grasped his hand in a hearty welcome and boomed, 'Doctor Hadleigh, my dear chap. How good to see you again. I hope all is well.'

Brushing aside any reply that Charles was about to make, he quickly turned his attention towards Augusta and said in a slightly insincere voice, 'My dear, what ails you? I have just heard from reliable sources that you are feeling unwell and that the good Doctor had to be prevailed upon.'

Although he sounded pleasant enough to an outsider, the malevolent look he thrust upon his wife was well written for her to decipher. It simply stated: Do not mention to the Doctor anything that had taken place of late.

'You are both to be congratulated,' cut in Charles. 'There is a child on the way. What a marvellous homecoming gift for you, Richard.'

It was as if an icy chill had swept through the room.

Augusta simpered and looked up at Richard, wondering what his reaction would be. His beady eyes narrowed until they became mere slits in his ashen face. His body, normally loose and flabby, instantly became rigid and taut.

With supreme effort and cunning effrontery he turned to Charles and added, 'Really, Doctor? Well, that is good news. A child you say. I'll be blessed. Fancy me a Father, to boot. Never thought it would happen to me.'

Spinning round and looking directly at Augusta, he muttered as an afterthought, 'Presumably everything is going to be just fine,' and without waiting for an answer, he strode towards the door and patting Charles heavily on the back, cried out, 'Come now, Doctor. We do not want to waste our time moping about in the damn bedroom. When downstairs I have some excellent vintage Port to celebrate with. It's a seventy-three by the way. A damn good year for it I believe.'

Doctor Hadleigh cast a furtive glance towards Augusta and lightly replied, 'That sounds fine, Richard, but what about your wife? Are you not concerned about her welfare? What about a little celebrating for her? A little tipple would not hurt her at this early stage.'

'Dear me, Doctor,' Fitzroy laughed forcedly, as he opened the door. 'Women partaking of port. Never heard the like. No, 'tis best she stays where she is. Out of harm's way I say. This is strictly between us men.'

And so saying he stomped out of the room, leaving a slightly bewildered Doctor Hadleigh to follow him.

7

Augusta was now well into the fifth month of her confinement. At last she was able to move about the place without the fear of constant nausea and those frightening dizzy spells. Her general well-being and even her poor appetite of late were beginning to improve slowly as the days wore on.

From the very first, since her condition had been confirmed, she had been a constant worry to everyone at Fairlawns, everyone that was, except her husband. After the first initial shock of finding out that he had sired a child, which needless to say necessitated the depletion of the entire stock of vintage Port, not to mention other convivial delights, it was no wonder he was fast becoming bored. Envy and irritation that his wife was the centre of so much fuss and attention prompted him to adopt the attitude that she could get on with it herself. Best to let nature take its own course. Child-bearing or rearing, to his way of thinking, had nothing whatsoever to do with a man. No, it was time to escape from the confines of the domestic scene, time to get away from the constant odour of sickness that seemed to pervade the entire house, time to escape from having to make seemingly polite and ineffectual conversation with a wife who never appeared out of her shapeless peignoir. Was she always going to look like this? So colourless, so drained, so insipid. Other women he knew had always appeared so bonny and robust-looking when with child. Why, oh why, did he have the misfortune to marry one who looked as if she were at death's door? Well, he was not going to ponder on it any more. It was time to get back to the fields, time to work hard at trying to transform this vast piece of uncultivated land by carving it into something that he and his future heirs could justifiably boast about.

Richard had been gone from the house about a week or more before Augusta really began to have serious doubts as to why he had not returned. Although she was still feeling well below par, she decided to make an effort and put her own feelings of discomfort to one side and concentrate more fully on what was going on around her. She knew that she had caused the servants a great deal of extra work and worry over the past few months and that she must snap out of it and carry on without adding to their ever-increasing burdens. So, this morning, she rose earlier than usual and thought she would take a stroll outside and find out what was going on that was so important to have kept her husband away from home. But when she finally ventured out of the house, it was much later than she had anticipated. The problem had been what to wear. For so long she had worn only her peignoir, because of being confined to her room so much, that when it actually came to trying on the gown, the shock she received at finding that not one entire outfit fitted her was a very depressing state of affairs indeed. Staring at herself in the cheval-mirror only heightened her fears. Was this really her? She looked atrocious. Her hair was straggly and unkempt, her face pallid and sickly. Her once slim and graceful body was now completely transformed. Where were the small, pointed breasts, the girlish waist, the flat stomach and the gently rounded hips? Vanished, they were now submerged into one big swollen lump. Tentatively placing her hands over the lump, it just seemed so incredible that one's figure could change so quickly and in so short a time. Oh, it was horrible. What did she look like? So this was having a baby, not at all what she imagined it might be like. Well, it was no good worrying over it now. The deed was done. She still had some time to go yet. Feeling sorry for herself was not the answer. No, she must try and make herself look as pretty as she could. The last thing she wanted was for anyone to think that she was incapable of carrying a child without any dignity or control over her appearance, or the manner in which she carried herself. Plucking up courage and pushing aside all self-centred and demoralising thoughts, she sent for Mrs Jameson to come in and unpick and loosen one of her morning-gowns, in the hope that it would hide the bulge more effectively. Betsy was sent for to try and do something with her lifeless hair.

It was now late in the morning as Augusta stood on the porch steps waiting for the buggy to appear around the corner of the carriage-way. Mrs Potts had just joined her and enquired if she wanted anyone to attend her, but Augusta replied firmly that she would be fine on her own. Greatly relieved was Mrs Potts to see that Augusta was looking better and seemed to be more in command of herself than had been of late. Then the buggy swung into full view and Augusta, not waiting for it to pull up at the porch steps, pushed open her parasol, held it high over her head and carefully made her way towards it.

The driver of the buggy was an old retainer of Fitzroy's, known simply as 'Old Amos' and scant else was known about him except that he had about as much grace as his master. A more querulous rapscallion had yet to be found. He was always seen to be wearing the same pair of dungaree trousers, with an outsized faded khaki shirt almost tucked inside it. Warts, boils and pimples all seemed to be fighting a war of their own for a more prominent position on his weather-beaten face. But needless to say, Richard Fitzroy apparently found him harmless enough.

Once seated inside the buggy, Augusta instructed Old Amos to drive her down towards the New Plantation. He scratched his head for a few seconds, spat out a piece of well chewed baccy and replied somewhat laconically, 'Are you sure that's where you want to go, Mrs Fitzroy?'

The cheek of the man. What right had he to question her whereabouts?

'Yes, I am sure, Amos. Is there some reason why I should not be?' she retorted back.

'Nay, Ma'am. Anything to oblige. 'Cept I wouldn't have thought that a lady in your condition would have wanted to risk a trip down there. Still, I only do's as I am asked to.'

Seeing Augusta preferred to ignore his comments, he flicked the whip across the horse's rump and set the buggy in motion.

The short journey was peaceful enough at first. It was so lovely to be out in the fresh air again. The temperature over the last few days had dropped fairly steeply, making the weather more bearable. It was still hot, but not that wicked

71

fierce heat that Augusta deplored so much. There was even a constant breeze about, to add to the quality of it all. She settled back against the hard cowhide seat and took in the sights and sounds surrounding her. The sky was azure with a few white puffy clouds filtering slowly by. Augusta tilted her parasol backwards, so as to obtain a clearer view of the smoky blue hills afar. Watching the wallabies and the frisky baby kangaroos tumbling and cavorting about in the under-growth was a sight she would never tire of. Now the buggy ran alongside the cool clear lake that eventually babbled and meandered its way into the frothy stream that fed through to the start of the New Plantation. Augusta stared back at the lake in enchantment. She loved this spot. She had loved it since the very first day that Richard had so proudly shown it to her. This was her favourite place, so peaceful, so tranquil and so green, so unlike the harsh and more glaring aspects of this country. Then suddenly, the peace and tranquility ceased. For in a matter of seconds, as they swung round a wide clump of trees, the New Plantation suddenly opened out before her.

Old Amos slowed the horses to a sedate trot.

'How far in do you want to go, Mrs Fitzroy?' he enquired, directing his cracked voice over one shoulder.

Augusta stared in amazement and disbelief at what she saw ahead of her. For they were now emerging into part of the area that was being cleared as the Plantation. She was stunned at the progress that had been achieved. A vast area had already been totally purged of those ghostly sparse gum trees. The once scrubby thicket was now transformed into innumerable acres of well ploughed fields. Then somewhere in the not too far distance, came the sounds of industrious activity.

Old Amos jumped and cried to Augusta, 'Sounds like they be coming back again now, Ma'am,' and without any apparent warning he suddenly lashed out at the poor beasts pulling the buggy and shouted, 'Get up there boys. Gee up there.' As the horses turned and bolted, Augusta was immediately thrown sideways. Struggling to regain her balance, she frantically called out for Amos to stop. But the crafty old devil pretended not to hear her and just kept on driving the horses forwards, but at a slightly reduced pace. It was not until they came in sight of the lake that he gradually tightened the reins. By this time Augusta was more than annoyed with him. How dare he disregard her commands! As a rule she was not one to lose her temper with the servants, but this time, due to her delicate condition, she lashed out at him in full fury.

'Amos, will you stop this instant?'

He did so and slowly and sulkily climbed down from his seat and sauntered towards her side of the buggy. He stood there for a few seconds. He looked a pathetic sight in his non too clean cheesecloth shirt, anchored in place with a pair of braces that must have been handed down from generation to generation, inside the usual pair of grimy dungarees. His dry, cracked knee-length boots creaked as he walked in them. His sparse, peppery-coloured hair fair matched the grizzled stubble protruding around his chin. But the most disgusting spectacle about him was the ugly brown trickle that oozed from the corners of his down-turned mouth from constantly chewing nicotine. Turning his head to one side, he carefully spat out a long gob then, wiping the remains away from his face with the back of his hand, he confronted Augusta again and continued to stand there with a mute expression on his face, as she gave full vent to her feelings.

'Amos. It was very wrong of you to drive the buggy at such a pace when you know full well that I am carrying a child. It was an extremely thoughtless action on your part. I could have been taken ill again,' she rushed on. 'And what would you have done, if I had been? Would you have run off and left me to my own devices?'

'No, Ma'am indeed not,' he sullenly replied. 'But I was not going to stay there with that lot just arriving.'

Augusta was slightly bewildered and enquired, 'With who arriving?'

'Why, them convicts. The Master has had them working up on the plantation ever since they arrived. Thought you heard them coming through the far fields. That's why I bolted off, Ma'am. Didn't want you to see 'em. They're not a pretty sight and I don't hold with mixing with them. They're a bad lot, Ma'am. Scum is what I calls 'em. Would have been best if they had all drowned at sea. Don't see why we have to have the likes of them over here,' he rambled on.

Augusta took a deep breath. She had been so preoccupied with her own feelings she had almost forgotten about them. Of course, that would explain why so much had been done on the land. She also wondered where they had been housed and what the conditions were like. Perhaps she ought to go and investigate for herself. She dare not ask Old Amos to take her. It would not be considered dignified for the Mistress of Fairlawns to concern herself in such matters. No, she would instruct him to drive her back to the house, then creep out some time later on the pretext of preferring to take a stroll around the grounds instead of a drive.

Later the same day, after Augusta had bathed and changed for the evening meal, who should chance to arrive at the house but Doctor Hadleigh. He had come to see how Augusta was faring and was also hoping that Fitzroy would be at home, as he had several things he wanted to discuss with him. But Richard Fitzroy, as usual, was not at home.

They were seated at the long, freshly polished oak dining-room table, not end to end but facing each other across the centre of the table. Delicate, sweet-smelling blooms in wide gaudy-painted bowls had been placed at regular intervals on the table in an attempt to lighten and soften the appearance of this normally drab and sombre room. This was the first time in many months that Augusta had actually managed to partake of her meals anywhere other than the bedroom. Doctor Hadleigh had been persuaded to take supper with her and the mere fact that she had someone else to converse with made her feel and look so much better. The conversation to begin with was light and full of reminiscences of their younger days spent in England, Augusta dreamily informing Doctor Hadleigh of what life was like for her during the last remaining years of George IV reign. How she used to love watching her mother dress up for the various balls and parties, father looking resplendent in full evening-dress to attend the many card games and gambling houses that he frequented. Trips to Ranelagh Gardens to hear the bands. Rides down Rotten Row and the exciting visits to the Annual Fair to buy coloured ribbons and fancy garters galore. The occasional boating trips to dear old Kew, where mother's favourite wigmaker lived. The day they even went to Brighthelmstone, to visit the Regent's new Palace, named the Pavilion. A chance meeting with his morganatic wife, Maria Fitzherbert. How fascinated and shocked they all were by the sudden rush of all the old King's sons to marry respectable wives in order to furnish him with legitimate heirs. Especially the account of how her own father was beset upon by Dorothy Jordan, the famous actress, who for many years was the mistress of the Duke of Clarence, trying to arrange a settlement for her. Notwithstanding, when Augusta was in her early teens, the eldest of the Fitz-clarence boys had been introduced to her as a future beau and mother had furiously proclaimed that there would be no bastard for her daughter. An Earl or a Viscount at least. But that was long before father took up with the drink and ruined it all. Of the conflicting troubles caused by the foreign wars. The shifting changes of mood that would suddenly erupt from his subjects. How on one hand the aristocrats and the wealthy lived a life of riotous indulgence, being able to have and attain everything possible, and how the poor had nothing. Not even their dignity. Charles was then quick to react to the fact that as he had spent most of his life tucked away in the rural shires, he had witnessed and lived through more than his fair share of deprivation. This then led him to discuss his hopes and plans for the future. Why he had deserted the Old Country, in order to try and change some of the wicked ways of the world. But after living here for only just a short while, he was beginning to feel disillusioned already. He could now see that it was not the fault of the country that affected the way people behaved but, sad to admit, it was the people themselves. He had desperately hoped that here, in this New Colony, the way in which a man worked and plied his trade would be by choice and not by force. That one man would not become the tool or weapon by means of attainment of another in a more lucrative or forceful position. When he first arrived at Fairlawns, at Richard Fitzroy's request, he was more than pleased at the way things had presented themselves. Fitzroy had housed him. Given him ample opportunity to travel freely around the colony, taking on new patients and been able to have lengthy discussions with all and sundry relating to illness and the types of diseases that were making their mark on the community. The biggest problem, though, for newcomers, seemed to be the heat, flies and the ever-pervading dust. Apparently this took a lifetime to overcome. He also had it in the back of his mind to set some time aside eventually to be able to venture out and explore the more wild and less habited parts, that is to say, the parts not occupied by the White Man, but by the true natives of this country, the aborigines. These breeds kept very much to themselves and inhabited the denser and lesser known parts. But Doctor Hadleigh secretly confessed to Augusta that he had a desire 'to go forth, seek out and try to make some sort of contact with them in order to find out how they ticked,' as he jokingly put it.

With supper over, Charles finally ventured on to the subject that he found most awkward to discuss, the question of the forced convict labour. He had not dared to mention it before, as he was not quite sure how Augusta would react to his feelings on this subject. A sense of relief flooded over him, for no sooner had he broached the subject, than Augusta exclaimed that her views were in accordance with his own. Taking the bull by its horns, Charles pursued the matter a trifle further by adding how he had on several occasions over the last few months intended to tackle Fitzroy about it, and therefore voice his own displeasure about the whole situation. After all, had he not left the Old Country to escape all these repressions? Augusta, on listening intently to Charles seized at once on the opportunity that now presented itself to her, actually to be able to do something about it herself.

'I am so glad that you have brought this subject to light, Charles, as I have been deeply distressed about it myself and I dearly want to see for myself what kind of conditions they are being kept in. The subject is taboo as far as Richard is concerned.'

'Extremely poor', butted in Charles dourly.

Augusta winced and was about to cut across his remark but Charles went on to say, 'Richard assures me that it is only temporary. He intends to erect something more permanent for them later on.'

Charles paused for a second, noticing how tense and pale she had suddenly become, he plausibly added, 'Augusta, if you are feeling up to it, we could take a sedate stroll in the direction of where the convicts are housed and this would, of course, enable you to have a bit of fresh air. Who knows, we may even meet up with your husband as well? He keeps very late hours I have noticed recently. Not altogether good for a man of his years to be out in this heat for such long periods at a time.'

Augusta silently agreed with him and also thought that a little walk would be beneficial to her.

They were strolling along the rough uneven pathway that led towards the enclosed area. They were forced to walk at a leisurely pace as Augusta still found it difficult to move around at too great a pace. Enjoying each other's company in a light-hearted manner, they soon approached the wide curved circuit that led directly into the enclosed working area. The workers were just finishing their toils of the day and Augusta and Charles could not help but notice the slow, apathetic movements as they packed away their tools and equipment of the day.

Down by the blacksmiths the big sweaty Smithy was busily extinguishing the burning coals 'neath the anvil, while the horses from the nearby stables could be heard chaffing at their bits. Passing by the huge water towers, the two noticed how with careful precision the open tanks were being covered in the hope that no-one would need any excess water until morning. All the time Augusta and Charles had been keeping a watchful eye about the place, in case they spotted Richard somewhere around.

Charles on reading her thoughts said flippantly, 'Mrs Fitzroy, would you have any idea at all where your husband might be?'

'No Charles, I do not. He would surely not be out in the fields this time of the evening.'

'I would hardly think so, as the light is now becoming quite poor. And where is that new overseer chap? I don't see or hear any evidence of him either.'

'Probably keeping his eye on his charges and no doubt extracting every ounce of work out of them, that he can manage,' Augusta grimly stated.

'Well, in that case, let us proceed further round the back of the stables to determine where they are,' said Charles as he gently took hold of Augusta's arm and carefully helped her over the rough cobbled ground, always careful to make sure that she did not accidentally place her kid boots into the numerous deposits of horse dung lying around.

The smell that exuded from the stables was unpleasant enough and most people considered it a healthy one, but the odour that penetrated from behind the stables and way beyond the stable area was indescribable. For Augusta and Charles now stood confronting rows upon rows of squalid mud and wattle thatched huts. These so-called huts consisted of one room, with hard-baked mud floors, with just a couple of rush-type mattresses strewn across them. The walls and roofs were daubed in some kind of sticky mixture that was only known to the natives of this country. There were several rows of them and all tightly packed together. A makeshift water hole had been dug at the far end of the huts, either to enable the convicts to drink from or wash in. Several copper pans had been placed on hooks jabbed into a crude piece of wood to represent some kind of shelf in which to hang their drinking or washing vessels.

All the huts were completely empty at this moment of time. Although it was now fairly late in the evening, it appeared that the convicts were still out working somewhere. Augusta and Charles were both having to resort to holding their kerchiefs under their nostrils. Augusta was beginning to feel extremely nauseous and faint. Charles suggested at once that they should return to the house, at the same time cursing himself for having exposed Augusta to such an unhealthy spectacle.

'No, no, Charles, I have made up my mind to investigate this situation to the full and I am not prepared to give in now,' she loudly retorted. 'We must find out where they are and what is happening to them.'

They hurried past the line of huts as fast as they could, with Augusta having to hitch her skirts up as high as she could. Fortunately, Charles was the perfect gentleman and carefully averted his eyes away from the yards of frilly underclothes that were now exposed.

Traversing on over ground that had once been full of ruts and rubble, it soon began to develop into a quagmire of slimy, evil smelling mire. Presently, a bit further on, there spread before them a fairly tall clump of straggly bushes, interspersed with patches of rough scrubby thicket and dotted around the area was the occasional eerie ghost gum tree. Then, before they could venture any further, a horse suddenly sprang out of nowhere in front of them. The rider of the horse, on seeing Mrs Fitzroy and Doctor Hadleigh making their way towards his line of direction, pulled sharply on the poor animal's reigns, causing its head to jerk upwards and snort profusely. The horse slithered to a halt and its rider, the new overseer, jumped to the ground. Augusta and Charles stopped in their tracks, somewhat taken aback by this unexpected intrusion.

Thrusting his wide-brimmed rancher's hat to the back of his head he exclaimed loudly, 'Good evening, Mrs Fitzroy, Doctor Hadleigh. Is there something the matter? For 'tis hardly the place that one would expect to find either of you. Does the Master know that you are here?'

Augusta hastily lowered her skirts and foolishly began to pick at the bits of burr that had stuck to her clothes. Charles just stood there with a slightly indolent look on his face.

'No, Mr Cookson, he does not. In fact we have not encountered him anywhere so far. I presume that you know of his whereabouts,' she answered him levelly.

Pushing his hat even further back and picking at his yellowish teeth with a dry twig he insolently said, 'Yes, Ma'am I do. He is visiting the Carters, the new settlers who are occupying the stretch of land to the west of Fairlawns.'

'The Carters,' she faltered. 'I do not think that I have heard Mr Fitzroy mention them to me. How long have they been here?'

He hesitated a moment before replying, 'About four to five months, Ma'am. But then seeing as you have been indisposed of late, the Master probably thought it best not to tire you with the details. He has been spending a lot of time with them lately, helping them to settle in and to adjust to their new surroundings. I think he hopes to involve them in some of his business schemes.'

'Them?' questioned Augusta. 'How many new arrivals are there? I trust that they are not more convicts. The place reeks with them now.'

'No, Mrs Fitzroy. They are most certainly not convicts.

79

These are God-fearing and respectable people. They are . . .' and here he broke off, to announce in clipped tones, 'But begging your pardon Ma'am, this is no concern of mine. It is not up to me to discuss the Master's business. I only do as I am instructed to and if you will excuse me, I have work to do. Must fetch the convicts back from having their victuals. By the way, Mrs Fitzroy, p'raps you would kindly tell your Doctor friend to keep his nose out of things that don't concern him. It might be to his own advantage if he were to spend his time trying to help those who deserve it and not those who don't. It's no business of his, to go poking about over there. It aint healthy for a start.'

During her conversation with the overseer she had not noticed that Charles had moved away from them and had been poking and prying about behind the long line of scrubby bushes. On hearing his name so rudely mentioned he quickly emerged and with a contorted, disapproving look on his face, he purposefully strode towards them. Charles was most careful to stand a few feet away from the other two, as his fine knee-length boots were partly covered in foul, highly pungent residue of human excrement, of which Augusta quickly became aware. Desperately trying hard not to embarrass Charles by creating a fuss about it, in the end she was forced to turn her back on him, staggered a few feet forwards and vomited and vomited until there was nothing left to bring up.

Charles himself felt wretched and hopelessly inadequate to deal with the situation. He longed to be able to rush over to her and help her. But he knew that he dare not. The state of the offending boots would only make matters worse. Instead he turned his fury on the overseer, who was just about to jump astride his horse and bolt off.

'Mr Cookson,' Doctor Hadleigh's voice reverberated through the air. 'Just a minute, if you please. What kind of man are you, who leaves the Lady of the House and a professional man as myself, in such a manner, with not so much as a by your leave or any consideration concerning both our predicaments? Would you please find Mrs Fitzroy something suitable for her to sit on. Even if it means that you have to unharness your horse and give her your own horse-hair blanket. And with as much grace as you can muster, I want you to remove these boots of mine and cleanse them to the best of your ability. I cannot possibly attend to Mrs Fitzroy until this highly offending footwear is a darned sight more presentable.'

The overseer slunk off towards his horse, muttering fiercely to himself. Pulling the rough haired blanket from off the animal, he searched around for a suitable tree stump to spread it out for Augusta to sit on. Cookson did his best in trying to settle her upon it, but his actions were clumsy and uncaring. Charles stood there watching, as this boor of a man ungraciously dumped Augusta on the ground. He dare not pull his boots off himself for fear of contaminating his hands and as there was no water near by to wash in, it would be impossible to examine her until he felt he was fit to do so. Fortunately, he did not have to wait too long as the overseer was impatient to be on his rounds. Doctor Hadleigh found a slab of rock to perch on, while Cookson yanked his boots off none too gently. Gingerly dragging them around the rough scrub, he then attempted to remove most of the muck. When he handed them back to Charles, they were at least dry if not altogether clean and by the time he had booted and dusted himself down he saw that Augusta was looking much better.

Kneeling down beside her he said very quietly, 'Mrs Fitzroy, I think you have had enough for to-day. I will see if I can find one of the boys to bring a horse around. There is no room for the buggy to pass through here. Will you be all right on your own?'

He had put one arm around her shoulders, and had very gently placed his forefinger under her chin and turned her face to his. His concern for her showed in his eyes and she longed to lean back in his arms and rest her head on his broad shoulders. Not since her Father had died had anyone looked at her like that before. Her heart was pounding beneath her ribs. She could feel the blood rushing to her cheeks and was beginning to feel a little light-headed. Taking her hand in his, Charles was attempting to take her pulse. She knew that her pulse-rate was racing ahead and was terrified that he might discover the real reason for her feeling this way. It was because he was so disturbingly close to her. Quickly averting her eyes from his, she turned her head sideways. If he had noticed anything untoward in her manner, he refrained from mentioning it. He merely stated that her pulse-rate was a little erratic, but that was only to be expected as she had walked further than she should have done, especially after spending so much time resting. Quickly rising to his feet, he moved away from her.

With the overseer gone some time beforehand and Charles now on his way to fetch a horse, Augusta was completely on her own. The temperature had dropped considerably and it was almost dark. Augusta felt relieved to be on her own for a short time, so as to allow her thoughts to calm down. But all did not stay peaceful for long. Coming towards her in the direction of the far ghostly, unfriendly gum trees, appeared the work-weary, grim-faced bunch of convicts, dragging themselves along at a painfully slow pace. Some were limping heavily where the chains had cut deeply into their rough flesh. Their tattered and torn makeshift garments were bloodstained from where they had wiped their cut and bleeding hands, caused by the rough and callous manual labouring that they had been forced to do. Having been fed the usual diet of greasy mutton stew, cooked in a heavy black cast-iron cauldron suspended on a pole over a blazing charcoal fire, they were forced to sit around this fire, holding their tin bowls, which at all times were fastened around their necks on thick chains, waiting for the overseer to slop the contents of the cauldron into them. He did this job himself, so as to make sure that everyone received their fair share, without causing any trouble or comment. After the meal, they were then led back to their huts. But before reaching them, the most inhuman act of all, was to take them, still chained, to the stinking putrid stretch of dug-out ground that served as the latrines. Women went first and then the men followed them. This was the place Doctor Hadleigh had the misfortune unwittingly to step into when he had gone exploring to find out from whence the unnatural stench has arisen. And all the time the overseer rode backwards and forwards, making sure that no-one had gone missing.

Oil lamps and tallow candles blazed forth from virtually every room in the house. As Doctor Hadleigh carried a fatigued and dispirited Augusta up the porch steps to the main door, Richard Fitzroy's voice could be heard sounding off all over the place. After kicking the bottom of the heavy door frantically for a while, the door was finally opened by Mr McTavish.

'She's here, sir, Madam has returned. God be praised, Mr Fitzroy, sir, she's here safe and sound.'

Normally Mr McTavish was not given to moving about at too great a speed, but now he ran through the house shouting the good news. Richard Fitzroy burst through the study door, just as Doctor Hadleigh was about to enter the small sitting-room, with Augusta still lying in his arms.

'My gad, sir, I hope you can explain your actions. Where do you think you have been with my wife?'

Fitzroy's face ws contorted with rage. His sparse hair was sticking up on end and his eyes glittered feverishly in his shiny face. Swiftly turning back into the hall, he bellowed at Mrs Potts and Betsy, who were both hovering wide-eyed at the bottom of the stairs, to take Augusta to her room and stay with her until the morning.

Doctor Hadleigh, who had by now set Augusta down on the couch, sprang towards her and went to lift her up to carry her upstairs, but Fitzroy, like something demented, flew at him and pushing him aside cried, 'No, you don't. We can manage without your assistance. You have caused enough trouble for one night. You and I have one or two things to discuss. I have not finished with you yet.'

Then turning to Mrs Potts and Betsy who were by now assisting their Mistress up the stairs he called out in his usual raised voice that Mr McTavish was to tell the rest of the servants to retire to their rooms and stay there till morning.

Richard stormed back into the sitting-room and slammed the door hard behind him. Doctor Hadleigh was leaning against the wall, feet well placed apart. The palms of his hands lay pressed against the wall for support. He could see by the contorted look on Richard's face that he was not in for an easy time with him.

With looks that could kill and a voice to match he hissed through his clenched teeth, 'Well, Doctor Hadleigh, I think it is high time that you and I came to some understanding as to how things stand between you and me. When you first arrived here at Fairlawns, you had nothing. Nothing that is apart from the clothes you stood up in, a collection of tatty so-called medical journals plus a well-worn bag of ineffectual medical instruments, but you did have the air and presence of a refined and well-bred English gentleman. Now, sadly, I can see that I was foolishly taken in by your charming manner and your cultured voice. I housed you, not in anything too comfortable, but certainly good enough for you. I even recommended you to my friends and colleagues. I gave you money to help with your researches and entrusted the care of my wife's health with you. I took you into my home and treated you like a close friend. You even had the privilege of standing in for me at the proxy marriage service between myself and Mrs Fitzroy. I suppose you thought that as you made my wife's acquaintance before I did, that gave you the right to a more informal relationship than would normally be permitted. I have also been informed that you even had the audacity to spend time with her out in the gardens on our wedding day. Then I am told that you and she have the occasional little *tete-a-tete* supper together. Not to mention the horse rides and so-called 'health enquiries' in order to find out whether I would be at home, as there were things you wished to discuss with me.'

Doctor Hadleigh moved away from the wall and went to make his way towards the door. He was not going to listen to anymore of this nonsense.

But Richard barred his way. 'No, you don't, you hear me out. Now this latest and most disgraceful episode of all. You actually insisted on taking my wife on a dangerous excursion on the pretence of wanting to talk to me. Where the hell have the pair of you been all this time and judging by the state of her when you carried her in, by God sir, I am almost afraid to ask?'

Fitzroy flopped his large frame on to the horsehair sofa and waited for the Doctor to reply. Doctor Hadleigh was so taken aback and angry at the vicious accusations that had been thrown at him, that it took some time before he could reply. Striding backwards and forwards across the room, he then forced his way towards the door. With one hand on the door knob he turned and faced Fitzroy and in tight clipped tones he answered.

'There is nothing that I have to apologise to you for. I have no desire to waste my breath on suitable excuses for my perfectly innocent actions. As for to-night, both Mrs Fitzroy and myself decided to find out for ourselves the plight of those poor souls that you have brought out here to do your dirty work. I may have nothing, as you say, but at least I do my own dirty work without involving the efforts of others. Well, we found out where you have kept them hidden and how you treat them, or perhaps I should say ill-treat them. Why, your own horses are kept in better conditions than they are. And the conditions of the convicts was what I really came to see you about and nothing else. Perhaps it has slipped your mind, Richard, that I am by profession a Doctor, nor is it just a handle to my name. I care about all the ills and misfortunes of everyone and not just the chosen few who can afford it.'

'Well, more fool you,' cut in Fitzroy. 'You will get no thanks or rewards from the peasants and wrong-doers of this world. They were a bad lot in the Old Country, so why should we make it easier for them now they are out here? And let me tell you something else, Doctor Hadleigh,' and the words Doctor Hadleigh were said with heavy sarcasm, 'When I came to this colony, I had one thing in my mind and one thing only. I was going to be king-pin around here. The Squire. The Lord of the Manor, call it what you will. Even though we are not allowed titles over here, I still want the biggest house. The best cultivated lands. The best set of stables. I want to do all the things here that I could not achieve anywhere else. But here, they will work, because I shall work day and night if necessary to find a way of achieving it. Now, if that means that I have the added fortune to be able to buy shiploads of convicts to do it, then by God, I will and no-one, mark me well, no-one will ever stop me from getting my own way. After all, Rome was not built in a day. And all things are rendered unto Caesar are they not? And that brings me back to Mrs Fitzroy. You will not see her again until it is time for the child to be delivered. I do need you for that particular function. There is no way that I want the future heir of Fairlawns being bungled into this world. I cannot stop you from practising in this colony, as we need a Doctor here. But from here on, keep your professional nose out of my private affairs.'

Charles went to turn the door knob. Could it be that

Richard Fitzroy had finally run out of steam. Turning the knob slowly, he pushed the door wide open and stared into the ill-lit gloomy hall. Seeing that no-one was in sight or hearing, he strode back to say something to Fitzroy but he was prevented from doing so, as he was stopped with a curt, 'Good night, Doctor Hadleigh. There is nothing more I wish to say to you.'

Turning his back on the Doctor, Fitzroy walked towards the nearest whisky decanter, poured himself a tankard full and gulped it back in one mouthful.

Charles watched him and, with a smirk on his face, he could not resist saying to the back of the bulky frame that stood within the lengthening shadows of the room, 'Good night to you too, Mr Fitzroy. Oh, and before I depart. Isn't there something in the Bible that says, What profiteth a man if he gains the whole world but in doing so loses his own soul?'

8

It was late afternoon and as Augusta was now in the final stages of her confinement, it had been her custom of late to retire to the day-bed in her room, in an attempt to finish off the tedious piece of embroidery that she had unwillingly taken upon herself to do. She hated needlework of any kind. It was such a painstaking task. How Mrs Jameson and her ilk had spent their entire lives dedicated to it she would never understand. Dropping the embroidery on the floor in despair, she lay her head back against the soft cushions. Placing her hands lightly either side of her stomach, she looked down to see if she could see her feet. But no, all she could see was this solid lump in front of her tired eyes. She was feeling thoroughly depressed and wretched. She was tired of sitting around all day with nothing of any importance to do. The weather had been unbearably hot these last few weeks. Raising her head a trifle, she looked out of the window and stared at the grounds in dismay. Everything was parched and dry. There was no grass left anywhere. The ground was rock hard, so hard that it hurt one's feet to walk over it. The distant trees were gaunt and bare. Nothing seemed to stir. It was as if the heat had exhausted everything in sight. The only things that seemed to move at any kind of speed at all were those damn eternal flies and mosquitoes. Those little beggars were able to seep in everywhere.

The air in the room was getting stuffier and more humid by the minute. Augusta's peignoir, although made of a flimsy material, was sticking to her everywhere. On the tiny bedside table lay a bowl of freshly-filled rose water, which she constantly dabbed herself all over with. How she wished that she could immerse herself in a cool refreshing tub of water. But that was out of the question as there was a tremendous water shortage due to the unusually long dry spell. Everyone was now fervently praying for rain. Augusta, on glancing around the bedroom, could not but help think what a depressing room it still was, even though she had tried in vain to make it more pleasing to the eye. Everywhere looked so mucky and granite-soiled. The constant lack of water made it nigh on impossible for the servants to clean thoroughly. Ringing the bell for Betsy, she thought at least a fresh gown and a vigorous brushing of her hair might help to relieve the boredom somewhat. Betsy took longer than usual to reach the room. Presently her pale and weary looking face appeared round the door frame.

'You rang for me, Ma'am,' she quietly asked.

'Yes, Betsy, you know I did,' replied Augusta testily. 'I would very much like a change of attire and my hair to be well brushed. I feel a mess.'

Betsy moved slowly towards her.

'I know how you feel, Ma'am. This fearful heat is getting to all of us. If it doesn't rain soon, I think we shall all go mad. I have heard as how the Master may have to shoot some of the livestock and his best horses, to boot, if things don't improve soon,' said Betsy, shaking her head sadly.

'Oh, no that would be too dreadful,' Augusta replied aghast. 'Those poor beasts, surely something can be done to prevent that happening.'

Pulling Augusta's hair back tightly from her forehead so that she could sponge her face properly, Betsy said, 'Well, it won't be just the animals that will suffer. It could be all of us next. Apparently Mr McTavish says that the water towers are bone-dry and our own domestic water-barrel is only half full and that is the only one left. Mrs Potts is sneaking bowls of water into the pantry in case of dire emergencies.'

As she was talking, Betsy was rummaging around in the closet for something cool for Augusta to wear.

'Do you know, Ma'am, there is not one clean thing left to wear. Everything is stained or too unsuitable for this climate.'

'Oh Betsy, I cannot sit around all day in this sticky peignoir,' Augusta wailed. 'You must be able to sort something out for me.'

Betsy shook her head. Then suddenly her eyes brightened as she cried out, 'Not to fret, Ma'am. I will go and find Mrs

Jameson and see if she can run you up something in a hurry. You know how good she is with her needle.'

So saying, Betsy went in search of her leaving Augusta to contemplate her own tatty piece of work.

Some time later, both Betsy and Mrs Jameson returned. Mrs Jameson had tucked under one arm a roll of white silken material which she suddenly threw across the patchwork rug for Augusta to inspect.

'Now then, Ma'am, let's see if there be enough material here to be able to make you something a little more fetching to wear.'

Augusta gazed at it. It was beautiful.

'Where on earth did you find this, Mrs Jameson?' Augusta enquired wide-eyed.

Mrs Jameson hesitated, then blushing quite profusely said, 'Why, Ma'am, it was left over from my own wedding gown. It was put away in case I ever needed it again. But I doubt if I ever will now. I had almost forgotten that I still had it. You are more than welcome to it, Ma'am.'

Augusta felt deeply touched by this simple woman's kindly gesture and gratefully answered her with, 'Thank you, Mrs Jameson, that is very thoughtful of you and I appreciate your kind offer.'

So between the two of them, Betsy and Mrs Jameson contrived to make for Augusta a loose-fitting but fairly fashionable new gown.

☆   ☆   ☆

It was early that evening as Richard stormed into the house and made his way up the stairs towards his dressing-room. Without waiting for his valet to attend him, he at once stripped off his sweaty, dust-stained clothes and, rubbing himself vigorously all over with a piece of linen, he then hastily changed into a set of fresh clothes. In so doing he could hear Augusta lightly humming away pleasantly in the adjoining bedroom. Silently unlocking and pushing the connecting door open, he stepped unobtrusively into the room to observe his wife sitting at her dressing-table having her long hair arranged by Betsy. She was, of course, now wearing the hastily made garment and feeling a little happier at having something fresh and clean to wear. Mrs Jameson was to be seen sprawling about on all fours, collecting up the fallen pins and the last remains of the discarded remnants from off the floor. Richard took in the scene and a sudden scowl spread across his hot perspiring face. Augusta immediately became aware of his presence and, noticing the look on his face through the looking glass, quickly dismissed Mrs Jameson and Betsy.

A little nervously she said, 'This is a surprise, Richard. It is not often that you are home this early in the evening. I trust everything is fine.'

Rising from her stool a little awkwardly she walked towards him.

'No, it is not fine,' he snapped back at her. 'This damnable heat and the constant lack of any rain is beginning to take its toll. Nothing is surviving. The stupid men have all stopped work. The ground is unworkable. Every damn pickaxe and hoe is beyond repair. The smith is now suffering from exhaustion at trying to mend so many broken implements. Half the wretched convicts are ill with some bloody bowel trouble. Nothing is working out according to plan. Furthermore, several weeks ago I lost my damn fool temper with your Doctor Hadleigh and that stupid ass hasn't set foot around the place since then. Just when I need him too.'

Slumping himself down on the bed and tearing at the buttons of his shirt, he pulled it over his head and began to wipe his chest and arms with it. Augusta on a sudden impulse came towards him and sat down beside him. This was the first time in their marriage that she had ever made any kind of approach towards him. She wondered what tempted her to do it. She certainly did not love this man, nor did she physically want him. But somehow, because she had felt so frustrated and cooped-up herself of late, she began to understand how he was feeling, he being a man who always had to be involved in something or other all the time. They both sat there on the edge of the bed, neither one saying anything. It was even too hot to talk. But presently Richard soon became impatient at sitting still. Turning towards her and raking his eyes fully over her face and body, he found he quite liked what he saw. She looked quite enticing this evening. There seemed to be something different about her.

He ran one finger alongside the side of her gown. It felt soft and luxuriant to his touch.

'I have not seen this before. Is it new?'

Richard's voice was of a lower pitch than normal.

She nodded her head and said, 'Yes, it is just something Mrs Jameson ran up this afternoon. I am afraid, Richard, I have nothing left to wear. Everything I possess is either too tight or extremely filthy. The material belonged to Mrs Jameson. Apparently, I have nothing left to make anything out of.'

Turning her eyes full on his face, she went on. 'Don't you think, Richard, that it was very sweet of her to offer it to me?'

Richard growled deeply and snatched his hand away from her side and in his customary gruff voice growled, 'Augusta are you trying to imply that I am neglectful of my responsibilities towards you as my wife? If you need new clothes, fancy hair ribbons, sashes, fans or whatever newfangled nonsensical fripperies that you women need to possess, you have only to ask me for them. God in heaven, woman, do you really think that I want to create the impression that we are paupers and that I cannot afford to dress my wife, Mrs Richard Henry Fitzroy, in the manner befitting her station in life?'

Augusta was amazed at this sudden concern for her well-being and decided to reward him for his pains by giving him one of her dazzling smiles.

This seemed to please him a little for he patted her knee and went on by saying, 'Now, what is it you need so desperately that you have to seek the help and charity from one of our servants?'

And before she could answer him, he continued to prattle on about how it would look down in the servants' quarters or around the outskirts of the colony, that the Lady of the House was being forced to walk about in the servants' left-offs.

'Surely, Augusta,' he went on, 'even you should know that it is the other way around. It is ladies of quality who give away their cast-offs. Are you quite sure that you came from the kind of background that you would have me believe? Was your father really such a great friend of Prinny's and your mother the Court 'Darling' that you have made her out to be?'

'Richard, how dare you speak to me like that.'

Angrily she started to rise from the bed but he quickly pulled her down on to it again. Her face was flushed. Her eyes were burning like two bright orbs. Her whole body was quivering with anger.

'Richard, that is the most wicked thing to say to me. Do I not look and behave like a lady? If you do not believe me, you only have to ask Doctor Hadleigh about my credentials, for he knew some of my parents' friends and acquaintances. He has never doubted me.'

She forced herself to say this knowing that it would only add fuel to the already over-heated flames.

'Hadleigh,' he stormed. 'Everyone quotes that man as if he were some sort of saint. I am sick of hearing how good Doctor Hadleigh is at this, that or the other. From what I can make out the man does not appear to be able to put a foot wrong in the place. It is not natural for a man to be like that. I like a man to be a man. Full of animal magnetism, rough and strong. One who can exert his will over others. That is what I call a man.'

'Not everyone would agree with you, Richard,' she timidly replied.

'Well, maybe not,' he retorted. Then in a softer tone of voice he added, 'What is it that you require for yourself, my dear?'

Augusta had calmed down a little and was now more in control of herself.

Pleadingly she said, 'There is such a lot I need Richard. New gowns for myself. But what is of the utmost importance is the layette for our baby that will soon be here. I have tried to crochet a few things myself, but I am not very good at it. Also, I would like my baby to have a proper crib and cradle. I do not want my baby to have to sleep in a top drawer of a cupboard, as so many seem to.'

But this last remark really set him in a spin.

'Good heavens, woman. What are you about? Sleeping in drawers. You must take me for a right bastard if you think that I would wish that. No, by God. The little one must have the best. I shall instruct that lazy son of a bitch Potts to put his back into it and have him make as much furniture as you need for the baby. And as for you, I will have someone ride over to the store to see what they may have in the way of materials and if that does not suit, I will send the overseer to the nearest harbour to see what has arrived on the latest clipper. He is just about the only one that I can trust here to take the money without bolting off into the blue with it. Though God only knows what he would come back with!'

'Thank you, Richard. I will be very grateful for whatever comes. I do realize, you know, that this is not the Court of St James.'

She had not meant that last remark to sting so. She meant it more as a joke. But Fitzroy did not possess a sense of humour and automatically took it the wrong way. He thought she was trying to snub him.

Augusta became acutely aware of the change that had come over him in the past few minutes. His anger had suddenly evaporated. He was almost conciliatory towards her. Rising slowly from the bed, she made her way towards the dressing-table and all the time she was conscious of the fact that he was watching her. Picking up the silver-backed hairbrush, she began to draw it idly through her hair. Glancing over her shoulder, she asked Richard if he would ring the bell for Betsy to come and arrange her hair and added, as an afterthought, that it might be a good idea if he were to put his shirt on and tidy his own hair. After all it was almost time for supper. But Richard made no attempt to move, so in frustration Augusta turned herself fully round and said, 'Richard, please could you ring . . .'

'Not now,' he quickly cut in. My God she looked so beautiful tonight, he thought to himself. The newness and the freshness of the silky white gown, had been fashioned to sit tightly on her shoulders, then plunge deeply down to her breasts and fall loosely over her stomach and hips, finally finishing up in soft flowing folds that barely covered her toes. If it were not for the bulge in the middle, she looked almost virginal. Of late he had not pressed himself upon her, but tonight, looking as she did, she was not going to escape.

'Come here, Augusta, and be a good girl. Supper can wait for a change.'

Augusta was rudely awoken the next morning by great flashes of light dancing around the room. She blinked, then closed her eyes tightly. Flash, there it was again. She was just about to waken Richard who was still sprawled out beside her, with his mouth wide open and snoring profusely, when a series of violent crashes resounded around the whole house. then, before she could move from the bed, she heard it. It started in large pattering drops, silently splaying onto the window sill. Faster and faster it became, then huge torrents of it were bursting forth in quicksilver crescendoes.

Richard was now awake.

'Great heavens,' he exclaimed, reaching out for his discarded breeches. 'Rain, rain at last. And by God, I hope it rains forever.'

Feverishly pulling on the rest of his clothes, he hopped madly about the room. Augusta had struggled out of bed and was watching from the window with fascination at the way everyone from the house and grounds were dancing about, some almost naked, all revelling in this glorious rain. She laughed to herself and thought how absurd this would sound to the people back home if they knew that they actually did their utmost to drench themselves in it.

Richard was now fully dressed and, leaping towards the door, he shouted over to her, 'I meant what I said last night. Make sure you get all those things you require. You will have to ask for them yourself, as I shall be too busy coping with all the problems that this deluge has caused. I shudder to think what it will be like up at The New Plantation.'

Then before leaving the room, he suddenly changed his mind and walked back towards her. Placing both hands heavily on her shoulders he muttered, 'Take care, my dear, and of the coming little one. Don't wait up for me. I shall probably be out and about for quite some time now.'

And before she could utter a word, he had swept through the open doorway and was dashing down the stairs out into the rain.

Slowly and methodically everything was slipping back into some sort of order. The past three weeks had been sheer chaos. Virtually everyone had been working day and night coping with the mopping up process. The main storm had been a particularly violent one, followed by several smaller outbursts that had lasted about three to four days. It had been due to extremely high temperatures of late. The rain had been incessant and the unusually high winds that had leapt up overnight had caused a great deal of damage. Inside the house the servants were seated around the kitchen table taking a well-earned break. The kitchen door had been flung open wide so as to enable the floor to dry out more quickly. Mr McTavish had turned his chair around and was looking straight through the open door onto the soggy stretch of ground directly in front of him.

'Well, at least everything smells a lot fresher. Damp maybe, but a fresh damp if you get my meaning,' he commented to anyone who happened to be listening to him.

''Bout time too,' replied Sally, the young kitchen maid. 'The pong here was beginning to make me feel quite queer.'

'Wouldn't have thought you would have noticed any peculiar smells, seeing as you spend so much of your time out in the stables with the stable lad,' someone poked in sarcastically.

'That will be enough,' snapped Mrs Potts. 'We are all tired, there is no need to make things worse by upsetting each other.'

'You still moaning, Ma?' voiced a weary Jack, as he suddenly entered the kitchen. 'Is there anything left to drink or has everybody swigged it all?'

'Here, have the rest of mine and less of your cheek,' Mrs Potts reprimanded her cheeky son, as she handed him a half full tankard of ale. 'And you can just take those boots off as well. Just look at them. Sally and I have spent hours trying to clean this kitchen floor.'

'Fast as we clean one bit, so someone walks in and messes it all up again,' moaned Mrs Soames.

Jack stared at his mother and Mrs Soames in amazement. The kitchen floor was not always noted for its cleanliness. As a rule it was the most unsavoury spot in the entire house. During the course of a busy day everything in sight from left over scraps of food, lumps of fat, discarded vegetable stumps, twirls of sugar, feathers from all types of fowl that had not been properly plucked, eventually found their way there. Not to mention the obvious bird droppings that were to be found lurking in hidden corners from the occasional chicken that would fly in every now and again just to root around. But the aftermath of the storm had intensified everything on a far greater scale. The water and the dirt seemed to have poured in from every nook and cranny in sight. The selfsame bowls and cans that Mrs Potts had carefully secreted into the pantry to hide the once precious water in, were now being used to catch the drips. So it was no wonder that after such a frantic and hectic period of additional work, and just as things were beginning to settle down and dry out, tempers were naturally beginning to fray at the least display of inconsideration of other's work.

The ultimate climax came, when on the following morning just as Betsy had removed Augusta's breakfast tray, the first of the pains started. Augusta was not too worried at first, as over the past few weeks she had experienced the occasional sharp twinge. Mrs Potts had assured her that this was quite normal and not to worry as there were still a couple of weeks to go, at least by her reckoning, before the baby was due. But as the morning wore on so the pains quickened and sharpened and Augusta started to feel more than just a little anxious. She knew that this was not the most appropriate time to start to go into labour. Everyone with the exception of Augusta herself had worn themselves to a frazzle lately. Richard she had barely seen at all. He was being kept busy on the land. Doctor Hadleigh had not been near the place since that dreadful day when Richard had upset him so. Goodness knows where he might be now, just when she needed him the most. He could be anywhere in the vicinity attending to all kinds of problems and plights. Still it was no use lying in bed worrying about such things. She had best summons Betsy right away. The frantic ringing of Augusta's bell could be heard all over the house as Mrs Potts and Betsy rushed upstairs in answer to it. Betsy had taken it on herself to mention to the rest of the servants, that after returning from her mistress's room earlier on, she looked as if she were in pain and that things might start to happen sooner than was expected.

Mrs Potts gave one look at Augusta and her worst fears were already realized. She reassuringly placed one cool hand onto Augusta's already fevered brow and placed the other onto her heaving stomach.

Breathing deeply she called out, 'Betsy, quick run fetch Jack and tell him to fetch Doctor Hadleigh straight away and make sure that you tell him that the Mistress's baby is on the way. Otherwise that dozy son of mine will tarry all day over it.'

Betsy did not need to be told, for she was already out of the room and running along the corridor.

Back in the bedroom Augusta was plaintively complaining to Mrs Potts, that she was sorry to be such a nuisance.

'Nuisance, that you are not, these things cannot be helped. You can't stop nature Ma'am,' replied Mrs Potts gently. 'Now you just rest quietly whilst I go and instruct them in the kitchen to boil up the water. Oh, I must get some fresh linen and plenty of towels from the linen-chest. Oh dear, so much to do. It will be another case of 'All hands on the Deck' as they say.'

And with that she scuttled out of the room, chattering and squawking to herself.

It had been the most dreadful day. Nothing had gone according to plan. It had started as soon as Mrs Potts left Augusta's room and went to collect the fresh linen and towels from the linen-chest and to her dismay she found it almost bereft of them. It had slipped her mind that due to the wet weather more linen had been used and had not been replaced. Clicking her tongue in annoyance, she hastened down to the kitchen where horror of horrors, she found that Mr McTavish and Mrs Soames were carefully dismantling the kitchen range. Apparently the old thing had been working overtime lately and they had decided to give it a really good clean.

'Oh my goodness!' exclaimed Mrs Potts, 'How long are you going to be on that thing? The mistress has gone into labour and I shall need plenty of hot water.'

'Oh no, so soon,' puffed Mrs Soames.

'Well, we cannot carry on with the cleaning of this monster,' pointing a finger in the direction of the black sooty range.

'Leave that now, Mr McTavish, and find Jack and tell him to bring up plenty of wood for burning.'

'Oh, that's torn it,' wailed Mrs Potts, slumping down on the nearest chair.

'You will have to get someone else to fetch the wood. Jack I hope is on his way to find the Doctor. And where is that dratted girl Sally? I need to know what has happened to the clean linen.'

'Hm, you are not the only one who wants to know where Sally is. I shall be needing her soon to start on the vegetables,' Mrs Soames wearily answered as she and Mr McTavish were hastily putting the partially cleaned range back to its previous state.

'There that will have to do, Mr McTavish. Now will you please be off and get some dry wood for me. Sooner we get this thing going again the better.' Mr McTavish virtually had an apopolectic fit as he bounced round the kitchen floor shouting, 'Me get the wood? Really Mrs Soames, I am not the errand boy around here. Perhaps you would like me to remind you as to what my duties actually are.'

'No we do not', interrupted Mrs Potts, as she neatly stuck one foot out in front of him, causing him to trip over and reflect on his haughtiness.

'Now get up off that floor Mr McTavish and please oblige.'

In all his years he had never been asked to fetch wood. Someone would answer for this. Yes, indeed.

He was halfway across to the woodpile when he spotted Sally sauntering along with a straw-coloured open basket on her arm. Her strawberry blonde locks had sprung free from the white lace mob-cap that had encircled them earlier on. Wispy pieces of straw clung to the bottom of her coarse black skirt. A dreamy far-away look was written all over her face for all the world to see.

'You will get caught good and proper one of these days, if you are not more careful,' he sternly reprimanded her.

'Don't know what you are talking about I'm sure,' she saucily answered him.

She was feeling in a wonderful relaxed mood, something she needed after all the hard work of late. And she was not going to have it ruined by this old sourpuss, so she quickly invented an excuse in the hope of keeping him quiet.

'I'm a good girl I am, have just been round to see if there were any more eggs lying around. They should be laying better now, seeing as how the weather has improved. Hens don't like the wet, you know.'

But Mr McTavish was not to be fooled and replied testily, 'Well, that's a good one I must say, especially at this time of the day.'

Coming up closer to him and batting her long silky lashes at him, she answered him wide-eyed and impudently, 'Come to think of it, I might just ask as to what you are doing venturing out in this direction. Not your usual place for a stroll is it.'

Suddenly he was reminded of the errand he had been sent on and contemptuously snapped back at her, 'You had best hurry back to the house, my girl. You are needed at once. Apparently the babe is on the way.'

'Oh lawks, why didn't you tell me sooner, you silly man,' she cried, dropping the empty basket and hared off towards the house.

Just as Sally reached the kitchen door she bumped full into Betsy, who was puffing and panting from the exertion of having to hunt all over the place for Jack.

'Has the Mistress had it yet?' Sally cried excitedly.' 'I jolly well hope not,' answered Betsy fervently. 'For nothing is ready for her.'

Mrs Potts, on hearing the two girls outside the kitchen door, called out to them to stop chattering and come inside and get on with their chores. Ordering Betsy to find out how Augusta was faring, she then sent Sally to collect the clean linen from wherever she had popped it to air.

Things went from bad to worse when Mr McTavish arrived back with the wood, all of it soaking wet. Nobody had thought to dry any in case it was needed in a hurry. The usual procedure after a wet spell was to dry a large supply in the wicker baskets, either side of the range. But this had been overlooked. Mrs Potts nearly went mad as she watched helplessly at the frantic actions of Mr McTavish and Mrs Soames as they tried to light the damp wood. Eventually, after a long tedious session with the aid of a pair of creaking bellows, they actually succeeded. The next duty to be performed on Mrs Potts mental list was to put a stop to Sally's excited prattlings and force her to sort out and prepare all the bedding and store it into its proper place. The fire at the bottom of the range was coughing, spluttering and belching out soot and smoke all over the freshly cleaned kitchen. Sally could be seen backing out of a cubby hole somewhere in the corner of the room, struggling under a pile of sheets which she intended to drape over the fender. Seconds later after she had neatly laid them out, Mrs Soames came puffing in with another copper pan filled with water to heat up. Struggling to place the heavy pan on top of the range, she noticed that the carefully ironed sheets were now spotted in flecks of black soot.

Dumping the pan down with a clumsy thud that caused much of its contents to slop onto the sheets, she screeched at Sally, 'You thoughtless chit. Look what you have done to those sheets. Waste of time washing them in the first place. Take them out of here and find somewhere else for them.'

Sally began to cry, 'Don't know where else to put them. Everywhere is still damp.'

Mrs Soames by now had completely lost control and began shaking the poor girl fiercely by the shoulders.

'You will have to wait till the fire has stopped smoking, otherwise you won't be able to use them at all.'

Leaving Sally choking away, Mrs Soames hauled them off the fender and plonked them down on a nearby vacant chair.

Upstairs Mrs Potts was questioning Betsy as to whether Jack had gone in search of the Doctor. Then she remembered that no-one had been sent to inform the Master. Augusta seemed to be holding her own for the time being and, apart from the pains becoming more acute, she felt that she could manage for a little longer without the aid of Doctor Hadleigh.

'Betsy leave the Mistress alone for a while, find Old Amos and tell him to inform the Master that the Mistress is about to have her baby.'

Betsy whirled around the room and wailed, 'Oh, no not again. I have only just recovered from dashing about trying to find Jack and you won't believe where I found him and who he was with.'

'Betsy, I am not in the least bit concerned where he was. Just do as you are told,' she cut in sharply.

'Sorry, Mrs Potts,' and turning to Augusta, 'Ever so sorry, Ma'am. I didn't mean to be rude,' and with an apologetic glance towards Augusta, took hold of her damp clammy hands and squeezing them gently, said in an unconvincing manner, 'Now, don't you fret, Ma'am. Everything is going to be fine. Just fine.'

But everything had been far from 'just fine', for young Jack, who after being caught around the back of the hen houses with young Sally, in a most uncompromising situation, one in which he was most embarrassed and upset about as he really preferred Betsy to Sally but since she had been elevated to the position of 'Mistress's personal maid', she now looked down her nose and even refused to speak to him. So, leaving Sally to fend for herself, he sulkily set off in search of Doctor Hadleigh.

Old Amos in trying to find the Master, decided not to go on his own enlisted the help of the stable boy. Neither of them had bothered with saddles, as very few of the workers did anyway. With a few hasty words, they set off in opposite directions. The stable boy shot off like a mad hare, for he was more than delighted at being able to escape from his normally tedious routine. Old Amos, on the other hand, went lumbering along, as he was wont when asked to do something other than routine.

The evening was wearing on and neither Fitzroy nor Doctor Hadleigh had arrived. Operations in the kitchen had now reached boiling point, in more ways than one.

Pans and kettles were steaming merrily away. The fire being stoked up at frequent intervals had now ceased to belch out smoke to all and sundry.

'Thank goodness for that,' said Mr McTavish loudly. 'The kitchen was beginning to look like a laundry room. Perhaps, Mrs Soames, you could clear the kitchen table and we could all settle down to a nice quiet drink.'

'Not to-day I don't. There is still far too much to do. I'm only half-way through getting the supper sorted out. Now come on move yourself from under my feet and go and make yourself useful.'

Then seeing Mrs Jameson standing in the passageway talking to Mrs Potts she called out, 'Well, I wondered where you had vanished to.'

Mrs Jameson was another one who thought she was above the kitchen staff and chose to ignore the cutting remark. Pushing her way past Mrs Soames she walked straight up to the kitchen range and with immaculate care and precision laid out an assorted array of little bits of crochet over the fender. Mr McTavish, on poking his head round the door, glanced towards the kitchen table, in hopeful anticipation that Mrs Soames had changed her mind and made a brew of some kind. But no, sadly enough, the table was now strewn with a pile of mud-caked vegetables. Mrs Soames, out of the corner of her eye caught him and knowing men only too well, guessed at what he had come back for. With a fixed set of head and in a very determined voice she announced.

'Mr McTavish, if you are that desperate for a drink, you will have to make it yourself.'

Mrs Potts on seeing the rear end of Mrs Jameson, once more bent over the stove moved up behind and pulling at her pinafore cried out, 'You will have to move away from there. I shall need clear access to it very shortly I fear. Things have taken a turn for the worse upstairs and if the Doctor does not arrive soon, I'm afraid we will have to manage without him.'

On hearing this, Mrs Jameson suddenly flew into a panic and seized all the baby clothes from off the fender. The rest of the servants gawped at her in amazement as she slowly waltzed around the room cradling them in her arms. In a frenzied tone she informed them that 'she knew absolutely nothing about bringing babes into the world. Crocheting and sewing was one thing but helping to deliver one successfully was another.' Then like the onset of a highly contagious disease, Mr McTavish also took fright. Carried away by Mrs Jameson's brilliant performance and grabbing hold of the poor woman he, also joined in the melee.

The whole charade came to an abrupt end when Betsy with her curly hair all awry under her lace cap and with perspiration running in rivulets down her forehead shrieked at the top of her voice.

'Mrs Potts, come quick. The Mistress is ever so bad. We must have the Doctor at once.'

Mrs Potts flew up the stairs behind her, 'Oh my God Betsy, what are we going to do?' she wailed, wringing her hands in despair.

'Where's that boy of mine? Hasn't been seen since I sent him off to find the Doctor. Trust a man. Never around when you need them most. Well, it is no use getting ourselves in a tither.' Standing at the top of the stairs, she called down to the rest of the servants, 'Come on now, all of you, let's have those hot water cans and as many towels as you can carry upstairs now.'

And so saying, they set to with more will than know-how.

Before they reached her room, they could hear Augusta's anguished cries.

'All I hope,' said a panting Mrs Soames, 'is that it is a fairly straight-forward birth. Any awkward turns at the last minute and we are all sunk.'

On entering the hot and stuffy room, the first thing Mrs Potts did, after placing the water can on top of the washstand, was to fling open wide all the windows. Betsy at once went over to the bed and continued her former task of trying to cool down Augusta's fevered brow. Augusta lay there, tossing and turning, her over-bright eyes constantly opening and closing in response to the spasmodic spasms of sharp pain. Her nightshift was soaked in perspiration and clung to her burning and swollen body . Several times she caught hold of Betsy's hand and in a gasping voice she cried out for the Doctor.

'Won't be long now Ma'am,' replied Betsy fervently.

Dusk was creeping upon them and still no sign of the Doctor. Mrs Potts was standing by the open window, just willing either the Doctor or the Master to appear. But neither ventured forth.

The pains were now coming at regular intervals and both Mrs Potts and Betsy were becoming more alarmed as each one passed. Mrs Soames, who was seated on the chaise-longue, with her head held in her hands, swaying backwards and forwards, suddenly clapped her hands together and thoughtfully announced that one of them ought to lift the bedcovers to see if anything was happening. Naturally enough there followed a heated discussion as to who should volunteer. As luck would have it, their arguments were swiftly cut short by the sound of horses hooves thundering up the carriage-way.

Mrs Potts flew back to the window and leaning her head out as far as it would go, she screamed out, 'I think it's the Doctor. Pray God, that it is.'

Doctor Hadleigh arrived not a second too early. For by now Augusta was completely incapable of holding on without the aid and experience of a Doctor to assist her. Sending everyone out of the room, Charles hurriedly removed his jacket, rolled up his sleeves tightly and swiftly went towards the bed.

103

The labour went on for at least another hour or so. Charles stood patiently by, one eye fixed intently on Augusta, the other watching the round face of the moon as it stared at him across the inky black sky. But not for long, for after an arduous and exhausting fight for life, Doctor Hadleigh finally triumphed and safely delivered into the world Augusta's baby, a tiny but perfectly formed girlchild.

9

Nestling contentedly amongst a pile of pillows, Augusta gazed fondly at the little bundle that lay fast asleep beside her. It was hard to believe looking at the baby's wispy golden hair, the lightly creased brow and the sweet rosebud mouth, with one minute finger resting under its chin and now blissfully peaceful after its feed, warm bath and a fresh change of linen, that only five days ago she had caused such consternation to its mother. Augusta was feeling much stronger but the birth had been a terrible ordeal, one that she would not care to go through again quite so willingly. It was reasonably quiet in the house. The traditional celebrations and wetting the baby's head as was customary had now died a natural death. Everyone had gone overboard at first, for this was the first child from the Fairlawns household to be born in the New Country. Mrs Potts would insist that it was a 'proper little foreigner' until Mr McTavish pointed out, that it was the rest of the household who were the foreigners, as they had left their country of origin to settle in a new one. The baby heralded a new breed amongst the community. Charles had ridden over every day so far just to make sure that all was well. Each visit had been a very disconcerting experience for him, for he still felt uncomfortable in the house, nor had he encountered Fitzroy since their last stormy meeting. There were certain things concerning Augusta's well-being that, as her husband, Fitzroy ought to be informed about. But, although he had enquired several times regarding his whereabouts, no-one seemed prepared to enlighten him.

Fitzroy, true to himself, had behaved with his usual customary indifference to the birth. It was Old Amos who had eventually tracked him down to one of the more recent arrivals in the colony, a somewhat brash and slightly circumspect pair by the name of O'Rourke. They originated from some low-lying county in Ireland. Old Amos had found Fitzroy sitting out on their verandah swigging some ghastly home-made brew and swopping even ghastlier yarns with them. The sudden and unexpected appearance of the old timer, actually leaping about in front of him and shouting at the top of his rusty old voice that, 'You had best get home quick as the babe is on its way', completely threw him off his stroke. Annoyed and embarrassed at having been spoken to in front of his newly-acquired companions needless to say provoked a sharp and bitter response. He sent Old Amos off with a flea in his ear, telling him that he would return when it suited him and not before. Returning to his recently vacated chair, he pondered thoughfully for a while. Then to the amazement of his hosts, spontaneously announced that he was about to become a father. He also decided that as there was no-one back at Fairlawns with whom he could whole-heartedly rejoice with, he might as well make a night of it and stay in the already inebriate company of his new-found friends.

The celebrating had actually lasted three whole days, with Fitzroy circulating and partaking of 'a drop or two' at each and every place that he stopped off at on his way home.

It was Mr McTavish who had first spotted him, lying over the horse's neck, while the poor animal gingerly trod its way up the carriage-way. Waiting till the horse almost reached parallel with the front porch steps, he ran towards Fitzroy and tried to haul him off with as much dignity as the situation allowed. Surprisingly enough, he managed that part reasonably well, but his Master was so completely intoxicated that as soon as he had been shaken out of his reverie, he at once burst forth and began shouting incoherent noises in a strange and highly pitched voice. Poor Mr McTavish was at his wits end in trying to calm him down.

'Mr Fitzroy, sir, I beg of you, please contain yourself. Do you want to draw undue attention to yourself?' he fervently implored him.

But Fitzroy was too far gone to even bother.

'Let go of me, you impertinent being,' he roared.

Helplessly, he tried to dislocate himself from Mr McTavish's firm grip but this only caused him to trip and lose his balance. In a frantic effort he swayed violently from side to side and like a great galleon caught in the midst of a ferocious storm, he finally caved in and pathetically sank down. By now most of the servants had heard the commotion and surmised only too well what was going on. Seeing the Master the worse for the demon drink was nothing new to them. Although most of them thought that it was highly disgraceful that he should behave so, now that he had such a beautiful and charming wife to support. His valet had now appeared on the scene and between the pair of them they gradually managed to manoeuvre him up to his dressing-room and both silently prayed to God that their humiliating efforts would not awaken or disturb Augusta and the newly-born child.

On the fourth day he actually emerged through the dressing-room door, now somewhat more sober and less ebullient, to find out for himself how his wife and child were faring. Both were sleeping fitfully. The baby was lying in a hand-made wooden cradle by the foot of the bed.

Stooping forwards, he gazed down and stared at the baby's slightly wrinkled face. What a funny thing it looked, he thought to himself, and how ridiculous were those few strands of hair that seemed to be stretched taut scross its almost bald head. It almost resembled a wrinkled old man. If after nine long weary and troublesome months, this was all that Augusta could provide him with, what a disappointment it was all turning out to be. Moving away from the cradle, he stood beside the bed and, pulling back the covers from Augusta's face, he tapped her lightly on the cheek. Augusta opened her eyes and blinked several times at the bloated face that stared down at her.

Raising herself up on to her pillows, she said, 'Well, Richard, at last. I was beginning to think that you had gone for good. Did no-one manage to find you and inform you that we now have a daughter?'

Without waiting for his reply she went on to say, 'Have you seen her yet? Isn't she beautiful? A perfect little specimen, so Doctor Hadleigh said. She will be waking shortly for her next feed. Then you will be able to see her fully.'

Pausing momentarily, she added, 'Richard, you have not yet enquired as to my state of health.'

'Damn you, woman, you have given me precious little

chance. You have not stopped prattling since you opened your eyes,' he roughly threw back at her.

Augusta winced at his sharp remark.

On seeing this he himself felt a trifle contrite and in a more solicitous fashion said, 'Well, how are you? You look all right to me. A bit pale perhaps. But I guess that is only natural. I assume the Doctor arrived in time. Don't suppose it was too difficult a birth.'

'Actually, it was,' she gravely replied.

'But Doctor Hadleigh was absolutely marvellous to me. He is such a good Doctor, Richard. We are so lucky to have him. I just do not know what I would have done without him. He was perfection all the way through. You must make a point of being extra nice to him and reward him with a special bottle of something.'

Then, seeing the abrupt change of colour that had swiftly flown to his face, Augusta cut short what she was about to say. Richard coughed and shifted about uneasily from one foot to another. The last thing he wanted to hear was Augusta singing the praises of that fellow. He would not admit to himself that he was bitterly jealous of that good-looking and quiet-mannered Doctor, for he was everything that he would have wished to be. How he despised the way that Augusta's eyes shone when she spoke of him. Walking away from the bed he moved over to the open window and stared absentmindedly at the view in front of him. After a while, he felt slightly guilty about the churlish way he had spoken to her.

Turning his back on the view he faced her once more and tried to make amends by saying, 'Augusta, I'm delighted to hear that Doctor Hadleigh looked after you so well, but then that is what he is more than generously paid to do. It would be an unwise move on his part not to pander to your every whim and I suppose it would appear most inconsiderate of me if I did not contribute a little something myself in gratitude in presenting me with a child. What would you like? You name it and I shall endeavour to do my best to afford it for you.'

Augusta clapped her hands together excitedly.

'Thank you, Richard, that is most kind of you,' she coyly exclaimed.

'But there is no need to go to any extravagant lengths. Any small gift would be more than graciously received. Perhaps I could drop a slight hint and suggest that some new gowns would come in most useful. I have very few left that fit me anymore.'

Richard looked at her levelly, shrugged his broad shoulders and uttered, 'If that is all you require, I shall see to it next time I ride over to the store. So two or three bolts of some pretty material would please you then,' he condescendingly replied.

Augusta nodded her head in agreement. She was about to ask him how things were going on the plantation when the new arrival suddenly opened her mouth and started to exercise her lungs. Fitzroy spun round to see where this dreadful wailing was erupting from.

Augusta laughingly said, 'It is all right, Richard. She is letting us know that she is very hungry. It is time for her feed. Do you think, that if you are very careful, you could lift her from her cot and pass her to me?'

Hesitantly, Richard walked over to the cradle and contemplated the tiny mite that was now bellowing away with all its might. No, he could not pick that squawking thing up. Whatever next? If he did not extricate himself from this unaccustomed domestic scene, who knows what he might be called upon to do? Could even end up by holding the little monster.

Beating a hasty retreat, he raced over to the bedroom door and spluttered out to a bewildered Augusta, 'I will send Betsy or Mrs Potts to administer to the baby's needs.'

It was about two weeks later and Doctor Hadleigh was on one of his routine visits. Seated on the chaise-longue in Augusta's bedroom, he was telling her how pleased he was both with the baby's and Augusta's progress.

'Have you decided on a name yet?' he quizically enquired.

'Well, not yet. I have one or two that I have given some consideration to but nothing definite so far,' she thoughtfully answered him.

Glancing idly around the room, Doctor Hadleigh's eyes rested on the tiny gurgling infant that lay before them.

'What about Fitzroy, has he anything in mind?' Charles cautiously ventured.

Augusta turned her face away so that he could not see the hurt in her eyes.

'No,' she quietly answered.

Charles paused for a while before he put his next question to her.

'And what has he to say about his lovely little daughter?'

Augusta turned restlessly in the bed.

'Nothing, that's it. Just nothing. As far as he is concerned, she does not even exist. He has seen her but once since she was born. Oh, I hear how he brags about her to outsiders but the stark fact is he does not really want her,' she tearfully replied.

Doctor Hadleigh rose from his seat and went over to Augusta's side.

'My dear,' he said reassuringly, 'you must not upset yourself. I am sure he does care. He is just not the sort of man who can show paternal feelings very well. He will come round, you see. After all it is early days yet. You have to understand that he has been a confirmed bachelor for some years now. Accepting these kinds of responsibilities probably comes hard to him. Just give him time.'

'Yes, you are probably right, Charles,' Augusta said smiling through her tears.

Charles patted her hand and quickly said, 'Now I must be on my way. I have several more calls to make. but before I leave, let us try to find a suitable name for your child. How do you fancy Hannah?'

'Oh no, not that. I thought of Sophia or Rose, even Amelia,' she said, wishing him to say Amelia.

Shaking his head in mock dismay, he placatingly said, 'Sophia is nice. Yes, I like that. But I have just thought of another one. Ever since I met you I have been reminded of Tamarisk Roses. You wore them on your wedding day, remember? They were even in the house. You look just like a beautiful Tamarisk Rose lying there, delicate and pure. The little one looks just like you. Why don't you call her Tamarisk, or even better still, Tamara?'

'Oh, Charles, what a lovely thought. Yes, I do like the name Tamara. I think it will suit her beautifully. Yes, I have decided. Tamara it is.'

Charles got up and bent over Augusta's hand and kissed it

lightly, as was the custom, saying, 'Now I really must go, Augusta.'

She was about to reply when the bedroom door burst open and in walked Richard.

'I might have guessed it was you,' he snarled at Doctor Hadleigh.

Charles straightened up and backed away from the bedside.

Turning to face Fitzroy, he carefully said, 'Good-day, Richard. How are you? I am pleased to see that your wife is making such a splendid recovery. She is looking well, don't you think?'

'Yes indeed.' was the reply as Richard cast a cursory glance in Augusta's direction.

'And what about the child?' added Charles.

'No doubt you have not been neglectful of her welfare.'

Fitzroy rounded on him.

'Most certainly not. She is coming along nicely,' he said in a tight clipped tone.

'Now if you will excuse me, Richard, I just have time to partake of a drink that was offered to me by Mrs Potts when I first arrived.'

'I shall be pleased to,' Richard grudgingly answered him.

'For I wish to speak to my wife alone anyway.'

Charles left the room and hastened down towards the kitchen area.

It was hot in the room and Richard undid his jacket and threw it onto the chair.

'God, what a day I have had. Nothing seems to be going right at the moment,' he said, pacing aound the room.

'Those damned stupid convicts. They still have not completed the work on the New Plantation. If they do not get a move on it will be too late to plant anything at all this season. That new overseer has tried everything to make them work faster but to no avail.'

Augusta, on sensing the mood he was working himself up into and not wanting to prolong this any further, quickly cut in with, 'I'm sorry that you feel so upset, Richard. Perhaps I can cheer you up a bit by telling you that I have decided on a lovely name for the baby. It is Tamara. Do you approve?'

Augusta waited anxiously for his approval. He was only

111

half listening to her as his mind was occupied on other matters.

'Yes if you like. It makes no difference to me. Oh, by the way, Mr Greene who owns the store asked me to give you this and he sends his felicitations.'

Diving into his breeches pocket, he pulled out a length of shiny pink ribbon and threw it onto the bed. She picked up the ribbon and ran it joyously through her fingers.

'Well, that was nice of him,' Augusta murmured.

Throwing back the covers, she gingerly sat on the edge of the bed.

'So you did get to the store. I wonder, Richard, were you able to purchase any material for me, as you promised?'

'Any what?' he absently answered her.

'You know, Richard, material for some new gowns. Do you remember?'

'Oh that. No, as a matter of fact. I'm sorry, Augusta, I completely forgot but I did purchase an exceedingly well-made pair of knee—length riding boots. Just the kind I have always wanted. They are of an unbelievably soft leather. Never for one moment did I think to obtain such a pair over here. Couldn't resist putting them on to show you.'

Lifting one booted leg on the bed, he carried on for all the world like a naughty schoolboy playing his first school prank.

'See what I mean?' he said, patting them lovingly.

Suddenly the air was rent by an hysterical scream, but it did not come from the crib in the far corner of the room, but from the double bed from whence, for the first time in many months, Augusta was at last giving full vent to her pent up and frustrated feelings concerning her husband's constant lack of them.

10

Two full years had drifted by and it was now another perfect summer's day with the sky cobalt blue with just the merest whiff of a few tiny wispy puffs of white cloud dotted about here and there, almost so fine that one hardly noticed them. The golden rays of the hot sun beamed down upon the two very happy beings chasing a friendly and playful baby kangaroo around several of the tall sparse gum trees.

'Tamara, do please be careful. Try not to get too near to him,' Augusta called from behind one of the trees at the excited and aventurous little two year old, who was trying without too much success to catch hold of the baby kangaroo's tail.

Watching her closely, Augusta could still not believe that this delightful child with her brilliantly blue eyes, lightly freckled round face, springy golden curls with a happy bubbly nature to match was really hers. The first two years of her babyhood had simply flown by. Almost every hour of the waking day had been spent in this adorable child's company. Everyone made such a fuss of her. It was a wonder that she was not overly precocious. However, this tiny tot seemed to take it all in her stride. Augusta had never visualized how strong the maternal instinct could be. She was fiercely protective towards her daughter. Perhaps she felt she had to be, as Fitzroy could not bring himself to foster the same kind of affection towards her. She knew that as time went by he was gradually becoming more and more proud of her little achievements but did not always necessarily show his pride in her progress to Tamara. Added to the fact that during the working day he saw very little of Tamara or of Augusta herself for that matter. Still, as long as Augusta had all the time in the world to spend with her child, she seemed to be thoroughly happy and contented. Augusta on reverting her attention to Tamara called out again but the child was far too engrossed in a wonderful game of hide and seek to take any notice of her mother. Tamara lunged out again and very briefly, for a few short seconds, managed to grab a handful of fine hairs from its quirky tail. The kangaroo reacted to the slight tugging and swiftly whirled around and instantly leaped at Tamara, clasped his hairy paws around Tamara and playfully knocked her to the ground. The child, naturally enough, was frightened and began screaming and kicking her chubby little legs frantically in the air. The baby kangaroo thought that this was great fun. The child's wailing noise only added to the excitement. Augusta, suddenly seeing this happen, was horrified and rushed over to where her precious daughter lay, only to be hampered by constantly tripping over her long gown.

'Lie still, darling. Lie still,' she shouted.

Stopping some feet away from the animal, Augusta hoisted her gown around her waist and slowly and carefully crept towards it. She did not want to frighten the kangaroo as it might well do intense harm to the now still child. The funny thing was that after the first initial shock of being put to the ground by the kangaroo, Tamara was not scared of him anymore, for he was being rather gentle with her in slobbering all over her face with his great wet tongue. Then with one massive tug, Augusta succeeded in lifting the baby kangaroo off her gurgling daughter. Tapping the kangaroo's bottom lightly, she at once pushed him off into the direction of the long grass. Picking up Tamara and holding her tightly, Augusta lightly scolded the child and told her to be more careful where wild animals were concerned. Tamara tried to struggle free and cast her eyes about for her latest playmate. But Augusta had decided that they had experienced enough excitement for one day and with Tamara still clutched tightly in her arms, proceeded to make her way back home.

They had entered the house from the rear so they did not notice the pony and trap parked outside the front porch. On entering the hallway, Augusta could hear strange voices drifting from the drawing-room. Who could be visiting them? She was not expecting anyone to call. Catching sight of Mr McTavish coming along the corridor carrying a silver tray with several tall glasses upon it, she walked towards him and enquired who was visiting the house.

'I believe they are new arrivals, Ma'am. They have come over to pay their respects.'

'Thank you, Mr McTavish. Will you tell them that I have just returned to the house and I will be with them shortly?' she hastily replied.

Quickly grabbing Tamara by the hand, she flew up the stairs and sped along the corridor to the nursery. Mrs Jameson since suffering from failing eyesight was no longer the seamstress, but had become the child's nanny. On entering the room, she found Mrs Jameson slumped in a rocking chair, having her 'forty winks' as she put it.

'Mrs Jameson, will you please put Tamara down for her afternoon nap for me?' cried out Augusta nervously.

Mrs Jameson opened her eyes and scrambled out of the chair to attend to her charge. Augusta kissed Tamara swiftly and bade her be a good girl and told her that she would play with her again presently.

Returning to her own room, she summoned Betsy to help her change into something more fitting for receiving visitors. On entering the drawing-room, she was amazed to find a small group of people seated on various sofas and easy chairs. Fitzroy was standing with his back to the mantel-shelf.

Looking towards her he said, 'Why Augusta, I'm so glad that you are here at last. I have some very charming people for you to meet.'

One by one they all stood up as Augusta moved over to stand by Fitzroy's side.

Placing one arm around her shoulders and in a deep resonant voice he announced, 'This is my wife, Mrs Augusta Fitzroy.'

He then turned to the group before him and introduced them as Mr and Mrs Carter and their offspring. The offspring consisted of four sons and two daughters. The four boys ranged in ages somewhere between sixteen and twenty-five and were all fine strapping specimens. One could tell at a glance that they had been reared on the land. There was Tom, the eldest, then George, followed by Robert, and the youngest was a highly freckled-faced lad named Edgar. The two girls were such a contrast to each other. The eldest, Clara, was fairly tall, with straight jet black hair peeping from underneath a large straw bonnet adorned with coloured ribbons and a large pheasant's tail dangling down the side of it. She was dressed in a gown of russet and black, with a cream lace-edged collar just to give the sombre colours a bit of light relief. Her eyes were small and light brown. Her overall appearance was not one of great beauty but passable, to say the least. Her manner seemed quiet and pleasant though. On shaking her hand, Augusta noticed how smooth her skin was and how unnaturally long were her fingers. Obviously this member of the family was not used to rough hard work. The younger of the two, Clarissa, was the exact opposite. For she was of the nicely rounded type with masses of unruly and wiry red hair. She also had freckles but nowhere near as many as her younger brother. Her large blue eyes sparkled mischievously in her very pretty and plump rosy-cheeked face. This one looked as if she could be quite a handful if allowed to be. She was dressed in what could only be described as 'an assortment of varying colours', but nevertheless still contriving to look fairly neat. By contrast, the 'boys' looked a strange sight in their homespun jackets and breeches and all clutching those terrible flat caps that they all wore in the country. Mr Carter appeared to be a man well into his late forties or early fifties. He also was powerfully built and although attired in a reasonably well-cut jacket with trews to match and sporting a fine walking cane, the impression that came across was of a farm-hand who by some quirk or good fortune had acquired, God knows how, a sizeable amount of capital to enable him and his family to move up in the social scale. His wife, on the other hand, even though she was dressed in her Sunday best of black moire, with a string of passable pearls around her thick neck and with an old-fashioned poke bonet crammed on top of a pile of dingy grey hair, looked a typical farmer's wife, red-faced, red-nosed and red-eyed from too much toil and hardship. All of them, perhaps with the exception of their eldest daughter Clara, spoke in a heavy North country accent. Augusta seated herself on a chair directly facing Mrs Carter so that she could take in more clearly Richard's explanation that the Carters had just bought a piece of land adjoining theirs.

'We shall be neighbours, so as to speak,' Mrs Carter pertly

informed her.

Pausing briefly to take a quick gulp of madeira from the tall-stemmed wineglass that she continuously twirled about in her fat square-shaped hands, she rattled on with, 'The last place we stayed at was even remoter than this. It was the wildest, most desolate piece of country I have ever had the misfortune to be in. It was just full of plain nothingness. If we had stayed there much longer, we would all have gone right off our heads.'

It was now apparent for all to see that Mr Carter was becoming faintly irritated by his wife's tirade and ordered her to still her tongue. Fidgeting about with the lapels of his jacket, he started to carry on where his wife left off, but in a more conciliatory tone. Amidst the clinking of glasses and the crunching of tiny oblong shaped wheat-cakes, he tried to convey his feelings and intentions as to what his family intended to do now they had finally decided to settle in this part of the world. Only recently, had they started to build their own house.

'Nothing as grand as this though,' hastily put in Mrs Carter, as her face changed into varying shades of purple, at the thought of incurring her husband's wrath later on.

Her husband chose to ignore this latest remark and with the occasional swipe at his youngest son, who seemed to be having some difficulty in sitting still, he proceeded on with his story.

'At the moment, we are of course living fairly rough. Home for the time being is a covered wagon. But not for much longer, I hope. Soon as the house is completed, it will be back to work on the land. There is, of course, as you well know, Mr Fitzroy, sir, such a devil of a lot of clearing to do, but with these four strapping lads of mine, who are well and truly capable of hard work and know what's what, well shouldn't take no time at all in conquering the land in readiness for the planting of crops. Why in a year or two, everything should be fully productive.'

Fitzroy smiled to himself, thinking how long it had taken him to get on his feet. To think that one could conquer these harsh lands with just a mere handful of men was too ludicrous for words. If he had not thought of the brilliant idea of having convicts to do the dirty work, he would never even have started the plantation. No, he had to admit that things in that area were going along quite nicely now.

'Water and the weather will be your biggest problem,' Fitzroy finally broke through with.

'We are going to build water towers, like you have here,' suddenly burst out Tom, the eldest lad.

'That is not what I meant,' replied Fitzroy tersely.

'I mean water for drainage. You must irrigate the land from the streams, otherwise you will soon be in serious trouble. I lost so much during the early years due to intense heat and lack of constant water. Finding water holes and running streams here is not as easy as you think. I was lucky with my find. Then there is the question of workers. You need a goodly supply of them. You must hire yourselves as many hands as you can afford.'

Mr Carter got up and started to pace slowly round the room. Augusta and Mrs Carter were by now deep in conversation concerning the pros and cons of this new country, each one carefully skirting around the delicate question of why they had left the Mother Country to settle in a competely alien one. Mrs Carter opted for playing it safe this time and deftly started to throw in numerous pieces of gossip, and sometimes fairly accurate bits of information, as to what had been occurring in the Old Country when 'that dreadful old French ogre Bonaparte had deemed fit to shatter the world's peace.' The state of affairs seemed to be on a more even keel, once 'Old Pineapple' came to the Throne'. That was the nickname given to William IV by many of his subjects because of his peculiar dome-shaped head.

'Especially after he disentangled himself from that 'Jordan woman' and settled down with dear old Adelaide, he soon became quite a reformed character.'

Still, everyone was in complete accord as to the outstanding success achieved by the young Queen Victoria. However, not all could be said for her German Consort, another foreigner linked to the power of the Throne.

'Although I daresay, some of them could be considered reasonable enough,' Mr Carter lamely put in.

Fitzroy jumped out of his chair and bouncing round the room jauntily, boomed sardonically, 'Perhaps you should ask my wife what she thinks about the Hanoverian rulers. After all, her own father, when still only a young man, was ruined by his preference for them. Fell into disgrace towards the end of Prinny's reign and had little option but to make amends and come out here.'

Augusta's face turned scarlet, but before she could raise her voice in defence of her father's actions, Mrs Carter, who was now enjoying this heated conversation to the fullest, swiftly caught out Fitzroy with, 'Pray tell me, Mr Fitzroy, what was your main reason for leaving the land of your birth. Did you fall foul of the monarchy too? Or like so many others before you, perhaps you chose to escape from financial hardships?'

A deathly hush ensued. Nobody dared speak, let alone move. Fitzroy was rendered completely speechless. Turning smartly on his heel, he glowered at the poor frightened woman, who had moved over to sit next to her eldest daughter, now sitting perched on the arm of a small sofa. A mauvish tinge was creeping slowly towards the roots of his gingery scalp. His eyes looked like two slits of steel as his gaze penetrated backwards and forwards between his wife and Mrs Carter.

Then in a granite like tone he snarled, 'It's none of your damn business, woman, how I came to be here.'

With that he turned and focussed his attention upon Mr Carter, who sat there with an excruciatingly embarrassed look upon his face. Fitzroy helped himself to another drink. He threw it back quickly, before offering Mr Carter another. Mr Carter silently refused by spreading his hands firmly over the top of his empty glass.

Trying to make light of his previous angry outburst, he jocularly concluded with, 'Now look what happens, when a woman is allowed the upper hand. If they were all allowed to get away with it, where would us men be, I ask you?'

Mr Carter still sat there slightly dumbfounded. He seemed to be having difficulty finding the right words. He knew whatever he said would, without the slightest doubt, cause offence one way or the other.

Augusta came to the rescue by placing one finger gently on her husband's arm and placatingly saying, 'Richard, I am sure Mrs Carter meant no offence. I think she was just a little carried away on the spur of the moment.'

'Yes, yes, Mrs Fitzroy is so right,' cried the poor woman,

hastily dabbing at her eyes.

Standing up and silently motioning to one and all that it was about time they left, she added, 'I'm afraid the excitement of being with new people went to my head, didn't it, Mr Carter?'

So saying, she imploringly looked at her husband for moral support. But he was not going to give her any. He was already pushing his family anxiously out of the room in order to beat a hasty retreat.

Holding out his hand to Fitzroy, he somehow managed to say, 'Thank you for your hospitality, Mr Fitzroy. I apologise profusely for anything that my wife has inadvertently said to cause you offence. But I'm afraid my wife is one of those women who will never learn the art of keeping her mouth closed. To my way of thinking, they should never have got rid of the iron tongue. Furthermore, I sincerely hope that this will not stand in the way of our friendship. I shall be needing to pick your brains over several matters, I am thinking.'

By this time Fitzroy had calmed down quite considerably.

Clasping Mr Carter's hand tightly in his own he announced in a falsified jocular tone, 'No, of course not, my man. I'm sorry I let off a bit of steam myself. Anytime you need my advice, I shall be more than pleased to give it to you. Perhaps we could come to some arrangement at a future date about sharing the work force between us.'

Mr Carter, not realising that Fitzroy meant the use of enforced convict workers, seemed delighted by the prospect. The rest of the company appeared less than amused. The Carter offspring were either fidgeting with their caps and bonnets or scuffing their feet over the already well-worn piece of carpet. The occasional cough or hiccup was easily perceived. The time had come, of course, for the perfunctory goodbyes to be said. Augusta, on squeezing Mrs Carter's hand lightly, insisted that they should all come again shortly. Whereupon, Mrs Carter took the liberty of hugging Augusta to her breast and replied that she would be more than delighted. Then filing out of the room one by one, the entire Carter ensemble left the Fitzroy household in far less ebullient spirits than when they had arrived.

11

It was the middle of yet another scorching hot summer. During the past five months another two more consignments of convicts had arrived. This time, mainly to Doctor Hadleigh's insistence, the mud and wattle huts that were to house them had miraculously been built in advance. Even so, he could not have done it all on his own without the grudging help from the overseer. Although he was a hard taskmaster and cared little, if anything at all, for the plight and well-being of the convicts, nevertheless he had been forced to realize, through Doctor Hadleigh, that they were entitled to park their arses in some kind of dwelling and, not least of all, something fitting to fill their bellies with. The situation between Fitzroy and Doctor Hadleigh had not improved, to say the least. The Doctor rarely visited Fairlawns now. Augusta had not set eyes on him for months. It therefore came as a tremendous shock to her as one afternoon, Mrs Carter, having made one of her infrequent calls to Fairlawns, had boasted to Augusta how the dashing Doctor Hadleigh seemed to be paying an unusual amount of attention towards her eldest daughter Clara.

'Clara', she went on to say, 'has this marvellous idea of starting some kind of school to help the children from the nearby farms and colonies to become more learned. Reading and writing is just as important as learning how to plough the land she reckons.'

'Why yes, I fully agree with her,' said Augusta, somewhat abstractedly.

Pinching Augusta's arm lightly in an attempt to gain her full attention, she gaily nattered on, 'Naturally, Doctor Hadleigh has offered her all the help and support that she may need. He has spent most of his spare time with Clara, trying to find the right location. My Clara is very clever herself, you know. She was always the 'special' one in the family. Plays the piano beautifully. Self-taught too, would you believe? Where she gets it from, Heaven only knows. Neither Mr Carter nor myself show any inclinations towards that kind of thing. That's probably what the good Doctor sees in her. Don't you just agree with me?'

On and on she went, leaving Augusta to nod here and there or wherever it suited her to do so.

Several hours after she had gone and Augusta was left alone to ponder over her visitor's conversation, it was with some trepidation that Mrs Carter's imparted news regarding Doctor Hadleigh's frequent outings with Clara, resulted in Augusta feeling strangely perplexed and utterly depressed.

The noise, of course, was quite deafening, but nobody seemed to mind that much. After all, social gatherings in most circumstances are quite frequently pretty rumbustious affairs. This occasion was to be no exception. There were about thirty to forty people, all crowded inside a fairly large, roughly hewn, wooden hut. The hut, some twenty feet long, with just four large gaping holes, positioned somewhere around the middle of its frame, barely let in the daylight. A great hole had been hacked almost in the centre of the rough and amateurish-looking thatched roof, the idea being either to allow more daylight to flood in or to let any stale air flee out. Although the hut itself was something of an eyesore, it had naturally enough, been constructed and built in their sparetime by Clara Carter's brothers. Jutting out like a sore thumb on a carefully selected spot, not too far away from the New Reformed Church and the recently enlarged local store, was of course Clara's pride and joy, the New Schoolhouse, the first known schoolhouse in all of this region. Proudly, she stood by the side of her latest acquisition, a handmade high-fronted desk lovingly put together by her favourite brother George, who had excelled himself by achieving a very high standard of French polishing. The desk completely outshone everything else in the room. Behind the prize desk stood a high, hard-backed wicker chair. The children, of course, were expected to sit on the plain wooden forms in front of the desk. Appropriately enough and by a most strenuous effort on Mrs Carter's part, she had over the years carefully secreted away quite a number of the old slates that Clara had used when she had been a scholar. So with a little bit of gentle persuasion from Clara, she eventually succumbed and handed them over to be used by her daughter's future charges. At the far end of the hut near the open door, several youngsters could be seen gleefully prancing about. Seated on the low wooden frame, placed end to end in the centre of the room, sat some of the parents, only too glad to be able to sit and chit-chat with many of their far-off neighbours. It all made quite a pleasant change from the usual humdrum existence of their daily life. A handful of mothers had crowded around Clara, plying her with questions concerning the schooling of their offspring. Differential age groups deemed it nigh impossible to hold separate classes, so Clara had opted for one big class only. That way some of the elder children could help to look after the younger ones. Surprisingly enough, most interest emanated from the parents who attended the New Reformed Church, possibly because it was fairly nearby and the break-away reformers hoped and probably prayed that more and more converts would join their flock.

Pushing back a loose and fairly damp strand of hair, Clara stood patiently illustrating her well-intentiond plans to a particularly awkward and highly critical mother, when a firm hand suddenly gripped her elbow, forcing her to spin around and confront its owner. The tall frame of Doctor Hadleigh loomed in front of her.

'Doctor Hadleigh,' she cried out. 'This is a surprise. I am honoured that you found time to come here. What do you think of my first effort?'

Doctor Hadleigh took Clara's outstretched hand, mockingly bowed over it, and replied graciously, 'It will do very nicely for the time being, Miss Carter, and I am very happy for you.'

Firmly taking hold of Clara's arm, he then whisked her away from her desk and, turning towards the ladies present, he charmingly ventured, 'Will you excuse us for a while, as my time is rather precious. I am expected at another call very shortly and I do need to discuss various matters with Miss Carter here.'

Both Doctor Hadleigh and Clara swept out of the room,

completely oblivious of the knowing winks and sly looks that flew around the room faster than any fly.

Doctor Hadleigh held on to Clara's arm until they were well away from prying eyes. Somehow they had managed to find a quiet, peaceful spot where only the occasional sleepy starling fluttered gracefully in the warm, hazy afternoon sun. Crickets chirped and bleeped. Mudlarks sang their pretty songs. Iridescent shafts of light soared through tall blades of grass, effecting such a contrast to the fragile blossoms of the overhanging acacia bushes. While they had been walking along, Clara had noticed that Doctor Hadleigh had been carrying rather a bulky brown paper parcel, tied up with a piece of string and, needless to say, it had intrigued her a trifle as to what was inside.

As if reading her thoughts, he stopped abruptly and shyly handed it to Clara saying, 'I thought perhaps you might be glad of these.'

Carefully removing the wrapping, Clara was surprised and slightly taken aback to find six beautiful leather-bound books inside.

Tears sprang to her eyes immediately and with a slight catch in her voice, she exclaimed, 'Why Doctor Hadleigh, this is most kind and so very thoughful of you. I could not have wished for a finer and more useful gift. I shall treasure them always. They will be of great assistance to me in my work here.'

Taking her hand in his, he squeezed it momentarily and gravely replied, 'Clara,' then hesitating for a second he added, 'may I take the liberty of calling you that? Clara, for what you are trying to achieve here in this community, these books are a small token indeed. I only wish I could offer you more.'

Clara blushed deeply. Never before had anyone spoken to her in such an intimate way.

Steadying her voice with some difficulty, she tearfully cried, 'Oh, but you have, by giving me these books and attending this afternoon. You have given me your support in this little venture of mine and that to me is worth more than anything else on earth.'

Doctor Hadleigh, on hearing Clara's rapturous reply, felt a little emotional himself and had an uneasy feeling that all this could be leading off into another direction. Clara, however, also realised the same and firmly pointed out that it was time that they went back to join the others.

By the time Augusta had arrived on the scene, everyone apart from Clara and Doctor Hadleigh, was now seated at several rows of makeshift trestle tables. These had been lined up as neatly as was possible under a row of overhanging branches. Even if the shade from the trees was sparse in places, very few complained.

Crisp, freshly starched, plain white damask cloths had been draped artistically over the trestles so as to conceal their crudeness. Here and there amongst the plates of home-made pies and fancy tarts lay small posies of wild flowers, their heady scent combining with the aromatic smells coming from the slightly sweating game pies. Needless to say, Mrs Carter, with the aid of her four sons, was in her element as she went around filling up the assembled guests' drinking vessels with an assortment of home-made brews and jugs of freshly-squashed limeade. As everyone present had been asked to bring their own drinking vessels with them, owing to a vast shortage of Mrs Carter's own, she quite rightly, in judging by the enormity of some of the tankards, knew who would stay the course the longest. Shifting her eyes away from the table for a short respite, she suddenly noticed Augusta making her way towards the gathering. Thrusting the heavy pewter jug into her son George's hand and telling him to take over, she bustled towards Augusta.

'My dear, Mrs Fitzroy,' she breathlessly spouted at her, 'this is most cordial of you. You are most welcome at our happy gathering.'

Pointing a finger in the direction of the schoolhouse, she proudly exclaimed, 'What do you think of my Clara's little school? Of course, it is not much yet, but there is plenty of time for improvement. I am afraid we have already started with the 'tea' and you are more than welcome to join in.'

Glancing around at the motley crew who were now wholeheartedly indulging themselves with the prepared spread, and noticing that many of the table habits were somewhat uncouth, Augusta politely refrained. But because she did not want to appear stand-offish, she gratefully accepted a tankard of fruit squash. This tankard had been provided by Mrs Carter as she did not think it fitting that a lady of Augusta's ilk should have to demean herself by bringing her own. After Augusta had finished the cool drink and had made the acquaintance of several of the ensemble, she asked if Mrs Carter would permit her to view the inside of the schoolhouse. Mrs Carter could hardly wait and hustled Augusta up the steps of the schoolhouse, for all the world as if she were guiding her around The Tower of London.

Once inside the building and after a quick scrutiny, Augusta had the greatest difficulty in trying not to show her obvious disappointment. It was all so bare and terribly gloomy. But to give Clara her due, she had created this building, almost by her own efforts, no mean feat for a woman to do. None of the men around had thought of building a schoolhouse, not even Fitzroy. Mrs Carter could instantly see that her visitor was not overly impressed. Racing ahead, she took it upon herself to inform Augusta that the place would look so much better once the walls had been whitewashed, the chimneystack put in place and the half-finished shutters inserted in the now gaping holes. On this note Augusta readily agreed.

The door swung open again and in bounced Clara with Doctor Hadleigh close on her heels. As they were conversing deeply with each other, neither of them noticed anyone else standing in the room, not until Mrs Carter, on seeing her daughter suddenly emerging into the room, uttered, 'Clara, there you are. I was wondering where you had disappeared to. Look who has honoured us with her presence! Mrs Fitzroy.'

Startled by her mother's voice, both Clara and Doctor Hadleigh made their way over to where the two women stood. They all greeted each other warmly. Augusta thought that Clara seemed a little overwrought and uncommonly jittery. But on reflection, she thought it was probably due to the excitement of having so many new faces around her. Was it just her imagination playing tricks or was Doctor Hadleigh looking a little flustered also?

An uneasy silence spread around the place but Doctor Hadleigh quickly broke through it by leaping forwards and saying, 'It is so nice to make your acquaintance again, Mrs Fitzroy. I trust all is well at Fairlawns.'

Augusta felt slightly miffed at being addressed so formally, so she replied in the same vein.

'Yes, thank you, Doctor Hadleigh, and I trust all goes well with you.'

And turning her back abruptly on him, she coolly focused her attention on Clara. Was there anything that Clara would like for the school? Some cupboards perhaps? No, her father was going to provide those. Perhaps one or two old books, that were badly in need of repair? She would be more than welcome to those. No, thank you for the thought but Doctor Hadleigh had just presented her with six really lovely books. Clara could not contain her pleasure at being given them and promptly showed them to Augusta. Turning them over in her hands, she could just make out a few of the titles in the dim light. Bunyans *Pilgrim's Progress*, Shakespeare's *Sonnets*, Milton's *On the Death of a Fair Infant*.

'Yes, very nice indeed.'

There must be something she could give her, something that might be of more assistance than the books. Walking away from there and glancing towards the hole in the roof, like a flash of lightning it struck her. Yes, she had thought of it now. Lamps, several bright lamps that would brighten up the room indeed.

'Clara,' she called. 'I have thought of something that is badly needed here. Especially as you are to teach children. Lamps.'

'Lamps,' called back Clara.

'Yes, oil lamps. You will certainly need those. I will send Old Amos over with some as soon as is possible. After all, children must be able to see what they are about to be taught.'

And with that, she swept haughtily out of the building.

On the way back to Fairlawns, she reflected on why she had been so bitchy and unkind to Clara. After all, she had not asked for that kind of behaviour. Everything had been fine, until she suddenly saw Doctor Hadleigh and Clara alone. Could it be that in the midst of the noisy gathering outside the schoolhouse, Clara and he had managed to find a quiet spot where they could, to the eye of the onlooker, be in a world of their own? Yes, that was it. She was forced to admit it. The feeling she was now encountering was one of envy. She was envious of Clara Carter, not because she was to become the first school mistress in the colony, but because she had caught the attention of Charles Hadleigh.

☆   ☆   ☆

The long hot summer was just nearing its end when tragedy broke. Augusta had barely seen Fitzroy anywhere around the house or the immediate vicinity for at least five days. Needless to say, on the few infrequent times that she had, she sensed that something pretty awful was transpiring. It was not anything that Richard had said that brought on this premonition, but more how he looked and behaved when he thought no-one was observing him. Richard Fitzroy was a strange man, moody and totally indefferent to other people's feelings. He had precious little time for 'small talk', except when he needed to have his say. Most people tried to avoid any kind of discussion with him, as it usually ended up with him losing his extremely short and volatile temper with them. Once having the misfortune of incurring his wrath, one was not easily tempted to come back for a second helping. It did not seem to matter how hard anyone worked for him or how they tried to satify his many whims, he was insatiable. Most people who knew him thought he was the luckiest devil alive. He had the finest house around, the best lands and all of them nearly cultivated. His latest achievement was the very successful vineyard he had managed to nurture, and many would have given their eye-teeth to have been lucky enough to grow their own vines, let alone be able to sell the produce thereof. He had an uncanny knack whereby everything he turned his hand to automatically prospered. The majority of new settlers to this land failed time and time again. Notwithstanding that, the larger percentage of them usually gave up half way through and ended up in worse straits than they ever imagined possible. But not Richard Fitzroy. There seemed to be gold in everything he touched. Then there was his wife. She apparently was the envy of all. Every woman around tried to aspire to Augusta's heights. No wonder the old buffer waited so long to tie the knot. He knew the wait was well worthwhile. Married by proxy too. What a risk. But even the risk proved too good to be true and finally, to complete the picture, she had presented him with a beautiful,

128

spirited child, Tamara. Sadly, although everyone else admired and adored Tamara, her father spent precious little time with her, if any at all. Sons were the order of the day. A man needed sons. What good were daughters? Just a lot of useless trouble. A man could talk and boast of things to a son. How could a man communicate with a daughter? Same thing went for his wife. The only thing she seemed any good at was managing the house, sorting out the servants and fussing over Tamara. The fact that Richard Fitzroy spent so much time away from his home and family somewhat mystified the servants as well. Why, in fact did he spend so much time on the land? After all he had plenty of enforced hands to do all the menial tasks and they seemed to be arriving by the wagon load at indecently frequent intervals. Where they were being housed and fed was a constant discussion between the household servants.

'Shouldn't wonder if we don't have an entire Penal Colony of our own before much longer,' Mrs Potts sourly remarked one day.

The answer to all those questions was that Richard Fitzroy actually enjoyed being away from the rigours of domestic life. Basically he was a loner. He loved being the 'Big Boss of Fairlawns Estate'. To say he was an insomniac was nothing short of the truth. For he could just not wait to be able to get up at the crack of dawn, have the stable boy bring round one of his finest mounts and gallop off on his exhausting rounds giving orders and generally cracking the whip to all and sundry beneath him. So it came as something of a surprise as late one morning, Augusta discovered Richard aimlessly mooching about the house. Normally Richard took very little interest, if any of the tasks, however large or small, that his wife involved herself in, but this particular morning, as she was preoccupied with an ornate flower arrangement, he sailed up to her side several times and proceeded distractedly to poke a number of scarlet blooms into Augusta's carefully arranged display. Slightly irritated at having her work interfered with, Augusta laid down the magenta spray she was holding, turned and stared hard at her husband's troubled face.

'Richard, Richard,' she finally penetrated through, 'Is there something that is troubling you unnecessarily? Perhaps I might be able to help. Something that you may wish to enlighten me with.'

Abstractedly he replied, 'Not really, my dear. Just a few problems with the workers and a little bit of a hassle with the overseer. Nothing that I cannot sort out and control.'

Racking her brains for something to take his mind away from his problems, if only temporary, the situation was swiftly alleviated by the noisy appearance of Tamara as she was leading Mrs Jameson a merry dance around the house. The over-excited child ran up to her mother and demanded that she should join in the fun as well. A puffing and panting Mrs Jameson, on seeing both Tamara's parents in the same room and so early in the day, suddenly whisked Tamara from under her mother's feet and chased her back upstairs again. This unexpected action gave Augusta food for thought. Richard was now turning a piece of carved ivory in his hands, pretending to be intent upon it.

With as much tact as she could muster, Augusta walked over to him and said, 'Richard, may I be so bold as to suggest that you forsake your work this day and spend a few hours with your daughter? She is a delightful child, you know, and who knows, you may even enjoy her company for a while. I do not wish to sound like the proverbial nagging wife, but you really should show a little more interest in Tamara. After all, she is your child too.'

Thumping his hand on top of the table and scattering the broken-off stems and discarded leaves onto the floor, he brutishly said, 'Oh, very well. Bring the child down to me and I will endeavour to try and amuse her for a few hours, though God alone knows how.'

12

The following day the storm broke. Cholera had broken out amongst the convicts. Doctor Hadleigh had been sent for and regretfully was forced to confirm it. That, of course, explained the reason why Fitzroy had stayed away from the fields. He had left it to his overseer to deal with. Richard Fitzroy was not going to have that smart-arsed Doctor putting him in his place. Best let some other poor devil suffer the vent of his spleen. He had tried to prevent Augusta finding out, knowing that she would be petrified and disgusted at such a catastrophe occurring at Fairlawns, but in his customary bull-headed way and lacking the foresight in such matters, he had, like an ostrich buried his head in the sand. Therefore, it came as quite a shock to Mr McTavish, who on hearing Doctor Hadleigh standing on the front porch steps shouting at the top of his voice and in a very agitated state indeed, opened the door and was almost knocked over by the Doctor as he thrust past him and demanded to speak with the Master.

'I'm afraid he is not yet risen, sir,' Mr McTavish replied apologetically.

'No, I bet he is not. Probably doing his best to stay out of harm's way,' snapped back the Doctor.

Then, noticing how increasingly more irritated the Doctor was becoming, Mr McTavish suggested that the Mistress should be sent for instead, as he knew that she was already up and about.

Augusta, still attired in her morning wrapover, found Charles hastily pacing up and down in the study.

'Charles,' she cried, as she ran towards him.

'Whatever brings you here this early in the morning? Has something untoward happened?'

Not daring to look her in the face, he clenched his hands

131

tightly behind his back.

'Yes, Augusta, I'm afraid something terrible has happened. Cholera has broken out amongst your husband's precious convicts,' he threw at her.

'Oh no, Charles,'

This sudden and unexpected news had actually taken the wind out of her sails. Small beads of perspiration oozed through her slightly creased forehead. Turning her now ashen face towards Charles' angry one, she falteringly asked if Fitzroy was aware of the situation.

'Of course he is, Augusta,' he angrily replied, 'Why do you think he avoided seeing me yesterday, and where is he this morning? He should be up and out with his overseer, trying to do something about this frightening problem. You know he left it for the overseer to ride over and tell me.'

Shakily Augusta murmured, 'No, I did not.'

Then things slowly began to slot into place.

Almost to herself she uttered, 'But of course, that now explains why he spent so much time with Tamara yesterday. As a rule he merely pats the back of her head, or condescends to give her the occasional nod of the head.'

Charles could hardly believe his own ears.

Grabbing Augusta fiercely by the shoulders, he shouted, 'He did what? The fool, the bloody fool. Pardon me for my language, Augusta, but that is just about the worst thing he could have done.'

By now Charles was totally unable to control his anger. Whirling about the room like a mad dog, he went on.

'You know what this means? I am forced to tell you that there is every chance that Tamara may contract this dreadful disease. It attacks the young and the old first, you know. I had been hoping and praying that he might have had the good sense to have stayed away from you and Tamara for a while. If only till things die down a bit.'

Augusta sat there, still unable to comprehend it all. She was hoping against hope that this was all a bad dream and when she awoke it would all go away but in reality she knew different.

In a barely audible voice, she whispered, 'Charles, I do not wish to undermine your integrity but are you absolutely sure that it is cholera?'

Seeing her anguished face looking up at him, he longed to be able to ease the pain therein, but he was forced to say, 'Oh Augusta, I know cholera when I see it. After all I saw enough of it back home and in my travels on the Continent to be more than convinced.'

Charles had quietened down considerably and he was about to leave the room to have words with Fitzroy when Augusta stopped him by saying, 'How many confirmed cases are there at the moment?'

'About fifteen at present and they are all amongst the latest lot of arrivals, so I have been told,' he retorted.

Augusta jumped out of the chair and followed Charles over towards the door.

'But I thought Richard had instructed the overseeer to be more careful over the sanitary arrangements. Not to house too many together. Ever since that dreadful day when Richard accused you of unspeakable things concerning our being with each other, I have tried to intervene and do my best to persuade him to abandon the whole idea. But you know how stubborn he is.'

Charles, looking up swiftly, noted that Augusta had turned her face away from him, in order that he should not notice the sudden embarrassed flush that had crept over it. Stalling for a second, he then said in a far quieter tone.

'How did you know about the heated conversation which took place that night? I brought you home in a state of shock. I thought you went straight to bed.'

'I did,' she girlishly replied. 'But walls have ears you know, Charles.' Then with a knowing wink, she added, 'Servants miss nothing.'

'Hm. yes.' he thoughtfully answered her. 'And talking of servants, do you think that any of them know about the cholera outbreak? We don't want any unnecessary panic at this stage.'

'No, I'm sure they do not. Otherwise I would have heard by now,' she quickly reassured him.

Charles grabbed hold of the door handle and pulled it free.

'Look Augusta, as dearly as I would like to, I must not waste any more time talking about this. I must start to put some plans of my own into action. With or without your husband's help.'

'No, Charles, you must discuss this with Richard. You know how he reacts if he thinks things are being done behind his back. Stay a while, while I go up and rouse him. By the way, help yourself to a drink if you feel like one.'

Then stepping lightly out of the room, she fled upstairs to wake her tiresome and arrogant husband out of his fitful sleep.

By the time Fitzroy had entered the room, with just his dressing robe over a pair of hastily donned breeches and his hair unbrushed, Doctor Hadleigh, aided by a large brandy had calmed down somewhat, although the calmness quickly evaporated the moment he saw Fitzroy standing just inside the door jamb, with a deep scowl upon his thickset jaws. Richard was feeling thoroughly chagrined about being summoned by the Doctor to discuss what to do about the sickness of some worthless convicts. Sighing deeply and rubbing his eyes in feigned tiredness, he muttered something to Charles about how tired he was due to the long hours spent in the fields and making up all sorts of useless excuses as to why he was still abed.

'Pray let us stop this pretence, Richard, and let us get down to the matter in hand,' Doctor Hadleigh demanded.

Augusta hovered in the background, not knowing whether to stay and participate or to disappear for a while. Judging by her husband's irritable demeanour and Charles's apparent lack of tact and humour, she opted for the latter and speedily fled out of earshot.

Barely waiting for Augusta to vanish, Richard drawled sullenly, 'Very well, have it your own way. What is on your mind?'

Flexing his taut muscles, Charles moved towards Fitzroy and stared squarely at him, man to man. Nothing seemed to stir in the airless room, not even the numerous flies. It was like the calm before the storm.

Slowly and with great deliberation, Charles pronounced in a croaking voice, 'There is a cholera outbreak amongst your convicts. Something has to be done about it immediately before it rages all over the Colony.' He eased off and waited expectantly for Richard's reply. Fitzroy pretended to be stunned by this announcement but Doctor Hadleigh, shrewd man that he was, could see right through him.

'Well, what do you suggest that I do about it?' he growled.

Doctor Hadleigh heaved a sigh of relief. At least the man seemed content for once to be able to take some advice.

'The first thing we have to do is to move all of them out of those stinking holes that you have bundled them in. Find them somewhere dry and warm for a while, at least till you have built new places for them, then . . .'

'Wait a minute, wait a minute,' interjected Fitzroy, frantically waving his arms in the air.

'Build new places? Have you taken leave of your senses, man? All I shall do is to get some of the workers to fumigate the huts, leave them empty for a week or so. By that time they should be fit for habitation again.'

Charles could hardly believe his ears. Was this man really so insensitive and stupid.

'No, you do not,' Charles shouted at him. 'You must burn the lot down and if you do not, then I will. The only way to stop the disease is by burning everything in sight.'

This time it was Fitzroy's turn to lose control of his temper.

'If you think that I am going to take the risk of setting fire to those miserable huts, knowing full well that in these deplorable dry conditions the fire could easily spread and cause me to lose all my crops, no, Doctor Hadleigh, I refuse to do it.'

Doctor Hadleigh threw up his hand in despair.

'You have no choice,' he snapped back. 'May I remind you, sir, that I am the Doctor here and it is my duty to try to save these poor souls from any further misfortunes that may come their way, and to prevent the rest of the community from catching it.'

The loud and over-heated voices could now be heard in most parts of the house and presently not one keyhole was left vacant.

'I know that this is not merry England and that over here there are no hard and fast rules about punishing offenders for not upholding their responsibilities towards their workers, but rest assured; I shall do my utmost to make things damned difficult for you in the future.'

Fitzroy was at a loss for words. Deep down he knew that the Doctor was right in his assumption, even though he was not going to admit it. He stood silently pulling at his rough unshaven beard.

Then in a more conciliatory tone he said, 'Very well, do what you have to do. I wash my hands of the whole affair. Use what medications you may need. I will reimburse you. May I suggest that you get my overseer to start the burnings and let him have the worry of finding somewhere else for them.'

Charles coughed contemptuously.

'Is that not putting rather a lot of responsibility onto someone else's shoulders?' Charles sneered slightly.

Fitzroy spat heavily across the room, almost missing the tall spittoon leaning against the fireside.

'Damn me man. Isn't that what I pay him for? You don't get things done properly if you go soft on your workers. Anyway, I ought to spend a bit more of my time around the house. Let someone else have a few of the worries.'

Doctor Hadleigh heaved a deep sigh. Just like Fitzroy to run out when there was any sign of real trouble brewing. Picking his hat up from the leather-studded chair, he placed it on the back of his head and strode out into the hall.

Fitzroy with his back turned against the Doctor, called out in a gruff voice, 'Good of you to call, Doctor Hadleigh. You don't have to waste too much of your time trying to save their souls. After all, I can soon round up another bunch. There are plenty more from where they came from.'

Doctor Hadleigh gritted his teeth tightly and with his jaw firmly set, marched out of the house, without even a backward glance to see if Augusta was nearby. Snatching his horse from the hitching post, he galloped off at a furious pace down the carriage-way and out towards the fields, spurring his horse on faster and faster until he managed to drive some of the anger out of his system and thinking all the time that never in all his life had he met quite such a callous bastard as Richard Henry Fitzroy.

Tethering his horse to a wide tree stump outside the overseer's shack, Doctor Hadleigh wasted no time in calling out for Mr Cookson, but no-one answered him. So kicking the door wide open with his foot, he stepped in. It was dark inside and casting his eyes about for a piece of tallow wax to light, his gaze gradually settled upon a round tin dish containing a mound of congealed wax pressed firmly into it.

Gingerly lighting the wax from the tinder box beside it, he held it up high allowing him to scrutinize the inside of the shack properly. He had often wondered what the overseer's place looked like. For he was standing in a fairly square compact part of it. Narrow wooden shelves ran alongside three parts of it, with a door on one side. There were, of course, no proper windows but gaps had been left for enough air and light to ventilate through. Under one of these gaps on the hard-baked earthen floor stood a wooden table piled high with papers and lumps of charcoal. The shelves were littered with pieces of string, twists of unsmoked tobacco, jars of wax, several large clay pipes and at the far end near the door hung a small quantity of bull whips. This section obviously was used as an office of some sort. Behind the desk, Doctor Hadleigh noticed that a length of canvas had been carelessly draped over a pole that was attached to the ceiling. On pulling it aside and casting the light from the candle in front of him, he found himself in what could only be described as the living quarters. Here the floor had been partially covered by a large square of coconut matting. In the far corner was an un-made iron-framed bed, beside it stood a washstand with a plain white chipped basin and ewer. Underneath the washstand, not even enclosed by the customary cupboard doors, sat an un-emptied chamber pot. 'Ugh,' thought Doctor Hadleigh, 'how these types live.' The roughly hewn hand-made table that had been placed somewhere in the centre of the room still had the remains of the previous meal scattered about it. Cursing himself for having wasted so much time in the shack, he extinguished the candle, popped it back on the shelf and making sure that the piece of sacking was seen to be in the same position as he found it, he stealthily departed from the miserable place and set off once again.

Tired and pent-up from his recent outburst with Fitzroy and the hard riding, he at last came upon the overseer in one of the far-off fields. Riding swiftly up to him and almost suffocating the man in clouds of red dust, he anxiously called out to him.

'Mr Cookson, Mr Cookson, I must have a word with you.'

The overseer who had been kneeling beside a small water hole filling his water pouch leapt up with sudden relief at the sound of the Doctor's voice.

Brushing the dust away with his slouch hat he cried out, 'Thank God, to see you, sir.'

Clutching hold of the Doctor's arm and nearly unseating him, he said, 'I do believe Divine Providence must have sent you. Quick come over here, would you Doctor?'

Without waiting for the Doctor to dismount, Mr Cookson led the way over ground that was covered with rough gorse bushes and cruel spiky thistles to a wide clearing that was fairly flat and completely scrub-free. There, squatting about on the ground, were about twenty to thirty of the convicts, their hands free but their feet still shackled together. Further afield lay several men, writhing about in agony, gripping their stomachs and with their knees knotted up under their chins and all the time moaning and groaning to themselves. On seeing the plight of these poor devils, Doctor Hadleigh at once alighted from his horse. Pausing only to grab his medicine bag from behind the saddle, he rushed over to attend them. Huge sighs of relief emanated from the rest of the onlookers at the sight of the Doctor being in the midst of them. The overseer, shifted about uncomfortably from one foot to another just behind the Doctor.

'It's the same as the others have got, isn't it?' he said as Doctor Hadleigh finished his cursory examination and stood up.

'Yes, I am afraid it is,' he gravely replied. 'Do you know what it is, Mr Cookson?'

The overseer's eyes lolled slightly in their sockets and in a fearful voice he cried, 'Well, I'm not too sure, but I reckon it's some kind of jail fever mebbe.'

Doctor Hadleigh motioned Cookson to follow him to a quiet spot some distance away from the convicts, so that he could have a straight talk with him. Without wasting any further time, he quickly and firmly gleaned from Cookson several vital pieces of information, such as how several of the newly-arrived convicts had mentioned that this kind of fever had been running rife on the ship that had brought them over. Small wonder that it spread so, when they were known to be herded together in rat-infested holes, deep in the bowels of the ships, left to survive as if they were no better than caged animals. Doctor Hadleigh also made it perfectly clear that to all intent purposes, Richard Fitzroy had little intention of doing anything constructive himself. Therefore, he informed the overseer, that it was now left to him to decide what to do about their plight. Cookson panicked at once and began blubbering about what to do for the best. This, of course, gave the Doctor the prime opportunity that he had been waiting for. Swiftly and curtly, he ordered Cookson to move all the sick men back to their huts. This would have to be done by getting the rest of the convicts to knock up some kind of hurdle to carry them on. Secondly, it was decided that they had to be isolated far away from anyone else, but somewhere nearby so that the Doctor could administer to them properly. It meant finding somewhere where he could heat up water and mix powders and purges properly. Running his fingers through his hair and racking his brains as to where he could put them, when all of a sudden the idea flooded through to him.

'Great heavens, why didn't I think of it before? Yes it would be perfect,' he called out.

But the overseer was appalled when Doctor Hadleigh suggested that they should use Mr Cookson's own place. Cookson stood there dumbfounded as he listened to the Doctor explaining to him how he could lay out rows of mattresses for them to lie upon, in the back room, behind the canvas door. Next he was required to have a plentiful supply of freshly-drawn water for the Doctor to use each time he came on his rounds.

At first Cookson stubbornly refused by saying, 'I am not going to have a lot of shit arse convicts dossing down in my place.'

He was not going to lay down his weary head next to them. But Doctor Hadleigh smoothed his way around that situation by forcibly telling him that he would personally find him somewhere to stay till a more permanent place could be found. The final blow came when Cookson was informed that all the huts, not to mention his own shack, would have to be burned to the ground and that new ones would have to be erected almost immediately.

'Burn everything,' squawked Cookson, 'I can't do that. Mr Fitzroy would never forgive me. Not for setting fire to his land. Why he has spent months and months working in these fields, just getting everything right for harvesting. We dare not destroy all those crops just like that.'

Tears of rage were now flowing down Cookson's sweaty cheeks. The word 'fire' had also spread fear into the minds of some of the convicts who had been silently listening to the fierce exchanges between the two men. Now they were making noises of protest. But to no avail. The Doctor swung round and, taking several long strides towards them, ordered them all to be quiet. Cookson had also heard enough and started to saunter off towards his horse. Doctor Hadleigh on seeing him do so, followed him and grabbed him by his arm.

'Mr Cookson, I know this is a difficult job for you. But you really have no choice. In these circumstances, fire is the only fool proof method we have of terminating the epidemic. If you are extra careful and take a few precautions, the fire should not spread too far. I'm sorry but your boss had left me no alternative but to act drastically. And now I suggest that we stop talking and get on with the deed in hand. We have wasted enough time already.'

The overseer, who had by now extricated his arm from the Doctor's firm grip, nodded his head slowly in assent. Soon he was shouting instructions to the rest of the convicts.

It was not until he had reached his own shack, that it strangely occurred to the overseer that the Doctor seemed to know an awful lot about where and how he lived. Funny because, he could not ever remember him being invited there.

'Next time I get the chance, I must question him about it.'

And so, making a mental note of this, he forcefully turned his mind away from the subject and focused it on the unpleasant task that was now at hand.

Melodious refrains of Schubert wafted sweetly throughout the house. Golden shafts of bright sunlight filtered onto the slightly parted drapes and danced wickedly all around the crystal candle holders that sat perched on top of the grand piano. The rays bounced back and forth catching the sparkling brilliance from the precious stones set in Augusta's rings. Her nimble fingers barely touched the ivory keyboard as her thoughts submerged into the unconscious regions of her mind, lost in the beauty of the music. But the tranquil moment was over in a trice. Bursting into the room and wringing her hands in despair, Mrs Jameson's agitated voice rose shrilly over the top of the cadenza. Augusta finished the piece and, spreading the palms of her hands flat alongside the top of the piano, leant forward and stared in undisguised annoyance at Mrs Jameson. Knowing that Augusta did not like her privacy invaded when playing the piano, the distraught woman made it appear far worse by hopping about from one foot to another and rolling her piggy eyes around in their sockets.

'Is it of vast importance, Mrs Jameson?' enquired Augusta, who was by now quite used to the woman's sudden dramatic outbursts.

'Why yes, Ma'am it is. Otherwise I would not have bothered you so,' cried back the older woman.

Augusta reluctantly rose up from the piano stool. Then placing the precious sheets of music back into their folders, she walked over towards Mrs Jameson.

'Now, Mrs Jameson. Pray tell me, what is the matter now?'

Mrs Jameson was not quite sure how to tell Augusta what was causing her such alarm. So quickly and incoherently she went on and on about the peculiar behaviour of Tamara.

Yesterday, apparently she had been very listless. Her appetite poor. 'All through the night she had suffered bouts of restlessness. This morning she was all hot and feverish and complaining of nasty pains in her tummy and now Betsy has just told me that Tamara had thrown up all over the counterpane.'

Augusta screamed and threw up her hands in horror.

'Oh no, Mrs Jameson, why did you not tell me before?' she cried.

The clock in the hall suddenly chimed out eleven of the clock.

Twisting a piece of linen in her damp hands, Mrs Jameson replied morosely, 'I thought I could handle the situation myself, Ma'am. I presumed that she was just cutting another tooth at first. Now I am not so sure.'

Augusta shifted about nervously.

Pulling at the ribbons at the front of her silken blouse, she apologetically exclaimed, 'Yes of course. I am sorry, Mrs Jameson. You obviously did your best.' Swiftly pausing for breath, Augusta carried on, 'Now let's go up at once and attend to Tamara together.'

141

Augusta and Fitzroy sat facing each other across the study floor. Doctor Hadleigh had just departed.

Pulling and twisting at the corners of her lace kerchief Augusta cried out wildly, 'This is dreadful news, Richard. Cholera, Tamara is desperately ill with cholera and Doctor Hadleigh forbids me to sit with her. How could this happen to our child? I have always taken such care of her. I just do not know what to do.'

Richard crossed and uncrossed his legs and, sighing deeply, said, 'Control yourself, Augusta. It is not any fault of yours.'

Augusta bounced out of her seat and, storming round the tiny room, shouted at him accusingly, 'No, it is all your fault. You and those wretched convicts. You should never have brought them here in the first place. We could have managed without them.'

Now it was Richard's turn to shout back.

'No, we could not. I needed them to assist me in enlarging my estate properly. I now have the finest cultivated lands around.'

Augusta could hardly believe what she was hearing.

'Yes, and you also have a very sick child lying upstairs. One who could very well die because of your whims and demands.'

Richard stood up and moved towards the open window.

'Oh don't be so melodramatic, Augusta. You sound like one of those ridiculous heroines out of those damn fool books that you spend so much of your time reading,' he sneered at her.

'Richard,' she seethed, as she came to stand directly behind him, 'if anything happens to Tamara, I will never forgive you for it. Never, do you hear?'

Richard moved away from the window and sat down heavily in his usual chair. For a while he sat there, with his head sunk deep upon his chest, trying to absolve himself from having to listen to the rantings and ravings of his near demented wife. Eventually he was forced to reply.

'I hear you, Augusta. But there is nothing that I can do about it now.'

Over the next few hours Augusta had plenty of time to reflect on Richard's attitude of late. His sitting moping about the place for the past week or so had not improved matters. Nor did the fact that he had left all the unpleasant tasks in the hands of Doctor Hadleigh and Cookson the overseer to tackle. Charles had just informed her that Cookson had burnt all the huts and that half of Richard's precious wheat had gone up in smoke as well. It was this last piece of imparted news that was eating away at Richard's inside this very moment. Augusta was deeply concerned and upset to see how tired and ill Charles was looking. All this extra work involved in caring for the sick convicts was taking its toll upon his health. Augusta could not let the matter drop. It was wrong of her husband to opt out of everything.

'Richard, you are impossible,' she shrieked at him later that evening. 'All you seem to care about is your own self-interest. Nothing else seems to matter. People and their sufferings have no place in your life,'

There, she had said it. Nervously she waited for his reaction. Richard, with a thunderous look on his face, had been going over his accounts. Suddenly he threw the heavy leather bound book across the floor. Jumping up he snapped back at her.

'That's right and why should I care? People have never given a damn about me. Everything I have or wanted I have achieved by my own means. If you go round studying other people's feelings before your own, you will never get anything in life. Now get out of here, Augusta, and leave me in peace for, unlike you, I have a lot of paperwork to catch up with.'

Augusta stared at him dumbfounded. This man she had married was a monster. Humiliation and fear swept through her entire being. How could she have stooped so low as to tie herself to someone as coarse as he?

Flouncing out of the room, she said under her breath, 'Don't worry, Richard. I have no desire to be in your company for any longer than is absolutely necessary.'

Betsy came out of Augusta's bedroom carrying the untouched breakfast tray. A heavy pall of silence hung over the entire place. With her head held high and her hands gripped tightly around the handles of the tray, she managed this time to decend the stairs and enter the kitchen without breaking down.

None of the staff even observed her entrance or answered her, as placing the tray upon the well-scrubbed kitchen table, she mutely said, 'The Mistress has not touched a thing.'

The servants stood or sat slumped around the kitchen in a state of complete shock. None of them was able to force themselves into saying anything. They all kept their grief tightly locked inside them. Only a few days ago, the house had rung with Tamara's excited, piping voice, the excitement generating from the fact that she was just about to celebrate her fourth birthday. The birthday cake that Mrs Soames had made for her was still waiting to be iced. Mrs Jameson had just five more tiny seed-pearl buttons to sew on the exquisite little velveteen jacket. The rocking-horse that her parents had so lovingly and carefully hid in the linen cupboard, lay on its side, and out in the stables, smashed and scattered amongst the straw, was the painted wooden dog on castors, which Jack had been working on when his mother imparted the terrible news to him. He had sat there, paintbrush in one hand and wooden mallet in the other. As soon as his mother left him, he had lifted the mallet and totally destroyed the toy. He loved little Tamara and had been looking forward to witnessing the joyous look on her pretty little face when he presented her with the wooden animal. He had visualized her pushing it playfully around the garden. Now he had been denied the chance of giving it to her.

Inside the hall, Mr McTavish was expressing his deep felt sympathy with Doctor Hadleigh. The Doctor had just returned after spending most of the night in Tamara's bedroom. Mr McTavish could not help thinking how dreadful the Doctor looked. His skin was a ghastly grey, his face unshaven. His eyes were lifeless and sunk in their sockets. His crumpled clothes looked as though he had not removed them for days on end and his stance, normally so upright and proud, was now bent and sagging. The tending of the convicts had been bad enough. Forty-one had died so far. But in the last two days there had been no new cases of deaths. He thought that things were on the mend. At last, he might be able to have a good night's sleep. Then this shattering thing had to happen. He had tried everything in his power to save her. But all in vain. For somewhere around the early hours of the morning, Tamara Amelia, the names

144

that he had helped to choose at birth, lay dead in his tired arms, unable to survive the exceptionally high fever from the cholera infection.

For three whole days, Augusta stayed within the confines of her room. The only person allowed in or out of it was Mrs Jameson. As Tamara's nursemaid, she had come to love and cherish the little girl dearly and this fact greatly comforted Augusta. Knowing that she could share her grief with someone who had loved her daughter as much as she did was a comfort indeed. By rights, she should have had the comfort and support of her husband, but since the day of Tamara's death, she had not set eyes on him and neither had anyone else for that matter. He had slunk out of the house, in the early hours of the morning, shortly after the Doctor had pronounced that 'there was nothing more he could do for the child.' He knew full well that his behaviour would be judged as cowardly and despicable but the look of hatred and contempt that Augusta had flashed at him as she sat with their dead child's head in her lap, would haunt him for the rest of his life.

The burial took place three days later. Mercifully the weather was a good deal cooler. Only a handful of people turned up at the tiny cemetery, high on a craggy and dust-ridden plateau. More people would have attended, as was only rightly expected of them, but due to the fear that the cholera might spread amongst the rest of the community, they stayed within the confines of their own dwellings. So it was only Doctor Hadleigh, Mrs Carter, Clara and Mrs Jameson who followed on morosely in the wake of Augusta, Richard and the newly-appointed Parson of the church, Father O'Mallaghan.

After the tiny coffin had been lowered in the ground and the last rites said over it, Father O'Mallaghan stepped back and under partially closed lids, eyed the grieving mourners piteously, as they hopelessly tried to comfort each other. Life was strange, he thought. He had only recently arrived in this New Country. Foresaking his native Ireland in the hope of finding a little more happiness and less misery in this 'Brand New World', and here he was conducting his umpteenth burial before he had even completed his unpacking. On the face of it, death seemed constantly to follow him around. He liked the look of Mrs Fitzroy. She seemed genuinely distressed by the loss of her child. The Doctor, judging from the past few weeks, was a good and honest man, one who really cared about his 'people'. Not like most he knew, who had spent most of their time drinking themselves into oblivion, in order to escape from the more horrific and degrading aspects of their profession. Then snapping his well-worn leather-bound bible shut with a sharp bang, he caught the bleary eyes of Richard Fitzroy. The man was visibly swaying from side to side, whether from grief or too much of the demon drink, Father O'Mallaghan was not too sure. Only Augusta knew that he had only just made it for the burial. He had been drowning his sorrows, with his old cronies, the Smiths. Somehow he had sobered up and even managed to conduct himself in a manner befitting the occasion. To give him his due, he had taken the whole thing pretty badly, only he was not the type to let his feelings show to those closely related to him.

Augusta stood weeping uncontrollably as the last shovelfull of dry earth hit the top of the coffin. Gradually, with the aid of Mrs Carter and Mrs Jameson, she slowly and painfully followed Father O'Mallaghan and her husband back down the narrow and twisting pathway. Bringing up the rear and quite some way behind the others, came Doctor Hadleigh and Clara Carter.

Around the estate and on the perimeter surrounding the colony, things slowly crept back into place. Only one new case of cholera had been reported of late and the men working in the fields toiled earnestly away at their labours in a feverish attempt to patch things up. Some of the crops had been saved but unfortunately the vast majority of them had been destroyed, along with many other things in the fire. Inside the Fairlawns household life slowly dragged by. Richard Fitzroy had lost no time in getting back to work. To his way of thinking, hard work ws the remedy for all ills. For the past few days Doctor Hadleigh had been relieved of some of his duties by a travelling 'quack' who had turned up on his doorstep at a most opportune moment. Leaving most of his cases to the gentleman in question, Charles relished the thought of having a few spare hours to himself. He therefore decided on one of these occasions to ride over and see how

Augusta was coping. Also he thought that it would be a good idea to take the long route round and stop off at the schoolhouse to pay Clara a social visit. Sadly though, on this particular morning, Clara had decided to take her pupils on some sort of nature ramble. Naturally enough, he arrivd at Fairlawns a good deal earlier than he anticipated.

Knocking sharply on the front door, he waited patiently for Mr McTavish to let him in. After the usual enquiries were over, Doctor Hadleigh asked if he could be permitted to see Augusta. Some minutes later, Mr McTavish escorted him up stairs.

On reaching Augusta's room, the Doctor hesitated for a moment before knocking. Suppose Fitzroy were in there with her. He did not want another confrontation with the man, especially this morning. As luck would have it, Betsy just happened to appear on the top of the landing. Seeing her there, he quietly beckoned her to come thither. Listlessly she walked towards him. Her eyes, normally merry and bright, appeared heavy and cloudy. She looked as if she had shed quite a few pounds in weight as well. He guessed rightly that poor Betsy was taking Tamara's death to heart as well.

Lifting one finger swiftly to his lips, he whispered, 'Good morning, Betsy. Is your Mistress alone?'

Betsy nodded in assent and quietly vanished down the stairs leaving him to face Augusta alone.

He found her sitting on the side of the bed, still in her night attire. Strands of auburn hair clung damply round her neck and shoulders. The face she turned towards him was almost frightening. She was so white. Her eyes were red and swollen from so much weeping and great black smudges lay underneath them. She looked so forlorn and lost. They stared at each other for a while, then Charles, unable to bear the look of pain any longer, rushed towards her and flung his arms tightly about her.

'Oh, Charles,' she finally sobbed, 'what am I going to do? I cannot go on.'

How long he sat there rocking her in his arms, smoothing back her matted hair and constantly dabbing at her tear-drenched eyes, he could not comprehend. He just sat there, holding her close to him, so close, closer than was permitted for a Doctor to hold his patient. Several times that

147

conscience-pricking thought had flickered through his tired mind and once or twice he had tried to lessen his hold upon her, but Augusta had immediately sensed it and clung on to him all the harder. Relentlessly, he gave up the inner struggle and responded by holding her closer to him than before. Then the previous shared moments were brought to an end by several loud knocks on the bedroom door. Doctor Hadleigh on releasing Augusta, leapt off the side of the bed and in a sharp tone bade whoever it was to enter.

Mrs Potts hesitantly entered, carrying a large silver tray. While carefully placing the heavy tray on the dressing-table, she very expertly managed to give the Doctor a long cool calculating look. It was plain for all to see that she was not one to let even the slightest occurrence go undetected.

'I have brought up some nourishments for the Mistress. She has not partaken of anything for such a long while,' she informed the Doctor, firmly.

Augusta still could not face the thought of eating. Sobbing quietly to herself, she waved her hands in protest at the mere sight of it. But she had not reckoned on the stubborn persistence of Mrs Potts and Charles's persuasiveness, as bit by bit, they managed to coax her into sipping several spoonfuls of hot nourishing broth.

'Now, if you take my advice, Ma'am,' said Mrs Potts, standing beside Augusta, her arms akimbo, 'a nice hot bath is what you need now and perhaps I can persuade Betsy to wash and curl your hair, just the way you like it. Then maybe that will relax you enough to catch up with a few hours well-deserved sleep.'

Mrs Potts gathered up the dirty utensils and returned them to the tray. Smiling to herself she thought she had graciously won the battle where Augusta's moods were concerned.

But no, the victory was short-lived, for just as she was about to disappear out of the room, Augusta suddenly wailed out, 'No, no, I cannot sleep. Every time I close my eyes, I keep seeing her dear precious face before me. I shall never sleep again. I will never, never get over her death. I still cannot believe that she has gone. My baby. Oh Tamara, Tamara.'

The recurrence of the outburst unnerved Charles as well. Forcefully opening his bag, he took out two small phials and handed them to Mrs Potts.

'Here, give one of these potions to her in a little water after she has bathed and another one before she retires tonight. These will help her to sleep.'

Then, taking her hot little hands into his he said in a very gentle tone, 'Augusta, you will get over this tragedy eventually and who knows, perhaps one day you may end up with many children? Accepting death is part of life, I am afraid. I know that this is not perhaps the best time to tell you, but you are not alone in your grief. There have been quite a number who have lost their lives through this outbreak. You are one of the lucky ones. There are plenty of people around you who care enough to make sure that you will not have to suffer your grief on your own.'

Looking up at him and sighing deeply, she uttered, 'Yes, Charles, you are so right. You make me feel very ashamed. I will do as you prescribe.'

Turning to Mrs Potts she added, 'I will have that bath and my hair washed. I must look an awful sight.'

Breathing a sigh of relief and winking at the Doctor as if to say, 'I think all will be better now,' Mrs Potts walked over and pushed open wide the door, but for reasons best known to herself, she did not go out straight away. Standing there, with her feet firmly planted on the ground and with a fixed look on her face, she glanced first at her Mistress then at the doctor.

'Hm, hm,' she coughed loudly.

Realization slowly crept over Augusta as to why Mrs Potts was behaving somewhat out of character. It was the fact that Doctor Hadleigh was still in the bedroom and had not made any evident attempt to follow her out of it.

Rising to the occasion, Augusta said pompously, 'Doctor Hadleigh, I thank you for all the care, your concern and most of all your time, but I would greatly appreciate it very much if you would be so good as to leave me now.'

Mrs Potts smiled benignly and walked out. Doctor Hadleigh did not though. He just stared in disbelief at Augusta.

Gripping hold of the iron bedstead, so tightly that the whites of his knuckles showed through, he said in a highly controlled voice, 'Augusta, you need not be quite so pompous with me. After all, I am only trying to help you.'

Dispirited though she was and distraught with grief, she did however manage to see the funny side of the situation. Charles was right. Pain could not last for ever. There had to be a turning-point somewhere. Perhaps she had even reached hers. Gradually the sad expresiion on her face slowly started to melt away. Tears of bitterness quickly evaporated and were replaced by tears of laughter. Charles was instantly aware that she might be losing her reasoning altogether.

Augusta childishly caught at his outstretched hand and said quite coquettishly, 'Oh, Charles, please don't look so shocked. I only said it for Mrs Potts benefit. She obviously does not approve of you being here.'

'Well I am your Doctor, for God's sake,' he replied quite tersely, although secretly he was more than relieved at seeing the sudden change in her.

Letting go of his hand a trifle reluctantly she answered him with, 'Yes you know that and I know it, but to the servants, we must openly display propriety. You know how everything has to be 'proper' with them.'

Charles smiled warmly at her, kissed her hand lightly and promised to call again very shortly.

As soon as he had gone, Augusta rang the bell for Betsy, miraculously feeling more than ever the desperate need for a bath and a change of clothing.

13

For most of the people in and around the colony, the pattern of their lives weaved on in its usual routine way. That is, with the exception of Richard Fitzroy's. Many more convicts had been hired to replace the ones he had lost. The cholera infection had seemingly died a natural death. At first Richard had intended to carry out Doctor Hadleigh's plan to find a new site and erect huts on a much larger and more charitable scale. This all seemed a grand idea until the overseer handed him the plans and the costings. One did not have to be a brilliant mathematician to speculate on how great the cost would be, let alone the invaluable time lost on such a venture. All this was quickly waved aside and it was decided to rebuild on the old foundations, thereby wisely saving time and money, or so he thought. As usual, there was still an abundance of work to get through on the land. The seasons were on the change and a wet spell seemed imminent.

Augusta had rallied round and was slowly and painstakingly attempting to carry on as well as her unhappy way of life permitted. At least she and Richard were now on speaking terms, if only perfunctorily. They rarely saw each other during the course of the day. On very rare occasions they sometimes supped together, Augusta preferring to have a light supper in the small sitting-room, leaving Richard to spend most of his evenings drinking and cavorting with his disreputable neighbours. Like most men of his kind, it never occurred to him to concern himself with his wife's social welfare. In his opinion, and he was not alone in this, once wed, women were destined only to run a home, see to their Master's every whim and content themselves with their embroidery, tapestry work and endless afternoon tea-parties. All this, of course, was coupled with the tedious chore of raising enough healthy brats to carry on the family tradition.

The winter months came and went and Augusta was more than glad to see the back of them. She hated the winter here. It came upon the place so suddenly and the dramatic drop in the temperature was more than noticeable in this New Country than in the Old One. With the warmer weather, one soon became accustomed to the hot sun penetrating deeply into one's body, generating a goodly effect. During the winter months the house was forever cold, even though huge peat and log fires burned in almost every room. All houses were built with the long, hot, dry summers in mind. Therefore, nowhere was draughtproof or particularly cosy. The cold and wind seeped in through large gaps beneath the wooden planked floors. At night, people would lie in their beds listening to the wind whistling and whining as it passed through the large gaps between the rotting window frames. The servants were always ill-tempered and miserable as they hated having to leave the warm confines of the kitchen range to do the menial tasks in the coldest nether parts of the house. When the rains came, they were not so forceful or devastating as the previous year. But travelling around was always a nightmare in the rainy season. All the paths and tracks eventually became oozing quagmires. During this period Mrs Carter had actually braved the elements and paid several afternoon visits to Augusta, mainly to boast about the completion and furnishings of her new home. For two or three hours at a time, Augusta was virtually forced to listen to a non-stop recital of the wonderful achievements of the Carter family. The gains they had snatched from the land as a result of Fitzroy's sound advice about using convict labour was at last paying off with great dividends. They were now thinking about buying more land for the sole purpose of sheep rearing. This would mean that more and more enforced labour would be required. They just hoped that there would be enough convicts to go round.

It was on such an afternoon that Augusta asked Mrs Carter whether she actually condoned this disgusting trade on her own homestead.

'Well, I didn't at first, Mrs Fitzroy,' she sheepishly replied. 'But as my husband says, if you have to break someone else's back in order to clothe one's own, then I guess it's acceptable.

After all it is a case of needs must.'

Somehow, though, Augusta could not come to terms with this idea, no matter how hard she tried to put it in to perspective. She hated them being used on her husband's land.

Some weeks later, when Mrs Carter called again, Augusta noticed that she was not her usual chirpy self. After carefully prising the truth out of her, it soon emerged that all was not going too well for Clara. After the opening of the school house and all the fuss that had centred around it, things had not happened as Clara had envisaged. Precious little had been done on the maintenance of the building. The chimney-stack had never been inserted. The temporary window gaps were still minus their shutters. The floors and walls had not been flattened out properly and, far worse, the makeshift earthen closets were still not attended to. It was not that the men in the Carter family would not help her, but that they were far too busy trying to keep up with their own numerous tasks. So it was not altogether surprising to learn that when the rains came, things took a turn for the worse. When the schoolhouse was finally flooded out, Clara had no alternative but to close it down for the time being. The children were of course euphoric about the decision. To them this meant no more having to endure splintery old forms, having to suffer the sights and smells of such a small enclosed building, no more having to strain precious eyesight in the near dark over the cracked slates that had the habit of constantly slipping through tired and aching fingers and no more having to listen to Miss Carter, 'Ma'am', as she preached and dictated her views through the course of the day. It had been heavenly to be able to escape through that loosely-hinged door and tear off home. For the fathers of these delighted scamps, it was a blessing in disguise. Now they could get down to some real work and help out on the land.

'I do believe the weather is on the change at last,' commented Augusta to Richard, one bright Sunday morning, as she tied the ribbons of her new bonnet tightly under her chin.

The weather was the one subject that was considered

153

reliably safe to talk about without causing Richard to fly off the handle. Richard grunted in reply.

Anxious to engage him in conversation, she casually continued, 'I suppose there is no point in asking whether you intend to go to church this morning, Richard. Or are you going to have a change of heart for once?'

Fitzroy was engrossed in an article he had found in an old journal. All he wanted to do was sit in peace and absorb it. Sunday was his day of rest and to hear his wife nagging him again to go to church was like the repeat performance of a very bad play. Why couldn't she go on her own. Other women did. Flinging aside the journal; he brutishly echoed, 'No, Augusta, I am not. I will never sit amongst that congregation again and have them looking at me as if I were the Devil Incarnate. Nor do I wish to experience those cod-fish eyes of the Rector glaring down at me or hear his fire and brimstone text about the walls of Jericho falling down on those who pursue immoral and profligate ways of life. No, you can go and suffer him if you must. But I shall be off to 'Pastures new', as they say.'

They were both in the morning-room. Richard sat sprawled on the Chesterfield surrounded by paperwork, while Augusta was patiently waiting for the buggy to be brought round to take her to the Sunday Meeting House. Richard lifted the pile of papers to one side with the toe of his boot, as Augusta demurely swept past him. Observing her from underneath his shaggy eyebrows, he quickly took in the slenderness of her figure, the long-sleeved, tight-fitting bottle-green velvet jacket, with its shimmering skirt to match and the whiteness of the frothy lace high-necked blouse which accentuated her slenderness even more. Her feet were shod in knee-length black lace-up boots, with kid gloves to match. The wide-brimmed green bonnet, rakishly set at an angle topping her rich auburn hair contrasted with the rich creamy complexion of her skin. Never before had she looked so desirable. Augusta turned away from the window sharply and in doing so, caught Richard's eyes wandering over her.

A little anxiously she asked, 'Is there something wrong, Richard. You seem to be staring at me trifle overlong.'

Feeling somewhat bolder, he replied, 'Not at all, Augusta. I was just thinking how well you look at the moment. It would seem that you have recovered very quickly from your ordeal. Perhaps now is the time to put the past behind us and start again.'

Clutching tightly at the Prayer Book in her hands, she fearfully retorted. 'I am not sure what you mean, Richard.'

Slowly rising from the Chesterfield, he then swiftly caught her in his arms and pressed his mouth hard upon hers thickly whispering, 'Yes, you do, my dear. Don't play games with me. Forget about church this morning and Father O'Mallaghan preaching about the 'sowing of the seeds'. I suggest that we go upstairs and sow some seeds of our own.'

'Richard, no.'

She managed to struggle free and push him away.

'Please do not be so uncouth with me,' she gasped.

Grabbing at her wrists and holding them firmer than he realised, he blurted back at her, 'Uncouth with you? damn me, woman, you are my wife. I can do what I like with you. Here, take that stupid outfit off and give yourself to me as is your duty.'

Twisting her hands backwards and forwards, till she finally released her wrists, she spat out at him, 'Never, never will you use me again for your own pleasure. I am not a a whore.'

As if by divine intervention, the wheels of the buggy could be heard crunching along the gravelled carriage-way. On hearing them, Augusta ran towards the door and pulled it open sharply.

Richard suddenly crossed her pathway and cried in her ears, 'No, you are not, though I sometimes wish you were.'

He was about to bear down on her again, when voices could be heard in the hallway. He moved slowly away from the door, allowing Augusta to walk haughtily through it.

Minutes later, watching her depart in the buggy, he laughed to himself scornfully as she sat there, trying to re-arrange her bonnet and fiddling with her gloves. Poor Augusta, he thought, How hard she had taken the death of their child. What he could not fathom out was why? Women lost babies all the time. It was a common occurence. So why should his wife be caused such consternation? Not to mention all the stupid fuss about conceiving another one. Well, if she did not want to oblige, there were plenty around who would.

155

Straightening his mulberry cravat and smoothing the creases out of his breeches, he decided to venture out and find one, knowing full well that he would not have to go too far. For thank God, the whorehouses opened on Sunday mornings too.

Thick pungent smells of beeswax, sandalwood, and vinegar water mingled with the more delicate fragrances from freshly picked sprigs of rosemary. The heady and exotic perfume emanating from the coral hibiscus plants swiftly assailed Augusta's nostrils as she entered the drawing-room. Following closely behind her was Mrs Potts.

'It all looks so much cleaner and it certainly smells a lot better,' Augusta exclaimed, swinging her arms widely about, in an attempt to convey an air of geniality.

'Not before time, Ma'am,' Mrs Potts answered her stiffly.

Augusta was feeling greatly relieved and very pleased now that the house had been thoroughly spring-cleaned. The winter months always took their toll on the place. Augusta could not make up her mind which she disliked most: the filth in the winter or the dust and flies during the summer. She was now looking out of one of the long windows. The drapes had been tied back as far as was possible to let the late morning sunshine warm the room.

'Talking of flies,' said Augusta abstractedly to herself, 'I must see if they have started to spring-clean the kitchen yet.' She knew only too well how quickly populated that area was with them. As she was about to leave Mrs Potts with a host of instructions, her attention was suddenly alerted and out of the corner of her eye she saw something moving about on the far perimeter of the garden. Seconds later, a baby kangaroo bounced out of the bushes and began frisking around the grounds. Watching it closely, she could not help remembering another such moment, when Tamara was alive, that happy afternoon both of them spent frolicking around with the baby kangaroo. It might even be the same one. Perhaps he had come back to find his excited little playmate. The mere thought of Tamara instantly revived painful memories. She had tried hard to keep her emotions in check, but in vain. Hot tears were now scalding her eyelids. She was frantically searching for her kerchief when Mrs Potts, sensing that something was wrong, came towards her and placed a reassuring arm around her shoulders. It was not her place to probe into her Mistress's private affairs. No doubt she would be told in good time. Augusta dried her tears and walked away from the window towards the china cabinet in the far corner of the room. Taking them out one by one, she half-heartedly, began checking the pieces for breakages.

Some were quite pretty. She found herself staring at a porcelain figure of a young girl with flaxen hair streaming out behind her. She was clothed in a pale blue gown and carrying a small puppy in her bare arms. Dancing around the girl were a couple of village yokels downing large tankards of foaming ale. It was her mother's last birthday gift to her and it reminded her very strongly of dear old England.

Placing the piece carefully back in its place, she spun round quickly and quite surprised the housekeeper by announcing, 'Mrs Potts, I have just thought of something wonderful to do. I think I shall give a small soirée.'

Mrs Potts looked startled. She had never even heard of the word.

'A soirée was something that my Mama used to give many years ago. They used to be great fun. Mama was very lucky in that she knew so many famous people. She was absolutely wonderful at persuading some of the most talented musicians and romantic young poets to entertain her guests. One evening she even persuaded the great Mendelssohn to play.'

'Well I never,' commented Mrs Potts, raising her eyebrows to the sky, in a fashion that indicated that she and Mendelssohn were bosom friends. As it happened, she had never heard of the fellow. Still it did not do to plead ignorance in too many quarters. Augusta, on recalling these little anecdotes, felt her unhappy feelings slowly melt away. The mere thought of having a little party cheered her up no end.

Now that she had engaged Mrs Potts' full attention she gaily carried on by saying, 'You should have seen the titbits that were served during the course of an evening. They were often quite a surprise. Mama would go to great lengths to make even the most mundane dish appear faintly exotic and grand. Most of them she had copied from the Prince Regent's soirées. She herself never went to any of them, but Papa, attended them frequently. He would come home and tell

Mama all about the grandness and the lavishness of the food and she, of course, would do her best to concoct something similar at her next soirée.'

'Just a minute, Ma'am,' interrupted a sceptical Mrs Potts. 'Aren't you getting a bit too carried away? I mean, all that may have been very well back in old England. But out here it is quite a different kettle of fish. How on earth is anyone going to be able to concoct those weird and wonderful dishes? Can you just imagine Mrs Soames trying to come up with a royal dish? It's an effort for her just to prepare the ordinary fare of the day and as for entertainments, well that's just out of the question. This is a land of farmers, not dandies.'

Augusta nodded her head in agreement. Perhaps she had allowed her heart to rule her head this time. Still, there was no reason why she should not invite a few friends and acquaintances over for a small intimate party. Perhaps with a little determination she might be able to persuade Mrs Soames to bake some tasty little biscuits and a quantity of small wine cakes. As for the musical interlude, well no doubt she would have to think hard about that.

Some hours later, as she was surveying the silver candlesticks on top of the spinet, an idea sprang to mind. According to Mrs Carter, Clara was exceptionally musical and played the piano extraordinarily well. Yes, the problem could be easily solved. She would invite Clara Carter to play at her first little soirée. After giving the matter thought she wasted no further time in putting her plan into action.

The weeks ahead were fairly busy ones for Augusta as there was organising to do with the little soirée she had planned. All the guests had pleasantly replied and so far no one had cancelled. She had mentioned it several times to Richard, hoping that some of her enthusiasm would rub off on to him, but unfortunately it did not. Richard seemed to be preoccupied of late, so much so, that both Mrs Potts and Betsy had dared to mention it to her. At first Augusta had brushed the suggestion aside by stating that it was probably due to some worry or other concerning the estate. But even she realised that there might be more to it when his mood became increasingly more sullen and broody. Strange, too, that he was leaving the house later and later each day and returning to it far earlier than he normally did. The previous day his behaviour was even stranger. Maybe imagination was playing tricks on her but it seemed that every time that she happened to appear in any part of the house where he was, he automatically made some kind of feeble excuse to leave it immediately. Once or twice she had tried to pin him down to discuss the guest list for the coming party. Who knows, she thought, he may even be able to add to it? But even this resulted in him bolting from the room. Could it be that he was feeling vexed because she was doing something on her own at last? On trying to approach him in order to explain her feelings, she was once again met with the same lack of response.

The night of the party loomed up sooner than she realised and there was so much to think of that Richard's tiresome moods soon passed into oblivion.

14

So far, so good, thought Augusta as she wandered amiably amongst the guests who had turned up for her first soirée. Dressed in a wide-hooped gown, of the palest green. The bodice was tight-fitting and had rows of bewitching little bows running down the front of it. Festooned around her bare neck and shoulders hung a magnificent emerald and filigree necklace. Her rich auburn hair had been so skilfully brushed by Betsy that it practically outshone the brilliance of her gems. Augusta had decided to wear her hair long this evening and sported the latest fashion by having it parted down the back and half of it draped boldly over one shoulder. She looked exceptionally captivating and everyone commented on the fact. To her surprise, she had learnt that, with the exception of one or two guests, the majority of the people invited had not the faintest idea what was meant by a soirée. They were generally held by the more artistic members of the upper-class society. But as most of the guests reflected once they had entered into the swing of things, any social gathering was more agreeable than none at all.

At first Augusta noticed that her guests seemed to lump themselves together in tight little groups. To the right of her stood Doctor Hadleigh, who looked very resplendent and handsome in his evening clothes, which contrasted deeply with the somber frock-coat, his companion, Father O'Mallaghan, was wearing. Both men were deeply absorbed in discussing the plight of the Aborigines.

At the far end of the room, Fitzroy's voice could be heard loudly talking above the voices of his friends the Smiths. In the centre of the room, sat the Carter family. All but the youngest one had turned up and Augusta, on seeing them sitting so close to one another, could not help smiling to herself and thinking that they were a perfect group. A new family had just arrived to the colony and had been standing awkwardly by the door until she ushered them gently in. They were Mr and Mrs Cameron, with their twin sons Edmund and Fergus.

The only flies in the ointment, so as to speak, were the infamous Smiths. This pair had obviously been invited at Richard's insistence. Augusta had hoped that they would not bother to attend, as this was not their kind of gathering. But no, they turned up in all their vulgarity, delighting in being able to nose around and poke fun at Augusta's attempts to try and bring a little culture into the 'Outback', as it was now generally called.

The women, thought Augusta, had all made such a tremendous effort to look really elegant and suitably attired. This was no easy task as there were no fashionable shops from which to buy fancy and exotic silks or fabrics, only the local store that stocked several shelves of mostly plain and durable materials. To purchase anything more grand, one would have to ask the storekeeper to send off to one of the towns for it, or wait for some travelling pedlar to emerge, flaunting his usual gawdy wares. These normally consisted of bolts of brilliantly hued shot silk, reams of tawdry laces, yards of richly coloured velvet ribbons, packets of decorative combs and imitation jewelled hairpins. If one searched hard enough one might be lucky enough to come across a yard or two of something quite respectable. Where the pedlars acquired their wares, God alone knew. Wickedly, Augusta could not help thinking that Mrs Smith, attired in that awful gown of flaming red that clashed horribly with her flaming red hair, must have relied heavily on the arrival of the travelling pedlars. Still, at least for the time being their behaviour was not quite so raucous.

Richard, she had observed, barely mingled with the other guests. He had opted to spend his evening socialising in a far-off corner with the Smiths. Somehow, he did not appear to be his usual ebullient, rumbustious self. Normally he liked to be the life and soul of the party, always drinking heartily and laughing gustily at the top of his deep resonant voice. But tonight he seemed more than just a little perplexed and troubled. Perhaps he was worrying about the recent heavy

161

expenditure on the estate. Or could it be that the death of Tamara had upset him more than he cared to admit. Since their last encounter, he had not said anything more and still carried on in his usual way, if not more distant than ever before. He seemed to be staying out later and found it necessary to travel further afield. Still it was not her immediate worry now. Her concern was for the welfare of her guests.

Mrs Soames had excelled herself, although it had taken a lot of forceful persuasion on Augusta's part to cajole her into attempting such delectable dishes. But after a lot of nail-biting and frequent stormy outbursts in the kitchen, she had managed to surprise Augusta's guests by her efforts: mounds of pastel coloured custards and creams. Fruit compotes, swirling trifles, spiced biscuits, dainty ratafia cakes and macaroons juggled for space between the more savoury and subtle fish and cheese delights. Huge bowls of hot spicy punches had been placed at both ends of the table so that the guests could help themselves more freely. This, Augusta surmised, would make a pleasant change from the usual beverages of mead, ale and the more rough and heady home-made wines.

Judging by the relaxed and congenial atmosphere she sensed that this would be the most appropriate moment to entertain everyone. Strolling over towards the spinet she sat down and began, hesitantly at first, to play some of her favourite Beethoven Sonatas. She adored Beethoven and it was not long before she found herself being swept along by the magical beauty of his music. Her guests, slowly, one by one, settled themselves in small groups around the spinet to listen more intently to her playing.

Then it was Clara's turn to play. With her long black hair knotted very loosely down her back and dressed in palest lavender, she looked very attractive and demure this evening. Of the two, Clara without doubt gave the finer performance. Her excessively long, nimble fingers flitted over the keyboard, astounding and delighting her awe-struck audience with several well-chosen pieces by Liszt and Mozart. At the end of the performance she was slightly taken aback by the warm and rapturous response.

Someone standing at the back of the group was immensely

proud of her. For all through Clara's recital, Doctor Hadleigh had been turning matters over in his mind. This pleasant and convivial evening, spent in this if not grand but comfortable house, amongst a group of people who seemed to be enjoying themselves as much as he was, started to trigger off all kinds of emotions. Perhaps it was, after all, time to settle down with a nice, quiet, domesticated and talented wife. Maybe he ought to be thinking about acquiring some property of his own. Could it be that he ought to be establishing his own roots somewhere, make a mark on the landscape, as they say? After all, he could not live indefinitely off the gratitude of others. It was strange because the thought of settling down had never occurred to him since he had arrived here. The whole land was so vast and uncultivated, except for the small colonies that were springing up out of nowhere. One could travel for months on end, without ever coming across another human soul. Another more likely explanation, as far as he was concerned, was that he loved the complete freedom of being able to do what he wanted, without any kind of restrictions. But he knew, deep down, that he could not go on being a wanderer for ever. Strangely, he realized that at this moment he was experiencing the same kind of emotions that he felt on the day when he and Augusta stood side by side in that brash little church in Sydney, taking those absurd proxy vows. Many times that feeling had passed through his mind. There had been moments when he imagined that he had been legally married to Augusta and the thought had sent his senses reeling. Over the past few years he had come to realise only too well how much he cared for Augusta but the one thing he would not admit to himself or anyone else, was the fact that he was deeply in love with her. But he also knew that she could never be his, not while Fitzroy was alive, and he was not prepared to spend the rest of his time waiting for him to die. Who knows, he might be rejected anyway. No, far better to cut his losses and start again. So, why not Clara? She was attractive and highly thought of. More to the point, he enjoyed her company greatly. He knew he did not love her, not in the passionate demonstrative way that he should. But then, Clara herself had never betrayed any sign that she needed a man purely in the physical sense. He guessed that Clara needed a man to match her sensibilities and commonsense. With care, concern and a mutual liking, such a relationship might just work.

Later on, after the entertainments were finished and the guests had assembled themselves in varying groups to discuss topical matters, Doctor Hadleigh finally found himself with a slightly flushed and excited Clara. Placing his hand under her elbow he gently led her through the open doors onto the verandah. It was a beautiful, balmy night. The tall exotic blooms tantalized as they stood very close to each other. Dramatically highlighting the romantic atmosphere were the hazy wisps of smoke drifting from the occasional cocoon-shaped flares placed around the verandah in an attempt to ward off mosquitoes.

Charles tightened his grip upon Clara's waist and pulled her closer still. They stared at each other for a few brief seconds, then their lips met.

Charles whispered, 'Clara, my love. You must know how I feel. I was so proud of you this evening. You played so convincingly that all kinds of emotions stirred my senses. Clara, I know, that I am rushing you and I know that I should court you properly, pay my respects to your parents and make my intentions known, but I confess I cannot wait. I need you. I would like you to marry me, Clara. Please say you will consider being my wife.'

He felt her stiffen, slightly under his grip. Slowly and painfully she eased herself away from him. A cold sweat broke out all over him. Was she rejecting him totally out of hand? Was she not even going to consider his proposal? She had not spoken. She did not need to say anything.

Charles slowly moved away from her and stared out over the grounds. Sensing his disappointment, Clara stepped towards him.

'Charles,' she whispered tenderly placing her arms around his neck and forcing him to face her.

He spoke first and quickly.

'Forgive me, Clara. I behaved ungentlemanly. It was wrong of me to thrust myself upon you like that. It will not happen again, I assure you.'

Clara laughed quietly to herself. He looked like a school-boy being severely reprimanded.

'Charles, there is nothing to apologise for. It is me who

should apologise.'

'You?' he exclaimed.

With her arms still around his neck, she said, 'Yes, me. Please listen to me very carefully. You must know how I feel about you, Charles. I think I love you very much and I feel flattered and honoured at the thought of being your wife. You must be the most admired and sought-after man in the whole of the country. I know everyone will say that I must be mad to refuse you. But, dear Charles, deep, inside there is a tiny part of me that forces me to say in all honesty that I cannot become your wife, at least, not for a very long while.'

Clasping her to him again, he cried, 'Why not, Clara? You must tell me.'

Pausing for a while so that she could pick her words carefully, she hesitantly replied, 'Charles, when I first arrived in this country, I wondered what we had let ourselves into. My feelings were a mixture of bewilderment and surprise. Bewilderment, at the nothingness of the land. The size of everything overwhelmed me. What would one do with all this virgin soil? I realised then that I could start completely afresh, do all the things I had always desired to do. Of course, I knew that this would probably take all my life to achieve even some of the things that I wanted. But one thing I decided then and there was that I wanted to be in the forefront of it all. That is why I tried to start a school of my own. I had heard stories about how so many well-educated girls came over here in the hope of becoming tutors or governesses, only to be treated like dirt and forced to live in unspeakable conditions. Well, Charles, that is not going to happen to me. My school collapsed before me, but I will rebuild it, and properly, if I have to do it with my bare hands. This is my challenge in life. I want to pass my skills on to the children here, who some day will be grateful for them. By the way, have you noticed, Charles, that the children who are born in this country are vastly different from those that have emigrated here?'

'In what way?' Charles asked.

As a Doctor, he had not noticed anything abnormal.

Clara dropped her arms from about his neck, paced slowly up and down the long verandah before she thoughtfully replied.

'The way they misbehave is more to the point. They are becoming more unmanageable. They have no interest in learning anything. Their only aim in life is to be completely free. I am afraid to say this, but I blame the parents. It's as if all this open space and wilderness matches their thoughts. Perhaps we are breeding a new race. Have you also noticed how drawn-out and nasal their speech is becoming? Some speak with a most peculiar twang.'

Here Charles nodded his head in agreement, but he did not think that it was of too much importance.

'Nevertheless,' carried on Clara, 'teaching children is to be my life's work. So, I have to confess to you that the one thing I wish to avoid is coming home at the end of a long long day and having to cope with my own little brood with running noses and dirty behinds. No, I intend to leave all that to those who are far better fitted for it than I am.'

Upset though he was, Charles found it impossible not to chuckle at this last remark.

Coming closer towards him, she added gently, 'That, dearest Charles, is why, though I love you, I cannot accept your proposal of marriage.'

She stopped suddenly. She had nothing more to say. She knew that she had hurt him enough. She wondered what his reaction would be.

Grateful for her honesty, Charles kissed her lightly on both cheeks and huskily whispered, 'Dear Clara, how I have misjudged you. You are more like me than I imagined. Maybe, one day, when you have succeeded in your mission, you will change your mind.'

With tears in her eyes, Clara flung her arms around Charles's neck and kissed him. They were interrupted by an agitated cry from within. Augusta burst through the doors onto the verandah, calling for Doctor Hadleigh. Richard had fallen heavily down the stairs and was lying prostrate across the hallway.

Charles went at once to Richard's aid. Mrs Carter was sat spread-eagled on his chest, one hand pulling and tugging at his constricting neck-piece, the other hand fumbling in vain to loosen the pearl buttons of his silken waistcoat. Both Cameron boys were frantically trying to wrench off his black boots. Mrs Smith, having lost her fan, was standing over

166

Richard and swishing her taffeta skirt from side to side, thinking that this heroic action would benefit him. The noise was deafening. Everything soon came to a standstill when Doctor Hadleigh shouted for all to move away and remain quiet, leaving Charles and Augusta to cope on their own.

Charles's immediate conclusion was that Fitzroy's condition was due to no more than a drunken stupor. However, on examining him more closely, he realized that this was not so. It was now abundantly clear that this was somthing of a more serious nature.

The guests were anxiously departing as Fitzroy was being carried up to his room. It had taken four of them to lift him, for he was no lightweight. Within seconds of depositing him, none too gently, on the narrow day bed, he started to come round. He lay there for some time, totally unable to utter anything comprehensible as his laboured and heavy breathing made it quite impossible. Doctor Hadleigh stared down into the sunken glazed eyes that rolled from side to side. Masses of unbroken sores lay grouped around his lower lip. On removing Richard's upper garments, it was noticeable that his body contained several unsightly rashes. Charles pointed one long finger in the direction of Richard's breeches, for those to be removed also. This proved to be more difficult, as Richard, ill as he was, managed to hold on to them. Panting and wheezing, he ordered Charles out of the room. In long-drawn out vituperative words, he insisted that there was nothing at all wrong with him and even went so far as to insult the Doctor and accuse him of interference and underhand deeds. Doctor Hadleigh froze where he was. This was not the first time that this arrogant man had insulted him in front of the servants. But, by God, it would be the last.

'Very well, Mr Fitzroy,' he tersely replied. 'Have it your own way. But let me just say this before I depart. You are a sick man, in more ways than one.'

Fitzroy gripped the sides of the bed and tried to raise himself up, but failed.

With all the strength he could muster, he cried out, 'I don't need a Doctor and, what is more, I don't need you. Get out of my house and out of my life. You are fired. Do you hear, fired? Get Augusta to pay you what is due to you, then get the hell out of here.'

Doctor Hadleigh turned on his heel and slammed shut the dressing-room door. Thundering down the stairway, he rushed past all those in sight of him, vowing never to set foot in the house again.

Some weeks later a letter had been delivered to Augusta. It was, of course, from Charles. He would like to have given her this information personally but at the last moment his courage failed him. It simply read: 'Dear Augusta, circumstances beyond my control have forced me to leave Fairlawns. I have decided to do some of the things that I set my heart on several years back: going into the 'Bush' to discover more about tropical diseases and the like. Eventually I will go to Sydney to find out what causes cholera and typhus. I hear a professor from the Sorbonne in Paris is giving lectures there. Have no idea when I shall return, if ever. Look after yourself. My love, as always, Charles. P.S. By the way, Clara also refused me.'

Augusta refused to set foot outside her room for the rest of that distressing day.

Richard Fitzroy slumped back heavily into the well-upholstered leather studded chair. Casting a laconic gaze around the unbearably hot and stuffy office, his eyes came to rest upon those of his overseer. Thick pungent tobacco smoke spiralled its way above their heads. The temperature inside the room was soaring but only Fitzroy was oblivious to the fact. The overseer had been called in to discuss the possibility of taking over some of Fitzroy's heavier responsibilities. Naturally enough, the very thought of placing Cookson in such an exalted position grieved him considerably. But he was forced to face facts. Shifting about in his seat, he began moving things around absentmindedly on his desk. Now and then he would pull out the gold fob watch, his wedding gift from Augusta, and sat idly swinging it. Then he opened one of the desk drawers, pulled out a large bunch of heavy keys and sat silently turning them over in his clenched hands.

Cookson, observing Fitzroy's actions contemptuously, inwardly debated how much longer he could endure his boss's infuriating behaviour. As if reading his mind, Fitzroy stopped fiddling with the keys and forced himself to look at the overseer. Coughing loudly and in a tired voice he started to ramble on about his plans for the future.

Cookson was only half listening to him. The atmosphere was extremely soporific and his mind was beginning to wander. The closeness and the stale odour in the room reminded him of another occasion, the time when he had been chained up in the hold of a convict ship. His mind flew back to the day when the ship crashed onto an unobserved barrier reef. Only three of his fellow convicts were saved. The ship, together with its entire crew, plunged fathoms deep and neither were seen or heard of again. By some strange quirk of events, he and two other convicts had been dragged from the bowels of the ship, and were forced to climb up the rigging to help with the unfurling of the sails. Because the majority of the crew had scurvy or were too exhausted from the overlong crossing, a number of the convicts had been forced to help out. He remembered little of the ship going down, for he had been knocked unconscious. All he remebered was that when he finally came round he was lying flat out on a length of rough timber, his arms pinioned firmly to his sides by two other convicts who had luckily managed to land on a large flat piece of floating debris. Somehow they had hauled him safely aboard and both were sitting astride him, this being the only sure way they could ensure that he did not wake up and roll over the side. How long they had drifted before they eventually reached the shore, no-one ever knew. After spending many years roaming, they decided to split up and go their separate ways. Cookson opted for working on the open land, as he could not bear the feeling of being confined. The longer he sat in Fitzroy's study, the more agitated he became. What had come over his boss lately? An enormous change had beset the man. He was nothing like the hardfaced, efficient, calculating, well-ordered land owner who had employed him as his overseer.

Something snapped inside him. If Fitzroy would not speak his mind plainly, then he would have to take the bull by the horns and charge in first. He agreed with Fitzroy that it

169

would be better if he were to take over some of the more tedious jobs. After all, he told him there was no reason why he should work so hard, when he could well afford to pay others to do it for him. The first thing he tried to get Fitzroy to agree to was the plan for the gulley streams. Should he still go ahead with the diversions or not? Fitzroy placed his hands squarely on top of the desk, and for a while sat staring nonchalantly into space. Cookson could not help noticing how violently his hands shook. He tried again to get him to answer his question, but Fitzroy seemed unable to give him a straight answer. 'Leave it with me for the time being,' was all he could say. Then he started rambling incoherently all over again.

Cookson stood up, realizing it was time for him to leave.

'Very well, have it your own way, Mr Fitzroy. After all, you are the boss.'

This comment seemed to stir him slightly. Yes he was the boss. It was his land, but at this particular moment it was the last thing he wished to be bothered with. He had far more important things on his mind. It was this thing he had contracted. There was a feeling he could not rid himself of. This thing was slowly killing him. He desperately needed to confide in someone, seek help. Was there perhaps a remedy he had not tried? But who could he ask?

Lifting his head slowly and wearily and staring straight past Cookson's head, so as to avoid his direct gaze, he said in a desperate tragic voice, 'Mr Cookson, what do you know about the pox?'

So that was it. It was out at last. It was not the drink, but something far, far worse. Cookson was rendered speechless. He took the liberty of clasping his arms around himself and then slumped back in the nearest chair.

Hesitantly he asked, 'Are you sure, sir?' Fitzroy nodded dumbly.

'So that's what the worry has been,' Cookson muttered under his breath. 'Have you seen the Doc? Is there no cure?'

Richard Fitzroy fixed him with a hostile stare.

'I have not seen anybody. How can I? It would be all over the place in no time. Oh, I know what it is, all right. I have seen it on other men. Never thought that it would happen to me though. I warn you Cookson, don't use that bastard whorehouse. I ought to have the place burnt down. Such creatures don't deserve to live.'

Cookson got up and made for the door. He left Fitzroy rambling on about how he was not like the rest of the riff-raff who used that place. He reckoned that he only went there the once and that was because Augusta had driven him to it. With Cookson gone, the worrying nagging thought kept on coming back to him: how to keep Augusta from finding out? He felt sure that she would kill him if she knew. He had to find some plausible excuse to leave Fairlawns indefinitely, or at least until a cure could be found. The only answer he could readily come up with was having to search further afield to find more workers for his present schemes. She would have to believe that one.

In the paddock Old Amos was strenuously putting a young colt through its paces. The colt was being broken in so that it could pull the new gig that Fitzroy had recently obtained for Augusta. It was meant as a peace-offering, to compensate for his leaving her while he and Cookson set off on their travels. Augusta had been complaining of late that it was nigh on impossible to leave the confines of Fairlawns. There was only one buggy and that was always in use by someone or other. Whenever she requested to have the buggy sent round, invariably it was not available. She rode herself, but there were times when she would have preferred the comfort of being driven. After a lot of persuasion, Richard had relented and bought a gig just for her convenience and after suffering a rare pang of conscience over the way he had mistreated her of late, he went the whole hog and added a fine colt to go with it.

So it was with some annoyance and frustration that Old Amos was suddenly dragged away from his frolics with the colt and obviously this was not going to be as easy as Augusta had visualized it would be. This was the first time she had used the gig. The weather had been exceptionally hot the last few days and the though of riding bareback in this heat was impossible. What had escaped her attention was that the frisky little colt had been harnessed once before and had not taken too well to it. It was with some trepidation that Old Amos actually managed to shackle the colt to the gig and succeeded in getting it to trot off in a somewhat ungainly manner round to its Mistress.

Once seated in the gig, Augusta instructed Old Amos to drive as fast as he could towards the main fields. Fitzroy and Cookson had only been gone a week and already mayhem had broken loose. Why, oh why, had Richard been so stubborn as to leave Fairlawns for any period of time? To her mind the last straw broke, when he insisted that the overseer went with him. In the past he had always made sure that the overseer stayed behind to manage the place for him. This time Richard had left everything under the control of a mere field hand. Richard should never have left Fairlawns. He looked so ill of late, not to mention his ugly moods and churlish behaviour. Augusta feared it was the drink, although it was a possibility that he had something physically wrong with him. Surely even he would have the commonsense to consult the doctor about it. Charles had not mentioned anything about his health before he left. Now, to make matters worse, he had gone haring off to acquire another load of convict workers. He must have had enough by now. What else did he want them for? What other schemes and plans had he in mind?

It came as no surprise when she learnt from young Jack that some kind of mutiny was taking place in the fields and she wasted no time in sending for Old Amos to take her there and find out for herself just what was happening. By the time she reached the main field, the worst of the fighting was over. Not waiting for Old Amos to place the steps in position for her to step down with ease, Augusta pushed hard on the side panel of the gig, causing the door to swing wide open and she leaped straight onto the hard-baked ground. The sight that met her eyes was not pretty. About a dozen convicts were sitting on the ground nursing their wounds: others had gathered together in small groups shouting and swearing at one another. But in the midst of all this, something even uglier was going on. Laying prone on the ground with his face pushed into the earth was the still figure of the recently appointed overseer deputising while Cookson was away. Prowling menacingly around him was a large bunch of bedraggled, bloodstained but triumphant looking convicts. Even though they were still fettered, they had successfully succeeded in overthrowing this bully and, like caged animals revelling in the final slaughter, they were not content just to leave him there to lick his wounds. They wanted to inflict further pain by humiliating swift kicks and well aimed spittle. The air was rent with cries of resentment and years of pent up frustration. Death was in the air.

Augusta began to run towards them, calling out for them to stop. But so intense were their feelings that they failed to notice her arrival. Quickly taking in the explosive situation around her, she turned and ran back towards Old Amos and the gig. She was annoyed to find him lolling back against the side of the gig with an amused look on his shiny face. He made no effort to move or offer her any assistance. This immediately infuriated Augusta.

'Amos, don't just stand there, gawping, come and help me. I cannot handle this situation on my own.'

Still not moving, he slowly uttered, 'Not me, Ma'am. This is not of my making. I always stay well out of other peoples squabbles.'

'This is not a squabble,' she fired back. 'They are intent on nothing short of murder.'

But still he made no attempt to move.

Now Augusta's patience was virtually uncontrollable. 'Amos,' she snapped, 'I cannot physically force you to take action. I am not a man, nor am I the boss. But when Mr Fitzroy is not here to sort things out, I have to do my utmost to control matters. And it is not easy, believe me.'

'No, Ma'am,' he answered. 'But, begging your pardon, Ma'am, if I go over there and start interfering, they will kill me as well. And I have always reckoned on spending the last few remaining years in peace.'

'You are impossible,' she cried. 'Well I will let Mr Fitzroy deal with you when he returns. In the meantime, ride back to the enclosed area and bring as many hands that you can find. Be as quick as you can.'

The moment the words were out of her mouth she knew that she had used the wrong words. Watching him drag his cumbersome frame away from the side of the gig and painfully mount the steps, she realised it would probably have been quicker to go herself. The fighting broke out again. The men had recovered their energy and were anxious to get back in the fray again. Old Amos turned his attention towards the convicts and nodded his head. Augusta was wringing her hands in agitation. She was beginning to feel sick with panic. Amos swore at the horse to move off, then leant forwards to lift the crop from its perch, when Augusta suddenly tore it from his hands.

'I will have that,' she cried. 'I may be forced to use it.'

Shouting at the top of her voice and lashing out violently with the riding crop, Augusta ran towards the fighting men and swiftly broke through to the centre of the disturbance. Slowly they backed away, scowling darkly at her, and muttering incoherent oaths under their breath.

Augusta knelt down by the side of the inert figure and slowly rolled him over. She gasped and stared in disbelief at the sight that confronted her. It took all her control not to vomit. The face of the overseer was completely smashed to pulp. There was no need to feel his pulse or test his heartbeat. Gingerly, she rolled him back again. The convicts crowded in to gloat over their handiwork, secretly pleased that it was Mrs Fitzroy who had found him and not the Master. But they had underestimated Augusta's strength of character.

With a new-found will, she leapt up from the ground, reached out for the fallen riding crop and lashed out once again in all directions.

'You animals,' she cried. 'You filthy disgusting animals. Get away from me, do you hear? Get back to the hovels where you belong. I will see that you all pay dearly for what you have done today. You are all guilty of murder. Do you hear me? Now move away.'

She stood there, outwardly composed and in command of herself but inwardly shaking with fright, not knowing which way to turn. She must stand her ground. If these people were to see her courage waver just one jot, all would be lost. Gradually they began to move away and the awful reality of the heinous crime that had been committed seeped into their minds.

Augusta relaxed a little and started to herd them together into a kind of semicircle on the ground. She hoped and prayed that she would not have to wait too long for reinforcements to arrive. After what seemed an eternity, the eerie silence was broken by the noisy arrival of Old Amos and a handful of workers, including the hefty bronzed blacksmith who was swinging his mighty anvil hammer high above his head.

Several hours later, after a refreshingly hot bath, Augusta sat propped up on a pile of cushions on the chaise-longue and reflected wearily on the day's events. How on earth would Fitzroy react when told, she shuddered to think. The dead man had been in Fitzroy's employ for some years, since before the days of Adam Smith. If it were true that he had sparked off the trouble by throwing his weight about and abusing his position by working the convicts far too hard, the situation should never have become so bad that it went beyond control. She felt angry and hurt that Richard no longer seemed to have the same grip on things he used to have. She felt lonely and dispirited. She wanted so much to be able to confide in someone close to her. She began to think of Tamara and how much she missed her. The pain was becoming unbearable again. She thought of her parents and realised she missed them dreadfully. Then she thought of Charles and of how much she had to tell him. But the thought of Charles made it far, far worse. Why did Charles have to leave, just when she needed him so. She longed to have his arms about her, to lay her weary head on his broad shoulders and to comfort her. She tried to cry but the tears would not come. She was too utterly exhausted.

15

Weeks went by and still Fitzroy had not returned, nor had she received any word concerning his whereabouts. Slowly everything was slipping back into place, but there was still an uneasy calm that hung about the place like a shroud. After Augusta had issued instructions that the deputy overseer was to receive a decent burial, she spent several fraught hours trying to cope with the many problems left behind in the aftermath of the trouble. Eventually she managed to persuade the men to return to their tedious routines, but not before she had sworn not to inform anyone that they had caused a man to die. This weighed heavily on Augusta's mind but she realized that it was the only way that things would return to some kind of normality.

For several nights she lay tossing and turning in her bed wondering how on earth Fitzroy would react to the news. Finally, she could stand the anguish no longer and sought advice and comfort from her own domestic staff. Instead of her summoning them to her rooms, she stole upon them as they were all busily engaged in eating their supper. Exclamations of surprise rippled through the room. Augusta who broke the ice first plunged in with a profusive apology for interrupting them at their supper, but within seconds they had brushed aside her apologies and in a genuine attempt to put her at her ease they all began talking loudly.

'Please, everyone,' she cried, 'I came down here this evening to seek your advice over a very worrying situation. Forget about everything else for a moment and spare me a few of your thoughts.' Very contritely, they settled back in their chairs to listen to what their Mistress had to say.

She began quite nervously at first, explaining what had happened over the past weeks since Fitzroy had been away.

When she recounted the scenes concerning the disruptive behaviour of the convicts, the fights, and the unfortunate death of one of Fitzroy's trusted workers, the sympathetic oohs and ahs that echoed around her helped to restore her confidence and she was able to share her worst fears with them, quite naturally.

They all too readily volunteered invaluable and practical advice on how to handle the situation. The solution was suggested by Mr McTavish and Mrs Potts. The death of that unfortunate man was due to all the extra responsibilities suddenly heaped up him, necessitating in him having to do two people's work. This led to him not being able to rest or eat properly and finally catching a feverish chill which resulted in his untimely death. The convicts revelled in the fact that they now had no one in charge of them and retaliated by going a little wild with each other and several ugly fights broke out, all of which Augusta had been called upon to stamp out. This 'story' was to be put about quickly and quietly to everyone who worked at Fairlawns, so that if the Master were to ask questions, everyone had the same answer.

'This tale will only hold water though,' warned Mrs Soames, 'so long as there is never any cause for the body to be exhumed.'

After thanking the staff for their loyalty and concern, Augusta left their quarters and made her way up to her own room, feeling more at ease and light hearted than she had for a long time.

16

Things drifted on in the same old routine. The only light relief in the household was caused by young Jack becoming betrothed to Sally, much to his mother's relief. There were whisperings behind Betsy's back as to whether she was really interested in the sudden attention being paid to her by Tom, the eldest of the Carter boys. She had confided to Mrs Potts that she did indeed like him very much, but was not too sure on whether she wanted to be a farmer's wife. After becoming Augusta's maid, Betsy had taken a liking to more relaxed and comfortable surrounds. She was not sure whether she wanted to throw all this up for the hard and precarious life that farming had to offer. Best bide her time a little longer, she thought.

Reflecting on what had come to pass in the last few weeks, Augusta thought now was the time for a change of scenery and decided to take the gig and ride over and visit Clara. She heard that the new schoolhouse was progressing very nicely. She opted to take the long route to the schoolhouse. She thought the longer she stayed away from Fairlawns the quicker the cobwebs in her mind would be blown away. This did not please Old Amos who was becoming more and more crotchety in his old age.

The long route meant having to pass the more built up part of the colony. Augusta carefully took in all the sights around her. The dozen or so tall wooden buildings that were all lumped together in a most higgledy-piggledy fashion were not at all well spaced out as they were in Sydney. The General Store, the first building to be erected, stood out from the others like a sore thumb. Someone then ventured to place a blacksmith's not too far away from it and haphazardly poked in between the two lay a flat-roofed rectangular building known as the 'Barber/Surgeon' which even boasted of a barber's pole. It was not long before two saloons, a couple of boarding houses, the newly-acquired Mission House and the Whorehouse appeared. Augusta cast her eyes demurely away from this den of iniquity, but not before she had caught sight of several of the women hanging out of the wide open casement windows. They stared at her in amusement. With their ridiculous hennaed hairstyles framing grotesquely painted faces and their low cut, gaudy, satin gowns they paraded their swelling bosoms.

Almost as soon as they had entered the place they were through it and winding their way upwards towards the tussocky hillock on which the small Baptist chapel precariously perched. On spotting the minister's wife hovering near the chapel door with a large bunch of brightly coloured blooms clutched to her breast, Augusta called out a greeting to her.

Suddenly the gig plummeted down the steep slope causing Augusta to gasp with delight and finally came to rest quietly some paces from the newly renovated schoolhouse.

Augusta sat staring at the greatly improved building. She could not help but admire Clara's efficient manner of dealing with things. A new roof and a chimney pot had replaced the makeshift one. The uneven wooden timbers had been strengthened and straightened and, miracle of miracles, glass had been fixed into the hollow gaps that had served as windows before. It had even been given a quick coating of whitewash so that it sparkled brightly under the glare of the hot rays of the sun. It was quite obvious to the passer-by that school had not reopened yet, for the area immediately around the front of the school house was littered with builders' refuse.

Augusta made her way gingerly over the debris, leaving Old Amos to find somewhere to water the colt. Pushing open the partly closed door that led into the schoolroom, she found Clara bent over a pile of books at the far end of the room. So engrossed was she in her work that she had failed to hear Augusta entering, but Clara soon realized that someone was moving towards her and looked up quickly.

'Augusta, how perfectly lovely to see you,' she exclaimed excitedly. 'This really is a surprise. What brings you here? I thought you would be far too busy to visit anyone at the moment, especially with Richard away.'

Embracing quickly and linking arms with her, Augusta replied, 'But not too busy to be able to visit you, Clara.'

'Well, I am glad you came. I need someone to cheer me up. I too have been working hard, as you can see. Let me show you around my new domain. What do you think of it now?'

'Well, judging from what I have already seen, I think you have done wonders. Now, tell me right from the beginning what have you been up to. I do not wish you to leave out one minute detail.'

Clara laughed happily. 'Well, nearly all my time has been devoted to the rebuilding and we are virtually finished. I have been so lucky, Augusta, with all the help I have received. The money to pay for all this was given to me by the church. The Minister and his wife have been so generous. Between them they have organized all kinds of collections and events to raise money.'

'Goodness,' exlaimed Augusta, 'that is good. I thought the church was only interested in collecting money for its own purposes.'

'Well, they are,' interrupted Clara, 'although, you see, their idea is for me to fill the school to capacity, pass on the good news about the redeeming qualities of the Reformed Church and how it is so conveniently placed near to the school, almost next door, one might say. Then the Minister hopes that this will swell his congregation.'

'Oh, Clara,' burst out Augusta, 'how could you become involved in such a scheme? It is not like you to be devious.'

'I know,' she replied, 'but if this is what I have to do in order to improve the literacy and waywardness of the next generation, well, so be it. Although others may judge me as being somewhat eccentric, especially when you think of the absurd lengths I have gone to.'

'What do you mean, pray?' asked Augusta, settling herself down on one of the rustic forms.

'Why, the laying of a woodblock floor, windows, a proper woodstove, and new forms, all for a bunch of rowdy and unkempt youngsters who within a few weeks will probably destroy the place.'

'Oh, no, surely not, Clara. They at least must see what you have achieved for them. If I were one of your pupils I would be extremely proud of my new school.'

'Bless you, Augusta, it is just like you to say such nice things about me.'

Swiftly changing the subject, Augusta inquired if Clara would care to drive back to Fairlawns with her and stay for supper. This Clara agreed to but not before she had shown Augusta her latest and most treasured acquisition, her own small sitting-room behind locked doors at the far end of the schoolhouse. She had made it look so homely and comfortable. One of the mothers had kindly made her a rag carpet that complemented a pair of richly coloured woven curtains. In front of a minute woodstove was a re-upholstered armchair that her mother had passed on. Two well-filled oak bookcases faced each other and, to complete the picture, in a tiny alcove stood a beautiful sewing table topped with a luminous smoked glass oil lamp.

'When do you intend to reopen the school, Clara?' Augusta enquired, as they were clambering into the gig.

'If all goes according to plan, Monday week. I still have a few accounts to settle and some further sorting out to do. But I must say, Augusta, I am really looking forward to it. This is my mission in life, one I intend to fulfil to the utmost.'

'I envy you in that, Clara. I think I am still looking for mine,' Augusta wistfully answered.

'Oh come now, Augusta, how could you say such a thing? You surely have everything you could want for. A husband, a nice home, pretty clothes, a new gig, money. What more could you want? Oh I know that you have lost Tamara, but it is not too late to have another child, is it?'

Augusta turned her head away from Clara's inquisitive eyes.

'Maybe not,' she echoed quietly.

The late evening sun was slowly disappearing as the two women sat facing each other across the verandah. A cool light breeze drifted around them. Only the chirpy sounds of the crickets and faint buzzings of the sleepy insects disturbed the tranquillity of that very pleasant evening.

'It has been a wonderful day,' said Clara at last. 'I have enjoyed your company so much, Augusta, but I really must be leaving, or they will be sending out a search party for me. You know how mother fusses so.'

'It has been so nice to see you again, Clara,' replied Augusta. 'We must try to visit each other more often.'

'I would like that, Augusta, always providing that Richard does not mind.'

'I do not see why not,' came back the firm retort.

'When do you expect Richard home?' Clara quietly questioned.

Augusta rose from her chair and stared out over the verandah.

'I have no idea,' she faintly replied. 'Do you know, Clara, strange as this may seem, I have this queer feeling inside me that he will not return.'

Clara hastened towards her friend and placed a comforting arm around her shoulders.

Kissing her lightly on both cheeks, she reassuringly murmured, 'Oh, you are a silly one, Augusta, of course he will return. You surely do not think that he is going to run away from all this. He will be home sooner than you think. Try to be brave dear. I know you must feel very lonely at times, but you could remedy that by helping me out at the schoolhouse.'

They both laughed and Augusta exlcaimed jovially, 'No thank you, Clara, I do not think I would make a very good schoolmistress.'

'Nonsense, you would make an excellent one,' rebuked Clara. Augusta walked to the front door with Clara and insisted on seeing her out herself. Clara kissed Augusta's cheek lightly and thanked her once again most profusely. She took her time settling herself in the gig, while Augusta patiently waited on the porch steps. She was just about to turn round and go in, when Clara leaned out of the gig and called out, 'Augusta, have you heard . . . ?' then stopped abruptly.

'Pardon, Clara,' called Augusta 'did you say something?'

There was no answer. Then just as the gig started to move.

Augusta on a sudden impulse cried out, 'Clara have you had any news from . . . ?' but the gig swiftly pulled away, leaving the fatal question unanswered.

All the way home Clara was annoyed with herself for not asking Augusta if she had heard from Charles. Augusta tossed and turned all night wishing she had had the courage to ask about Charles earlier on in the evening. Still on reflection, perhaps that question was best left unanswered.

17

The gig bounced lightly over the gravel carriage-way leading up to the front of the house. Augusta sat there not stirring, her mind completely lost on other matters. Old Amos strutted round and swung the door open wide, but still she sat there. Cursing silently to himself, he hesitated for a few seconds, then ambled back to talk to the colt.

Mrs Potts happened to be glancing out of an upstairs window and guessed that all was not as it should be. She hoped and prayed that it was not further trouble from the convicts. A few more minutes crept slowly by before she decided it was time to hurry downstairs and find out for herself what was troubling the Mistress. On reaching the gig, she found her Mistress sitting in the same position as before. She had not even noticed Mrs Potts' sudden arrival.

'Mrs Fitzroy, Ma'am, you should not be sitting out here in this fierce heat. Come inside where it is cooler.'

Taking Augusta's hand in hers, she tried to ease her out of the gig. Responding to the other woman's touch and awareness, Augusta's mind soon bounced back to normality. Smiling affectionately at the housekeeper, she thanked her for showing such concern for her well-being.

Once inside the house, Augusta bade Mrs Potts to send for cool refreshments as she felt hot and thirsty after the long drive to the fields and by the time Mrs Potts had re-entered the small sitting-room, Augusta was sitting at her bureau, quill in hand, penning a short but carefully composed letter.

After sipping a few sips of the iced cordial that Mrs Potts had just handed to her, she placed the glass on top of the bureau and calmly stated, 'This state of affairs cannot go on any longer. Normally, Mrs Potts, I would not discuss my personal affairs with the staff. But since I have been at

Fairlawns, it is fair to say that you have become my most trusted ally. As you may have guessed, no-one has heard from Mr Fitzroy or his overseer since they both left four months ago. I have tried to cope but to no avail. Since the death of that unfortunate man things have practically come to a standstill on the land. No one is bothering to do anything. True, things have quietened down. But I can sense a strong feeling of something or the other which I cannot quite put my finger on. I must track down Mr Fitzroy and demand that he return at once. But where to look for him? I just do not know where to begin.'

Mrs Potts sat with a worried look upon her dry wrinkled face.

'I know what you mean, Ma'am,' she stammered. 'One could search for years on end without ever having any luck. It is such a vast place. Where will you begin, Ma'am?'

Augusta took a sip of her drink and, pushing her chair away from the bureau, she wearily exclaimed, 'I really do not know where to begin. Oh, if only Charles were still here. He would be able to advise me.'

Mrs Potts stared at Augusta sharply whereupon Augusta blushed slightly, realizing her slip of the tongue in calling the Doctor by his first name. Recovering her former composure, she handed the housekeeper the letter that she had just penned.

'Will you send your Jack to deliver this to the general store and ask him to tell the storekeeper to have copies made to put on every stagecoach that leaves for whatever destination, in the hope that someone may have seen or heard of their whereabouts.'

Mrs Potts stood up and clutched the tiny envelope tightly to her bosom. 'Yes, of course, Ma'am. I must say, that sounds like a very sound idea. Let's hope it works.'

Two days later, as if in answer to her prayers, someone did turn up. Augusta was returning from a late morning ride and was still in the paddock with the horses when Betsy rushed over and informed her that the overseer, Mr Cookson, had just returned.

'Thank God,' breathed Augusta. 'Where have you put him, Betsy?'

Betsy shuffled her feet and looked down at the ground

before replying. 'He is in the study, Ma'am. Mr McTavish is with him. He looks quite dreadful though. All covered in mud and filth. I told Mr McTavish not to allow him inside. But he just brushed me aside.'

Closing the paddock gates behind her, Augusta hurriedly said, 'Thank you, Betsy, that will be all. I will deal with this now.' Gathering her skirt to one side, she hurried into the house.

She found Cookson leaning heavily against Fitzroy's desk. Betsy was right, he did indeed look quite dreadful. Mr McTavish was standing just inside the door eyeing him rather suspiciously. Taking in his mud stained appearance and dreadful pallor, she knew that something untoward had happened.

'Please sit down, Mr Cookson. You look as if you are about to drop.'

Turning to Mr McTavish, she asked him to fetch a chair and some ale for the poor man, which he did reluctantly. Cookson nodded his head and waited for Mr McTavish to depart before imparting his news.

'Mrs Fitzroy, I'm not quite sure how to break this to you, but I have to tell you your husband is not coming back.' He had intended to be a little less abrupt but fatigue and worry had stripped him of social niceties.

'Not coming back?' gasped Augusta. 'What do you mean? Where is he? Where have you left him?'

Cookson pushed on lamely, 'I mean, he can't come back. He is dead.'

'Dead? Oh no,' she faltered.

All at once the room seemed to sway around her. Fear clutched at her throat. Every muscle was constricted. Just then, Mr McTavish appeared with a pewter of ale intended for the overseer, but gave one look at Augusta and handed it straight to her instead. Dazedly she drank about half of it, then thrust the pewter into Mr Cookson's hands, who polished it off in one furious draught.

Perched on the edge of Richard's enormous leather-studded chair, she sat half listening to the overseer's stumbling account of what had happened to her husband, of how everything had been well at the beginning, how they had travelled many miles, seen many interesting sights, had

186

settled for a while at one of the largest cities and visited several large colonies, hoping to purchase a goodly quantity of convicts. However, luck ceased to be on their side when they were informed that all future convicts were now being requisitioned by the Government to lay foundations for all the military garrisons and outposts all over the country. The only convict workers employable for ordinary folk were women convicts. So rather than waste time and effort for nothing, they managed to buy forty women, ranging from fourteen to thirty years of age. Then just as they were about to leave, Fitzroy contracted some terrible stomach disorder which they were led to believe was incurable. Richard Fitzroy died from this complaint five days later. Cookson hesitated at this stage, not sure whether to go on.

Augusta dabbed at her eyes and said forlornly, 'What about the body? Have you brought it with you?'

The overseer looked flabbergasted. 'No Ma'am, I have not. I'm afraid I had to dispose of it pretty quickly.'

It was out before he had time to conjecture something more plausible to say. But he was deathly tired and uncomfortably hot and stale. His brain was not functioning at all well.

Augusta stood in a state of complete shock. Clutching fiercely at the strand of pearls around her neck, she was totally oblivious to the fact that one by one they slipped off their thread and cascaded noisily onto the wooden floor.

Forcing her lips to move and in a barely audible voice she stammered, 'Mr Cookson, am I hearing you correctly? Did I hear you say, dispose of the body? Are you trying to tell me, that my husband, Richard Henry Fitzroy, owner of Fairlawns Estate, was denied a decent and Christian burial?'

Augusta grabbed the back of the heavy leather chair and leant against it for support. With a nod of her head she dismissed Mr McTavish from the room. She did not want him to relay one more word than was necessary in the servants' quarters. No doubt they would have a field day over what had been gleaned already. Cookson, seeing how dreadful Augusta looked, realized at once the error of his words. The stark truth should never have slipped out in the first place. Racking his brain for something less harrowing to say was nightmarish. How could he tell her that her husband's death was caused by the ravages of syphilis?

Fitzroy had spent his last tortuous days on earth in a dingy room rented to him by the local gunsmith. His body was too decayed to be moved to the private graveyard on top of the hill. Even though Cookson had offered all the money that was left for him to be buried decently, the undertaker would not hear of it and had him shovelled into the paupers' open grave. To comfort Augusta, he lied and invented a story about how he had the Master buried with all due honour and respect in a 'very private cemetery', just outside a place called Woola-Wallanga on top of a beautiful lush hillside overlooking the valley, with purple covered mountains acting as a dramatic backdrop to a setting of serene tranquility. Whether she believed this he would never know, but the sudden easing of pain and tension that slowly crept over her face, causing it to soften a little, appeared to Cookson to have done the trick.

Dawn was breaking and the amber sun could be seen creeping through lightly scattered clouds on the horizon. Augusta was already awake. Pushing back the counterpane she stepped lightly onto the well-worn rug beside the bed. Another restless and sleepless night had passed by. After lazily stretching her body, she clambered out of bed and made her way slowly towards the window. Thrusting back the heavy curtains, she leant her head far out of the open window and drank in the sights and smells around her. This, she thought, was the best time of the day, the time she loved the most. Everywhere looked fresh and sparkling clean. Only the chirping of the brightly coloured birds and cries from the far off wild animals disturbed the peaceful scene in front of her. Then, all too soon, human noises could be heard afar off. The early field workers and farm hands were just setting off for another long day's hard toil. Augusta sighed deeply. Richard had been dead less than a month and there was still so much to do and think about. The affairs of the estate and adjoining lands had all been handed over to Augusta. Fortunately for her there were no debts to be paid. Richard Fitzroy, although a wealthy man, had also been an incredibly mean one. He had never spent one penny more than he was forced to. He had not left a will. The servants were put out to think that after years of service they had not been given even a cursory thought. Each night they all secretly prayed that Augusta would harbour far more charitable feelings towards them and not turn them away without a penny to bless themselves with. Augusta moved away from the window. She could not afford to spend any more time day dreaming. Purposefully she rang for Betsy to bring in her breakfast. She was quite some time answering Augusta's summons because her Mistress did not usually ring to so early in the morning. The girl staggered into the bedroom, looking dishevelled and heavy-eyed.

'Good morning, Ma'am,' she fairly yawned. 'Is there anything amiss?'

Augusta eyed her levelly. 'No, Betsy. Not with me. I am feeling perfectly well, thank you. But judging from your untidy appearance, not to mention your sleep-filled eyes, it seems to me that you have had some difficulty in rising this morning. You are getting sloppy lately, Betsy, and this will not do.'

Betsy eyed Augusta warily. 'No Ma'am, I'm sorry. It's just that you are a late riser yourself, and I normally have plenty of time to see to myself. But you caught me on the hop this morning.'

Augusta winced at this contrite remark, then not too unkindly said, 'That, shortly, is all coming to an end. From this moment on I fully intend to take the reins in my own hands and start to run this place as it should be run, efficiently. Everything in its place and a proper place for everything. I shall start with this dreary house. I have had enough of bare walls, threadbare carpets and these ghastly curtains.'

So saying, she moved towards the curtains, grabbed hold of them with both hands and tugged with all her might, then laughed with glee as they came away from their fixtures and fell about her feet in dusty heaps. Betsy looked on horrified. Had Augusta suddenly taken leave of her senses? Could it be that her husband's death had distorted her mind?

'I have not lost my reasoning. I am just asserting my long-lost authority and the sooner I start the better.'

Betsy replied a fearful 'Yes Ma'am' and moved towards the oaken cupboard, flung back its doors and held up a heavy black moire gown for Augusta's approval.

189

Augusta surveyed it thoughtfully and after a moment's hesitation she said, 'No, Betsy, it will not do. I have had enough of walking about in these dreary black sackcloths. From now on I shall only wear pastel coloured gowns of a lighter material.'

For the next few months events moved with such a speed under Augusta's direction that the staff could barely keep pace with it all. Every room in the house had been redecorated. New drapes and rugs had been installed. The old furniture had been tastefully refurbished, with one or two new items added. But the most spectacular change was in Augusta's bedroom and adjoining dressing room. Gone was every vestige of the past. A beautiful new four-poster bed occupied the centre of the room. At first she thought it was perhaps too ostentatious for Fairlawns, but then she remembered that her mother had not or would not have slept in anything less than a four-poster. Young Jack and Sally had spent hours fixing the brightly coloured drapes around it. All the old cupboards and the dressing-table had been replaced by the more fashionable walnut ones. Between them Jack and Mrs Jameson had worked like demons stripping and re-upholstering the dreadful old chaise-longue. Now it looked most luxurious swathed in rose coloured velvet, framed in wood the deepest mahogany. Fitzroy's belongings had been removed from the dressing-room which had been fitted out with plenty of cupboards and part of it sectioned off as a private closet for her own use. She had been well pleased so far with the progress and was extremely grateful to Mrs Carter without whose help very little would have been achieved. The four Carter boys had endured constant nagging and bullying from their mother as she coerced them into going over to assist Augusta with the more arduous tasks. But it went without saying that the servants' contributions were manifold.

Augusta was enjoying a few quiet moments respite penning the last few sentences in her diary, when there was a slight tap on the study door.

Mr McTavish entered with a queer look on his face and informed Augusta that, 'A rather strange Gentleman is standing on the front porch steps and asking for the Mistress of the House. He says he has something of interest to show you.'

She pursed her lips for a second or two. How annoying for someone to turn up now, just when she wanted to be on her own. Still, it could be of some importance. She asked McTavish to show the visitor in but also insisted that he stayed well within ear-shot. Augusta closed the diary and pushed it to the back of the drawer just as Mr McTavish returned with the strange Gentleman following quickly behind him. He burst into the tiny study before he could be properly announced. Augusta rose and stared at him. Rushing towards her, he swept off an enormous maroon slouch hat, almost sweeping the floor with it.

In a bracing voice he cried out, 'Galbraith, Ma'am, at your service. Tobias Galbraith. Charmed to be allowed to make your acquaintance.'

'Augusta Fitzroy,' she answered and held out her hand.

He gripped it tightly within his own.

'Ouch,' she cried, wincing with pain and cautiously prising away her crushed hand. She thought, here was a colourful figure if ever she saw one. He was a large burly man, somewhere around his early forties. The face, or what could be seen of it beneath bushy eyebrows, bristly moustache and flowing red beard, seemed very weather-beaten indeed. His hair was over-long and faintly reddish with silver-grey sideburns. The clothes he wore were peculiar, to say the least. He was dressed in a multi-coloured loose flowing shirt, rather like a farmer's smock, only far more flamboyant, that flapped about over a pair of dusty green check trousers which did not fit him anywhere at all. About three quarters of the way down and all around the trouser bottoms, wide crease marks were evident, obviously where the wearer had consistently rolled them up to his knee caps. But the large pair of excessively blue and twinkling eyes that smiled down at Augusta seemed friendly enough.

If Augusta thought his appearance a little eccentric, he was thinking how refreshingly different she was from any other female he had encountered on his travels. This one, to his way of thinking, looked too good to be true. Augusta was wearing one of her latest gowns, of the palest lavender and the finest lawn material that could be found. Normally material of such fine quality would be used for making blouses or summer underwear, never to make day-gowns.

191

Mrs Jameson, on being asked to make the gowns, thought they were thoroughly indecent and was not above saying so. However, Augusta's visitor thought that the square neckline with just a hint of white lace peeping above it, the tight waistline and the softly pleated folds falling away from slender hips in such a graceful fashion were positively delicious.

After the formal introductions were over, Augusta bade Mr Tobias Galbraith be seated, then enquired what was the purpose of his call. It transpired that he was none other than an artist and ornithologist who had emigrated to Australia some fifteen years ago. At first he had taken up farming with his young wife and five little ones. They drifted from one wilderness to another, hoping that each place they settled at would be different from the last. But, sad to say, they were one of the many families who suffered dreadfully from one of the worst droughts ever known. Only he had enough strength to survive it. After the loss of his dear wife and family, he vowed he would never work the land again, but rather that he should gain something out of it in replacement for all he had lost. So he eventually turned to bird watching and then finally rediscovered his long lost passion for water-colours. Hours and hours were spent patiently observing the habits and the beauty of the many birds he sought to capture on paper.

Just as she was least expecting it, he jumped up and dived at the bulky carpet bag that lay at his feet. With a burst of unsuppressed pride and a quick flourish of the wrist, he ripped open the bag and pulled forth a portfolio for Augusta to examine.

'Here, take a look at these and if there are any that interest you, tell me and perhaps we could come to some arrangement about them.'

Augusta sat and looked in awe as the pictures unfolded in front of her. They were some of the most beautiful and exotic water-colours she had ever set eyes upon, pages and pages of the most miraculous details of the birds, their colours vibrant and exciting. She had never dreamt that there were so many colourful varieties. Here were a crafty kookaburra straddled aside a large gum tree, a resplendent sulphur-crested cockatoo relishing fat juicy tree lice. She laughed with glee as she came across one of the birds recently seen, swooping low over her own grounds.

'Ah, that is a naughty one,' interjected the artist, 'for although very lovely to look at, he is a scavenger of sorts.'

'Really?' protested Augusta.

'Yes, really, because he devours every seed in sight and has even been known to attack the sheep just to get at the fat inside of their skins. It is known as the kea and I hear that the farmers are suffering badly from this little beauty. In fact, some of them are trying to persuade the Government to eradicate them.'

Augusta sighed sympathetically and remarked, 'Is it not sad, Mr Galbraith, to think that something so beautiful is so dangerous?'

Tobias Galbraith's eyes clouded over and his voice took on a solemn note as he replied, 'I am afraid that it is often the case with many things in life, Ma'am. That is where the old proverbs come in handy. All that glitters is not gold, beauty is only skin deep.'

'Never judge a book by its cover,' Augusta threw in quickly. Then she spotted something that really caught her attention.

'Pray tell me, what is this one known as?' she cried, holding a painting at a distance.

Tobias Galbraith looked over her shoulder and exclaimed excitedly, 'That, if I may be so bold as to say, is my favourite. It is known as the bird of paradise. It obviously will be of little surprise to know that they are rare indeed.'

Augusta clutched the painting to her breast and said, 'Mr Galbraith, I would dearly love to purchase some of your wonderful paintings, if you would kindly allow me.'

Tobias Galbraith threw back his head and laughed loudly.

'Mrs Fitzroy, Ma'am, I would be more than delighted to sell you all of my paintings. Now you take your choice and I will try not to influence you in any way.'

She hesitated for a while. It was a difficult choice.

All were equally beautiful.

Presently, she held up four paintings and announced, 'I think I have decided on these.'

Separating the bird of paradise from the others, she said hesitantly, 'This, Mr Galbraith, is also a favourite. I definitely

193

must have this one.'

Mr. Galbraith started to pack the rest of the pictures into the portfolio.

Looking up at her with troubled eyes he ventured, 'Oh dear, Mrs Fitzroy, I forgot to mention it to you but that painting is the one I never sell. It is my prize possession.'

Augusta looked very downcast, but still held onto the painting.

'Not even if I offered you double for it?' she asked.

Tobias Galbraith shook his head slowly. Augusta was not going to be beaten.

'Double the price and stay to supper as well,' she ventured further.

Tobias scratched the side of his nose and thought hard.

'Well, he mused, 'you are getting nearer. How about double the price and a bed for the night?'

Mortified, Augusta let go of the painting at once. This was not what she had in mind at all. Best to call Mr McTavish and let him handle the situation. Tobias Galbraith was quick to notice the sudden change that had come over her.

To allay her fears, he hastily placated her by saying in very serious tones, 'Now don't look so shocked. I shall be more than comfortable in a dry stable, or a barn come to that. May I take the liberty of informing you that I have not slept in a proper bed for years? To me sleeping rough is no hardship. In fact, I prefer it.'

Augusta felt a shade guilty at having jumped so quickly to the wrong conclusion. Still, one could not be too sure of strangers out here.

To make amends, she hastily added, 'Very well then. If you are content with the agreement, then so am I.'

Rising out of her chair to summon Mr McTavish, she smilingly said, 'Now what would you say to some liquid refreshment for the time being?' Spreading his long legs well under the study desk and with a contented look spreading across his hairy face, he looked up and gratefully said, 'That is most cordial of you, Mrs Fitzroy, most cordial indeed.'

So it was settled. Augusta was to acquire the paintings of her choice and Tobias Galbraith had managed to survive for another few more months.

18

Time passed and as each day crawled along, Augusta began to feel increasingly bored and restless, something she was not accustomed to. Living at Fairlawns was totally different from life in the new cities that were now springing up. In the cities there was plenty of socializing: tête a têtes over coffee, afternoon tea parties and the occasional dance or civic reception. Here at Fairlawns there was very little to escape to, at least in the way of entertainment. Pacing up and down the morning-room, she came to the conclusion that she ought to find something useful to occupy her time and mind. But what, was the question? Within days a situation developed which provided the answer.

Trouble had flared up again in the fields, so one morning the overseer had taken it upon himself to barge his way into the house, demanding to see Augusta straight away. When Augusta walked through the hallway to speak with the man, she found him, much to her consternation, snapping and snarling at poor Mr McTavish.

'Leave this to me,' she said as she coolly walked past him and into the study, with Cookson at her heels directly behind her.

Augusta sat herself squarely on the new plush velvet high-backed armchair that had recently replaced Fitzroy's old heavy leather one.

Running her fingertips slowly over the ornately carved arms of the chair, she said in a slightly agitated voice, 'What is it, Mr Cookson, that sends you rushing into my house? Has some great disaster suddenly occurred?' Cookson was somewhat taken aback by her directness. Looking around for the spittoon and finding it had been removed from the room, he walked towards the open window and spat into the garden.

Augusta was horrified and when he sat himself down on a chair directly facing her, without offering an apology, she decided that he had gone too far. 'Mr Cookson', she hissed through clenched teeth, 'How dare you use my home like a common taproom. If you cannot behave correctly, then I suggest you send someone who can.'

He glowered at her and his face turned a deep scarlet that was just visible underneath the dirt and grime.

'Begging your pardon, Ma'am,' he uttered, 'I forgot myself. Not used to doing business with a woman, you see. Can't get used to Mr Fitzroy not being here. He and I understood each other. I never had to stand on ceremony with him.'

Augusta breathed deeply and primly replied, 'Well, that is as maybe. But I am afraid Mr Fitzroy is no longer with us and I am the new owner here. I wish to be treated with all due respect.'

She calmly waited for the overseer to present his troubles.

It seemed that all the old problems were rearing their ugly heads again. Sickness was breaking out amongst the women convicts. The men were becoming sullen and resentful again, work was slackening off, the harvest had not been so fruitful this year. Added to this, several small fires had destroyed much of the crops. Grain and flour for the convicts was scarce and Cookson was having a difficult time controlling it all. He needed to make them work harder. Lashings and beatings were not effective enough, he desired something stronger.

Augusta had sat listening without saying a word or twitching a muscle. On looking into her eyes, after he had delivered his angry speech, he was amazed to see how clear and sharp they were.

Striking a purposeful stance, Augusta stood up and announced in strident tones, 'At crack of dawn tomorrow I will be up and ride out and assess the situation for myself.'

Once firmly mounted on her horse, she followed the overseer at a fast pace towards the problem areas of Fairlawns. As she neared the out buildings and passed by the blacksmith's, a feeling of distaste arose up in her throat. She remembered what had occurred previously and was in no mood for it to happen again.

On seeing Mrs Fitzroy riding through their midst, the workers stopped and stared at her, naked hostility showing in their eyes. It was almost time for the first break of the day and most of them were returning to the encampment for a quick brew. These were the field hands, the lucky ones who had found employment. Many of them lived in the colony nearby. They worked from sunrise to nigh on sunset, but were reasonably well paid for their labours.

Attired in a riding dress of bottle green, her long auburn hair piled high and crammed under a wide-brimmed straw hat, Augusta cantered off in the wake of the overseer, but at a far slower pace, so as to avoid being sprayed by the loose flying ochre dust. As soon as they entered the closed-in section, she shouted to the overseer to rein in his mount. He roughly jerked the animal to a standstill and pulled it sharply round, thereby causing the bit to cut cruelly into the side of its mouth. Sitting astride her horse, Augusta was taking a long look at all that was going on around her.

'Mr Cookson,' she said authoritively, 'it is my decision to take stock of all that I see here today. It is high time that I took a greater interest in the place. I want you to show me around. I need to know exactly how many workers are employed at Fairlawns, what each one does, where they live, their marital status, how much each is paid, so on and so forth.'

Cookson eyed her suspiciously, then quipped, 'Bit of a tall order, Ma'am, if I may say so. Mr Fitzroy never bothered his head with the like. His attitude was that as long as his work was done, he was not in the least bit bothered about their welfare.'

The horses' hooves pawed the ground impatiently. Augusta steadied the mare, and snapped back imperiously, 'Mr Cookson, how many times do I have to tell you, that I, not Mr Fitzroy am in charge now and I intend to run things my way from now on.'

Tapping her horse lightly with her crop, she shifted forward in the saddle and moved on.

First on the list was to inspect mundane items such as the water towers, the rustic fences and double barred gates. Then the barns and outbuildings were thoroughly checked. After spending a brief moment or two with the blacksmith and the farm hands, she decided it was time for Cookson to show her where the convicts were housed. The overseer was reluctant to do so, for he knew only too well what dreadful conditions they were forced to endure.

They rode slowly out and away towards the new plantations. Much had changed since Augusta last passed this way. The whole area was beginning to take on a new shape, but even the inexperienced eye could see that it had proved to be a long and arduous task. The crops at first sight seemed to be healthy enough and she hoped that they would stay that way until the harvesting was over.

A little further on the ground started to break up and they were soon penetrating into rougher and wilder contours. Slowing his horse down, Cookson waited for Augusta to catch him up.

'This is where I have the convicts working now, Ma'am. Down in those gulleys. They are clearing and trenching at the moment.'

He pointed a finger in their direction.

'Some way off yet, I'm afraid. But perhaps you had better see where they are housed. It is not so far away. That way, we can return by a different route. We'll come back through the trees, where it is a damn sight cooler. The noonday sun is a stinker today.'

Augusta silently agreed. It really was unbearably hot. Leaving the newly cultivated ground behind them, they soon ventured onto the more primitive parts of the estate. Little or nothing had been done to make pathways easier, though a score of more of the larger gum trees had been cut in an attempt to create a clearing. Nosing the mare cautiously forward, she followed Cookson towards the convicts' encampment.

When Richard Fitzroy had first brought the convicts here to work, he had the mud and wattle huts erected in some sort of semi-circle but because of the added influx they had now spread in a most haphazard fashion. The huts consisted of one dwelling room only and sometimes had as many as four inhabitants shackled together in each. The floors were hard-baked, with straw palliasses thrown down to relieve their hardness. All the walls were slimy and sticky to touch. Jagged holes in the wattle thatched roofs provided the only light and air. Augusta had not alighted from her horse as the stench that pervaded the whole area was overpowering. The overseer saw her clutching a perfumed lace kerchief to her nostrils and the look of horror in her eyes.

'They only sleep here. They have all their victuals dished up to them, twice a day, wherever they are working. All convicts are issued with a tin bowl and metal spoon, which is tied around their waists, so that they are neither lost nor stolen. Any man caught with nought goes with nought.'

Wrinkling up her nose and trying with great difficulty to fight off nausea, Augusta turned to the overseer.

'I have seen more than enough here. Let us proceed to where those poor devils are working.'

Lifting the brim of her straw hat, Augusta cast her eyes over the rows and rows of male convict workers before her. The fierce rays of the sun beat unmercifully down. Under the shade of a few large gum trees worked thirty or so female convicts. She stared at them in astonishment for she had completely forgotten that women convicts had been hired. So much had happened since Richard's death that she had given no thought to the outside workers. Mercifully, their tasks, in comparison with the men, were fairly light. Augusta was filled at once with pity at seeing them. Whatever crime they had committed, this surely was an inhuman way to punish them.

On seeing her near these women, Cookson rode over towards her and with an ugly grin spreading across his face commented, 'You will be pleased to know that at night time they are separated from the men.'

Before Augusta could check his crude line of talk, one of the women stood up straight, moved a few paces towards him and thrust an already extended belly in front of him. Cookson was furious and pushed her roughly away.

'Hm, seems as if that one escaped my attention. That means I'll have to get rid of her now. Otherwise all kinds of complications will flare up.'

Augusta just managed to catch the tail-end of his words and quickly asked, 'Mr Cookson, where will that poor creature go if you send her away?'

'None of your damn business where she goes,' he yelled at her.

Augusta was flabbergasted at his brutish and rude behaviour. If it was a fight with words he was intent on, then he had better watch out. The morning's outing had whipped up her normally placid temperament into something not far short of a raging inferno.

'Mr Cookson,' she whiplashed back at him, 'I have seen and heard more than enough already this morning.' Then swinging the horse full round in the direction from whence she came from, she coldly called out 'Be in my study early tomorrow morning. There are going to be some changes made. Yes indeed, some vast changes, and make no mistake about it.'

19

Later on that evening as Augusta sat resting quietly reflecting on the day's events, the miserable plight of the convict workers, especially the women, troubled her. Life for those who had erred against society was often cruel and unjust. Once cast aside, there was precious little they could do to redeem themselves. But surely, thought Augusta, it need not be so. It was within mankind's power to change events.

Gradually an idea began to form in her head. The more she thought about it, the more determined she became to put her plan into action. There was something that she could do without having to seek the advice of others. From now on she would focus all her attention on helping her own convict workers by trying to remove some of the unnecessary restrictions placed upon them. She would have liked to have been in a position to free them completely, but that was not allowed. All convicts had to serve their penal sentences to the bitter end. Augusta found that these thoughts had at least eased her conscience a little.

Lolling back in a chair, with his feet stretched out on top of his workshop shelf, the overseer suddenly threw back his head and laughed loudly to himself. He laughed till he thought he would never stop. Minutes later after wiping his eyes and his nose on the back of his filthy cheesecloth shirt tail, he heaved himself out of the chair and drew himself a tankard of frothy ale from a barrel half-hidden underneath the workbench. He swigged it down in one great gulp, then threw the tankard across the room. It landed in the midst of a pile of dirty bowls and platters on the tiny wooden drainingboard.

'Must clean that lot up soon, or there will be nothing left to eat or drink from.'

During the working day he took his meals with the rest of the workers, but in the evenings he preferred to cook himself something over an open charcoal fire and enjoy it in solitude. He was proud of his new abode. It was bigger and far more comfortable than the last one. He looked around and thought himself very important indeed. Then he thought again of Mrs Fitzroy's preposterous idea and laughed again to himself.

Picking up his bull whip and clay pipe, he kicked open the door and made his way towards his tethered horse. Once astride he spurred the docile animal into action. Bearing down on the convicts encampment, he pulled at the cord around his grimy neck, popped the bamboo whistle at the end of it in his mouth and blew shrilly down it. The convicts emerged from their huts like ants crawing out of their nests. Cookson recalled the absurdity of the Mistress's concern for their welfare.

Each day for the past two months or so Augusta had dutifully ridden over to see how the work was progressing. But of late it was becoming irritatingly tiresome and more of an ordeal than a pleasure. The main trouble stemmed from the overseer, who had been utterly opposed to the scheme right from the start. Cookson, like Fitzroy, was strongly of the opinion that women should be kept firmly in their place. Child-rearing was what she should be doing, not meddling about in men's work. Why the hell doesn't she remarry? he had angrily thought on more than one occasion, instead of stalking about like some prima donna. Grudgingly he was forced to admit, however, that she did get things done.

The winter months were fast approaching and the mornings were beginning to have a sharp nip about them. On Augusta's instructions, all the old mud huts had been levelled to the ground and new dwellings were already being erected for the convicts to live in, built of planked wood. She had settled on this idea after long discussions with Clara. Everyone thought she was insane for going to such elaborate lengths solely for a bunch of convicts. But as Clara wisely pointed out, if she had replaced them with similar materials, then the same problems would arise all over again. No, the answer was to build with wood. Sadly, it was proving to be an agonizingly slow affair. Crafty old Cookson only allowed the convicts to work on them after they had finished a hard day's toil in the fields. The overseer was totally opposed to Augusta's plans and had found a way of hitting back at her. He forced them to work harder and longer so that the majority became far too exhausted to carry on working late in the evenings.

For the time being Augusta had housed the convicts in two of the main barns, the men in one and the women in the other. The barns had been patched up, cleared and swept reasonably clean. Makeshift partitions down the centre of each barn served as a dual purpose. One half was used as the sleeping quarters, for the men this consisted of straw palliasses. The women however, were more fortunate in having truckle beds to sleep on. The other part of each barn was used for meals. Augusta had decided that the women should learn how to cook and fend for themselves. Two charcoal braziers installed just inside the entrance of the women's barn threw out enough heat to cook the mutton stews and flat rye bread on.

Augusta, on learning that the convict woman with child had once worked as a scullery maid, insisted that she should stay on and earn her keep by cooking for the others.

Although she remained aloof from them, partly from fear of appearing too concerned in case they took advantage of it, the women nevertheless responded to Augusta by behaving in a respectful and cordial manner. It fast became apparent to the convicts that the daily visits of Mrs Fitzroy were the only glimmers of light in their exceedingly dull days.

Riding back to the house late one morning, Augusta, although reasonably pleased with her efforts in controlling the estate, thought how lonely and empty it all was without having someone close to confide in, someone to boast of her achievements to. Because she had been so deep in thought, she had not noticed, leaving her horse at the post, that a strange one was already tethered there. Betsy, whom she had espied swiftly emerging from the small sitting-room, was just about to call out, 'You have a visitor Ma'am,' but thought better of it. Let the Mistress find out for herself.

Crossing the hall, and walking into the sitting-room, Augusta looked across the room towards the open casement window and sharply drew in her breath. Standing there, with his back towards her, was the familiar frame of Charles Hadleigh. He had been there for quite some time, observing Augusta as she thoughtfully walked through the grounds. He knew from the quick intake of breath, that it was she who had entered the room and not Betsy. With a bemused smile on his face, he waited for her to speak to him, wondering what her first words would be.

'Charles, oh Charles,' she cried in astonishment.

'Augusta, my dear,' he exclaimed, as he squeezed her hands tightly, 'it is so good to see you again. How are you? You are looking very well, but perhaps a little tight around the mouth.'

'Oh Charles,' she cried, 'trust you to notice so much, you with your professional eye. And what, may I ask, brings you back to Fairlawns? I thought you had left for good.'

Charles slowly released her hands and went over to the sofa. A boyish grin crept over his face. How handsome and fit he looks, Augusta thought to herself, dressed in a light linen jacket over a pair of soft beige cashmere trousers, sporting a green paisley cravat tucked inside a crisp white shirt, his dark hair curled neatly into the nape of his neck. And she, such a mess in her dusty riding clothes, hair scraped back and fresh dirt beneath her fingernails.

Averting her eyes quickly away from his face, she stared down as her hands as he laughingly replied, 'No, no, just a temporary departure. And am I glad to be back!'

Augusta then moved over and joined him on the sofa, albeit with a respectable distance between them.

'I hear quite a lot has happened since I left.'

Augusta lowered her eyelids.

'You have heard about Richard then.'

Charles nodded in assent.

'When did you know?' she queried.

Charles clasped his hands together and quietly replied, 'Two days ago, when I visited the Carters.'

Augusta went rigid, raised her eyes towards him and in a surprised tone commented, 'You have been to the Carters already.'

'Why yes,' he answered with a smile. 'Is there any reason why I should not have done so? After all, I was on very good terms with a certain member of the family.'

Augusta did not need reminding and meekly returned, 'Why yes, Charles, how remiss of me. How did you find Clara? Still full of her new schoolhouse?'

Charles laughed out loud and said, 'Why that? Would it surprise you to learn that she never stopped talking about it? I admire her so much, it really is a wonderful achievement.'

Augusta experienced a slight pang of envy and said quickly, 'Yes, she has worked so hard for her school, she really deserves it.'

Charles, noticing the piqued look on Augusta's face, gently added, 'And you deserve an accolade too, my dear. I am astounded at the improvements you have made around the house.'

This pleased her greatly and, jumping up and walking towards the window, she burst out, 'But that is not all. Just wait until you see what I have been doing out there.'

She pointed a finger in the direction of the outdoors. Charles got up and stood beside her.

With one hand resting lightly on her shoulder he carefully ventured, 'I am hoping that you will invite me over one day, so that I may compliment you even further on your efforts.'

Augusta spun round and hurriedly answered, 'Why, Charles, permit me to say that as there is no time like the present and I still have my riding dress on, let us go now.'

Taking his watch from out of his breast coat pocket and examining it carefully, he exclaimed slowly, 'I am afraid, Augusta, time does not permit at the moment, especially as I have not long returned. There is still so much to attend to. Perhaps another day, my dear. It has been good to see you again, but I must away. Duty calls, you know.'

He went to open the door, but she beat him to it, determined to have her own way.

'Charles,' she pleaded, 'you have only just arrived here. Can I not offer you some refreshment? Stay to luncheon. There is so much I want to hear about your travels.'

Tapping her shoulder lightly, he seriously replied, 'I am sorry to disappoint you, Augusta, but it will have to keep till another time.'

'Yes, yes, of course,' she answered, trying hard not to show how disappointed she felt.

Following him to the front porch, she watched him walk

unhurriedly along the gravel pathway, until he was out of sight. She crossed over to the large gilt mirror and studied herself carefully. Had she changed that much since Charles was last here? A little more drawn perhaps, but still the same slim figure and fiery eyes. His unexpected return had caused her heart to flutter and brought an excited flush to her cheeks.

To her amazement she found herself crying out loudly, 'How wonderful. How absolutely wonderful to see him again, but oh how I wish he felt the same way towards me.'

☆ ☆ ☆

Panic reigned supreme in the household for at least two days when Betsy suddenly took everyone by surprise and announced that she and the eldest Carter boy were to be married. Tom had managed to buy himself several hectares of land on the other side of the hillside and had successfully persuaded Betsy to marry him immediately so that they could set up on their own. Betsy pointed out to her Mistress that Tom was not going to wait for ever. It was now or never. Betsy knew that in her heart of hearts she would always miss Augusta and the comfort of Fairlawns but at the same time she was looking forward to a life of her own.

Augusta was pleased for Betsy but was nevertheless reluctant to part with her. It would be a long time before she found anyone as willing or as helpful as Betsy had been. The word was already being spread that Mrs Fitzroy would be requiring a new lady's maid.

20

Augusta enjoyed the hilarity of the harvesting but felt a little disappointed that Charles did not attend any of the gatherings. She later learnt that he had spent most of his free time either at the Carters or reorganizing his practice. Since his return, Doctor Hadleigh had wasted little time in asserting his position as the colony's most distinguished doctor. Old Doctor Trimble, who had been ambling along since Charles had left, was more than pleased to welcome him back into the fold. He intended to hand everything over to Charles and retreat to the incomparable tranquillity of a rustic cabin beside a swiftly flowing brook where he could fish and while his time away to his heart's content.

Charles had even managed to buy himself a pleasant property of his own. He did not wish to be employed on the Fairlawns Estate, his old dwelling-place having been given to the overseer, Cookson. Charles was more than pleased with his acquisition. The house was a fairly new one, part brick, part timber, and boasted of two storeys. It was in a pleasant spot, not too far away from the outskirts of the town, near enough to be in easy reach for those who needed him in an emergency and yet reasonably inaccessable for those few quiet hours when he needed to be on his own. The most difficult hurdle he had to overcome was finding the right person to keep house for him. As a bachelor he should have had little or no difficulty in securing someone to tend to his domestic wants, he thought. But the married women in the vicinity were firmly kept in their place by jealous husbands and the mothers of unattached females under twenty-five would not allow them to be in a position where their reputations could be tarnished.

On hearing through the grapevine that Augusta was also

looking for further staff, he decided to take the bull by the horns and see if she could help him to find someone suitable. As luck would have it, Augusta was taking considerable time over her appearance that evening, and was in a capricious mood, probably because while arranging her hair, Betsy had been bubbling excitedly over her plans for her forthcoming betrothal. Better than having to listen to the monotonous daily moans and groans from that odious overseer, Augusta thought to herself.

Betsy was just placing the last tortoise-shell comb firmly into Augusta's upswept hair when Mrs Potts poked her head around the door and announced that Doctor Hadleigh had arrived. Augusta's heart quickened and she knew instinctively that colour had risen to her cheeks. She hoped that neither Mrs Potts nor Betsy had noticed. Keeping her head fairly lowered, she bade Mrs Potts to ask the Doctor to wait in the sitting-room and say that she would be down presently.

Seated in one of the new chairs, Charles leant back lazily, spread his long legs out in front of him and gazed contentedly around the room. He was thinking how pleasant and attractive Augusta had made this room look. In fact, the whole house looked and felt entirely different since Fitzroy no longer ruled the roost. As Augusta slowly entered the room, Charles automatically stood up and greeted her warmly.

Reluctant to let go of her hand, he squeezed it lightly and said, 'Good evening, Augusta, and may I say how perfectly charming you look tonight? I do hope that I have not called at an inconvenient time. You are not about to entertain some lucky person, I trust.'

Slowly releasing her hand, she flashed him a brilliant smile and replied, 'No, Charles, I am not expecting anyone and you know that you are welcome any time. Please sit down again and let me offer you some refreshment.'

'That is most kind of you, Augusta. Anything would be more than welcome, I must confess. I have not had time to have a proper meal today, so much of my time has been taken up with all that needs doing in my new abode.'

Spinning round on her heels, Augusta replied mischievously, 'Why, yes, of course. A little bird tells me that you have been doing very well of late. I am so pleased for you. Why don't you stay to supper? Then you can tell me all that has happened since we last met.'

Charles let out a long sigh, gazed thoughtfully at her lovely face, jumped to his feet, and cried out, 'What a splendid idea. I was more than hoping that you would say that. Supper at Fairlawns is the perfect way to end a busy day.'

'Oh Charles, you really are impossible,' retorted Augusta. 'Now while you relax with a glass of my best Madeira, I will go and inform Mrs Soames that there is one extra for supper tonight.'

Several hours later peals of laughter could be heard from the sitting-room where the heavy drapes had been pulled together and the fiery embers from the log fire cast elongated shadows on the far walls. Mr McTavish had slipped in unnoticed, doused all but two of the lamps, placed a decanter of Cognac on one of the small occasional tables, removed the dirty glasses and slipped unobtrusively away.

Augusta and Charles reclined in easy chairs on either side of the fireplace, regaling each other with amusing stories. The heat from the fire, coupled with the wine and port consumed during and after the meal, not to mention the laughter, made the room seem overbearingly hot. Placing his glass of port on the card table beside him, Charles rose and loosened his neckerchief slightly. Then, seeking permission to remove his dark blue velveteen jacket, he casually cast it onto the back of the chair. His frilled white shirt gleamed in the firelight. Augusta watched him and thought how devastatingly attractive he was. The good food and wine and the chance to relax in a congenial atmosphere had miraculously eased away the lines of fatigue and tension from his face.

Crossing one leg idly over the other and thrusting his hands squarely on his narrow hips, Charles was about to ask the important question he had ridden over to put to Augusta: how to find the right housekeeper? He stopped short after uttering the words, 'Augusta, my dear, there is something of importance that I wish to ask you.'

All evening he had been trying to push to the back of his mind how exceptionally beautiful Augusta looked, how entertaining she had been, how totally rapt she had been by his idiotic stories. He could not get over the tremendous change that had come over Augusta since his return. Often he had imagined that since the death of Fitzroy she might at least be suffering from some sort of depression, even more painful without her beloved Tamara and having to cope with the everyday rigours of adapting to a completely new environment. But no, here she was, happy and confident, seemingly in control of everything and looking absolutely lovely. And here she is, thought Charles, staring up at me with eyes aflame . . . with what? Dare he find out?

Unable to control himself any longer, Charles, leant forward, took Augusta in his arms and kissed her very tenderly on the mouth. For a brief second confusion burst through Augusta's brain. Before she could make any sensible decision, something snapped inside her and she caved in and responded to his ardent advances. After a few moments it came as quite a shock to find that Charles had unbuttoned her gown and let it fall in crumpled pleats around her ankles. He quickly deposited her on the sofa. After struggling to free herself from his tight embrace, Augusta sat upright and panicked, fearful that someone should suddenly walk in the room. She blazed at Charles, 'What do you think you are doing? How can you use me like this?'

Groping around for her gown, she called out frantically, 'Charles, help me. Can you imagine what would happen if one of the servants were to walk in now?'

Charles leapt up and, seeing her wriggling frantically around the room, half in and half out of the dress, burst into uncontrollable laughter.

'Oh, Augusta,' he cried, 'if only you could see yourself now.' He gripped one of her wrists tightly and, still choking with mirth, cried out, 'Stand still you silly girl. You will never put that gown on properly if you keep hopping about. Here let me help you.' With eyes blazing and lips quivering, Augusta managed to stand still long enough for Charles to drag the gown up around her bare shoulders and fix it firmly in position.

Pinching her lightly on the cheek, and in a very serious tone, he stated, 'Forgive me, Augusta, I'm afraid I did behave very badly. Something just came over me which I was completely unable to control. If you are honest with yourself, Augusta, the same could be said for you.'

Hot with fury, Augusta raised her hand to strike at him but

Charles quickly checked it. Still holding on to her wrist, he managed to seat her once more on the sofa. But not himself.

Looking down at her flushed face, he muttered almost to himself, 'I never know when you are the more desirable, when you look like a Duchess or Shakespeare's Kate in *The Taming of the Shrew*.'

Wrenching her hand free, Augusta gasped, 'Let us forget this ever happened.'

Then something sprang to her mind. Did she not hear him say that he had something of importance to ask her? Could it possibly be that he was going to propose to her? Yes, of course that was the answer. That was why he reacted in such a way. How could she have been so stupid? Charles would never dare to compromise her unless he had marriage in mind.

She moved slowly towards him and said in a gentler tone,

'Charles, I fear that it is getting fearfully late, and I really must ask you to leave. I just cannot risk having my reputation ruined. But before you go I must say . . . '

Charles broke in swiftly with, 'No need to worry about your reputation on my account, Augusta. Just pass me my jacket, if you please, and I shall be on my way in a trice.'

Kissing her lightly on the cheek and thanking her for a lovely meal, he proceeded to move towards the door. Augusta watched him go, her heart pounding. Should she let him go without being asked the vital question? How could she force it out of him without seeming too forward, too concerned about his feelings towards her?

To her consternation, Charles suddenly spun round and said quite matter of factly, 'Oh, by the way Augusta, I almost forgot, there is something I must ask you before I depart, something that has been on my mind for most of the evening that is.'

Augusta just stood there, desperately praying that he could not hear her pounding heartbeats.

Pausing only slightly, Charles went on to say, 'Yes, my dear, I trust that you will not find this too personal, but I find that although I am well content with my new home, there appears to be one tiny problem that is irking me somewhat. I really need someone to help me out, someone I can rely on implicitly, someone who can attend to my needs without imposing themselves on me or my patients. Believe you me, Augusta, I am having the devil's most awful job finding someone really suitable. That is why I am asking you to help me.'

She wanted to laugh. How long-winded Charles sounded! All this pomposity, just to ask her to marry him. Men really were the strangest of creatures. She remembered Fitzroy and his fancy proposals, written on reams and reams of paper carefully stating what a fine catch he thought himself to be. And look how that ended up.

Because she could not contain her mirth or excitement any longer she burst out, 'Oh, Charles, you silly goose. Why go to such extreme lengths to say just a few magical words? Just ask me now.'

Charles stared at her in amazement. She seemed to be in a most peculiar mood tonight, not at all like her usual self.

'Very well, Augusta, I will not beat about the bush any longer. I hear that Betsy is leaving and that you are looking for a new maid, so I thought that as you are having to find new staff you could help me out by finding someone for me too. I need a housekeeper. I was hoping that you might know someone in the colony you could recommend.'

Augusta groaned inwardly. There was no way to describe how she felt. The colour in her face changed. It seemed an eternity before she could muster the strength to utter.

'I am sorry, Charles. I think I have been under a terrible misapprehension. I am sorry to say I cannot think of anyone at the moment. Please leave me now. I need time to consider your proposal.'

Charles smiled easily and said that she could take all the time in the world. There was no rush. Charles graciously opened the door and somehow she managed to gain enough control to walk sedately past him, leaving him to find his own way out.

21

Tom and Betsy had been married for three weeks and Augusta was still without a new maid. Several of the girls from the poorer parts of the colony had applied but none of them were what Augusta was looking for. Betsy was proving very hard to replace. Over the years Augusta had moulded her into a very fine lady's maid. Their temperaments had been perfectly matched.

The weather over the last few days had turned colder and Augusta had ventured to pay Mrs Carter a surprise visit before the weather became too bad to travel. Mrs Carter was very pleased to see her. Everything seemed so dull after the excitement of the past few months. There was so much she wanted to gossip about. Mrs Carter, although a good-hearted soul, thrived on gossip. Her husband reckoned that he could always tell when she had spent the day happily gossiping by the broad beam on her face when he returned from work. So when Augusta arrived unexpectedly, Mrs Carter fairly pounced on her, propelled her into the sitting-room, barely giving her time to remove her wide brimmed hat and shake the dust from her riding attire before poking a glass of Madeira into her hand, thrusting her into a chair and galloping headlong into speech.

The conversation centred around the wedding and how much Mrs Carter was missing her Tom. George, her second eldest boy was, of course, doing all he could to help his father but he lacked Tom's common-sense. George, on the other hand, always made heavy weather of most matters. Clara was still the apple of her eye and, according to her mother, could do no wrong. She seemed to go from strength to strength. The new schoolhouse was an immense success, not to mention the fact that the minister from the new Baptist

Church was more than pleased with her. According to Mrs Carter, Clara was afforded the privilege of supping with the minister and his invalid wife most evenings of the week. Yes, there were no complaints where Clara was concerned. Clarissa, however, was proving to be something of a problem. So unlike Clara in practically every way imaginable, Clarissa was not in the least interested in doing anything remotely worthwhile. Her sole aim in life was plaiting and unplaiting her unruly hair and flirting with the local boys.

'I just cannot get her to do anything around the home,' complained Mrs Carter bitterly, 'but if her father comes in and asks her to help out in the fields or fetch the men's midday food baskets, she's out and up there like a shot, and stays up there as bold as brass with them until they finish their work at the end of the day. What am I going to do with her, Mrs Fitzroy? That girl will be the death of me, you mark my words.'

Augusta sympathized with Mrs Carter and said that Clarissa would grow out of her wild ways soon enough. Then before either of them could discuss it any further, Betsy and Tom also made a surprise visit, which of course delighted Mrs Carter no end.

'This calls for a little celebration,' she announced cheerfully. 'Tom, fetch me out the best glasses and my strongest home-made wine. Then you can tell Mrs Fitzroy and I how you and your new wife are settling down to domestic bliss. You both look grand. Married life seems to be suiting you both.'

Betsy coloured deeply and simpered while Tom coughed to hide his embarrassment.

'Now come on, Tom, don't stand there idling. Fetch those glasses. Don't waste time. I want to hear all that has been happening since you left home.'

Not wishing to intrude on the family gathering Augusta suggested politely that it was time for her to leave. All expressed their regret at her leaving so early, especially Betsy, who had already experienced the odd twinge at having left the pleasant surroundings at Fairlawns.

'Have you found anyone to take my Betsy's place yet, Mrs Fitzroy?' enquired Tom as he helped Augusta into her riding-jacket.

'No, I'm afraid I have not. No doubt I shall find someone soon, although I must say this in your favour, Betsy, I warrant they will not be a patch on you.'

'That's very kind of you, Ma'am,' Betsy cried, quite overcome by Augusta's kind words.

Tom, quick to sense his wife's feelings, caught everyone by surprise by coming out with, 'Ye Gods, I have it. Why didn't I think of it before? Come to that, why didn't anyone else?'

'Think of what?' chimed in Mrs Carter impatiently.

'The answer to Mrs Fitzroy's predicament, Clarissa.'

'Clarissa?' they all screamed at once.

'Yes, Clarissa,' replied Tom. 'After all, she has nothing to do all day. You keep saying yourself, Mother, you wish that she would find herself something useful to do. Well, surely this could solve both problems at once. A new lady's maid for Mrs Fitzroy and something of importance for Clarissa. Working for a lady she might learn how to behave like one herself.'

'What a marvellous idea,' said Betsy. 'You really are very clever, Tom. Fancy you thinking of something like that.'

Augusta was not so convinced. If Clara had been suggested, that might have been different. But Clarissa . . . she would have to give this careful thought. Unfortunately, quite coincidentally, just as she was about to leave, Mr Carter and Clarissa entered the room and the whole idea was passed backwards and forwards. Mr Carter thought it was an excellent idea. He had been getting very anxious about the amount of time his youngest daughter was spending out in the fields with the farm hands. Clarissa, on the other hand, was not so enthusiastic, but after a few sharp exchanges with her father she reluctantly agreed.

So it was decided that Clarissa would move into Fairlawns at the beginning of the following week and commence training as a lady's maid.

22

On the way back from the Carters, Augusta thought she would pay another surprise visit, this time to see Clara at the schoolhouse. No doubt she would be pleased to hear that Clarissa was going to take Betsy's place. It was early in the afternoon and although the sun was still shining the temperature was beginning to drop rapidly. The ground was very heavy going and she wished that she had asked Old Amos to take her in the gig instead of galloping off on her own. As she raced down the steep slope and rounded the bend towards the schoolhouse she was just in time to make out the tall figure of Doctor Hadleigh galloping away in the opposite direction. She wondered what he was doing visiting Clara during school hours. Alighting quickly from her horse and hitching it to the post, she made her way up the steps of the schoolhouse. The door was closed but Augusta knew that the children were inside because of the noise. She knocked on the door and waited some time for someone to open it.

A tousled haired youngster popped his head out of the half opened door and shouted in a deafening voice, 'Someone to see yer, Miss.'

Seconds later Clara's voice could be heard crying out, 'Politely ask who it is, please Danny, and don't let them in until I say so.'

'It is Augusta, Clara, I trust I have not called at an inconvenient moment.'

Clara appeared before her, looking distraught. Specks of soot clung to her light grey dress and straggly hair, black streaks marked her face, and her hands were cut and bleeding. Finding her friend in such a state Augusta rushed over to her and took hold of her blood-stained hands. Clara hastily snatched them away.

'Oh, Augusta, please do not come any further. We think we have a measles epidemic in the school. Doctor Hadleigh has called and will be returning shortly with some medicine. In the meantime I am doing my best to keep this woodburner well-stocked without the stupid thing belching out sooty fumes everywhere, not to mention trying to make sure that the really sick ones are comfortable, warm and away from draughts. How he expects me to cope on my own is beyond comprehension.'

Clara cried as a sudden gust of wind caused more heavy smoke to swirl around the room. The children began to cough and whimper as the woodsmoke began to invade their already sore and dry lungs.

'Miss, miss, I don't feel well, I want my mama,' wailed one poor little mite, as he sat huddled up under his elder sister's woollen shawl.

Most of the children had grouped themselves around the spluttering woodburner for extra warmth. Looking down on the sickly and helpless little bunch around her, Augusta decided to ignore Clara's pleas and stay to help out as best she could.

Pulling off her long gloves, and hitching the hem of her riding skirt into the top of her riding boots, she moved purposefully towards Clara who was by now bent double over the fire trying desperately to coax some life into it by poking and prodding it with a long piece of charred wood.

'If I may make a suggestion, Clara, why not dampen the fire down and start all over again? At least the wood will be that much dryer.'

'It's not so much that the wood is damp as that something is blocking the flue.'

'Then we had better remedy that straightaway. Have you a broom anywhere, Clara?' asked Augusta.

'Yes, but you don't want to bother yourself with our problems, Augusta. Please go home, you will only end up covered in soot and possibly catch the infection as well. The worst thing about all this is that I should have spotted this complaint earlier on. Some of the children were away from school several weeks back. These others must have escaped their parents' attention. Now I have them affected and all under one roof.'

Augusta said she was determined to do her bit and help Clara out as much as she could. Completely ignoring the other's protestations, she calmly said, 'I am already mud-stained, so a little more grime will not come amiss. Besides, Clara, I cannot ride off and leave you all alone in this plight. I will get the broom while you put the fire out.'

Between them they managed to clear the flue of a dead bird and its already rotting nest. Clara filled the wood burner and this time the fire caught almost immediately. In the meantime, Augusta had dragged all the blankets from Clara's bed in the backroom and wrapped them snugly round the children. By now some of them were hot and feverish and were crying out for cool drinks or for something to relieve the pain in their heads.

'The Doctor will be here soon, then you will all start to feel a little better we hope,' said Clara.

'Perhaps we could try to sponge them down a little, Clara,' said Augusta wearily. 'It might help somewhat and there is nothing else that we can do right now.'

Clara agreed and asked Augusta to hold the fort while she slipped out to fetch some fresh water from the nearby brook. Augusta settled herself amongst the children and tried to comfort them as best she could. Looking down on their fevered brows and over-bright eyes, she remembered the day Tamara died. One little girl had nestled up as close as she could to Augusta and stared up at her with eyes that unmistakedly said, 'Please, Miss, make me better.' Augusta closed her eyes and offered up a silent prayer. 'Please God, save these children.' The death of her own child had caused her such deep grief, especially as she had been unable to do anything to help her, that she was impelled to pray for these little ones around her.

Clara soon returned with a bucket of cold water and placed it on top of her desk. Taking a small roll of white linen from the school chest, she tore it into wide strips and handed some to Augusta. How long they spent bathing the children's foreheads and pressing the damp cloths around their burning lips, goodness only knew. But at last some of them cooled down enough to drift into some kind of restless sleep.

Augusta and Clara decided to break off for a while to rest their aching backs and sore feet. Sitting on the hard floor with their backs against the wall, they talked together. Looking around the room with its bare walls and drab furniture, Augusta could not help wondering how Clara could incarcerate herself in a place like this for five days a week in order to educate other people's offspring.

Clara observed Augusta as her tired eyes took in the bleak surroundings and said slowly, 'I know what you are thinking, Augusta. Why do I do this, when I could have had a good husband, not to mention a home and possibly children of my own?'

'The thought had crossed my mind,' murmured Augusta.

'Well, strange though it may seem to you, I actually like my life. For the first time in my life I am beholden to no one but myself. For years I had to put up with my father always telling me what to do. Then there were all those boys. Mother lost three as well, you know. I was the eldest one so you can image what that was like, always having to help out with the others. Then when Clarissa came along I thought that she would take her share, but no, Clarissa was father's favourite and always managed somehow to avoid any hard work. If it had not been for my old Sunday School teacher back home who encouraged my reading, prose and piano playing, I know for certain that I would have ended up like some old drudge. In starting this little school, at least I can make my own decision. I cannot stand being told what to do. Can you understand that, Augusta?'

Augusta nodded her head in agreement. She knew only too well what it was like to live with someone who needed to assert authority over every situation that came along, not to mention the constant callousness and brutality that went with it.

'I have never mentioned this to anyone before,' said Augusta quietly, 'but Richard was very difficult to live with. There were times when he was more than unkind to me. I know that I should not be disloyal to his name for he did provide me with a decent home and a dearly loved child. But now all that has gone and I have to carry on alone.'

Augusta's eyes moistened as she once again thought of Tamara. Dashing away her tears in case Clara witnessed them, she clasped Clara's hand.

'I admire you, Clara, you are struggling hard to stand on

219

your own feet in a man's world. That really takes courage. Charles would have found a good wife in you. Do you ever think of him in that way, or have you put him out of your mind altogether?'

Clara blushed and laughed but not too loudly, lest she should disturb the sleeping children.

'Yes, I must admit I still think of Charles and I would be a fool if I did not. But if I give in to him and settle to be a good little wife, that is what he will expect, make no mistake about that, Augusta. Then all will be lost for me. I know that I could never live that kind of life. I am not cut out for that. I am quite a bossy-boots at heart myself. I have to be to keep these under control.'

The peace ended as the fire started smoking again and the fumes began to set the children off coughing and sneezing. They both jumped up and began frantically rushing about, not knowing whether to cope first with the wood burner or the distressed children. Amidst all the confusion, they did not hear the school door swing open wide or see the tall figure of Doctor Hadleigh standing just inside it.

The Doctor peered in and was amazed at the scene in front of him: Augusta cradling a sick child, Clara seemingly halfway up the wood burner.

'What do you two ladies think you are playing at? Clara, get away from that fire. Do you want to set light to yourself and add to my problems? And as for you, Augusta, how dare you involve yourself with these children. We have a measles epidemic here. Do you want to catch it yourself and become ill? Please go home, and leave this to Clara and me to cope with.'

Augusta spun round and with blazing eyes stared at Charles full in the face.

'I am helping Clara,' she stormed at him. 'She needs my help. She could not cope with this on her own. Somebody had to assist her while you went off.'

Brushing past Augusta, Doctor Hadleigh strode over to where Clara was disentangling herself from the wood burner.

Dusting herself down and pushing a strand of sooty hair away from her face, she exclaimed, 'Oh Doctor Hadleigh, thank goodness you have returned. Did you bring the medicine with you?'

Rummaging around in his black bag, he quickly found what he was looking for and pulled out a large green bottle marked 'The Mixture'.

'I am sorry it took so long but it takes quite a time for the ingredients to gel. Let us get to work and get these children to swallow as much of this stuff as they can.'

Moving towards the children he began at once to pour the foul tasting medicine down their throats. Loosening their blankets, he one by one quickly examined them, then turned to Clara.

'This was a good idea of yours to wrap them up so well. At least these blankets will keep them warm.'

Moments later, after making sure that all the children had been attended to, he slowly walked away from them and stood at the far end of the schoolroom. He needed to talk to Clara on her own, so he silently beckoned her to join him.

Standing by his side, she listened to what he had to say.

'The children are not in any immediate danger. They will recover, but I'm afraid I do have one piece of bad news. They cannot be sent home to infect their families. It also helps me if they are kept under one roof, but I shall need more supplies and extra blankets. That can all be sorted out later on. Your resourceful efforts have helped save the day, Clara.'

Grateful as she was in hearing Doctor Hadleigh sing her praises, she was not however going to allow him to think that she had achieved it single-handed.

'Actually, we have someone else to thank as well.' She did not want Augusta to think that her valuable help had been unappreciated.

Clara thought that Doctor Hadleigh had been a trifle hard on her. Charles, however, seemed unperturbed.

Straightening his back, he turned and saw that Augusta was bent over the fire piling more wood upon it. In two strides he was beside her and tried to remove the piece of driftwood from her hands.

'Augusta, I will not tell you again, please go home and stay there. There is nothing more you can do. This is no job for you. If your husband were alive today and knew what you have been up to, he would skin me alive and be well within his rights to do so. Now, as your Doctor, I command you to go.'

Augusta dropped the piece of wood expertly on his big toe. Before he could say more than 'ouch', she ran towards the end of the room, gathered up her belongings, called out a hasty farewell to a mystified Clara and escaped out into the cold, windy late afternoon air. How dare he order her around like a naughty schoolgirl. He never spoke to Clara in such a manner. Well, it only went to prove that Charles still regarded her as immature. Well, she would show him. She was beginning to feel thoroughly sick of all and sundry treating her as if she did not possess a mind of her own.

'To hell with the lot of you' she shouted, then chuckled at her own absurdity.

Dusk was beginning to settle in quite quickly and she whipped up the mare to make her move a little faster. It was growing much colder and she wished that she had not stayed so long at the schoolhouse. Coming upon the crossing that led straight into the town or towards Fairlawns, Augusta drew in the reins tightly and pondered for a few seconds which direction to take. She decided against going through the town. So, spurring the horse on, she galloped off over the hill and down through the fields towards home.

By the time she neared the outhouses, she was beginning to feel tired and her neck and back muscles were aching. Reining in the mare to a stop, she paused for a few quiet moments, moving her head forwards and sideways to relieve the tension. Gazing all around, she took in and savoured all the sights and smells of the vast acreage of land that was hers. Here she was mistress of all this vast virgin land and yet it had almost escaped her notice. She had been to preoccupied with thoughts elsewhere. She vowed that from tomorrow she would set aside some time to ride out and see for herself how things were progressing.

Her new-found enthusiasm was quickly shattered by the chilling sound of dragging chains as they echoed through the still evening air. Nosing the mare slowly forwards towards the rear of the outbuildings, she stayed half-hidden by the deepening shadows as she watched the long trail of weary convict workers shuffling along in the wake of the overseer who sat astride his massive stallion holding a lighted flare outstretched for all to see. A tall gangly youth appeared, banging what looked like two large tin plates together. This apparently was the cook's boy informing the workers that supper was ready. On nearing the lad, Cookson, the overseer, leapt from his horse, threw the reins at him, muttered a few crude oaths, walked past him and over to one of the wooden huts, obviously the cook's headquarters, and kicked the door open wide with his foot.

'We're back, so get out of there and dish up our grub.'

The convicts had flopped down on the hard cold ground, waiting anxiously for the last meal of the day. Within a matter of seconds steam could be seen circulating through the open hut and out into the cool air. The corpulent figure of the cook burst through the door clutching a heavy black cauldron which contained a greasy supply of muttonbone stew.

The unsavoury smell from the cooking pot soon assailed Augusta's delicate nostrils and, added to the pungent smell of the unwashed bodies that surrounded her, it was not at all surprising that she was forced to search out her perfumed lace kerchief, and rode out in front of the buildings where she could now be seen.

Cookson had removed his waistcoat and cap and was sitting hunched up on the ground with a plate of stew in front of him.

Augusta called out sharply, 'Mr Cookson, over here please, I wish to have words with you.'

Cookson looked up from his plate. Like the rest of the workers around him he was amazed at seeing their Mistress in their midst. He strode quickly over to her.

'Good God, Mrs Fitzroy, what are you up to, sneaking out amongst us at this time of night? This is no fit place for a woman to be in. Get along home at once. These men are dangerous and are likely to stop at nothing. I have more than enough on my plate to worry about without having to protect you as well.'

'Mr Cookson,' Augusta replied sharply, 'I was not sneaking about, as you put it. This is my land and I have every right to be on it, when and where I choose.'

'I beg to differ with you, Ma'am, but your place is in the house, not down here. This is my domain and I give the orders here.'

Augusta felt her blood boiling. The man was far more crass than she had ever imagined. She had never really liked him from the start but his present attitude towards her was downright rudeness. She was not prepared to have a showdown with him now, especially with the workers looking on. She would deal with this one in the fresh light of day.

'Mr Cookson, we will deal with this little matter tomorrow morning. In the meantime perhaps you would be so good as to escort me to the house. I am sure that you would not wish any harm to befall me before this evening is out.'

The workers cast sly grins at each other as they watched the overseer grimly pick up his slouch hat from the ground, dust it down, call for his horse to be brought back to him, snatch at the reins and follow Mrs Fitzroy all the way back to the house with a frozen look fixed firmly on his stubbly jaws.

True to her word, the following morning Augusta took everyone by surprise. Before she had even breakfasted or washed she had sent a note via Betsy to Old Amos instructing him to have the gig prepared and sent round to the front of the house within half an hour. Barely giving herself time to eat the sparse breakfast that she had requested and even less time for her toilette, she informed Mrs Potts that if anyone happened to call unexpectedly, the Mistress of the House would not be at home today to receive them.

'Where shall I say you be, Ma'am?' queried Mrs Potts, hoping that she would be able to glean the information for herself.

Augusta fixed her with a knowing look and added, 'Just tell whoever it is concerned, that I am out on business.'

23

Augusta stepped out on to the front porch to find that Old Amos and the gig were nowhere to be seen. How infuriating of the man, thought Augusta. I really must do something about his laziness. It's not as if he has that much to do around the place. After all, with Fitzroy dead there were only a few really good horses for him to care for. Impatiently she tapped one booted foot against the lower step of the porch. She waited a few seconds more, then decided it was time to send someone from the house over to see what was keeping him. Then she heard him. Cussing and swearing at the top of his crusty voice. Seconds later, the rear part of Old Amos emerged into view, with the colt and gig following somewhere behind. Something must have happened to the colt, for Old Amos appeared to be having a devil of a job trying to control him. Each time he tried to steady the reins and make him walk sedately, the young horse tossed his mane, snorted ferociously and side stepped, causing the gig to sway about uncontrollably.

Making her way towards him, Augusta cried out, 'Amos, what is the matter, what has upset Blaney?'

'Silly animal, a flock of wild cockatoos screeched past a while ago, and now he's got it into his head so as to follow them if you please.'

Augusta moved quietly towards Blaney to see if she could quieten the colt.

'Don't go near him, Mrs Fitzroy,' shouted Old Amos, 'he is likely to kick out at you while he is in this mood.'

'Well, do something,' replied Augusta, 'I am waiting to go out.'

'I shall have to take him back, Ma'am, and let him have the run of the paddock. He has to get this thing out of his blood.

225

Don't forget, he is still a young 'un. He needs to chase about a bit.'

'Very well, Amos, you old scoundrel, you win,' said Augusta, not unkindly. 'Take him back, and bring me the mare, perhaps she will cause me less trouble. You can meet me at the bottom by the clump of conifers.'

The early morning air still had a sharp nip and Augusta did not tarry as she strolled through the garden. Certain parts always brought back memories. Her favourite spot, where the spiky grass grew thickest, was where she and Tamara had so often roamed and picnicked. She still remembered with rising panic the moment when the baby kangaroo sprang on top of her darling child. It seemed to have happened only yesterday and how painful it still feels.

Amos cantered up from the other side of the conifers on the mare. Lazily, he swung himself out of the saddle and laconically moved to one side while he watched Augusta leap like quicksilver onto the mare's back.

Swishing her crop lightly over its rump, she called out to Amos, 'Hurry back and make sure that all is well with Blaney.'

Then like a bird on the wing she vanished quickly from sight.

First on her list was to be the overseer's place. She rode fairly quickly through the enclosed area but stayed long enough at the blacksmith's to enquire if he knew in which direction the overseer had taken his workers.

'Yes, Ma'am, they be up at Woomburra Copse logging for the winter months ahead,' was his forthright reply.

The copse was quite a distance away and to approach it she had to ride past the outbuildings and the two large barns that had been converted into temporary dwellings. As she neared the second barn she heard screaming. Pulling her horse to a standstill, she listened intently. There it was again. No mistaking it this time and it was definitely a woman screaming.

After slipping quietly from her horse and tying it loosely to a post, Augusta tiptoed the length of the barn and entered in through the half-open door. No-one heard her approach. The noise was coming from a far off corner. Augusta hurried towards where the screaming had now turned to exhausted

226

moaning sounds. Enough light was streaming through gaps in the roof for Augusta to take in what was happening amongst the bales of straw. A pair of naked brown legs were twisting wildly about as a man's heavy body lay prostrate between them.

In a choking voice Augusta cried out, 'Get off that woman, whoever you are.'

The man's body froze at the sound of Augusta's voice. Jerking himself free from his captive, he began frantically fumbling with his clothing and crying out at the same time.

'Begging your pardon, Ma'am, I did not think that anyone would be here.'

'Wait outside for me,' was all that Augusta could manage to say.

As he scuttled past her, with his face to the ground, too ashamed to look her in the eye, Augusta felt sick to the stomach and full of rage as she recognized the man. He was none other than Cookson, her own overseer.

When he had gone, Augusta ran towards the quivering figure of the petrified young girl still lying on the straw. Carefully, Augusta raised her up to a sitting position. The girl stared mutely at her. Augusta guessed her to be no more than about fourteen or fifteen. She was very slim with a mane of straight black hair flowing around a pale and slightly grubby face.

'Here, let me help you,' Augusta said gently, as she hastily bent down beside the trembling figure before her.

A pair of large, lucid eyes stared straight ahead as Augusta attempted to straighten and rearrange the girl's torn clothing. 'How old are you?' asked Augusta softly.

There was no immediate reply, so she asked again, a little louder. The girl did not say anything but slowly held up her fingers for Augusta to count. She was still in a state of shock.

Augusta muttered under her breath, 'Fourteen, he ought to be horsewhipped. Now listen carefully. I am going to take you back to the house with me, so that I can tend to you properly. Do you think that you will be able to sit on my horse?' The girl nodded. Augusta then placed one arm around her skinny waist and one underneath her knees and tried to lift her from the ground, but as soon as she touched her, the poor thing suddenly went to pieces and began crying

227

hysterically and shaking uncontrollably.

'There, there,' Augusta said gently, 'I am not going to hurt you. You are quite safe now, but I must be able to move you.'

The girl was not only shivering with fright but also with cold. Augusta hastily looked around for something to wrap around her. Lying across some bales of straw were several old horse blankets. Grabbing at one and shaking it she placed it around the girl's thin shoulders. Eventually she succeeded in calming her down a little and even managed to settle her on the mare. Before mounting herself, Augusta took a quick look around to see if Cookson was about, but there was no sign of him. He had scampered off like a thief in the night.

24

Tongues were still wagging for weeks after the event, not so much over the fact that the overseer from Fairlawns had raped one of the convicts, but that such an unworthy creature had been shown such kindness by the Mistress. Augusta had cut them all to the quick by insisting on the child being examined by Doctor Hadleigh, but not before Mrs Potts and Sally had forced her into a tub of carbolic suds.

Charles had duly examined her and had stated that only time would tell whether any issue would be forthcoming from the rape.

Augusta had felt a little disconcerted by Charles' attitude towards her of late, especially when after spending a few moments with him in the sitting-room he had enquired what she would do with the child when she recovered from her ordeal. On answering that she would probably take her in and find her some light tasks to do around the house, he had then looked sideways at her and commented in a droll tone, 'You and your lost causes, Augusta, will they never end?'

To her surprise, she discovered that most people were annoyed by the way she had spoken to Cookson. She had been informed on more than one occasion that a man had to find his pleasures somewhere. There was precious little to do around Fairlawns.

Cookson had lain low for a week or so and was still licking his wounds. He was not in the least bit concerned about the wretch he had forced himself upon, nor the fact that everyone was talking about it. What really galled him was the way that Miss high and mighty had read the riot act to him, so as to speak. Who was she to denounce his way of life? If only she knew what her late husband had got up to. After witnessing what had happened to Fitzroy, he would not risk contamination with the women at the local whorehouse.

His pride really took a tumble when Augusta accused him of behaving worse than the wild beasts in the fields. If he did not look to mend his ways then she, Mrs Richard Henry Fitzroy, would be left with no alternative but to replace him with someone more responsible and less despicable. He wished he could find some way to wipe that contemptuous look from her face. It did not take him too long to find his opportunity. Because of his pent-up anger he had taken to spending his evenings drinking an illicit brew at the back of one of the disused barns. He was staggering back to his hut when he was overcome by dizziness and sank heavily to the ground. He lay there for some time.

Slowly coming to, he rubbed his sore eyes and stared ahead of him. He could make out small tongues of fire spasmodically bursting through a mound of hot molten ash. The Cook's lazy and half-witted boy had not bothered to douse it properly. Mesmerized by the flames, an evil notion began to form in his befuddled brain. He loped towards the burning embers and with the sole of his boot began to drag the ash from side to side, causing the fire to leap into full play. Only a few more dry twigs, he thought, then it would burn brighter still. Soon it was burning fiercely. The spreading of the fire excited him immensely. The heat was exhilarating. The result was catastrophic.

Staggering away from the flames, he veered lopsidedly along the track towards the first section of the newly completed huts which housed the convicts. It was apparent that all the occupants were fast asleep. How dare they sleep, he thought when he wanted to play? The more he thought about it, the angier he became. These were convicts, scum of the earth, murderers, cut-throats, thieves, pick pockets, blasphemers, fallen women and their fallen daughters. He remembered all to vividly how Mrs Fitzroy had humiliated him.

Strange things were now happening to him beyond his control. All kinds of tricks were being played upon his emotions. In an uncontrollable fit of hatred, he knew that he had to do something. Like a wounded animal he drunkenly made his way towards the heart of the fire. Without thought or care he thrust an arm into the midst of it and pulled out a

230

half-burnt piece of timber. He charged forward and thrust the flaming torch onto the nearest matted roof.

With a spiteful look on his face he watched as the flame snaked its way through the loosely bound thatch of the hut.

Within minutes all hell was let loose. The terrified occupants, with their feet still manacled together, were depserately trying to escape. It was only when Cookson looked down on the poor devils, crying and screaming at each other for help, that he realized how far he had gone. Turning tail, he staggered towards the enclosed area. As he went, he prayed that he would be able to wake the workers before it was too late.

'Fire! Fire! Quick, get up you lazy lot! There is a fire raging outside.'

He ran from hut to hut, bashing on the doors until his skin was torn from his knuckles.

By now the smoke from the fire could clearly be seen. The smith was the first to act. He began issuing orders.

'Come on men, follow me and let's have this thing under control before the sun is up.'

They worked like Trojans, beating and stamping for all they were worth but the majority of the huts had been completely destroyed and the rest badly charred before the fire was finally under control. Two of the convicts had been burnt alive, many of them suffered severe burns and fear reigned supreme.

Cookson dragged himself off to his own place to sleep off an overpowering hangover, not realizing the tragedy that his jealousy and anger had caused.

The following morning Augusta was regaled by horrific stories of the night's events. She sent for Cookson as soon as she had heard about the fire but he had not turned up and she decided to venture out and see the damage for herself. The sight filled her with revulsion. It mortified her to think that every moment spent building the dwellings was wasted, that they had been utterly destroyed in one night. The whole area was just as the men had left it. All that remained amongst the smouldering heaps of straw and charred timber was half a hut. Of the occupants there was no sign.

25

Languidly brushing a solitary fly away from her face as she lingered over a late supper, Augusta reflected on the events of the past weeks: the fire, the confrontation with Cookson, and the arrival of Clarissa whose airs and graces had upset the servants. They were still up in arms at having the young convict girl in their midst. Then just as things started to improve, Clara rode over early one morning to inform them that Betsy had miscarried and was very poorly and Clarissa was needed at home. Augusta had suggested that Lisette, the young convict waif should be trained to do some of Clarissa's tasks, which sent Mrs Potts and Mrs Jameson into fits of pique.

The re-organization of the buildings for the remaining convicts had left her feeling thoroughly drained and depressed. She was beginning to learn how harsh and cruel life really was. This was a hard country to settle in. Nobody seemed to care about anyone else. She noticed how sullen and crude the field hands were. They worked six days a week and part of the one day they could spend with their families was given up to the Congregational Church. No wonder they resented her. She could choose what to do with her life. They had no choice.

But her biggest bugbear was the overseer. She hated having to spend time with him. Their dislike for each other grew daily. Cookson had the annoying habit of whistling through clenched teeth each time she spoke to him about improvements on the estate. The last time she had mentioned that she thought the convicts' dwellings were far behind schedule he laconically answered, 'These things take their time, Ma'am. They take their time.' And she knew that he would see to it that they did indeed take their time.

She instinctively knew that she needed to get away from Fairlawns, to escape from the endless problems for a while. But where should she go? Leaping out of the chair, she flew upstairs, raked a comb through her flying hair, pinched colour into her cheeks, grabbed a shawl and ran out of the house, without a thought as to where she was going. Creeping round the back of the stable, she thanked God that Old Amos could be heard snoring his head off, enabling her to sneak off with the mare without him realizing.

Her nearest friend was, of course, Charles. The dirt track leading to his house was the safest route to take. So she decided on this one. All the way along the narrow and muddy pathway she pondered. Over-fatigue and recent upsets had overturned her normally cheerful disposition and there were times when she felt as if she were climbing a high mountain peak, without ever having placed her feet firmly upon the lower edges of it. Now, at this unexpected moment, she began to experience great pain, not pain of the body, but pain of the soul. How could one explain or express to another the acute feelings of pain? She thought she had failed over many things: as a wife, as a mother and as a woman in a man's world. Then there was this uncanny and unusual feeling of pity for the convicts. Why should *she* go out of her way to relieve their suffering, when the rest of the community despised them? Was there some inexplicable gulf between her and other mortals so that people failed to see the real goodness within her heart?

When she had arrived at Charles' front porch the heavy drapes were pulled closely together and she hoped that he would be at home. Only the heavy bronze lamp hanging over the portals of the front door burned brightly amidst the darkening shadows. She crashed the knocker loudly. She did not have to wait too long. Charles, being a Doctor, was always quick off the mark when anyone knocked loudly on his door. He stood there, with the full light of the lamp beaming softly down on him. He had obviously finished work for the day for he was casually attired in a pair of buff-coloured, tight-fitting breeches. A colourful necktie was knotted loosely inside a cream coloured, open-necked, collarless shirt, and his sleeves rolled up. He was clearly surprised to see Augusta.

'Good evening, Charles,' she blurted out. 'I am sorry to trouble you at this time of the evening, but I do need to talk to you for a while.'

'Yes, of course, Augusta, do come in. Please come through to the sitting-room.'

Charles led the way. No sooner had she entered the room than she felt quite at peace with the place. The room, although spotlessly clean, had a lived-in air about it.

'Do sit down, there is no need to stand on ceremony. I am completely on my own tonight.'

Augusta hesitated slightly. Then, tossing her fringed shawl lightly over the back of a fireside chair, she did as she was bid.

'Well, what is it this time, my dear? Fire, flood, plague, brawling convicts, damsels in distress?' he mockingly threw at her.

'Please, Charles,' she held up one hand to silence him. 'It is nothing like that. I am managing quite well at the moment. How can you be so unkind as to mock me so? I will admit that I do not always find life easy and I daresay I make many mistakes, but I do try hard not to. It is hard enough when one's enemies snigger, let alone your friends.'

Charles straightened his back and burst out indignantly, 'Come now, Augusta, I hope that you are not suggesting that I snigger behind your back. For if you do, then my dear girl, you are greatly mistaken. I happen to have the highest regard for you.'

Before he could say another word, she broke in quickly and said apologetically, 'Oh, Charles, no, that is not what I meant to say. Please, let us not quarrel with each other. At least not now. I need someone to cheer me up, someone to talk to. That is why I rode over here tonight. Fairlawns at the moment is weighing me down.'

'Damn,' uttered Charles silently, then moving closer towards he, he gently added, 'What an ass I am when alone with you. I do not mean to be so insensitive. Now come on, tell Uncle, all that is bothering you.'

Augusta laughed and placed one finger lightly on his bare arm.

'That is better, Charles, you have made me laugh and I feel better already.'

They sat there, quietly discussing her problems. Uppermost on her mind was how to deal with Cookson and his unpleasant ways. What should she do about the convicts? She did not entirely agree with slave-labour, but at the same time, needed them to carry out the necessary fieldwork.

Charles listened intently, only moving away once or twice to fetch her a glass of Madeira. Gradually she felt much more relaxed. When she felt she had finally explained her problems, she waited patiently for Charles to come up with appropriate answers to them.

'Well, one thing is for certain, Augusta, a resolution to your problems must be found fairly promptly. It is not right that you should have to carry the burden of all those distressing worries yourself. To my mind, Cookson is your main worry. I suggest that you fire him and look for someone else. I know good overseers are hard to find, but no doubt someone will turn up. It was a pity that Adam Smith left the way he did. Now he was a good man. Trustworthy too. Richard was a fool to let him go.'

Augusta stretched lazily and replied thoughtfully, 'I wish I knew where he was now. Perhaps I could tempt him back.'

Suddenly an idea leapt into her retentive mind.

'Charles, you don't think that enquiries could be made to find him. I mean, is there any possible way that one could find out? Of course, if I knew how to go about it myself, I would, but I am only a woman and . . . '

'Well really Augusta,' cut in Charles before she had time to finish. 'I have to hand it to you. What a crafty little minx you are. Now don't pretend to me that you are incapable of doing anything for yourself. After all, I seem to remember you advertising your own services once.'

'Please Charles, do not remind me on that score,' she instantly retaliated. There was no way that she wanted old wounds re-opened now.

Then seeing as she looked slightly crestfallen, Charles quickly replied, 'Don't worry my dear, I shall make enquiries for you. I also intend to do something about those convicts of yours. Only recently I have heard how some do-gooders over here are trying to badger the Governor, with some kind of proposal or petition enabling him to pass some sort of legislation, whereby the convicts can either buy their freedom, that is after so many years of penal servitude, or better still, owners can try to obtain a hearing in which to plea for their causes. Providing that you can vouch for their good behaviour and trustworthiness, one is able to purchase their freedom for them.'

Augusta jumped up and clapped her hands together excitedly. Charles jumped up and pulled her back down onto the chair again, 'Here hold your horses Augusta, you must not get too carried away. It is still only a suggestion. These matters normally take years to implement. One step at a time. To raise one's hopes too high would be sheer folly right now.'

'Oh I know you are right Charles, but thank you all the same for at least trying to raise my hopes.'

On hearing the hall clock chime the hour of ten she sprang out of the chair and suddenly exclaimed. 'Gracious, is that the time. I had no idea it was so late. I must leave at once.'

Half-heartedly, Charles arose from his seat and reluctantly said, 'Yes, of course, you must.'

As she moved towards the door Augusta sensed that he was reluctant to see her go. Oh why was it so necessary to return home, when she felt so happy and relaxed here? What was it about Charles that made her feel this way?

Charles picked up her discarded shawl and draped it lightly about her shoulders. Looking down at her he gravely said, 'I think I had better escort you back to Fairlawns. It is not safe for you to travel about so late on your own.'

Flashing him one of her brilliant smiles, she replied graciously, 'No Charles, there is no need. I shall be quite safe going alone.' Without realizing what the consequences would be she turned round and kissed him more than fondly on his right cheek. Within seconds she was in his arms and responding impulsively to his ardent kisses.

He was about to cry out, 'Augusta don't go, stay with me,' when there came a violent crashing on the front door knocker. Cursing loudly, Charles gently put her from him and rushed to the door. On opening it, the frantic figure of the Rector rushed in and declared that his wife had fallen down the stairs and that no one was able to move her.

Charles pushed the poor man back outside, while he ran back to explain to Augusta what had happened. Running through the house and shouting at the same time, Charles called out. 'I must go Augusta, don't wait for me. I do not know how long I shall be gone.' Quick as a flash, he disappeared from the house leaving her feeling disturbingly lonely and cold.

26

'Ashes to ashes, dust to dust,' the Rector's droning voice echoed throughout the dusty plateau on which stood the tiny graveyard. The chapel below had been packed with mourners and by now most of them had managed to trudge their way, more out of pity than sorrow, to pay their last respects to the Rector's wife. Having been an invalid for so long her untimely death had not come as such a shock to those closest to her.

With the service coming to its final close Augusta could not help noticing that she was not the only one who was openly grieving. Her grief however, was not attributed solely towards the Rector's recently departed wife but more for the fact that it was now exactly three years ago to the day when Tamara had been laid to rest.

Swiftly all the painful memories came flooding back to her. Looking up quickly and trying to concentrate on what was happening around her Augusta suddenly caught Charles' tender gaze upon her. Nodding his head slightly he deftly moved to her side and placed a comforting hand beneath her elbow. He wished he could reassure her by adding a few consoling words of his own but secretly he knew that any words said at this particular moment, would not be the right ones. However, he did feel extremely moved when Augusta secretly pressed his hand tightly to her side and held it there for a few precious seconds. They both knew deep in their hearts that words were not always necessary.

Silently the band of relatives and friends trundled back down the narrow, stony pathway that led directly to the Rector's house, with the sun beating mercilessly down upon their backs.

Nearing the stone wall encasing the perimeter round the

Rector's house the Rector stopped in his tracks and asked if Augusta would honour them with her presence and partake of the repast that he had provided for in remembrance of his dear wife.

She hesitated at first for she did not know this particular Rector and his family all that well as she attended the official church, still it would probably appear churlish and un-gracious if she were to refuse.

Inside the Rector's small and shabby parlour Augusta began to have second thoughts on accepting his invitation, for she had been jostled on several occasions and the hem of her best day gown trod on more times than she could remember.

Most of the guests made hurried attempts at squeezing themselves into the more comfortable chairs and settles, Augusta who was not normally used to being exposed to this sort of behaviour, curiously found herself the only one left standing in the midst of the room. Hastily looking at the swell of sombre faces in front of her she felt a trifle ill at ease, probably because she scarcely recognized anyone that she knew at all well.

She also noticed that most of the congregation looked very homespun and poorly, even though they were dressed in their black fustian Sunday best. She, on the other hand, was attired in a long, sweeping, black silken skirt, topped by a pure, white, frilly, lace blouse, with full puffed sleeves and a tiny black bolero, showing her graceful figure off to perfec-tion. Several strands of creamy pearls glistened around her throat and her rich auburn-hair piled high at the back of her head, gleamed vibrantly for all to see. Looking slightly out of place and what was worse, she was acutely aware of it, she hopefully glanced around again to see if she could spot either Clara, Charles, or even Mrs Carter. But no, they were nowhere to be seen. Trying to muster up enough courage in allowing herself to become engaged in some kind of repartee, with one over large and bewhiskered gentleman, to her relief she was thwarted in her tracks, as the Rector strode into the room and announced in a deep voice, 'a little cold collation had generously been prepared for all by the extremely kind-hearted efforts of our dear Clara and Mrs Carter.'

That is where they are, thought Augusta, busy overseeing

the preparations for the tea. This explained where Clara and her mother were, but not Charles. Surely he had not gone straight home. The moment for contemplating these things came to an end, for like a stampede of elephants suddenly everyone rose at once and herded off to the next room to gorge themselves silly.

Augusta suddenly found herself being propelled by a pair of large hairy hands towards a vacant chair and was thrust most unceremoniously upon it. Turning her head around to see who the hands belonged to she discovered they were no less than those of the owner of the local corn store. 'Can't have you standing this time Mrs Fitzroy, can we?' he drawlingly bellowed in her delicate ears. His accent verging on the same idiom as was fast becoming the new way of talking.

The centre of the table was filled with all kinds of savoury-filled tarts and tartlets. Numerous dishes of relish and chutneys were inter-dispersed amongst various plates of cold chicken and mutton pies. At the far end of the table, nearest the window, rested an enormous richly-glazed, roasted ham. Hovering over it with a giant pair of bone-handled carvers and with saliva already dribbling down the sides of his mouth, accentuated by the mouth-watering aroma exuding from the ham, stood the Rector looking for all the world, like a fox ready for the kill.

Augusta was suitably impressed with the collation and guessed quite rightly, how hard the two women had worked on achieving this. She was about to take a slice of chicken pie, when Clara was seen to pop her head around the door and after carefully scrutinizing all in sight, espied Augusta sitting meekly there and weaved her way towards her.

'It is so good of you to come, Augusta, and how well you look. The dear Rector has just confided in me that your presence here today has greatly lessened his pain.'

Augusta smiled and thanked Clara for the kind words and added, 'I barely knew his wife, but even so I thought it my duty to attend.'

Clara bent forward and whispered in Augusta's ear lest she should be overheard. How dreadfully the Rector's wife had suffered in the end and perhaps her death had been a blessing in disguise. For as Clara carefully put it, the man needed a practical helpmeet to assist with church affairs and not one who had fast become a burden to him. It has been very hard on him of late. Here she broke off for the Rector suddenly stood up and banged noisily on the table with his fork. The flow of conversation came to an abrupt halt. Looking rather flushed in the face, due to immoderate sips of red wine, and with his clerical collar slightly askew, he nevertheless managed to stand long enough to deliver a very flowery speech. Seeing him there in full flight, Clara excused herself from Augusta's side and hastily tore over to stand next to him. Firmly believing that he urgently required her services, she faithfully remained standing there, until she heard him say, 'And now we come to Clara, without whose loyal and spontaneous support in more ways than I could mention, has stoically helped me through my terrible ordeal. All credit must be given to her.'

A few titters and the occasional cough echoed round the room.

As the speech meandered on, Augusta found herself staring at Clara. Augusta observed that she had never looked lovelier, even though she was dressed from head to foot in deepest black. Clara's eyes, she noted, never for one moment left the Rector's face and he in turn, kept on turning to look at her. If other mourners had noticed anything, it did not appear to be showing on their faces. They all seemed far too preoccupied with their own thoughts, wondering how long it would be before they all got down to the serious business of eating.

Eventually, with a wide sweep of his hands, the Rector gave his blessing and urged his congregation to start. Everyone began talking and shrieking at the tops of their voices. After a while Augusta found she could endure it no longer. Pushing her half-eaten food to one side, she begged to be excused and gingerly made her escape. Minutes later, she found herself breathing in great gulps of fresh air. Looking around, she saw that she was standing on a patch of rough grass in a small walled area, obviously the Rector's private garden. Small clumps of mimosa and lobelia mingled amongst the lilac bushes at the bottom of the garden. The grass was long and needed scything.

She was quite stunned when a concerned voice behind

her said, 'Feeling all right are you, Mrs Fitzroy?' She turned round and came face to face with Mrs Carter.

Relieved at seeing this friendly soul, she uttered, 'Yes, thank you, Mrs Carter. I am fine really. Just hot, that is all. And how are you?'

Mrs Carter ran a hand through her damp hair and wearily said, 'Worn to a frazzle, you might say, and I guess twice as hot as you.'

Mrs Carter was most inappropriately dressed and it was no wonder her feet and ankles had swollen up. Augusta felt sorry to see Mrs Carter in such a weary state and was prompted to suggest that the only way to deal with the problem would be to find somewhere shady to sit down and remove their offending shoes. Sitting back to back underneath a straggly yew hedge, both women dangled their toes, closed their eyes and slowly let the strange happenings of the day gently wash over them.

Inside the house, only the Rector, Clara and one or two of the few remaining guests stuck out the flies, cockroaches and sultry heat of that soon-forgotten afternoon. Only Doctor Hadleigh had done the sensible thing in slipping quietly away to sit beside the little stream that ran past the church, to rest his aching head. Funeral gatherings were not for him. He was more concerned with the saving of lives than being pressed into witnessing an end to them.

27

Another year had passed, with the winter months ebbing by peaceably enough, but the following summer was one of the worst that anyone could remember. It was the beginning of the Great Drought and Augusta had never experienced anything like it and never wanted to again. The heat all through that long hot summer was fierce and scorched everything in sight to mere black and sinster shapes. The trees stood gaunt and bare. The bushes sprouted out their pitiful, sparse branches and the few hardy animals that had barely survived lay prone on the dust-choking ground, too sick and exhausted to move. The water holes, brooks, streams and the lake had completely dried up. Only the main well was just about functioning properly. Augusta had been forced into issuing strict instructions to all the workers that if they were not careful about the amount of water being pulled daily from the well, it would soon run dry.

Everyone was tense and irritable and things became steadily worse. The house was unbearably hot and oppressive and to venture outside was worse still. Gritty dust flew around everything and everybody and it was becoming nigh on impossible to rid oneself of it. Flies and termites impinged on such a gigantic scale that it was nothing short of miraculous that more harm had not been produced by them.

For the past month or so Augusta had felt a virtual prisoner at Fairlawns. For although the house was unbearably hot, the thought of having to leave it and endure the agonies that beset her outside filled her with dismay. She had not set eyes on anyone, save for those nearest around her, and the rest of the folk were like her, too busy having to cope with their own day-to-day problems. Fresh meat was a rarity and Mrs Soames was at her wits' end trying to find something nourishing and appetizing to feed so many mouths. If it were not for the availability of wild hare, peacock and some new-fangled species new to the country, rabbit, they might well be eating kangaroo.

For the rest of the community and the small-time farmers, life was exceptionally harsh. It had been ages since Augusta last ventured out to oversee her land. For once she had been pleased to leave all that with Cookson to contend with. With a pricking conscience she knew that she ought to make more of an effort to try and manage things herself, but whenever they met and she put forward new proposals, Cookson, in his usual quarrelsome manner, cut her down to size as it were, and never failed to remind her that a woman's place was in the home.

At the end of the summer, not one but two miraculous events occurred, one after the other. It was the night the storm broke and ended the worst drought recorded so far.

Augusta had just finished a rather tasteless supper. There had been no meat for weeks. Meals consisted of anything that could be made from bran, wheat or half-rotting vegetables. On finishing her sparse meal, Augusta pushed the tray to one side and strolled over to the open French windows. For days now the air had been totally still. Everything seemed to be the same colour. The brittle and lifeless branches of the bushes and the gaunt frames of the gum trees mingled with the scorched earth and the ever-swirling dust, presenting a picture of dull reddish browns and smoky greys. Looking far to the horizon, the contours of the once blue hills loomed black and ominous in the distance. The heat was intolerable and she was beginning to feel more than irritable and depressed at always feeling so sticky, dirty and uncomfortable. Closing her eyes briefly, her thoughts immediately sprang back to England, to the peace of English country life, to the greens and yellows, the rich, gently rolling pastures, the cool, leafy lanes, with the sweet smelling roses and jasmine that had clung tightly around her window frames. Oh, to feel the cool breezes and the sudden splashing of sparkling raindrops.

'Rain, rain, oh, why in God's name does it not rain? How much longer can I endure this suffocating climate?'

Suddenly she felt angry and hurt. Why oh why, did she

have to come to this dreadful country in the first place? Oh, how she hated her life here. Hate turned into venom. She began to hate her mother, her silly, vain mother, who had been so spoilt and petted all her life, and her father, whom once she had loved and would have sacrificed everything for. What had he done to deserve her loyalty and trust? Gambled and drunk himself to death, leaving her to cope with life in a strange country with no friends, on her own. Then there was her husband and what a disaster he had turned out to be. There was another one who had wasted his life. True he had obviously worked hard in his early years, but for what? To end up no better than her own father. Tears began to flow down her cheeks, quite slowly at first, then her· thoughts drifted on to Tamara, the only real happiness that she had known in such a long time, and the tears soon turned into torrents. Loneliness and despair engulfed her. She longed to turn to someone for comfort, but to whom could she turn? Everyone around her had so many horrifying problems of their own. Last time she had felt like this, she had dashed off to see Charles. She thought of him, tall, straight, handsome, so intense and caring in everything that he did. It was Charles that she needed more than anything or anybody. Was she in love with him? Possibly so. But she could not keep running to him everytime she felt dispirited. Charles would quickly tire of her. Charles, being a doctor, was always busy with his experiments . Her constant problems would fast become a burden and she a liability. No, this had to be faced alone.

Great silver flashes lit up the sky, following each other in quick succession, terrifying thunderbolts echoing in their wake. Sudden activity burst out all over the house as all the servants stopped work and rushed to the open windows to witness the scene. Then the first miracle happened. The heavens opened and down poured the long-awaited blessed rain. Within seconds everyone stumbled outside and tearing off as much of their garments as modesty would allow, danced, pranced and leapt around in the warm and wonderful rain, laughing and crying with sheer joy and utter relief until they were too exhausted to cavort about anymore.

'This calls for a celebration, does it not Mrs Fitzroy,' shouted an almost incoherent Mr McTavish. 'What say, we all descend on the kitchen, with your kind permission, of course, Ma'am.'

'An excellent idea,' spluttered Augusta. 'You lead the way, Mr McTavish.'

Grabbing up their sodden cast off clothes, everybody struggled back into them and in a jovial fashion trouped behind Mr McTavish along the flagged pathway towards the rear end of the kitchen. Suddenly, their high spirits and raucous laughter came to an abrupt halt, as the bedraggled figure of a man slowly loomed in front of them. His outstretched hand fell limply to one side as he tried to stop the oncoming group of people crashing into him. Before their startled eyes, he sunk slowly and wearily to the floor.

Half an hour later, after they had revived the stranger with many a tankard of strong ale, they all agreed that this must surely be the second miracle of the day. For, sitting propped up against the kitchen table, with a look of relief spreading over his drawn face, was the long departed, almost forgotten figure of Adam Smith.

28

Adam Smith's health was slowly restored by Mrs Soames, willingly helped by Clarissa and Lysette. His life since leaving Fairlawns had not been easy, as he painfully confided to Augusta one early evening when they were both seated in the study.

'You have made this room very comfortable and tidy,' said Adam Smith, taking in the newly acquired leaded-light bookcases, the finely sanded woodblock floor, partially covered by a creamy sheepskin rug. On the mantelpiece, that he last remembered littered with Fitzroy's belongings stood tall, statuesque, bronze oraments that gleamed.

'You have done wonders with this place, Mrs Fitzroy,' he went on, nodding his head in approval. 'Pity that Mr Fitzroy did not live long enough to appreciate it.'

There was a pause.

'Yes, I can see that quite a lot has changed since I left, and all for the best.'

Adam Smith settled deeper in the leather chair and very quietly began to unfold the story of what had happened to him since they had last met.

'You know, after I left here with my wife and family, we moved around from place to place for quite a while. We covered a lot of ground and that's not easy when you have a wife and a handful of youngsters around you all the time. For a while it was not too bad, in fact, quite an adventure. We lived reasonably well to start with. As you probably know, Mr Fitzroy was good enough to provide me with a substantial amount of money, "something to get you started with", as he put it. So we splashed out a bit at first, swanking around and all that.

I got a job on a sheepfarm up at Woomburra. But I soon

got fed up with the long back-breaking hours and the sheer hard work of it all, so I decided to try my luck and branch out on my own. Sure as hell didn't know what I wanted to do, mind, just felt I had to do something on my own. Like a fool, I threw everything in, sold up, bought a covered wagon and a team of well-shod horses, loaded the rest of our possessions in the back and set off.'

'Set off where?' interjected Augusta.

Tight-lipped he replied, 'Anywhere that came my way. A bit of farming, odd jobbing, tree-felling, sheep-shearing, ditching and, the final ruination of it all, – gold-mining.'

'Mining!' cried Augusta. 'You must have travelled far. I hear the mining areas are hundreds of miles away.'

'You hear right, Mrs Fitzroy, for they sure are hundreds of miles away and, what's more, they are the most miserable and soul-destroying areas on God's earth. In the summer months just blinding red dust as far as the eye can see and in the winter months, everywhere becomes completely water-logged. No wonder the natives call it "Bad Man's Land". Funny blighters they are, Ma'am, pardon the expression. Have you seen any of them since you came here?'

Augusta wriggled slightly in her seat.

'Not close to, Mr Smith, but I have just caught the occasional glimpse of them on my journey from Sydney to here. My first reaction to them was that they looked very savage and nasty. However, I have it on good authority from Doctor Hadleigh, who pays fairly regular visits to the bushlands and seeks them out for medical research, that they are not so savage as they used to be. Some of them, he reckons are quite friendly and extremely fascinating to watch.'

'Well, so much for the good Doctor's opinion of them, but I am bound to say that mixing with the native is not in my line of country, nor ever will be.'

'Mr Smith,' interrupted Augusta again, 'I do not wish to appear uninterested, but have we not strayed from the tracks? What happened to your wife and family when you took to mining?' Adam Smith fidgeted in his seat then, slowly spreading his palms out flat on top of his knees, sighed deeply and said in flat voice, 'They are all dead, Mrs Fitzroy. They died of hunger and disease. I left them on a small homestead with the owner's wife and family, while Jim, he was the owner, and I went off to make our fortunes in the mines, or so we thought. When we left, conditions at the homestead were not too bad. The drought had not really begun. Naturally, the women did not want us to go. The previous harvest had been a bad one and the ground was yielding very little. Then to make matters worse, the majority of his sheep contacted a disease and had to be destroyed. So Jim and I decided to try our luck at mining, thought it would be more rewarding.'

'And was it?' demanded Augusta.

'Well yes and no. We worked like blacks, to start with,' carried on Adam Smith in reply to her question, 'we even started to show a profit, but events soon caught up with us. Conditions there were hell. The food was more than disgusting. The owners of the mines had everything tightly under their control, no loopholes anywhere.'

'How do you mean?' Augusta enquired, wide-eyed.

'Oh, things happened there that I just could not repeat in front of a lady, but let's say that a man had a hell of a time hanging on to whatever he happened to possess.

We had been gone about ten to twelve months before we decided to go back to the homestead. When Jim and I set off to the mining area, I left behind a pretty little wife and five children. When I returned it was to bury my wife and six children. Apparently one was born while I was away. Never even saw it alive, just a pile of tiny bones was all that remained of it. Don't even know whether it was a boy or a girl. Would have liked a boy. We had all girls, you see.'

Adam Smith stopped briefly, drew out a large piece of red flannel and blew his nose fiercely upon it. He gradually managed to carry on. Augusta had turned her head away from him, so that he could not readily see her own tears.

'We had made some money, of course, and so we guessed it was about time to pack up and go back to our families. Jim had left several strapping sons in charge of the place and quite rightly thought that he had left them on their own long enough. There had not been a drop of rain for months and the drought was catching everyone unawares. When we finally reached the main camp, things were pretty crook. Food was scarce. In fact, some days it was non-existent. The water holes had all been pumped dry and the rivers and

249

streams had dried out. The men who ran the stores and the eating houses charged just what they liked for what they termed a "substantial meal" and bottles of raw whiskey was sold at crippling prices. Well, naturally enough, fights broke out. Men stole and some even killed each other. So it came as no surprise to anyone that through bad food, lack of water and just sheer filth all around, men were going down daily with some terrible illness. Luckily, Jim and I thought it best not to wait for the rest of our earnings, so we got the hell out of the place with just one old nag between us. All we had for our pains were the very clothes we stood up in and a few carefully conealed coins that would hopefully last us for a short while.

I couldn't begin to tell you the harrowing sights we witnessed on our return home. There were men and women looked like walking skeletons. The major parts of the inland stock routes were littered with dead cattle. At nights, when we used to camp down for a few hours much needed rest we had to take two hourly turns at sleeping, for fear of being murdered while we slept. The aborigines used to lie in wait along the far-off tracks that led to the minefields, with their long spears at the ready, gleefully anticipating the return of some wealthy digger in the hope of being able to spear him to death and relieving him of his hard-gotten gains and the angry farmers gave us malevolent looks as we cautiously sped past their pitiful barren lands. Thinking back, it was a pure miracle that we survived at all.'

He paused for a while and closed his eyes to shut out the ghastly thoughts.

'What on earth did you live on?' asked Augusta, anxious not to miss any detail

'Anything that moved, but very little actually. Any creature that had enough flesh on its bones to make a meal out of was the general order of the day. I chewed a lot of bark, that helped as well. I remember so well those last few days, before we reached the homestead. It was as if I was on the threshold of youth all over again. We joked about having our fill of good mutton and jar upon jar of home-brewed ale. We would take our wives out for a beanfeast that they would never forget. Never once in our state of hallucination did we ever think that they might be suffering the same miserable plight as everyone else.'

It was at this stage that Adam Smith broke down. Leaving her comfortable chair, Augusta walked round to his side, tenderly placed a clean kerchief to his glistening eyes, and said reassuringly, 'Do not upset yourself so. It is all over now. It is in the past. Try to push it to the back of your mind. Do not say anymore tonight.'

'No', he cried out vehemently, causing her to jump back against the wall, 'I have to tell someone. It is like a demon monster breathing fiery fumes upon my chest.'

The late evening air had grown strangely cold. It seemed a lifetime before anyone spoke. Then, suddenly, Adam Smith shrieked out in a frighteningly hoarse voice.

'It was my fault they died. All save Jim's eldest boy and he, poor lad, went right off his head trying to hold everything together. They just could not manage the homestead without us men. The drought and the poor harvest, followed by an outbreak of cholera, meant certain death for them all.'

He paused for a while, then in the most heart-rending voice imaginable, he sobbed out, 'Jim found his son, stark naked and almost withered away to nothing, hiding in one of the chicken runs, too sick in the mind and body to bury the corpses that lay strewn around the decaying house. We buried them all in one big grave, not far from the wooden-framed house. We were too exhausted ourselves to drag them any further. After erecting a makeshift cross and falling to our knees, we cried as two men have never cried before. Our tears rained upon that freshly dug grave until we were too spent to weep anymore.'

Augusta waited until Adam Smith had gained control of himself, rang the bell for Clarissa and ordered that her old servant be found a comfortable bed for the night.

29

It was the time of the year when womenfolk began to take stock and plan for the oncoming winter and those at Fairlawns were no exception. Augusta had personally supervised the domestic stock-piling herself this year. So for three whole weeks the servants were kept busy bottling fruit, preserving jams, making jellies, curds, cheeses, hanging hams, drying herbs, pulses and grains, making chutneys, sauces, rose and mint tea, syrups, corn dollies, that were later given as presents, salting beef and lamb and numerous other comestibles.

When that task had been completed, Augusta turned her attention once again to the convict workers. At least Adam Smith seemed to be in agreement with her on this subject. She had now re-hired him as a farmhand and he knew only too well, not being a landowner himself, what degradations and humiliations one had to contend with. When Fitzroy was alive, he had strongly objected to the use of forced labour. After all there were plenty of free men willing to break their backs for an honest wage, without having to resort to those measures.

She often wondered how he and Cookson were getting on together. When she was around, they kept up a pretence that all was going well but deep down they fiercely hated each other.

The beginning of this winter was a happy time for Augusta. Things were going along quite smoothly at Fairlawns. Clarissa's work was improving steadily and she seemed to be more content with her lot lately. She was asserting herself more as a companion to Augusta than just her maid. Little Lysette was also settling down well, now that she had learnt to obey and take notice of what Mrs Soames and Mrs Potts said to her. In fact, the hostile attitude that they had adopted towards her was slowly evaporating as time wore on. She was also proving to be quite useful to the household. Betsy was now expecting another addition to the family. This Augusta had gleaned from Clara when they met on their way to their respective churches the previous Sunday.

Augusta had hardly seen anything of Charles lately, as his work kept him constantly on the move. Clara had mentioned that he had gone off into the bush again to try out some more experiments on the aborigines and would no doubt be back when it suited him.

Mercifully all the stocktaking inside and out was now finished, enabling the staff to relax a little and get on with their own lives, and that is exactly what two members of the household did. For the following week Jack and Sally announced their intention of getting married the following Christmastide. This piece of news came as something of a blessing to his mother, who was overjoyed to think that her only son would be settling down at last. Augusta had given them her blessing and had stated that they could have a couple of small backrooms to themselves for as long as they wished. Frankly, she did not want to lose anymore of her staff at present.

On waking one crisp morning, she decided, quite on the spur of the moment, to pay a visit to the general store. She badly needed some new material for herself and several bolts of corduroy for the workers. This time Old Amos managed to harness the mare and bring her round and set off with Augusta sitting perkily in the back, without too many hiccups on the way. It was so good to be out again. The sun had just started to break through the clouds and she felt pleased to be alive. She revelled in the luxury of having nothing to do but relax and watch the wild life teeming around her.

On her arrival at the store, she was quite taken by surprise to find no other customers inside. Therefore she was fortunate enough to have the undivided attention of Mr Brownlow, the storekeeper.

'Stocks are already running low,' he hastily informed her. 'Soon as there is a sharp nip in the air, folks rush in and buy up everything in sight. Blue merino is still very popular,' he went on, as he deftly thrust a bolt of it onto the glass-topped counter.

Augusta pinched the material between her fingers, exclaiming over the fine quality and texture.

'Or this.' He broadly smiled at her. 'This is what all the fashionable ladies are wearing this year,' and, winking slyly at her, he crooned, 'even the saloon girls are trying it out. Plaid, the latest thing from England. Everyone is sporting it now.'

Augusta hesitated for a while as the storekeepr unleashed a plaid of vivid reds, purples, green and blacks.

In his best salesman patter he cunningly said, 'Now this is nice and I just have enough left to make a very fetching frock.'

Augusta pursed her lips and thoughtfully replied, 'No, I do not think so. The colour is too vivid for my taste.'

Another piece was slowly unfolded in front of her.

'Well, what about this one then?' Browns, yellows and greys. This is popular with many of the older women.'

Augusta winced.

'No, not that one either.'

Not to be deterred, he fished out a colourful remnant from under the counter.

'You might just be able to make a skirt with this piece, that is if you don't waste too much on the cutting out,' he knowingly remarked as he swished it backwards and forwards over the counter. But again, this was not to her liking.

'Surely you must like one of them. After all, Ma'am, I am informed that everyone is wearing plaid this year,' he tactfully added.

Augusta looked a little downcast and replied, 'Then I am pleased to say, Mr Brownlow, that is one good reason why I shall not be wanting to wear it. I have always tried to maintain some sort of individuality in my dress, so as not to look like all and sundry.'

Pushing the offending materials out of sight, he quickly reassured her by saying, 'And a very pleasant picture you present, if I may be so bold to say so.'

She thanked him warmly and turned away.

Wandering around the store by herself, she stopped to examine a few of the brightly coloured laces and trimmings that lay draped upon the various shelves and boxes. Mr

Brownlow, who considered himself something of an expert where women were concerned, raised his eyebrows as he ran an experienced eye over the graceful figure of his customer. Augusta, who was completely unaware of his appraisal, was fetchingly attired in a well-cut, oatmeal morning dress and beautifully shaped, russet fringed cape. Her newly-washed and scented hair was neatly wound up under a matching bonnet. Mr Brownlow slowly came to the conclusion that this was no ordinary housewife or settler. This was a woman of quality and deserved to be treated as such. At all costs he must not lose her custom. Was she not the sole owner of Fairlawns Estate? How could he have made such a blunder as to offer her the same material that everyone else had ordered. No, if he wanted to keep her custom, he must quickly find something of the utmost quality that would arouse her interest.

It came to his mind that out in the back of the store room stood several bales of material that his wife had ordered some time ago and neither of them had got around to unpacking it. Excusing himself politely, he tore round the back and within minutes, he returned with two large unopened packages.

'Now, Mrs Fitzroy, if I may gain your attention for a brief moment,' he loudly exclaimed.

With bated breath and simultaneously offering up a silent prayer, in case the materials he was about to expose, proved to be less than worthy of his troubles, he fervently added, 'What about these?' Quickly tearing off the outer wrappings, he deftly unfurled a bolt of material that made Augusta's eyes blink. She ran over and gently caught at the gently swaying material and held it up against her. The tawny greens and golden threads amongst a background of softly muted browns accentuated her creamy complexion and added a warm lustre to her eyes and hair.

'This is perfect,' she announced happily. 'I will take some of this gladly.'

The other bolt, when unwrapped, turned out to be black alpalca, which she disliked intensely.

'Is it just one bolt of material you will be acquiring, Mrs Fitzroy?' said Mr Brownlow hesitantly.

Augusta pondered for a while, then casually replied, 'Well no, I think perhaps I had better have the blue merino as well and some ribbons and laces to add to it.'

Mr Brownlow thanked her profusely and hastily set about wrapping up her purchases in case she changed her mind. After she had settled her account and picked up her packages, she bade Mr Brownlow a very good day and departed from the store, hoping that Old Amos, who could rarely be trusted to stay in one place for any length of time, was not too far away.

As usual, he was not by the gig, or anywhere to be seen. Slightly aggrieved, she threw her heavy parcels into the back of the gig and set about looking for him. If he had stayed over long in any of the saloons at the far end of town, she would give him a piece of her tongue that he would never forget. She was half way up the narrow muddy street, when a sudden and terrifying commotion could be heard afar off. The sounds of gunfire, blood-curdling screams, howling dogs and the thunder of horses' hooves began to disturb this usually quiet little township. Within in a flash, the storekeepers and saloon owners, joined by their customers and general layabouts, fell out of every nook and cranny onto the almost deserted street.

From out of nowhere a lone voice cried out, 'For God's sake take cover, you fools.'

Terrified people ran about in all directions, leaving Augusta hopelessly bewildered and not quite knowing where to run to. Then, just as a band of troublemakers swept into the town and before she knew what was happening, a pair of strong arms whisked her up and ran back with her along the now empty street. Before she had time to recover her breath, she found herself flung most unladylike onto the front part of a horse. With the stirrups still dangling down the frightened beast's side, it was frantically kicked into action, after someone else had landed behind her, and sped off hell for leather in the direction of the outlying Rectory.

Augusta was so petrified that it was not until the low stone wall of the Rectory shot into view that she realized it was actually the Rector who had come to her rescue. Some moments later, crouching well behind a huge boulder on top of the hillock overlooking the town below them and with their hands shading the glare of the mid-day sun, were Augusta, Clara and the Rector. Luckily, Clara had been there to witness Augusta's unseemly arrival. The schoolhouse had closed down for a short holiday. They now watched horror-stricken as hordes of convicts who had somehow managed to escape from the large penal colony some sixty miles away clambered over the open terrain below them. They had been on the run for four to five days at least. Somewhere along the route they had encountered a group of aborigines and inevitably violent clashes had broken out between them. The convicts could clearly be seen now, as they broke through the sparsley covered ridges below chased by the spear waving aborigines. Presently all hell was let loose, as more gunsmoke swirled around the area. A troop of men on horseback, firing wildly into the air, thundered town the hillside towards them.

These were the local farmers and tradesmen, headed by the Justice of the Peace who had quickly rounded up a posse in an attempt to capture the runaway trouble makers. Fearfully clinging to each other, the two women begged the Rector to take them back to the safety of the Rectory. But he claimed, authoritively, they were perfectly safe where they were, providing they did not turn tail and clamber up the hillside for all to see.

All three endured their cramped positions long enough to witness the rounding-up of nearly all the convicts, who in all probability were now quite willing to forgo their short burst of freedom. The excitable aborigines were given a short, sharp dressing-down from the Justice of the Peace himself, who in turn promptly turned a blind eye as the fearsome warriors ran whooping away to their primitive and well-concealed lairs.

Just as things were beginning to quieten down a little, several more riders descended upon the scene from the opposite direction. To her consternation, Augusta recognized them to be her overseer and several farmhands. What on earth were they doing getting themselves mixed up with such a rabble? While she was meditating upon this matter, another lone rider edged his way through to join the throng. Clara, stood up from her crouched position and cried out.

'Look, isn't that Doctor Hadleigh down there? Oh I do hope he will be careful.'

Augusta threw all caution to the wind herself and leapt up

shouting, 'Where, I cannot see him at all? There are far too many people down there.'

Clara pointed her finger in his direction. The Rector, poking his head around the boulder, also spotted him.

'There he is, over there, just behind the JP,' he spouted out.

Then she saw him, sitting tall and straight in the saddle, with the amber rays of the sun casting long shadows around him. 'Yes, yes, I see him now', Augusta thankfully replied.

Just as she said this, Cookson thrust his way through the crowd and started hectoring the Justice of the Peace and the Doctor.

To Cookson, it had seemed as good a time as any to try to hire some more convict workers. He had connived with the other men and they all agreed that it would be well worth the effort to drag a number of them back to Fairlawns. However, the Justice of the Peace disagreed with him, stating that, by rights, these men should be returned from whence they came. For the newly-appointed Commandant of the Penal Colony was following in the firm footsteps of his infamous predecessor, Captain Patrick Logan, who had earned the reputation of being an extremely tough disciplinarian. It was well-known that this man often meted out sentences of up to a hundred lashes to any convict that had managed to escape his steely clutches. The Justice of the Peace promptly informed Doctor Hadleigh that the new Commandant would probably have a field day once this lot were safely returned to him.

Despite the refusal from the Justice of the Peace, Cookson took no notice and at the top of his rasping voice issued a volley of curt instructions to his men to round up as many convicts as they could and drag them back to Fairlawns. No sooner had these words fallen from his lips, than a bout of fierce fighting broke out between the convicts and Cookson's workers. Within seconds, the majority of the posse had joined in the fray as well. These men were not going to allow this usurper to charge in and take the law into his own hands.

A single gun shot echoed around the hillside. The Justice of the Peace sat astride his horse, with his smoking pistol held high above his head. A bunch of fighters broke apart, others fought on. Another gun shot rent the air. This time the fighting ceased abruptly. Without more ado the Justice of the Peace then spurred his horse right through the mêlée. Swiftly and curtly, he ordered the men to behave like responsible citizens and to channel their energy into helping him place the convicts safely behind prison bars.

On seeing the convicts being whisked away from under his nose, Cookson became so enraged that he started shouting obscenities at the Justice of the Peace all over again. But this time Doctor Hadleigh, who had endured more than enough of this man's disgusting behaviour, thrust out his arm in an attempt to ward him off. Quick off the mark, Cookson recoiled and retaliated. Drawing out a long-handled sheath-knife from an inside pocket, he slashed it savagely down the Doctor's right arm and across his chest, causing him to cry out in pain and slowly sink to his knees.

Both Augusta and Clara let out frantic screams and, gathering their long skirts tightly about themselves, ran, tripped and stumbled down the slope. The Rector, now a frightened man suddenly lost his footing, plummeted down and ended up at the bottom before anyone could stop him.

30

How strange was the tide of events, Augusta mused to herself, as she rode down the muddy track towards the Doctor's house. Moments beforehand, at the crossways, she had paused for a few quick words with Clara, who was about to pay the Rector a fleeting visit, before returning to the schoolhouse. Both women deemed themselves to be on missions of mercy where these two eminent men were concerned. For Clara was rushing over with a large jar of foul-smelling lineament, which she thought would help to ease the Rector's bruises, while Augusta had carefully strapped onto the mare's back a large bowl containing calves' liver jelly which she hoped would be the remedy that Charles would need to regain his lost strength. Only a few months ago she had complained that life was tedious but the unexpected happenings of the last few days certainly proved her wrong.

The housekeeper held the door open for Augusta and at the same time cooed, 'Another visitor for you, Doctor.'

Charles raised himself into a sitting position as soon as he saw Augusta and smiled broadly. He still looked very wan and the wound in his chest, although not deep, was considerably sore. His injured arm, supported by a heavy sling, had been securely bandaged but still felt stiff whenever he tried to move it. His housekeeper, a shade surprised at seeing Mrs Fitzroy in person, hovered around the Doctor's bedside and began straightening the covers and plumping up his pillows. Charles seemed a trifle disconcerted, and tried to push her away, but not too unkindly. Augusta came to his rescue by thrusting the bowl of jelly into the housekeeper's hands and firmly insisting that the Doctor be given some straight away. She plodded back to the kitchen, thus enabling Augusta to give her full attention to the patient.

'How are you feeling this morning?' she enquired cheerfully, as she lightly rested her hands on a nearby chair.

'Much better this morning, my dear,' he gratefully answered.

With his one good arm he patted the side of the bed for her to sit upon, but Augusta resisted and decided to stay where she was.

With the door now closed and the windows firmly shuttered, the overpowering reek of carbolic fluid, commonly used in all sick rooms, caused Augusta to vacate her seat and force the windows wide open, letting the warm rays of the sun stream in.

Returning to her chair, she idly commented, 'This room badly needed light and plenty of fresh air.'

Charles agreed with her and then as an afterthought graciously added, 'Thank you for the flowers and fruit which you sent over with Amos yesterday, and might I add how pleased I was to see that he is still with you. For it would not have come as any great surprise to me to learn that you had fired him as well.'

Augusta winced slightly and pulled a wry face.

'Now Charles, do not start goading me now. Under the circumstances I had precious little alternative.'

Charles grinned at the piqued look slowly spreading over her upturned face.

Turning her back to him she said chidingly, 'Anyway I had been waiting for this chance for some time now and this turned out to be just the right one. But nevertheless, I am truly sorry that it was you who was hurt the most amongst the fray.'

She was, of course, referring to the fact, that she had been given no alternative other than to fire Cookson on the spot. She had not minced her words when she ordered him to collect his belongings and be off by the end of the week. Old Amos, who had deserted his post outside the local store, leaving Augusta exposed to great danger, had been severely reprimanded. If it were not for the fact that he was getting on in years, she would have fired him as well. He was not really a bad man, just irresponsible at times.

Turning round to face Charles again and this time sitting on the edge of the bed, she gauged that now was the right

261

time to tell him her one really good piece of news. Adam Smith had been restored to his old job as overseer of Fairlawns Estate. Cookson would be officially dismissed and paid off at the end of the day. In a very dignified manner she ended up by saying, 'I just hope and pray that he does not cause any further trouble before he finally departs and that he goes away quietly.'

Charles grinned widely. If it had not been for the fact that his wounds still pained him, he would dearly have loved to have laughed out loud.

However, he did manage to say quite dramatically, 'Augusta, my dear, you really are quite wonderful. You dismiss a man in no uncertain terms, in front of all and sundry, knowing full well what type of animal he is, and you expect him to creep away from Fairlawns as if he had merely committed a naughty schoolboy prank.'

Augusta sighed heavily, knowing that Charles' words were all too true.

'You must make sure that Adam Smith has everything tightly under his control when Cookson leaves,' he went on, even though he was unsure whether she really wanted his advice.

Charles wagged a finger sternly and resolutely said, 'Make doubly sure that you are not alone. I just wish, my dear, that I could be with you at that particular moment, but as you can see, I shall be completely laid up here for a while.'

Augusta felt positively contrite over Charles' concern for her. Gently patting his bandaged arm, she whispered quietly, 'Oh, Charles, you should not be so concerned for me. It really ought to be the other way around. All my concern should be for you, as it was one of my employees who caused all this pain in the first place. If anything really serious had happened to you, I would never have forgiven myself. In fact, to tell the truth, I do not know how I would have reacted.'

From underneath his long, thick, curling eyelashes he looked at her and, pointing to his heavily bandaged arm and the deep wound in his chest, he mockingly replied, 'So you do not think that this is serious enough? With my right hand lacerated and a hole in my chest, I could be finished as a doctor for life.'

Knowing only too well that he was mocking her, also

realizing that many a true word is said in jest, she quietly answered, 'Charles, I never fully realized until this moment, how dreadful that situation could have been. I really ought to have had Cookson horsewhipped. Quite frankly, I was astonished to find out that the JP had let him get away with only paying a fine. By rights, he should have locked him up for a few days. That would have cooled him down for a while.'

Before she could continue, Charles quickly interrupted her by saying forthrightly, 'Augusta the poor JP had quite enough on his plate at that moment. The entire gaol was at bursting point with unwanted convicts. There was nowhere to put Cookson. Besides, I gave my word, for all to hear, that he would be severely dealt with once and for all.' Augusta nodded her head in agreement.

'Yes, of course Charles, how silly of me.'

A tap on the door brought their conversation to a halt, as the tall figure of the housekeeper trotted in. Going straight to the bedside table, she placed upon it a tray containing the promised calves' liver jelly and a glass of water.

Turning to Augusta she sourly commented, 'Perhaps you would care to feed him as well.'

This comment caused Augusta to bite her lip and glance helplessly in Charles' direction. He did not approve of the woman's tone and was about to admonish her with a curt reply, but thought better of it. Augusta passed him the glass of water, which he drank thirstily. The jelly he decided to try later on. 'Tell me, Augusta,' Charles began a little wearily, 'did Clara return to Fairlawns with you as you wished her to? I daresay I am fast becoming woolly-headed, but I seem to recollect the pair of you talking about it some time after my accident. Did you not suggest that she would be far safer staying with you and Clarissa than stuck out at the school-house on her own?'

Augusta could not give him an answer straight away. She gathered from the way that he was talking that Clara had not even bothered to enquire about his recovery in person.

Lowering her eyes, so as to avoid Charles's hurt gaze, she answered, 'No, Charles, she did not come back with Amos and me. Apparently she returned to the Rector's house.'

Charles muttered a feeble, 'Oh I see,' and then closed his

aching eyes.

Seeing how deathly pale and tired Charles looked, Augusta thought it would be best to leave him to sleep undisturbed. However, before she had time to move away from the bedside, Charles opened and fluttered his sleepy eyelids.

In a voice overcome with drowsiness he managed to say, 'Anyway, enough of this morbid talk. As you can see, I am improving daily and these what can only be described as flesh wounds will soon heal.'

Augusta smiled at him and said that she really ought to be returning home. Charles caught at her hand and holding it lightly in his own, he whispered, 'By the by, I have not yet thanked you or Clara for coming so speedily to my rescue. How on earth did you both get there so quickly?' Augusta laughed lightly at the memory of that fateful day.

'Well,' she giggled, 'Clara, the Rector and myself witnessed the whole ghastly episode from the top of the Rectory grounds. We saw it all. The Rector, I may tell you, saved me from a fate worse than death.'

There she stopped, for she saw that there was no reason why she should bother him about their strange behaviour now. Best to forget it for a while. After all, what did it matter where Clara went? It was her business and hers alone.

To change the subject, she continued by saying, 'I expect your patients are all missing you dreadfully and I trust that no one is about to die or give birth at this moment?'

Augusta stopped, realizing that her words had been wasted. Charles had dropped off into a deep slumber. Slowly moving from the edge of the bed, she leant forward, lightly planted a kiss on his forehead and tiptoed quietly out of the room.

31

Later that same day, Augusta and Clarissa were to be found lazily browsing through a pile of patterns in the hope of finding something that could be termed 'eye-catching'. Pausing for a while and arching her back in order to ease her aching muscles, Augusta's mind flew back to that never-forgotten day when she had purchased the material that now lay strewn about her. In so doing, she was reminded of the fact that there had been a small matter which she had needed to question Clarissa about. She was anxious to know why the two sisters had stopped visiting each other. However, before she could put her thoughts into words, the sitting-room door burst open and an agitated Mr McTavish bolted through it, followed in hot pursuit by the extremely inebriated form of the overseer.

'I told him to wait outside, Ma'am,' panted a heavily perspiring Mr McTavish, 'but he refused. He even threatened to get violent with me if I didn't take him to you personally. I'm truly sorry, Ma'am.'

Augusta leapt to her feet and took one look at the sickening figure of her overseer, as he lurched from side to side.

Quickly turning to Mr McTavish she replied authoritively, 'That is quite all right, Mr McTavish. I understand perfectly. You obviously did your best. But I would prefer you to leave us alone for a while.'

On hearing this the poor man's eyeballs suddenly swivelled around inside their sockets and tears started oozing along the lapels of his linen jacket.

Spluttering and stuttering he jerked out, 'But Ma'am, I can't leave you at the mercy of this, this, . . . ' words seemed to fail him.

Augusta held up her hand to silence him, while Cookson

staggered into the centre of the room and slumped himself across one of the chairs. Unable to conceal his loathing towards the wretched oaf, Mr McTavish once again attempted to rid Augusta of his presence. But Cookson was not going to allow anyone to remove him. Augusta was livid and she feared if she were not careful she would soon lose all control. She had to act firmly.

With a determined look on her face, she nodded in the direction of the open door and in a dignified tone she uttered, 'Please, Mr McTavish, and you too, Clarissa, I think I can manage Mr Cookson on my own.'

They were completely astounded. Clarissa reacted at once and scuttled away as fast as her short legs would allow. Mr McTavish followed, with some reluctance. Once outside the room, Clarissa bolted up the stairs to comparative safety. While to say that Mr McTavish actually hooked an ear to the keyhole might be something of an exaggeration, it has to be said that that was not that far from the truth.

Augusta eyed her prey with lips pinched and her head erect. If her outward stance presented a picture of control inwardly she was feeling the reverse. She kept her back towards him for as long as she could so that he could not see the little beads of perspiration breaking out upon her forehead. Finally her control snapped.

'Are you going to sit all day in my chair without saying a word now that you have forced your way in here?'

There was no reply. She was dying to turn around and confront this man face to face. Before repeating the question, she decided on a new approach.

'Please be so kind as to inform me why you are here.'

Still there was no response.

Tapping her fingers lightly against the window pane, she rigidly said, 'I assume that you have been paid off. I left instructions with Adam Smith to act on my behalf.'

He did not answer immediately but by the shuffling sounds that were coming from the opposite end of the room, she gathered that he was about to remove himself from the chair. She turned and confronted him.

Heaving himself out of the chair, he lolloped over to where she was standing. He looked and smelt disgusting. His greasy hair hung lankly around his grey stubbly face. A pair of

266

bleary and bloodshot eyes bobbed about in front of her. His mouth hung open loosely and his breath reeked from drinking too much rye whiskey. The clothes he wore were crumpled and hung shapelessly about his person. Mud and grime lay caked in the folds of his thick, leather boots and as he moved deposits of it were spoiling the creamy lambskin rugs.

With as much force as he could muster he drunkenly slurred at her, 'So you think you are real smart, don't you?' Augusta was shocked and completely taken aback.

'How dare you talk to me like that,' she cried out in ringing tones.

Lurching towards her, he sarcastically sneered, 'Now don't get all hoity-toity with me, Mrs Fitzroy, Ma'am.'

Then, before she could reproach him, he breathed at her, 'All right, so you fired me. You put that po-faced Adam Smith in my place, got him to pay me off and do your dirty work and that's all the thanks I get. I was only trying to get more help for you. But no, you rejected my help out of hand, rejected me in front of all those people, made me look a complete fool.'

'No,' Augusta burst out angrily, 'you made a fool of yourself. You always have done so.'

Augusta tried to back away from him, but there was hardly any room to do so.

Hoisting up his baggy trousers, he replied sullenly, 'Never have liked me, have you, Mrs Fitzroy? Wasn't good enough for the likes of you, was I?. You had it in for me since the first day you set eyes on me. Well, I will make sure that you pay for this.'

'Very well,' cried out Augusta with relief, 'so you are not satisfied with your pay-off. How much more do you require?'

Suddenly he let out a loud, crude, belly laugh that seemed to rock the entire room.

'Oh, no, little lady. 'Tis not as simple as that,' he jeeringly swung back at her. 'You cannot fob me off just like that.'

By now Augusta had endured enough. Perhaps it was time to let Mr McTavish deal with him. Skirting quickly around him and running towards the closed door, she angrily snapped at him, 'Take your grievances elsewhere and get out of my house and out of my life.' He stared at her from out of

his swollen eyes then threw back his head and bellowed forth
the most frighteningly devilish sound that Augusta had ever
heard. It jolted every nerve in her body.

'Oh I'm going all right,' he spat at her, 'but not before I
leave you with this,' and in so saying, he momentarily averted
his eyes from Augusta's pinched white face and with shaking
hands, he fumbled beneath his breastcoat pocket and pulled
out a small round object and threw it down at her feet.
Augusta jumped back, for she thought he was going to hit her
with it.

She stared at it for a while, then cautiously bent down to
pick it up. She recognized it instantly and let out a piercing
scream. It was Richard Fitzroy's gold fob watch.

'Where did you get this from?' she said inaudibly.

'Wouldn't yer like to know?' he sneered at her.

'Yes, I very much would,' replied Augusta shakily.

Cookson swayed in front of her. All his pent-up hate
flooded out as he gleefully croaked, 'From his death bed, if
one could call it that.'

Augusta stumbled slightly as she rose from the floor. Her
heart felt as if it were in her mouth and her throat felt dry and
constricted. Her whole being felt as if it were on fire. She
managed to take three steps then collapsed down on the
settle, still clutching the watch in her hands. It had originally
belonged to her father and she had often wondered what had
become of it. She had presented it to Richard on their
wedding day, it had been her only wedding gift to him. A
slow sickening smile spread across Cookson's contorted face
as he craftily guessed that she was wondering how he came to
possess it. Looking up and seeing that awful grin, she knew
instinctively that something bad was about to befall her. The
room had suddenly grown cold and dark.

He stood there, swaying on his heels, and with eyes as
bright as burning coals, he gloatingly cried, 'I took it off his
body. His stinking, rotten body. That's all he had left in the
world. He had spent everything else on trying to get himself
cured. But he was so far gone that no-one could help him.'

Oh how he was enjoying this! He was loving every second
as he watched her face change with every spiteful word that
he could vent upon her. She just sat motionless as he spewed
out his bile.

'Thought we were taking off to hire more hands, didn't you? But we took all those moneybags and belongings for something different though.'

Augusta clapped her hands to her ears. She did not want to hear anymore. Cookson raised his voice even higher.

'Yeah,' he went on, 'we went to all the quacks we could find. Spent a fortune on useless cures, potions, stones, powders, bars, saloons, dens, whorehouses, flea-pits.'

'Stop it, stop it,' cried out Augusta painfully. 'I do not want to hear anymore.'

But still he gabbled on. 'It did him no good though. No-one wanted to know in the end. He finished his life in some sleezy lodging-house, too poor to pay for a proper funeral. What a laugh! The one-time rich and powerful Richard Fitzroy ended up in a pauper's grave, miles from anywhere. When they buried him, I found the watch still dangling on him, so I took it as a fitting reward for my devotion to duty. Devotion to a pox-ridden old sod.'

And here he stopped, too exhausted by spent passion to carry on.

For Augusta the nightmare was not over, however, Nor ever would be. Wringing her hands in total despair, she cried out hysterically for Mr McTavish, who all this time had been eavesdropping. Flinging the door open, he stumbled inside, too astounded at what he had just learned to do anything positive other than gawp at the evil man now lying almost prostrate on the floor. Augusta looked up wild-eyed and frightened.

'Send Mrs Potts to me,' she said almost fainting away. But Mrs Potts did not have to be summoned as she and the rest of the staff had been hovering in the hallway for some time, knowing that something very unpleasant was going on. Mrs Potts rushed in and caught Augusta to her.

'Oh you poor dear,' she wailed, 'you look so dreadful. What in heaven's name has been going on here?' Then, catching sight of Mr McTavish, she screamed at him, 'Don't just stand there gawping, man, throw this treacherous villain out.'

Mr McTavish was shaking so much he did not know which end to pick up first. Then a deep booming voice was heard just inside the doorway, as the tall figure of Adam Smith

269

swiftly strode through.

'That's all right, Mr McTavish, you can leave me the pleasure of doing that.'

They all stared in disbelief at seeing him, and could not understand as to how he came to be there, until he gravely explained that Clarissa, on being sent from her Mistress's room, had lost no time in running to his hut to tell him that Cookson, in a drunken and violent stupor, had fought his way inside the house and was now all alone with Mrs Fitzroy.

32

A year or so had passed quite uneventfully although Augusta's life had been reasonably busy and enterprising at times.

More and more free settlers were slowly drifting in alongside the Hunter River and on finding the nearby Darling Downs extremely lush and fertile, they soon settled down to growing rich crops and raising healthy cattle.

Doctor Hadleigh, now fully recovered from his injuries, had plunged back into work with renewed vitality. As the old adage has it, 'out of something bad comes something good', and good did materialize in his case. During his tedious weeks of convalescence he had been searching for something beneficial to occupy his mind. As chance would have it, he did not have to wait too long. One of the causes that he had long been championing began to ferment. Frequent disturbances over the last few months had brought the plight of both the aborigines and the convicts to a head, which was greatly welcomed by most of the community.

After many tiring and traumatic meetings with the Justice of the Peace, followed by countless hours spent penning letters and studying medical journals, he concluded that enough information had been gathered that the Governor Elect personally would champion his proposals. He proposed that some sort of settlement or encampment, assisted by Government aid, should be under some kind of control and supervision. In a forthright manner, he stated that, although Australia was the aborigine's land by birthright, nothing was being done to protect them against the steady influx of white settlers trampling over their domain. Conflicts and battles were inevitable as the aborigine was made to feel that he was being forced off his land. Surely to goodness, no one in their

271

right minds wanted here what had previously happened to their American counterparts. The lesson learnt from that newly-found Continent's obsession over land ownership, which resulted in wars and constant strife with the native Red Indian, was that their mode of life must never be accepted in Australasia.

Months and months of hard work had finally resulted in him being able to tie up all the necessary paperwork, bind and seal it and despatch it to the Governor Elect via one of the passing mail-coaches. His efforts did not pass unrewarded. Toward the end of the year he did in fact receive a reply and, what was more to the point, it was in the Governor's own hand. On reading the Governor's letter, Doctor Hadleigh learned that a Special Bill had been passed, resulting in a separate piece of hunting and grazing ground being awarded to a local tribe of aborigines some thirty to forty miles away. A copy of the 'Bill' had also been forwarded. How long this arrangement stood was not stated, but permission had been granted to Doctor Hadleigh and the Justice of the Peace, allowing them full authority to act upon it. It was not quite what Doctor Hadleigh had wished for, nevertheless he had felt impressed and, if nothing else, it was a step in the right direction.

As to the plight of the convicts, even greater news had emerged. In 1833 there were more than eleven thousand convicts in the local Penal Colony. As the years wore on, this number, of course, lessened. It had become increasingly difficult to put a stop on the numerous break-outs so, with the upsurge of free settlers spreading through all parts of the country, more and more labour was required and settlers were accustomed to taking on workers with suspect characters. Gradually the reins relaxed and the convicts who were considered to be less of a risk once outside of the gaol were hired out to the wealthier landowners. Now reports had filtered through that a new law was about to be passed, so that all remaining convicts would be given their rightful freedom, which would enable them to set about regaining their long-lost dignity.

With a little badgering from Charles, Augusta had written numerous letters to the Governor. She was especially concerned with the pardoning of her own convict workers. To set them free would have been against the Law. By rights, they were to serve their sentences. Then, just when Augusta had least expected it, Adam Smith informed her early one morning that notices had been pinned on all the buildings in Town, requesting everyone in the community to attend the Reformed Church on Sunday morning next.

The church, needless to say, was packed to overflowing, some late-comers having to be content with sitting on hassocks outside. As the owner of Fairlawns, Augusta was fortunate enough to have a private pew to herself. She did not have to worry about arriving early in order to gain a good seat. All through the prolonged Service, people fidgeted and craned their necks trying to see who the great personage was in their midst. But they had to wait for the final rendering of the Lord's Prayer before all was revealed.

With as much pomp and style as he could muster, the Minister dramatically flung aside the moth-eaten velvet drapes that partially concealed the vestry door and roared, 'My friends,' and waving one arm high above his head, while tightly clutching the Holy Book in the other, suddenly ran out of steam and with his mouth wide open and eyes cast heavenwards, patiently waited for the right words to say.

Augusta, who like the rest of the congregation had been sitting in rapt attention, suddenly found herself having to suppress the need to giggle. One moment the Minister looked as if he were about to pull rabbits out of a hat, the next as if he were in a state of holy trance. However, he soon came back to life as he started again.

'My friends, we are greatly blessed as we gather here today to listen to and welcome into our midst the Surveyor General of New South Wales, Sir Thomas Mitchell.'

Mouths gaped and eyes rolled in wonder. Never had such an important personage stood before them. How his presence had been kept such a guarded secret, nobody could imagine. His reasonably formal and short reply to the Minister's overflowing sentiments was delivered in a thick brusque tone.

'Members of the community, I take this opportunity to inform you that as from twelve o'clock today, in this free state, all convicts have been graciously pardoned by the Governor General and all those still in bondage are to be given their freedom henceforth.'

This was the news that Augusta had waited so long to hear. Loud clapping or cheering were totally forbidden in the Church. However, deep sighs of relief and the occasional hushed, 'Thank God,' could definitely be heard echoing around the white washed walls. After the Surveyor General had offered his sincere thanks to all those who had turned out to hear the 'Declaration' the congregation lost no time in jostling each other as they hastened out of the Church.

Augusta, being no exception to the rule, forced her way through the ranks in a helpless attempt at trying to find Charles as she wished to thank him for all the past help that he had so readily given her. She saw him at last, standing under an overhanging mulberry tree, conversing with Clara, Mrs Carter and the Rector. Judging by the twinkling light in his eyes and the wide grin on his handsome face, she sensed at once that Charles was more than pleased with the morning's news. Cautiously darting through the noisy gathering, she succeeded in catching them up just before they were about to move off in different directions. After congratulating and embracing each other most warmly because there was still a certain sense of expectancy and jubilation in the air, Charles surprised them by insisting that all four should join him back at his place for a quick celebration. To this they all agreed most spontaneously.

Because the bridle path was packed with horses and carts of all descriptions, they decided on a leisurely and pleasant stroll along the footpath that meandered its way right up to Charles's front door. They soon fell into an easy pattern of conversation, Clara with the Rector, Mrs Carter struggling along somewhere in the middle and Augusta with Charles following on behind.

Charles had casually mentioned to Augusta earlier on that as the next few weeks would prove to be hectic for her, if she needed any assistance she only had to ask and it would be given without a moment's delay. They had by now reached the Doctor's house and were politely ushered in by the housekeeper. No sooner had they removed their cloaks and hats and hung them on a row of outsized wooden pegs that served as a cloakroom, than they were shown into his small and cluttered sitting-room.

Charles lost no time in handing around large glassfuls of golden madeira accompanied by dishes of tasty wheatcakes and tempting cookies. The toasts came next, followed by euphoric singing of each other's praises and the clinking of glasses. For Augusta and Charles, the day's news had significance, and they more than anyone were undoubtedly relieved by the Surveyor General's good news. After the first flood of conversation had died down a little Augusta, who had been patiently waiting for the right moment to discuss several weighty matters with Charles, found to her annoyance, that Clara seemed to be claiming all of his attention. Mrs Carter had taken it upon herself to slink off into a corner, seat herself deep inside a wide, spacious, winged chair and gorge herself with sweetmeats.

Augusta was fast becoming bored, having to listen to a round of footling topics discussed by the fiercely perspiring Rector. It was not that she disliked the man, far from it. He was a very pleasant person. Feigning sufferance from the heat, she strolled over to the open window and stood quietly observing both men.

The Rector, well into middle-age, was portly, with dappled grey hair slightly receding, piggy eyes, a bulbous nose, over-large ears and a florid face. Dressed entirely in sombre black, he was a picture of quiet, rustic, learned, mystical affability. Charles, in his well-cut morning suit, sporting a pure white silk neck-band gleaming atop his maroon, watered silk, paisley waistcoat, with his long sideburns and equally long, black, curly eyelashes, looked almost Byronic. Although he always cut a dashing figure, Charles was also quietly spoken, well-mannered, faintly sardonic and always highly intellectual. It was this last trait that Augusta adored in him the most. True, his looks and humorous asides could set her heart aflutter but it was his intellect that transported her more.

Watching Clara with him now, she realized quite painfully why they got on so well together. Clara was extremely intelligent herself. Why Clara had turned him down she would never comprehend. However, who could say that she was not having second thoughts right at this very moment? Here she was, flirting quite outrageously with him, not at all in keeping with Clara's normally reserved nature. Augusta

275

was feeling rather peeved and yes, she had to admit it, envious of Clara's hold over Charles. Still, what could she do about it? Clara had more right to his attention than she had.

The Rector, bored at being left to his own devices, ambled over and stood behind the totally absorbed pair. They seemed completely oblivious of him, however, feeling ignored, he shuffled away from them with a disdainful look and craftily sought out Mrs Carter. This proved to be something of a disaster, too, as the over-indulgent woman had now succumbed to a spasm of heavy snoring. Disgusted by this, he then meaningfully trotted over and caught up with Augusta once again. With an amused look on her face, she had been watching him doing the rounds. She knew that this time she could not escape and therefore felt obliged to stay and listen to him. However, it was a mistake on her part for it turned out that he had nothing worthwhile to say.

At last, Charles and Clara managed to tear themselves away from each other's company, leaving Augusta feeling overjoyed and very much relieved. Disappointingly, though, all did not work out as she had visualized. Mrs Carter suddenly awoke from her reverie and announced sleepily, 'I have so much enjoyed myself, but I really must return home as Lord knows what that artful lot of mine will get up to while I'm away.' Kissing her daughter fondly on the cheek and telling her not to work too hard, she quickly embraced the others and went in search of the rest of her family.

The Rector, who was by now looking quite despondent, kept on repeating to himself that he really ought to be concentrating on his next sermon and asking if Clara was ready to leave and that he would kindly escort her to the schoolhouse if need be. Clara said she did have to return to the schoolhouse to prepare extra work for the following morning, which only left Charles, who exclaimed thoughtfully that he still had several medical matters to attend to before the Surveyor General returned to New South Wales. However, he did manage to persuade his last three guests to partake of one last drink before they set off to their various destinations.

33

Three days later, an Official Officer, acting on instructions issued from the Governor Surveyor himself, rode over and personally delivered to Augusta the relevant paperwork required to set free the convict workers at Fairlawns. The following morning she arose early and before breakfasting rode with all speed straight over to Adam Smith's hut, hoping that she would catch him before he set off for another day's toil. The previous evening she had carefully sorted out all the official papers that had been delivered to her.

Seated well in the saddle, for she still insisted on using one, she drank in the good, clean air and wonderingly observed the thick verdure everywhere, due to the recent rainfalls. Here and there on the edge of the wood, the grass-cutting wombats could be seen burrowing into their snug abodes. Kangaroos, dasyures and flying phalangers plunged and danced about with incredible grace and agility. High above and around her, wheeled numerous large birds. Their specacultar and gorgeous plumage was a constant delight for the beholder. Macaws, cockatoos, parrots, parakeets, pigeons, kookaburras and lyre birds soared high up in the sky, then plunged down to settle and feed from the hedgerows and undergrowth below. The wattle trees, with their countless myriads of yellow, tufted flowers and beak-like pods, almost outflanked the ever-spreading wild figtrees and the delicate fronds of the occasional tree-fern. Nearer the ground spread wood-sorrel, fig-marigolds, sweet smelling honeysuckle and the sparse patches of orach, the wild parsley that exuded a wonderful and uplifting fragrance.

Past the stream and the rushing waterfall the ground evened out over flatter, stonier and plainer views and Augusta could not resist clutching at a wayward frond from the huge weeping willow that dipped the water's edge with its pendulous branches.

'Oh yes,' she sang to herself, 'this is going to be a memorable day indeed.'

No sooner had she left the water's edge and swung out over the ridge, when she quickly spotted her overseer as he cantered on some distance ahead of her. Spurring on her horse and pitching her voice loudly, she was forced to call his name several times before he finally heard her. On hearing and then seeing Augusta thundering behind him, he turned his horse full round and galloped towards her. Coming alongside her, Adam Smith swiftly dismounted and manfully helped Augusta to do the same. In breathless tones, she hurriedly explained why she was there and the scheme she expected him to put into action.

Adam Smith listened to her impassioned plea with an incredulous look upon his face. Secretly he thought that she was making quite a heavy drama out of the entire affair. Still, with a twist of irony in his voice, he touched his slouched hat and crisply commented, 'You're the boss, ma'am. Anything you say, I shall be pleased to do.'

After stating that she would return in exactly two hours time to the place she had previously mentioned to him, Augusta swung herself back into the saddle and galloped back in the direction of the house, leaving a bemused but willing Adam Smith to carry out her wishes.

Without a minute to spare and on the precise spot where Richard Fitzroy first brought these people so many years back, Augusta rode up and confronted the expectant group bunched before her. Seconds later, standing by Adam Smith's side, she held up a hand for absolute attention, not that any was lacking. Since being dragged to this position, all the convicts had been pondering on what this apparently important meeting was about. Few dreamt it was for their total freedom. Augusta, looking smart and businesslike, yet still radiantly attractive in her emerald green, narrow fitting, riding-dress with a jaunty peacock-feathered hat to match, found it immensely hard to control her inner feelings of pride and achievement as she quickly handed out the Official Papers to each of her convict workers. Not one of them could read or write, so it was left to her to verbally pronounce them

278

'free citizens'. Adam Smith then moved towards them and ceremoniously unlocked the cruel fetters around their ankles that had savagely united them in bondage.

With this tedious and lengthy task finished, he strode back to face Augusta and with a slight mocking bow promptly handed the heavy, evil-looking key to her. Taking the key in both hands, she held it out in front of her, so that all gathered could see it. Then with a determined look upon her face and a quick thrust of the wrist, she flung the offending object as far away as the naked eye could see. She had expected shouts of jubilation, backslapping or frenzied whelps and yelps but, strange to say, none of this materialized. Instead, the dirty, weather-beaten and grizzled bunch of some fifty· to sixty workers assembled together in her midst just stood, looking utterly dumbfounded and perplexed at the neatly written sheets of parchment that had been thrust into their hands.

'Do you think they fully understand what is happening?' the overseer asked Augusta, for he too was amazed by their lack of warmth and spontaneity.

'I am asking myself the same question,' she replied thoughtfully.

Adam Smith eyed the lack-lustre and mindless cluster of society's rejects standing apprehensively before him. Taking the bull by the horns, he leapt amongst them and fiercely proclaimed, 'You are free. Do you understand? Free. The Governor General of this State has granted pardons for you all. You can now choose whether you wish to stay and work as free men and women and be paid a modest wage for doing so, or you can walk away and start a free life for yourselves. Those of you who decide to stay on here at Fairlawns will be treated in the same way as the rest of the hired hands.'

Augusta, now completely carried away by the overseer's sterling speech, suddenly interrupted his steady flow by crying out, 'Listen to me all of you. Mr Smith has promised that he will do good by you. He also assures me that fair play will be the order of the day. You have all served your penal sentences. Now you must put the past well and truly behind you and forge ahead as only free souls can.'

The Official Papers had meant virtually nothing to them. Seeing their release written down in black and white did little to stir their blood. But witnessing the Mistress of Fairlawns standing there on no more than a dustheap, tall and straight, eyes aflame, voice so clear and resonant and with so much promise and conviction finally brought the truth home to them.

Slowly, one by one they sank upon the dusty ground, the very ground on which they had given so much, thanked God in his Heaven and unashamedly wept tears of joy and relief.

34

The following weeks had been full of excitement and activity. The unexpected visit made by the Surveyor General was still the main topic of conversation on everyone's lips. Augusta decided that it was time that she held a little celebratory party, nothing pretentious, just a small gathering of her closest friends and acquaintances. It seemed ages since she had last entertained a number of people all at once. She had made full use of Jack's services, as he had been scurrying around from one place to another delivering invitation cards. Finding a box of these cards tucked away in one of the recesses in the study bureau and putting them to use once more had afforded her great pleasure.

On the day prior to the party, Charles managed to find time to ride over and visit the Fairlawns Estate. It was late afternoon as he swung his roan horse through the wide gates. His excuse was that he needed to check the health of the ex-convicts. He was also going to enquire if Augusta needed any assistance with the travel arrangements of her guests, in connection with the party planned for the following day, knowing full well that he did not have to concern himself on either score, as she was more than capable of handling both situations. Nevertheless, it was a perfect ruse for seeing her again.

After completing the necessary task with the workers and stopping off for a few words with Adam Smith, he hurriedly made his way towards the house. He found Augusta sitting on the verandah sipping a long, cool drink.

'Charles, I was not expecting you until tomorrow,' she languidly exclaimed. 'I was just enjoying a glass of fresh lemonade, perhaps you would care for one as well.'

Charles nodded appreciatively and swung himself into the wicker chair facing her. Augusta poured him the lemonade which he drank thirstily.

Staring at his tense face, she cautiously ventured, 'I trust you are not the bearer of bad news. Nothing has happened to prevent you from coming tomorrow, has it?'

Charles placed his glass beside him and ruefully replied, 'Good Heavens, no. In fact, I am looking forward to that. No, I am just paying you a courtesy call and I also took it upon myself to look into the welfare of your workers.'

Augusta raised her delicately arched eyebrows at him. This was not like Charles to interfere with the way she ran her estate.

Seeing the contrite look on her face, he hastily added, 'Nothing much to complain about though. Adam Smith appears to have everything under control.'

Augusta heaved a sigh of relief.

'Nice man Adam Smith, I get on well with him. Things should improve for you, my dear, now that he holds the reins. Not like that other wretch,' Charles seriously added.

Augusta pursed her lips and tightly replied, 'I hope you are right, Charles, for I seem to have had my fair share of troubles in the past.'

Refilling both their glasses with the lemonade and handing one to her, Charles firmly answered, 'Yes I know, but you and I both have something to be grateful for.' Augusta abstractedly swatted at a fly on her face, as Charles carried on saying, 'You have won the case over the release of your convict workers and I have made a concrete start concerning the plight of the aborigines.'

'You are so right, Charles, we have both achieved something of importance,' she cried winningly.

She was about to say something else when the slight figure of Lysette appeared before them carrying a tray of freshly picked limes and wild figs. Augusta quietly thanked the girl as she turned and wide-eyed slipped away. Charles smiled to himself as he tried to visualize what the young girl had looked like when first brought to his attention. Augusta had certainly worked wonders in that direction.

Taking up from where he left off, he casually added, 'I have to confess, Augusta, my cause with the aborigines is still in its infancy. There is a long way to go yet and who knows how things will develop in the end? I fear only time will tell.'

Pausing for a while as she bit into a juicy fig, Augusta then replied earnestly, 'If it were not for people like you, Charles, precious little would be done for the less fortunate members of mankind. The majority are only concerned with their own welfare and conforming to patterns, whatever the cost. I sometimes wonder whether they will ever be free, or will they always be forced to roam wild over this land?'

'To my way of thinking,' cut in Charles, 'it will largely depend on how the rest of mankind treats them. If they continue to treat them like savages, doubtless they will remain so. After all, we are what life makes us, my dear.'

Augusta sprang out of her chair and suggested that they went inside as the flies were now becoming most bothersome. Charles agreed and as they passed through into the sitting-room, she graciously said, 'I just love discussing politics and life in general with you, Charles. Perhaps it is because it reminds me of my old life back home in Surrey. With father being a politician and mother constantly at Court, one was always getting involved in some lengthy discussion or over-heated argument. I think, inwardly, I still miss those exciting and stimulating days.'

Charles patted her arm lightly and answered with a knowing look on his face, 'I know what you mean. But that reminds me, Augusta, that much as I would dearly love our conversation to continue, I am afraid I must leave you. I still have some important papers to despatch to the Governor General. However, I promise to spend more time with you tomorrow evening for, as I said before, I am immensely looking forward to it.'

Kissing her lightly on the cheek, he then strode through the hallway and dashed off to his awaiting horse, leaving Augusta silently reflecting on the past.

35

The buffet supper was proving to be a great success. Everyone so far had turned up with the exception of the Carters. But no sooner had she mentioned this to Charles, who was one of the first on the scene, than the crunching of wheels could unmistakedly be heard jolting along the carriage-way. Augusta went to the front door to greet them and gasped in amazement as she watched the entire Carter family arrive in some sort of style, in their closed-in, newly painted wagon. Watching them tumbling out one by one, she wondered how on earth they all managed to get in there in the first place.

She naturally enough had invited the Minister and had felt obliged to invite the Rctor as well. At first both men, being of divided religions, eyed each other warily from either side of the room. However, as the evening wore on and the constant supply of rich ruby wine ran free, their suspicions dissolved and conviviality reigned supreme.

Adam Smith, on Augusta's insistence, was also there and one could not help but notice how much of his time was spent in Clarissa's company. He appeared most relaxed and at ease with her and she looked calmer and full of confidence in her appreciably modest style of dress.

As a reminder to everyone that this little gathering was given to celebrate the reward of her hard-earned efforts over the past few years, Augusta had cunningly allowed Lysette to be groomed and suitably dressed so that she could wait on guests in the dining-room and not hide herself amongst the dirty pots and pans in the kitchen. Notwithstanding, to make amends for this little bit of folly, Augusta had hired local girls from the colony to help Mrs Soames with the preparations and the inevitable dish washing.

Augusta moved amongst her guests, looking absolutely stunning in her newest gown. It had been artfully contrived by herself and Mrs Jameson. The overall effect was quite sensational. After finishing one new winter's cape and dress, from the tawny, gold threaded material, just enough material was left over to make something else. On turning the material inside out, the pattern on the opposite side was completely smooth and shiny. It was a warm, irridescent, russet colour and straightway an idea had infused Augusta's mind. She had Mrs Jameson cut the material into four widths tapering off at each end. These strips were then gathered onto a wide cummerbund made of the same material and carefully inserted between yards of creamy Chantilly lace. The low cut bodice made entirely of lace was attached to the cummerbund and held tightly in place by a long streaming bow. The final touch to this awe-inspiring creation was a huge pendant encasing a dropped pearl, threaded on a brown, velvet ribbon which hung precariously around her delicately arched neck. Everyone had complimented her on her superb choice of gown. Some had been persistently trying to coax out of her from whence it came, but neither she nor Mrs Jameson would confess.

Charles had earlier informed her that tonight she was looking her loveliest. His eyes had constantly followed her around the room. Seeing her like this tonight made him think how amazing she really was. Life dwelt on this rugged land, with its scorching heat and the constant battles of everyday life quickly took their toll on most newcomers. But not, it would seem, where Augusta was concerned. She positively thrived on it. He wished he knew her secret for survival. Later on in the evening, when mingling with the Carter family, he swiftly noticed how fast Clara was ageing. She was looking more and more like an old maid each time he saw her. He surmised that it was all those schoolhouse brats weighing her down. Betsy still looked good though, even if she had just recently been delivered of another child. Several months ago, George the second eldest son, found himself marching up the aisle with the gunsmith's youngest daughter, but on seeing them waltzing around together, there appeared to be no obvious tell-tale signs to show that they were about to become parents.

As usual the house looked grand and the food was plentiful. Towards the end of the evening, Augusta more than once congratulated herself on having placed Lysette on hand to attend to the guests, as Clarissa was constantly nowhere to be seen. Where did that girl keep disappearing to? Even Mrs Carter had remarked that she had not seen overmuch of her youngest daughter of late. Most of the time Clara, however, seemed either to be fussing over the Rector or conversing lightly with Charles. Then Tom and Betsy politely indicated that they had seen little of Clarissa and wondered if all was well with her. All was revealed an hour or so before the party broke up. As the rest of the guests stood merrily clustered around in small groups, the French windows were noisily flung aside and a radiant looking Clarissa entered through them dragging the nervous and slightly hesitant figure of Adam Smith closely behind her.

To the astonishment of those gathered in the room, she refused to lessen her grip on the poor man until he called out for everyone's undivided attention. Clearing his throat and coughing loudly, he waited until the buzz of conversation ebbed away. With Clarissa at his side to egg him on, he shyly but proudly announced that he and Clarissa were to be wed. To say that this had come as a surprise was an understatement. Nevertheless, glasses were refilled once again, toasts were made and spontaneous congratulations were heaped upon the happy couple.

Not everyone was so excited about the news, however. Mrs Carter later on confided to Augusta that although Mr Smith seemed a fine chap, he had been married before and therefore she would have preferred her youngest daughter to have found someone nearer her own age and not so experienced, as she delicately put it. Mr Carter, on the other hand, when pressed for his comments, thought it was an excellent idea. 'Might knock a bit of sense into that feckless brain of hers,' he muttered ostentatiously to the Reverend.

Clara, understandably enough, was rather non-committal and stated that it would probably take some time in adjusting to the suddenness of it all.

Charles lost no time in congratulating Adam heartily and warmly responded by saying, 'Best thing for you, my man. One certainly needs the support of a wife and children, especially out here.'

Augusta recoiled slightly. Oh no, surely not. Was Charles still harbouring those thoughts about Clara and himself? She hoped that he was not. Come to think of it, they had been together quite a lot recently, not to mention the amount of time spent with her this evening. Her thoughts were suddenly broken, when Tom, full of exuberance, shouted out, 'Come on Clara, let's have a tune before we go.'

Clara hesitated and shook her head wildly, but Tom was not going to be put off. Lifting her up bodily, he smacked her down on the piano stool, and coaxingly said, 'you are the musical one in the family, Clara, best not to let us down.'

Clara laughed gaily and needed no second · bidding. Augusta stepped over and lifted the lid off the spinnet, stood back and waited for Clara to play. As the notes tinkled off the keyboard, Charles suddenly swept Augusta in his arms and slowly began swirling around the room with her. Soon all the others excitedly took to the floor and joined in.

'You have come a long way since we first met,' he whispered in her ear, as he drew her closer towards him. 'No longer the timid and fearful young woman of yesteryear. For in her place I see a strong willed, determined and ravishing one. Although, I will add, underneath all that, there still beats a heart of pure gold.'

Augusta laughed outright and, pushing him away from her slightly, she spluttered, 'Really, Charles, sometimes I wonder if there is not a streak of Irish that runs through your blood. Are you sure that you were not born on top of the Blarney Stone itself?'

In reply he squeezed her waist lightly and whispered, 'This is a lovely evening, Augusta, and one full of surprises.'

A feeling of pure happiness flowed through her veins and she felt not in the least bit tired. She wanted this evening to go on forever and to stay blissfully locked in Charles's arms. With Clara dreamily tinkling away on the spinet and the rest of the company enjoying themselves to the hilt, she fervently prayed that nothing would happen to spoil this marvellous feeling.

The evening naturally enough had come to a close and the guests were now departing. The Carters were still laughing and singing as they bundled themselves into the back of the

287

wagon.

'Goodnight, Augusta and bless you dear,' called out Mrs Carter as she flopped back against the shiny, leather seat.

'We've all had a grand time,' shouted Mr Carter. 'Watch over that girl of mine and make sure she behaves herself at least until she is properly wed.'

'I will,' Augusta promised him.

Augusta waited until they had popped their heads back inside the wagon before returning to those still left behind. The Rector and the Minister, arm in arm, came jauntily swinging along the hallway.

'Got on like bosom pals,' said the Minister as he bade Augusta a hearty good night.

'A most enjoyable evening, Mrs Fitzroy,' waffled the Rector.

Charles would have preferred to stay on but for the sake of Augusta's reputation, he decided to leave with the others. With several members of her household hovering in the hallway, he was forced to keep his goodbyes fairly formal, just a polite kiss on either side of her cheeks and then he was gone.

Clarissa was somewhere on the verandah, saying her fond fairwells to Adam Smith. Augusta, on returning to the sitting-room to tell Lysette to finish her chores and retire to bed, realized that Clarissa was not to be seen. Halfway up the stairs, she spotted Mr McTavish coming out of the study and told him to find Clarissa and order her to bed immediately. At the top of the stairway, she paused to reflect on the announcement made by Adam Smith earlier on. Sly old fox. It had not taken him long to find a new love. As she opened her bedroom, door, her heart cried out. 'Please God not Charles and Clara.' That was something she could not bear to think about.

Waiting for Clarissa to help her out of her evening gown, she sat on the side of the bed and romantically let her thoughts dwell on the party, but they all centred on the same theme and one person in particular. Why could she not erase his memory from her mind? The answer was simple. Yet somehow she was afraid to face up to it. Deep down, she knew without a shadow of doubt that it was Charles she really loved and there was precious little that she could do about it.

36

The weather was just perfect and all around Augusta the birds could be heard chirping and singing on the lawns. Crickets cheeped and the multi-coloured butterflies fluttered lightly in the gentle breeze. She was trimming the wisteria around the verandah, a job she really enjoyed doing. All was peaceful until Mr McTavish appeared with a note on a silver tray.

'Jack brought this back from town just a few minutes ago,' he said as he handed her the tray.

Stopping to remove her gardening gloves and placing the cutters on the verandah ledge, she lifted the note from the tray and before she had a chance to glance at it, Mr McTavish knowingly uttered, 'It is from Doctor Hadleigh.' Augusta flashed him a sharp look and he disappeared out of sight before she could rebuke him for his forward manner.

Tearing the letter open she hastily read, 'Dear Augusta, please accept my deepest apologies for not telling you in person. I shall be away for some weeks. Have urgent business in Sydney. I will see you on my return. Yours affec. Charles.' Augusta bit her lip and wondered what he could be doing in Sydney. Well, it must be of great importance. Probably to do with his schemes for the aborigines. She returned to trimming the wisteria but without the same enthusiasm.

Over the next few months Augusta devoted most of her time helping with the re-organization of the estate. Adam Smith had quickly readapted to the swing of things. So far, only seventeen ex-convicts had left to find employment elsewhere. It seemed that the rest of them could be relied upon to stay on. Naturally enough, new conditions and living arrangements had to be made for them. Augusta had talked this matter over with Adam Smith and they both came to the same conclusion: that it would be best if the old huts that had previously housed them should now be destroyed. Adam suggested that two large workhouses should be erected where the men could live in reasonable warmth and comfort. They would always be on hand and less likely to cause further trouble. Augusta agreed that it was an excellent idea and she had the men put it into action almost immediately.

The plight of the womenfolk, however, was causing her another problem. Something had to be done, and fast, about their way of life. Now that they were free citizens they could not be expected to work on the land as before. After supper one evening, Augusta and Clarissa sat discussing this very topic. The only answer was to find them some sort of work outside Fairlawns. This was not going to be an easy task as most of them were untrained for anything other than hard labour.

Several times Augusta had approached local dignitaries to see if they could assist in any way but nobody offered any practical help. She had also made enquiries around the colony but the new settlers were suspicious of having ex-convicts in their homes. After many a sleepless night and a great deal of brain racking, Augusta finally hit upon a solution. Whether it would work or not she had no idea, but she was determined to give it a try. Before the women could be reasonably employed, they had to learn some kind of trade. They must be taught how to look after and fend for themselves properly. Teaching them cooking, sewing, cleaning, needlepoint, even to scribble their own names if need be, would be a necessary start for setting them on the right road. Augusta decided she would hold classes to instruct them in those subjects.

With the exception of Clarissa and Lysette, the rest of the servants thought she had lost her reason and put it down to the fact that she was bored and looking for something to amuse herself with. Nevertheless Augusta was not to be thwarted and twice a week the women would congregate at the rear of the house, where they would be expected to try their hands at whatever Augusta gave them to do. At first it was extremely hard going, but as the weeks went by and with more of the household staff helping out, the future did not look quite so dim.

Christmas came and everyone enjoyed the outdoor celebrations. Augusta still found the situation comical as turkey and plum-pudding were eaten by the entire household sitting in the centre of the front lawn. As predicted Jack and Sally married two days later and more jollifications ensued. Clarissa and Adam Smith had also set a date for their forthcoming nuptials. It was to be in precisely two months' time. Clarissa had been restless and irritable of late, so Augusta allowed her to visit her home every Thursday afternoon. It was probably due to pre-wedding nerves and the girl undoubtedly needed her mother's care and advice.

During the first month of her regular afternoon visits to her home, Clarissa always returned looking cheerful, relaxed and eager to see her fiancé. But on this particular evening of her return, she sauntered into Augusta's bedroom with a very glum look on her face.

'You are not looking your usual happy self tonight,' Augusta said thoughtfully. Clarissa shrugged her shoulders helplessly. 'Have you and Adam quarrelled?' Augusta tried again.

Clarissa spun round on her and gulped, 'Oh, no. Far worse than that.'

Augusta clenched her fists and prayed that she was not about to hear Clarissa say that she was with child. That would be the last straw. So much for her father entrusting his daughter to her keeping.

Clarissa hesitated and Augusta impatiently cried out, 'Well, come on out with it. You can tell me, you know. I shall not throw you out, if that is what concerns you.'

The silly girl was far to upset to take in what Augusta had implied.

'It's Clara,' she blurted out. 'She is going to be wed. Oh, of all the stupid things to do.'

Augusta felt the room swaying before her. Sinking on to the chaise-longue she sat there motionless while Clarissa babbled on. So that was it. That was why Charles had gone to Sydney. That was why he had sent that silly note to her all those months ago and nothing since. O, how polite of him! How formal! Just like Charles who must do everything properly. No wonder he could not tell her himself. He was afraid that

291

she might just be upset at the news. What a coward he had turned out to be. Then there was Clara. Oh, how devious she had been in not confiding in her. She had certainly given the impression that she too was surprised to learn that Charles was still in Sydney. In all probability he went to buy Clara her wedding trousseau.

'When did you find this out, Clarissa?' asked Augusta shakily.

'This afternoon,' the girl replied sullenly. 'Mother told me as soon as I arrived.'

Augusta twisted her hands nervously and bitterly cried, 'Well, I expect your mother is over the moon. Especially as she loves weddings. No doubt this will be the wedding to outdo all weddings. Your mother has long been an admirer of his and made no secret of persuading Clara at setting her cap at him.'

'Admirer,' burst out Clarissa. 'Mother hates him. He is old and fat. Saintly and boring. Fancy having a man of the cloth for one's brother-in-law. Ugh, we shall all have to watch our p's and q's now.'

Augusta could hardly believe her own ears. Old, saintly, a man of the cloth. What was this stupid girl talking about?

Moving swiftly towards her, she shook Clarissa by the shoulders and fervently cried, 'Are you trying to tell me that Clara is not marrying Doctor Hadleigh?'

Clarissa looked thunderstruck.

'Doctor Hadleigh?' shrieked the girl. 'Who said anything about him?'

Augusta slowly released her grip on Clarissa's shoulders and sighed inwardly.

Tears welled in Clarissa's eyes as she brokenly said, 'I only wish it were the Doctor she was marrying. Oh, how she could have rejected him for the fat, old Rector? She must be insane.'

Augusta kept on repeating those last few words to herself, until they finally sank in. Taking Clarissa's hand in hers, she hesitantly enquired 'Are you absolutely sure that Clara intends to marry the Rector?'

Clarissa whispered a faint 'yes', then threw herself down upon the floor and poured out more tears, because she felt so utterly miserable. Augusta threw herself upon the bed and cried abandoned tears of utter relief.

☆   ☆   ☆

Two days later, Augusta heard via the grapevine that Charles had returned home. All day she pondered on how Charles would receive the news about Clara and the Rector. If he still carried a torch for Clara, and it was quite possible that he did, then he would be devastated by the news. Perhaps she ought to ride over and forewarn him. It might help in lessening the blow a little. The thought preyed on her mind until the early evening, when she found she could bear it no longer. Slipping a warm shawl over her pretty evening dress, she ran round to the stables, forced Old Amos to set up the gig and clambered aboard.

'Where to Ma'am,' he grumpily asked.

'Doctor Hadleigh's house and for once in your life, be quick about it,' she fiercely replied.

The house appeared in almost complete darkness as the gig drew up close to it. Not waiting for Amos to assist her, she jumped down and ran straight to the door. Knowing that Charles's housekeeper was slightly deaf, she rapidly crashed the knocker. The door opened almost immediately and behind it stood Charles, clad in just a plain white lawn shirt and a pair of riding breeches.

'Augusta . . . what on earth?' he exclaimed. 'What is the matter now?'

Hastily peering from side to side, in case anyone should notice her, she firmly replied, 'May I come in, or must I stand here for all to see?'

Charles politely stepped aside. 'No, please come in. The house is in a state. Mrs Smith was not expecting me back for another week. She is away at the moment, staying with her sister.'

Augusta followed him through to his sitting-room.

'How did your trip go, Charles? Was it successful?' she questioned.

'Yes, very,' he replied, still a little nonplussed at why she had descended on him so late in the evening.

'Would you care for a drink?' offered Charles.

Augusta coughed behind her hand and firmly replied,

'Thank you all the same, but not right now.'

Charles pulled up a chair for her, then seating himself beside the fireplace he wearily asked, 'Now Augusta, tell me what has happened. Is everything in order at Fairlawns?'

'Everything is fine at Fairlawns, Charles. However, it is not about Fairlawns or me that I have come to see you.'

Charles twisted himself about in the chair and fixed her with a hard stare. 'Well, I am all ears,' he said tritely.

'Charles,' began Augusta, 'I do not know how to put this to you, without hurting your feelings. But I thought I ought to tell you first, that is, before you find out from other people who just may not be as considerate of your well-being, as I am.'

Charles stared even harder at her and in exasperation cried, 'Augusta, my dear, will you stop twittering and please come straight to the point?' What has happened since I have been away?'

Taking a deep breath and in a voice full of compassion, she gently said, 'Charles, I have just learnt that Clara is to wed the Rector. Now, I know how much you care about her, so I came here hoping to soften the blow. I am so sorry for you, Charles. You really do have my deepest sympathy. I hope that in time you will forgive her. Do not be too hard on her, for she obviously has her reasons.'

Charles stared at Augusta in disbelief. His face suddenly went white with shock. 'Augusta, am I hearing you correctly?' he faltered.

'Yes Charles, it is true,' she cried back. She waited for him to digest this piece of unnerving news before saying, 'I think perhaps it would be best if I left you now, to be alone with your sorrow.'

'Augusta,' he cried out, 'stop it, stop this nonsense at once. Are you playing games with me?'

'Games,' she hurled back. 'Oh how cruel you can be. I came here to help you and all you can do is accuse me of playing games.'

Charles quietened down a shade, then reproachfully said, 'Augusta, I am truly sorry. I did not mean to hurt you. But, my dear, you seem to be under some misapprehension concerning Clara and me. It is not Clara I love, nor even care for, at least not in the way you imply. I like her, yes, and I always will. There was a time when I thought we might have been good for each other, but that is all in the past now. If what you say is true about her marriage to the Rector, then if that is what Clara wants, then I am happy for her. She will probably make a good Rector's wife. They are ideally suited.'

Here he paused for a while, allowing her to say in an overheated tone, 'Then why did you rush off to Sydney like that? What was so important? I thought you had gone for Clara's sake.'

Charles threw back his head and laughed. 'Oh my dear, I meant to tell you but there was no time. I was ordered to go by the Premier himself. I have been offered a wonderful position in medicine at the new Medical School ·they are building. The work itself is based entirely on research. It is a big thank you for the efforts I have put in my work in relation to the aborigines. A sort of peace offering if you like.'

'Charles, I think I will have that drink now,' said Augusta shakily.

Chuckling to himself, he heaved himself out of his chair and walking towards the wall cupboard, took out two large glasses and filled them with port wine. Handing Augusta hers and resuming his seat he slowly uttered, 'Until I went to see the Premier I had no idea what it could be. Now are you satisfied?'

She nodded slowly as she sipped her wine.

'Are you going to accept the post?' she ventured.

'That depends on many things,' he seriously replied.

'Such as?' questioned Augusta.

Charles stretched his legs and ruefully commented, 'Well, on whether you would consider moving back to Sydney with me.'

Augusta was astounded. 'Back to Sydney, Charles, you cannot be serious. What is there for me in Sydney? My place is at Fairlawns where I belong. That is my home now, where I am my own mistress. What in God's name would I be at Sydney, your housekeeper or something like that?'

Charles placed his glass on the side table and then carefully took hers as well. Kneeling down in front of her and in all seriousness he explained, 'No, Augusta, I want you to be my wife. It is you I love. You I have always loved, right from that very first day when I stood as proxy for your marriage to

Fitzroy. I fell in love with you then and I have never stopped loving you. I wanted to tell you this so many times, but each time I tried to tell you, something happened to prevent it.' He paused to catch his breath. 'God, Augusta, don't sit there looking at me like that. Say something, please.'

She was so overcome by his words as to be rendered speechless. Never in her wildest moments had she dreamt that this moment would come true. Her heart was pumping away beneath her ribs and she felt extremely light-headed as she somehow floated towards his open arms.

'I love you too, Charles. I always have done,' was all he allowed her to say, before he swept her into his arms and kissed her with a passion that she never knew existed.

Pausing for breath, he managed to say, 'Will you marry me, Augusta? Please say you will.'

She did not need any coaxing as she readily responded by saying, 'Yes, oh yes, I will marry you, Charles, and I will go anywhere with you. I will sell Fairlawns, for in a way I shall be glad to be rid of it. Although it is a beautiful place, it can be very lonely for one.'

Relaxing his hold on her for a while, he tenderly said, 'There is no need to sell Fairlawns, Augusta, I would not ask that of you. No, you must keep it. Why don't you leave it in the good hands of Adam Smith and Clarissa? They will care for it as if it were their own. We can always visit it from time to time. No doubt, it will be something grand to show our children, if we are lucky enough to have any.'

Throwing her arms wildly around his neck she kissed him tenderly and whispered, 'Thank you, Charles, for everything. You seem to have worked everything out very well so far.'

Charles clasped her to him once again and happily cried, 'Just the beginning, my darling, just the beginning. Now come here, and I shall prove to you how very romantic I can be as well.'